IDIOTS
IN THE
MACHINE

A Novel

15TH
ANNIVERSARY
EDITION
16 YEARS LATER

EDWARD SAVIO

BABELFISH
P R E S S

SAN FRANCISCO • NEW YORK

101 Montgomery Street, 800, San Francisco, CA 94104

ISBN 978-1-63124-010-2

Library of Congress Card Number: 2001-116133

Cover design and illustration by Ethan Stone
Back cover photo © Tommaso Lizzul

The talking fish logo is a trademark of
Babelfish Press.

For reprint permission: permission@babelfishpress.com
All other information: info@babelfishpress.com

10 11 12 13 14

Printed in the United States of America

IDIOTS
IN THE
MACHINE

Introduction
To The 15th Anniversary Edition (One Year Late)

I don't like introductions. Too often, they ruin the story, reveal a twist, give away an ending. I won't do that to you. I'll simply tell you *another* story.

Some years ago, I walked into a bookstore and quite by accident grabbed a book off the bottom shelf solely because the cover caught my eye. It had an odd-looking man with a bushy mustache and a bird on his head. I had never heard of the book or the writer, but then I wasn't very smart back then. I read the back cover (books still had back covers then), read the first few pages, and decided to buy it. Over the next few days, I devoured *A Confederacy of Dunces*. It's a wonderful book. Funny, literate, unique. It's also *not* the book I thought it would be. A few years later—while stranded in Chicago for two days during a snowstorm—I decided to write *that* book. You're holding it now.

The first few paragraphs of *Idiots in the Machine* are an homage to John Kennedy Toole's opening. But the underlying premise of *Idiots* was born two years earlier while I was co-writing a film about contact with a race of humans living inside the earth in an Eden-like society—sort of a *Close Encounters With Our Own Kind*. I was in a script meeting one day when I suddenly realized two of the producers *and* the financier responsible for half of our budget genuinely believed the U.S. Government was hiding the truth of this Inner World's existence. Now, I'm not above taking money from crackpots. This is Hollywood, after all. But there was an *actual* line item in the budget for "lead shielding" in the ceiling of the production offices. I guess so spy satellites on the lookout for those who knew the truth would see only an innocently blacked-out rectangle.

My partner and I were writing a subterranean fiction script. These producers were looking to expose a *global conspiracy*. Needless to say, that movie never got made.

But a question got lodged in my head. What could make a person believe something so ridiculous? What in their past, what misinterpretation of fact could allow such a fantasy to take hold?

That is how two unrelated events came to inspire this novel.

Where scripts are tightly controlled works of specific lengths with rigid rules—like page-per-minute Haiku—and unforgiving formats (down to the one font you can use), I wrote *Idiots* as an "anti-screenplay" with the certain belief that no one could make it into a movie. Not even me. It was more than surprising when Sony Pictures bought the movie rights for over a million dollars. Mainly because my agent, Lisa Lindo, and I said "no" to their first ten offers.

This is the fifteenth-anniversary edition of *Idiots* (and in keeping with its lead character, it's a year late). I've heard from many people in that decade and a half plus one who love this book. And some who hate it. To both sets of readers, I say thank you. The worst thing that can happen to a writer is that no one likes their work. The second worst thing is when everyone does.

I was a writer before I was a reader. It's not that I didn't like to read when I was young, I did—sort of—it's just that most kids books were horrible back then. So, I created my own stories. Which is how I started writing screenplays. But even as an adult, I labored through books. Each time I finished one, I spent weeks, months—sometimes longer—searching for the next halfway decent read I could tolerate.

And that's what I was doing when I walked into that little bookstore in L.A. and found hiding on the bottom shelf the next thing. The thing that changed the way I viewed reading forever.

From that day on, I begged anyone who would talk to me to tell me their all-time top five books. I'd been searching alone in the wilderness, and like most men, I had flatly refused to ask for directions. When I finally did, I was shown treasures I never imagined. Serious novels that are hysterically funny. Classics that have action and adventure that put most movies to shame. Thousand pagers I mourned as I turned the last page. These books pushed me to refine and broaden my craft, beginning a process that made me see that prose on a page could be as powerful as images on film, and many times, more so. I was a lover of movies and scripts and plays, of banter and dialogue. I became a lover of *words*.

The writers I love to read, the ones I admire, whether playwrights, screenwriters, or novelists, those are very big shoes to fill. But I'm hoping if I walk long enough, my feet might swell.

March 2017

To Natalie.
See, I told you so.

"THE TROUBLE WITH THE WORLD IS THAT THE STUPID ARE COCKSURE AND THE INTELLIGENT ARE FULL OF DOUBT."

—BERTRAND RUSSELL

I. OUT OF THE LOOP

A mittened hand reached up and tucked in the errant flap of tin foil escaping from under the knit cap covering the large head. A loose yarn on the mitten tangled itself on the corner of the foil before it was rescued by a second mitten. Liquid blue eyes, translucent, captivating, sat behind a set of dense lashes, pulling attention away from an unremarkable face.

Satan stood on the corner of Dearborn and Adams, looking down with disdain at the brown slush underfoot, then the mass of humanity surrounding him, thinking how horrible it was to have been born in the last half of the twentieth century—too late for the simple life, too early for android love slaves.

A cold wind whipped past him, and he wished he was in the Caribbean somewhere, only he hated humidity, planes, the ocean, and poverty. A year over thirty, and a measure over six feet, Satan, a.k.a. Magma Head, a.k.a. Lava Brain, born Noel Dorobek, put a padded hand to his hat once again to confirm the aluminum was in place.

Keeps out the gamma rays.

A couple of sheets of Arnolds™ brand aluminum foil shiny side up also protected Satan's brain from those as-yet-undiscovered frequencies bombarding the planet. As surely as he was standing in the freezing cold on the Godforsaken soil deemed Chicago—Windy City, Big Shoulders, Slaughterhouse to America—he and everyone within a billion mile radius of that wondrous star Sol was being irradiated.

Killed. Murdered. Cell by cell by cell.

The thought sent a cold shiver up his spine. He hated to think about it, but thinking about it, he remembered something: He was almost out of Arnolds. He made a mental note to stop off at the market on the way home.

Satan looked at the stoplight, covered up and down with the ornamentation of the season, covered with garland and strings of lights forming a cone. As if someone might really mistake it for a Christmas tree. Before he could calculate the exact number of watt-hours being wasted, the "star" at the top of the "tree" turned green and instantly, the walk sign changed from an open palm to a featureless man in a geriatric pose.

Satan stepped off the curb and crossed the street.

With all these distractions, it was a wonder nobody had gotten run over yet. You could hardly distinguish the twinkling decorations from the traffic signals. All it would take was a little too much eggnog hitting an unprotected, irradiated brain and somebody was going to have an early Christmas present under their front bumper.

He just hoped it wasn't anyone he knew.

Luckily, he didn't have many friends.

Satan made his way down Dearborn, grabbing the top of his coat near his Adam's apple to keep the wind from getting inside. It had been a cold fall. Winter would officially arrive in a few short weeks, although it had already shown up as far as most people were concerned. As he fought past the droves of men and women rushing to get home to a microwave dinner and 600 channels of Must-See TV, Satan paused against one of the buildings along the street and glanced up at a reindeer strung between two light posts, one on either side of the roadway.

They don't have this crap *inside* the Earth, he thought.

Satan got his nickname because he believed deep beneath the Earth's crust resided a race of hyper-sapien beings, living and flourishing under the warmth and glow of the planet's molten core, even though virtually all scientific data refuted this possibility. The government had suppressed other truths, why not this one?

None of the few friends he had gave credence to any of this, but he had amassed an incredible library on the subject, and they found some amusement in his dissertations on the paradise which lay beneath. Satan was convinced these beings were the planet's salvation, and he was determined to someday make contact.

His gut told him these Inner-worlders were much too advanced for mutant red-nosed caribou or Visa cards. Although, until he could gain passage to the world below, he would somehow have to deal with these botherations on the surface.

He made another mental note: pick up Arnolds, defame this Santa guy, blow up CreditDat, Trans Union, and Equifax.

Suddenly, the sound of screeching tires resonating from the alley to his right jarred Satan out of his thoughts. A sneering hood ornament expatriated from some eighteen-wheeler came to rest two inches from Satan's underdeveloped crotch. Perched there, frozen atop the barge-sized rusting Oldsmobile, the gray metal dog looked as though it might attack. A slight tingle languished in his mid-section, reminding him he still had feeling there. Pondering the silvery canine, Satan considered bestiality as an alternative to his lack of female companionship. But it sounded so...so base. Bestiality. People inside the earth, if they did such things, would have a much more pleasant word for it. *Frivialocity*, or something as cordial. If only it had a name like that, he might give it a try. But *bestiality*...

"Hey, asshole, why don't you watch where you're going."

"Excuse me," Satan replied, "are you speaking to me?"

"Yeah, I'm speakin to you, ass*hole*," screamed the faceless driver as he stared at the grown man wearing big red mittens, an overused down jacket with all its feathers settled at the bottom, and a red knit cap with a white fuzzy ball on top. The driver thought he saw something flash near the man's half-covered ears—something shiny, perhaps, but he couldn't be sure.

Satan stared at his reflection in the chrome bumper for a moment.

"Forgive my limited scholarship in the ways of terra firma, but it's my understanding that pedestrians have the right of way when it comes to the sidewalk."

"You gettin smart, buddy?" asked the stranger, his voice taking on a hint of delight as a receding power window began to reveal him.

"Actually, I started out smart." Satan aimed the words toward the widening breach. "However with a seriously degenerating ozone, microwave ovens, and pop music constantly bombarding us all, I've been getting dumber. *Much* dumber."

The hood ornament took a snap at Satan's crotch as the driver's foot slipped off the brake. A chuckle emanated from inside.

"What are you, some kinda faggot?" the stranger asked.

"Why is it that anyone who disagrees with somebody is a faggot? Last century, they were Communists. Now, they're homosexuals. I can't wait to see what comes next."

"A Commie-faggot," said the voice.

"Communism's dead, or haven't you read the papers in a decade or two? They traded it in for a Maytag and a Honda."

"You gonna get outta my fuckin way," asked the man who now was sticking his head fully out the window, "or am I gonna havta run your ass over?"

Satan stared at the man's dark hair, the little scar that ran under his nose, the three moles that added to, rather than took away from, his face. "You must have a sunroof that you use a great deal," Satan said, trying to get a glimpse inside.

"What the fuck's that supposed to mean?"

Seeing the electric three-way sunroof, Satan nodded. "Just as I thought."

"You don't get outta the fuckin way, I'll put a tire track across your forehead."

With a tiny bow, Satan took a step back. "I'm glad to see you haven't lost the Holiday Spirit."

"Fuck you."

Satan watched as the man squealed out of the alley, tires spinning, splashing a wave of frigid slush on his legs as the car went past. When the Netherworlders appeared on the surface to rid the Earth of the mentally incompetent and socially inept, this man was sure to be the first pitched into the flames.

Satan's mission was simple: spread the word, save as much of mankind as he could, and buy more foil. He made a final mental note: purchase Arnolds stock. Once he told the world his secret, they wouldn't be able to keep the stuff on the shelves.

•

A pop rang out as the wood in the fireplace crackled. It was warm in the room. At least that part of the room the heat from the fire reached. Barris wasn't in one of those parts. He sat huddled over his notepad in a way not wholly human. One leg was stuck under his buttocks; the other resting on the cold wood floor, twisted out at a right angle from his hip. A shiver ran through him as he looked over to see Kelsey sitting before the fire, wrapping presents and sipping at a mug of hot spiced cider. The light from the flames illuminated her tangled blonde mane.

Barris glanced down at the notepad. It was almost entirely empty except for a small doodle in the top left that had once been an "A." Nothing was coming to him. "A" always seemed a cunning way to start a sentence when you couldn't think of anything else. He peeked over at Kelsey once more. She snuggled up to a blanket, flaunting the fact that she was warm in front

of the hearth, while he sat here in the frozen tundra cutting off his circulation in an attempt to use his buttocks to bring some warmth to his icy toes.
It was, to say the least, a trade off of dubious merit.

He placed the tip of the pen to the notepad once again and began to form
a new letter.

P...

Not a very good letter to begin a sentence with, but he was getting
frustrated.

People suck...

"Barris, what do you think of giving the Marshalls a membership to the
gym?" Kelsey said, interrupting the first true thought Barris had had all
evening.

"What?"

"What do you think about getting a gym membership for the Marshalls?"

"As a Christmas present?"

"Yeah, I thought it might be nice." Kelsey sipped at her cider.

"The Marshalls are fat. Why would you get them a gym membership?"
Barris looked at the two words he had scribbled on the pad. He was quickly
losing his muse.

"So they could get in shape."

"Are you purposely trying to have these people never speak to you again?
Or is your brain cooked from too many nights by the fireplace?"

"I just thought they could stand to lose a few pounds. It's good for their
health."

"Why don't you buy them a hundred pound bag of feed. You could simi-
larly insult them and at a cheaper price."

"You don't have to be sarcastic," Kelsey said as she reached up to the sofa
and scratched out "GYM MEMBERSHIPS" beside the Marshalls' name.

Barris started to return to his two words when—

"What should we get for Satan?"

Barris sighed loudly enough for Kelsey to hear. "A padded room?"

"Barris...be nice." Kelsey gave him a less than angry eye over the rim of
her cider. "I like Satan."

"Don't say that too loud, dear. The neighbors'll get the wrong idea and start blaming us for their missing cats."

"I *mean* it," more than a little anger this time. "Satan is a sweetheart. More than I can say for you at the moment."

"I got it, a shovel. He can dig his way to the center of the earth."

"Barris, you're such an insensitive prick. Show a little compassion. He's had a tough life. It couldn't have been easy, what, with his father leaving him and his mother like that."

Barris lifted his head from the notepad. "Like how?"

"Oh, so now you're interested. He's only been our friend for five years," Kelsey said, going back to her cider and blanket and warm fire without another word.

"Like how?" Barris put a bit more inflection on his words.

Kelsey sat humming to the beat of the crackling cinders.

"Kelsey." Like a safecracker searching for the correct combination, he tried it softer this time. "Like how?"

Chink, the lock sprung.

"Like this," began Kelsey. "Satan's father told them he'd gotten a new job in the city. He went on ahead—"

"And never came back."

"Oh, so you know this story now?" Kelsey said sarcastically. "Actually, Barris, as usual, you're wrong. He did send for them. Had them sell the house and get on a train to Chicago, saying he would meet them at Union Station. Only he wasn't there."

Barris wished he smoked because this seemed as if it might be a long one. Kelsey was known for her ramblings. In fact, whenever he wanted to end a party quickly so he could get back to his writing, all he'd have to do was ask her to tell one of her stories. After a quarter hour of her droning on about insignificant details—"...and their house, which by the way sold for a hundred and sixty-three thousand and was bought by a Cuban man who came over when Castro released all those people from prison and put them on boats. No one knows what he was in for. But the Cuban court system is supposedly one of the strictest in the world. Anyway their house..."—everyone was asking for their coats and apologizing for being such party poopers, saying they had an early day tomorrow or some such excuse.

Barris watched Kelsey for a moment waiting for her to continue the story. She sat there, silent.

"So?"

"So, what?"

"So, what happened?"

"That's all I was going to say. You always complain that I take too long to tell stories. So…I gave just the facts this time."

Barris grumbled something under his breath and went back to his notepad.

People suck shit.

•

Satan pushed the shopping cart as straight as he could down the aisle, but the wheels kept forcing him into the shelves. Two aisles over he had already knocked a bottle of pickles to the linoleum. Luckily he had made it around the corner before anyone noticed him. Surely the Food King's management had found the mess by now and was alerting the police who would soon be on the scene taking wheel prints and following the trail of pickle juice seen intermittently on the white tiles. It was only a matter of time before they matched the tracks to the wheels on his cart. Then the cops would turn him over to the manager who was a huge, ugly man with hair growing out of his ears in patterns defying gravity. His only chance was to keep his purchases to fewer than twelve and hope the express lane was open.

"Clean up on aisle nine," bellowed a voice over the store's P.A.

The cat was out of the bag now. He'd have to hurry. Satan could picture the manager running toward the massacred pickles, hair flopping from his ears, thinking of the loss column, realizing that forfeited bottle of pickles could have paid one of his cashiers for eleven minutes of work. Steaming with anger, the manager would be searching for the progenitor of this mark-down, hoping to beat those eleven minutes out of him.

Satan wasn't paying attention to the fact that the cart was yawing even more violently to the right than normal. The front corner of the cart nicked the shelf and plowed several jars of spaghetti sauce to the floor. The splatter pattern was actually quite interesting. Heavy on the near side, fanning out clear across the aisle until the sauce collided with the molding under the opposite shelves.

It sort of reminded Satan of the Fourth of July.

The manager heard several pops like the crackling of firecrackers. He turned his head toward the noise, the excess skin under his jaw arriving a few seconds after the rest of his oversized face. Immediately he knew what was afoot. Some degenerate, hoodlum, or small band of teenagers was in his store, wreaking havoc with his bottom line. He pointed to the mangled pickles on the floor. "Save as many of those as you can," he told the pimpled-face teen at his feet. Most likely, it was some of the teen's friends that were behind all this. The manager turned on his heels and headed quickly toward the sound. The hair sprouting at odd angles from his ears waggled as he struggled to pick up the pace.

Satan knew he had only a small window of opportunity to escape with his life. He steered the unruly cart past the tomato, garlic and basil sauce along a route that would get the least amount of the red paste on the tires. Spaghetti sauce was easily traceable. Leaving a dotted line of crimson on the tiles, Satan had one chance. And in a flash, it hit him: Return to the scene of the crime. Go back to the pickles. Satan made a beeline for aisle nine, praying that the sauce would wear off the wheels before he got there.

Turning the corner of aisle nine, Satan glanced ahead to see the blemished teenager bent over the last remnants of the accident, which looked minor in comparison to the one two aisles back. Luckily, the manager was nowhere in sight. On the verge of a cold for nearly three weeks, Satan's sigh of relief sounded less than healthy as a bit of phlegm got caught in his esophagus. He hacked a few times in an attempt to dislodge the mucus. Once in his mouth, he searched around for a safe place to rid himself of it. Just then, the teenager lifted his head to reveal a bright red face, obviously gotten from using too many acne cremes at once or just a bit too much scrubbing. Satan could see the boy's name stitched into his white smock. *Ted*, it said. The young man was looking at him now, and there was nothing Satan could do with the foul-tasting mucus but hold on to it.

Ted stared at the strange man as he wiped the last of the pickle juice from the floor. Mittens and knit cap. The man looked like an oversized version of a six-year-old sent out to play in the snow by an overprotective mother. And there was something escaping from under the cap. Shiny, metallic. The man seemed to have a cold, perhaps full-blown pneumonia. It was Ted's first week at the Food King, and he didn't want to get sick.

"Can I help you, sir?" he said, trying not to breathe.

Without a word, the man shook his head, no. Still, Ted thought the man looked lost.

"Cold medicines are on the next aisle."

As the man nodded a thank you, and rolled his cart past, Ted noticed a faint trail of red stripes leading down the aisle in the direction the man had come. On his knees, he gave a sidelong glance at the man's cart and saw that its hobbling wheels were laying down the pattern. Suspiciously, he raised his eyes to the man turning the corner. Something strange was going on. Ted knew one thing, no matter what it was he'd be the one that'd have to clean it up.

Wheezing and out of breath, the manager stood over the fallen Italians that lay bleeding on his floor. His eyes followed the path of sauce down the aisle. The hulking man scratched at one of the brussel-sprout-like tufts of hair that protruded from each of his ears and decided to pursue. Navigating past the mess, he tiptoed around the chunky bits of tomato and "fresh-cut" mushrooms.

Satan had made it past the boy and found himself beside an end display of Saltine's that was stacked ten feet tall in the shape of a Christmas tree. He surveyed the area, making sure no one was watching, then spat on the floor at the foot of the display. Glancing back at his handiwork as he rounded the corner, he thought the yellow-green phlegm added something.

A little present under the tree.

In a dark, empty room lit only by flickering blue-gray light, a bank of monitors displayed the movements of shoppers and shoplifters alike. On one screen, a bundled up man spat on the floor. On another, a young boy began cleaning up a set of red tire tracks. On a third, an oversized man with visible ear hair followed a second path of red as fast as his body would let him.

Satan looked into his cart for the first time since wrestling it away from the ungiving grip of the stack at the front of the store. It was empty, save for a few splatterings of sauce and a single gherkin that hung on precariously at the bottom. Pushing the empty carriage halfway down the aisle, Satan came to the section of shelving that housed his purpose for being in the Food King. He stopped his cart, knocking a box of trash bags to the ground. He picked up the package and studied it, concluded he had done no discernible damage to the item, then replaced it on the shelf.

Putting his mittened hands into the pocket of his down coat, Satan stepped back and viewed the wall of aluminum foil before him. Hundred yard boxes. Boxes of two hundred yards with seventy-five yards free. Restaurant width, standard size, double fold, Gatorback for extra freezer protection. All bearing the Arnolds name. Sure there were other brands, most of them bigger, with flashier advertising campaigns that featured beautifully enticing "housewives" using their products, but none of them matched the concern, the commitment to foil that Arnolds ennobled. The other brands had cheapened the faith by expanding into plastic wraps and freezer bags with special locking strips. Arnolds was the aluminum foil specialist.

Satan had only seconds to spare before the cops would arrive to take him away. He grabbed one of each kind, eight in all, and took the balance in 250-yd double fold, taking a dozen total. Making a quick decision, he put one of the boxes back. He wanted to make room for one other item and still qualify for the more-than-likely-closed express lane.

The manager was hot on the trail. The theme from "The Good, the Bad, and the Ugly" played in his head. His eyes moved from one red stripe to the next with incredible concentration. One led to another led to another led to—a young man's hand. The manager put on the brakes, almost crushing his new employee's soft white fingers. For a week now, the manager wondered if the boy only took the job to get twenty percent off acne medication.

The manager glared down at the boy. "What are you doing?"

Ted looked from the huge shoe an inch from his index finger up to the manager's face. "Cleaning up."

"Who asked you to do that?" the manager shouted like a pig about to be slaughtered.

"No one. I just thought someone could get hurt if they slipped on the mess." Ted eyed his employer suspiciously. The man had just yelled at Ted the day before, saying that he wasn't taking enough initiative on his own.

"Don't ever do anything unless I TELL you to," the hairs protruding from the manager's ears looked like smoke shooting from his head in anger. "UnderSTAND?"

"But you just told me to—"

"I don't care what I said." The manager looked up the aisle to see if he could pick up the scent, but the boy had cleaned every spot. A thought came to the hulking manager. He was now convinced that the conspirators were a band of teenagers and definitely friends of his spotted employee. An agent of the enemy had infiltrated his ranks and was covering up for his mischievous comrades by pretending to be a responsible worker. The manager knew that soon he would have to purge this turncoat from his payroll, but not just yet. He had been the only applicant willing to labor for minimum wage. He'd get two months work from the traitor before the kid had to join the union, which coincidentally forced the manager to nearly double his salary overnight. Then he'd cut him loose. But for now, he was on to the boy's true allegiance.

Satan pushed his cart toward the front of the store. To his amazement, the express lane was operating, albeit at less than "express" speed. Emptying his cart, Satan placed the eleven boxes of foil on the conveyor. Then reaching deep into the carriage, he pulled out a pair of Dr. Coal's charcoal odor absorbing shoe inserts and tossed them on top of the small pile of Arnolds boxes. An insert in each shoe on a bed of foil, and he'd be safe from radon gas and background radiation seeping up from underground. Satan wondered if these were somehow waste products from the Netherworlders. If so, they were but a minuscule smudge on their nearly perfect existence.

Dr. Coal's also served another purpose. Got rid of stinky feet. Kelsey had suggested, very sweetly, that he should pick some up.

Satan reached in his pocket and hoped he had enough cash to cover everything. Having to write a check in the Cash Only Xpress Lane would bring much unwanted attention to himself. The ugly manager/murderer might even have to approve the check. Satan continued to round up the crumpled wads of cash he knew were in the coat and prayed the manager had been held up by some elderly woman wanting to know where to find the saffron because she needed it for the special stuffing she made once a year.

The pickles and sauce added up to forty or more minutes of cashier time. In forty minutes, the manager could do some serious damage to several important internal organs. Missing the manager/maniac was the prudent choice since Satan's medical insurance had been canceled due to his refusal to undergo a mandatory chest X-ray for TB.

It was just like Modern Medicine to protect you from one disease by giving you another.

•

Armand Arnold sat back in the old leather chair and glanced at the report in front of him. A broken spring jutted into the small of his back, and his pant leg kept getting caught on a tear in the cushion. He had put in an order for a new chair a year ago, and then again every month since.

He reached for the intercom. "Tina, could you make out an order for a new chair?"

"Of course, Mr. Arnold," said the disembodied voice. "But you know what they'll say."

Armand sighed. "Just try. Thank you," he said, his voice rising a bit on the last word.

Returning to the report and the table full of men and women before him, Armand Arnold elbowed the broken spring, fixing it temporarily. The news was not good. The Arnolds Aluminum Company was in the straits of financial crisis. Sales were down, losses were up, and a strike loomed over the plant as contract negotiations were going nowhere.

Armand raised his eyes from the pages in front of him and glanced around the room. A board made up of a bunch of good-for-nothing relatives, less than good-for-nothing bankers, and a single light of hope. A hope in the form of a twenty-four-year-old snot-nosed college puke that happened to possess the only real marketing sense in the group.

Armand Arnold snorted and shifted in his chair. "I don't doubt your concern, your commitment to foil, ladies and gentlemen," he began, slowly.

The group nodded amongst themselves, proud of their commitment to foil.

"However, I doubt *any* of you have had an original thought in your lives." He looked up at the portrait of his grandfather and founder, Abner Arnold, for help, then slammed the report on the table. "We are sinking in a tidal wave of losses and debt, and you people bring me six more ways to roll aluminum! What's this one? Gatorback? What is that?"

One of the men sporting a bad toupee spoke up. "It's like our ribbed brand, but it looks like an alligator's back. It protects frozen food three percent better."

The man looked quite proud. Armand nodded calmly for a moment, a quiet, somewhat intrigued "three percent" slipped from his lips.

"Who the fuck cares!?! Three percent? *Three* percent? Jesus Christ." Armand reached for a cigar in the oak carved box—a gift from Allied Mines Corp. when times were better—that sat by the phone, but he found it empty. Slamming the top shut, he said, "How many times do I have to tell you bloodsuckers. People only buy so much fucking tin foil."

"Aluminum."

"Shut up," Armand screamed at a short, balding man who was one of the few people alive who would look better in a bad toupee. "Our market share hasn't gone anywhere with all these stupid gimmicks we've been trying.

We just spend more and more money to sell less and less *aluminum* foil."

He stopped for a moment, deciding to drop a bomb on these blood-sucking sycophants. "I've been talking to people for the last couple of months about selling Arnolds. And you know what? Nobody wants it! You know why? Because we lose too much money! We've got an R&D department that thinks we're working for NASA on the fuckin Space Station. We make foil you idiots!"

Armand tilted his head to the side, stretching the muscle that always seemed to be in spasm when he met with his board.

"Thanks to you people and ideas like this, the only offer I've gotten is so somebody can build a parking lot. You hear what I'm saying? We're worth more paved over! Lucky for you parasites no one's stupid enough to buy the actual company. But as soon as I find some moron with a big bank account, you're all history. Do you understand me?!"

Armand wanted to bite the tip off a good cigar, but had to settle for a ball-point pen instead. He hadn't really tried to sell the company, but he liked to say that every couple of years to put the Fear of God back in the board. He did get the parking lot offer—completely out of the blue. It was ridiculously low, even by Armand's degraded standards. Although, if things continued on their present course, he might just have to take it.

"Now, I want some ideas from you people. You hear me? *Ideas.* And none of these half-baked inspirations about alligator fuckin foil. What is that shit? You people actually get paid to come up with that crap? Jesus Christ."

He dismissed the meeting with a disgusted wave of his hand. As the rest of the good-for-nothings were walking out, his snot-nosed, college puke light of hope stepped up to him and tossed a letter of resignation on his desk.

II. BIODEGRADABLE PARENTS

It was well after eight when Satan dropped the plastic biodegradable grocery bag at the stoop of the thin graystone situated along Grace Street. It was a smallish two-bedroom rowhouse with windows that always seemed to be painted shut in the summer and drafty in the winter. He and his mom had found this place shortly after realizing that his dad wasn't ever coming to meet them at Union Station, that he hadn't just missed a train. But he was too young to remember much about the event, only flashes and what he heard in stories. His mother used to repeat the story every Friday evening at dinner. Satan thought about his mother's endless monologues, how she delivered them with religious zeal, reciting them by rote like a priest giving mass before his parish. The ramblings were always accompanied by fish in a sort of "no meat, no husband" ritual that seemed rooted in their Catholic faith and added to the spiritual tone. Satan recalled the terrifying day he realized all fatherless families, whether widowed, divorced or simply abandoned, didn't partake in the same ceremony. He was nine, and it came as quite a shock.

After finding his keys under an overdue jay walking ticket at the bottom of his coat pocket, Satan picked up the bag and started to climb the steps.

He credited that day so many years ago as the day he became disillusioned with his mother, his Church, and his life. But no matter how hard he tried to remove the story from his memory, it remained ingrained long after his mother was taken away in a padded wagon and could regurgitate it no more. As it turned out, she had started to take her show on the road as it were, preaching to people in the street about the dangers of wives allowing husbands to accept promotion, and eating meat on Fridays. To her, the two seemed inextricably connected.

She was diagnosed schizophrenic, phenolfrenic, parcelglasic, and about ten other unpronounceable things, then locked away as a possible menace to herself and society.

Somewhere uptown, his mother was at this moment eating fish. Where and how much, he didn't know. The only thing he was certain of was that she was still alive. And since it was Friday, if she was alive, she was eating fish—and most assuredly screaming at someone about husbands and promotions. Satan knew she was alive not because of the supernatural bond that is supposed to exist between mother and child. No, he knew because bills for her continuing care arrived every month and were placed by him in a stack in one corner of the living room. When one day a few weeks ago, he had noticed the pile was taking the shape of a Christmas tree, he rearranged the stacks to look like the Chicago skyline, complete with the Wrigley Building, Sears Tower, and John Hancock Center.

Satan opened the door of his home and went inside. He stepped over some spent Arnolds boxes lying on the floor. Several ends of foil also littered the ground, snip-its too small to be useful in his battle against irradiation. A note from his landlord lay just inside the door. He picked it off the floor and made a mental note to clean up the mess. Before opening the letter, he glanced at the stacks of bills from his mother's stay in the psychiatric ward of a hospital he had never seen. Had he not still been angry with her for leaving him like she did, he might have thought about getting her out, or at least visiting.

The skyline was his monument to abandonment.

The letters making up Chicago were all addressed to the same person, his absent father. Being such, Satan felt no need to pay them. Somewhere out there, his father couldn't get a car loan, a mortgage, or even a lousy Discover card because of late payments accruing on 180 months of medical bills. A small, but sweet revenge. Satan had often wanted to send away for his dad's credit report just to see how bad it was. But the fact that CreditDat wanted to gouge ten bucks out of him for the pleasure had so far kept him from doing so.

Satan reminded himself of the mental note he had made earlier on the street. He had to do something about these CreditDat people. What kind of tattletale mentality did it take for someone to have come up with such a thing? What kind of sick, twisted, revenge seeking soul would have visions of bad credit reports dancing in their head? Whoever this Mr. or Ms. CreditDat was had probably been made fun of by kids in school, or been the last kid picked for the team, or had never been asked to a prom. Whatever, he or she was definitely not well liked.

A face flashed in Satan's head.

Someone like Kenny Odorman.

Satan thought of the weird kid from his fourth grade class who smoked, hardly bathed, made fart noises under his arm in the presence of girls, and got his head shaved in a crew-cut exactly one year after it went out of style. This was a kid who bought his first pair of vertically striped elephant bell-bottom pants at a garage sale. It's a given throughout the known Universe that once something can be bought at a garage sale, it ceases to have any value of any kind to anyone on any planet.

In Kenny's defense, Satan had to admit one thing. Given his name, he could have turned out worse. How could one be expected to make it through life with a name like Kenny Odorman and not somehow get screwed up in the process? No matter how proud his parents were of the Odorman name and their family's contribution to America, it still was a rotten thing to do to a kid.

Satan's moment of compassion gave way to a sneer as he envisioned Kenny Odorman as he would be now: a chain-smoking, number crunching, tattle-telling fascist whose hate for credit shoppers was only outmatched by his love for his job and CreditDat.

Satan's solace came in knowing that all the Kenny Odorman's of the world would be swallowed by flames when the people of the Inner Earth reclaimed the planet. He rubbed his hands together in gleeful anticipation of that moment, then realized he was still holding the note. Ripping open the envelope, Satan read the enclosed:

Dear Mr. Dorobek...

He hated when surface dwellers addressed him by his birth name. He much preferred 'Satan' which was the idea of his friend Barris, a wordsmith working on his debut novel. The name lent itself to the Netherworlder theme Satan had chosen for his life. Yet, he had to admit to a bit of frustration at the tiresome task of having to explain to every ignorant that he was not a devil worshiper. How boorish it had become to deal with the masses. And yet, it was the masses that he would have to enlist if he were to achieve his goal. Surely, the Messiah would not be expected to lead the first and most dangerous trek into the center of the earth. As keeper of the secret, he would bestow upon the mindless followers the directions, and then when safe passage was secured, he could enter the inner world victorious.

Satan could do this. Noel Dorobek couldn't.

His landlord was but another Kenny Odorman of a different name.

Dear Mr....
I receive your check for month. Thank you for timeliness. I also receive note. No, you may not replace ceiling tile with lead plates.

Sincerely Your Best Regards,
Niromshi Nagasikima

Niro's family emigrated from Japan over a hundred years ago. He spoke perfect English, voted Republican. Still, every time Satan asked him for something, the communications came back missing determinants or verbs or pronouns or all of the above, and sounded like they had been written by some Japanese just arriving to buy his first piece of America.

It was annoying.

How does one answer a letter signed "Sincerely Your Best Regards?" That wasn't just haphazardly bad English; that was art. It also meant NO in a big way.

Satan looked up at the fiberglass ceiling panels which cleverly disguised what once had been three hundred and ninety-two rolls of Arnolds Aluminum, double fold. For now, they'd have to do—until he could convince his suddenly illiterate landlord to replace them with high-grade lead.

He felt safe in the mean time. The foil thickness had been calculated to block the greatest spectrum of radiation at the best possible price. It did an adequate job, eliminating most frequencies raining down from space. Satan had conceded to the existence of radio and television, and that their wavelengths were just too long to be stopped—unless he was prepared to encase himself in several feet of metal.

He had contemplated it, briefly. But after realizing he wouldn't be able to store up enough food to survive, he chose the long, slow death of gamma bombardment over the relatively short, painful death of starvation.

And in fact, Satan had learned to accept this small risk for technologies that brought news, sports, weather and Jeopardy.

There were, however, dangers Satan hadn't counted on; like cellular telephones. Every time he saw some driver put a handset to his money hungry ear, Satan felt a few million brain cells doing a death dance.

And then, there were those GPS navigation gizmos—an Orwellian device if ever there was one. The government was already trying to keep tabs on every living organism within its borders, and these people with their annoying pings and "turn heres" were actually paying someone to make it easier. Every time he watched the Space Shuttle lift off on one of those secret missions, he knew they were launching some new form of devious satellite meant to shrink people's already minuscule opportunity for privacy.

Satan smiled at the thought of what his house must look like on photos from the government's spy satellites.

Solid black. Not a detail to be spotted.

He felt safe from Big Brother.

But those damn cell phones…

•

A log on the fire settled, causing several sparks to fly out onto the hearth. Kelsey was lying quietly on the floor in front of the dying fire, her head resting comfortably on a fur rug. It was after midnight and Barris was still at the desk, his head lowered in that way it always was when he was deep in creative thought. Kelsey used to sit for hours when they first met, gazing at him in this pose, marveling at the writing process in action, in the flesh. However, that was two years ago, and the thrill of staring at an immobile, sullen, brooding man had lost most of its appeal since then. At first her awe had slowly given way to indifference, but more recently that indifference had turned to loathing when, after months of prodding, she was finally allowed to read something from his writings.

To say that Barris was a horrible writer was to overestimate the meaning of horrible. Not only was he a horrendous wordsmith in terms of content, but also in terms of volume. His debut novel scheduled to take a year to write had already taken two. The book slated for twenty-three chapters had one, and even that was only half finished.

Kelsey had wanted to be supportive of his work emotionally, as she had been financially, but reading the opening paragraphs, the words pounded at her sensibilities like a wooden club.

This story must be told. A man, a girl, a world of deaf people unwilling to listen. Hate so thick you could caress it, embrace it. Life so short, you might as well not measure.

It began in the streets of Chicago where the man, Barry, met her. Woman-girl, the embodiment of a Goddess, Kenya, blonde and built, made of sand and of steel.

She came to him from out of the deaf masses, the unfeeling numbers, which ruled the world. Came to him like Moses to the desert.

"I am Kenya," she announced to him as she stepped out of the moonless void of night. "I have come to make the music play once more."

He knew that she wanted to touch him, but he resisted her approach. He knew also that he would have to give in to the hunger before long. He was very hungry.

"Who cares if the music plays? No one can hear it."

"You can. You will be the one to make the people listen."

Barris stared at the yellow tablet in front of him.

People suck shit.

He stared at the words and wondered how he could fit them into his story. If he could find a way, he could retire knowing it had been a somewhat productive night. Contemplating his literary options, Barris looked toward the fire and saw Kelsey spread on the floor in a sexy pose as she waited for her man. An exquisitely smooth leg was peeking out from under the robe she had put on a few moments earlier and Barris could feel a stirring between his legs. He tried to remember the last time he and Kelsey had gone at it under the sheets.

It had been the night she pleaded with him to show her his work. She had buttered him up successfully with a candlelit dinner, great wine, and the best evening they had had in months.

Her face was so cute as she read the prose. A smile that suddenly changed to a frown as she realized the seriousness of the piece. Her interest was amazing, reading the eight pages three times before asking how he had come up with all of it.

Kelsey glanced over at her lover and saw that he was gazing at her leg. As their eyes met, she smiled, dreading what she had to tell him.

"Barris…"

"Yeah, Kelse…" He anticipated her offer to pull him away from his writing.

She held her forced smile for a moment. "I really think we should get something for Satan," she said, chickening out.

Barris stared at her. "I still say a couple of boxes of tin foil and he'd be happy."

"I guess…" she sighed, not really in response. "Barris?"

"Yes, dear?" he said, suspicious of her letting him off for his slight on Satan.

Kelsey glanced at the glowing cinders, then back at her lover. "Do you ever think about getting a job?"

"I don't understand what you're saying."

"I know you don't understand what I'm saying. I'm talking about a job, to make money. Have you ever considered taking one?"

"I thought we were going to give it a year and see what happened," he said, unsure why she was bringing this up now.

"It's been two years, Barris." She looked at the calendar on the wall. "Two years, thirteen days."

"Has it been that long?" Barris picked up the notepad and realized he'd have to revise his estimated completion date since his original deadline had passed unnoticed nearly thirteen months ago. "It couldn't be that long, could it?"

"Two years, Barris."

"I thought we were going to begin counting the year from when we moved in together," Barris said.

"Then it would be two years, nine days," said Kelsey matter-of-factly. "Remember? We moved in together on Monday, after meeting each other on Friday."

Barris somewhat recalled the event. He squinted his eyes, glaring suspiciously at Kelsey. "You're doing this because I thwarted your little plan to buy the Marshall's those gym memberships, aren't you?"

Kelsey shifted and deliberately pulled a bit more of the robe over her leg. "Barris, how old are you?"

"Thirty-two…" He thought about it. "…three?"

•

The face of Kenny Odorman filled Satan's field of view. Just a big head with little stubs of hair sticking straight up. Milky white skin spotted by three tiny brown dots that would someday be moles.

In fact, that was all that was visible of Kenny. His ten-year-old frame was disguised as a Goodyear blimp under seven layers of winter clothes and a pair of mittens Satan found himself somewhat envious of.

The mittened hands gripped tightly one on each of Satan's arms, Kenny was smiling one of those evil grins he displayed just before the toilets blew up or the class goldfish was found dead with a toothpick in the eye.

No note. No motive.

Satan wasn't really Satan, not yet having been given his prestigious pseudonym; he was just nine-year-old Noel Dorobek. It was cold and snowy and Kenny Odorman was about to push Noel and his metal coaster down the steep side of the school hill. The side you weren't supposed to slide down because of the trees at the bottom.

Kenny let out a menacing laugh, his eyes bulging with a crazed rapture as he shoved the coaster off. In a desperate act of survival, little Noel reached out for Kenny, grabbed the tips of his mittens that were clipped to the sleeves of his jacket and held on with locked fists.

The coaster raced down the hill, picking up speed as it headed into the steepest part, Noel on board, Kenny dragging behind. Out of control, both kids screaming at the top of their lungs, the metal saucer sped toward the row of oaks that waited at the bottom. Under the best conditions it took a deft hand to guide a coaster through the shrubs and trees, to give the proper shift of weight at the proper time. Even if he weren't careening down the slope backward, towing a yelping hunk of dead weight, Noel had none of the skills necessary.

Noel peeked over his shoulder to see the big oak he had carved his and Cindy Harper's name in dead ahead and approaching at just under the speed of sound. He tensed up, expecting a sonic boom at any minute—that is, if he and Kenny didn't hit the tree first.

Radical deceleration loomed about ten feet away.

Sonic boom on the verge of sounding, all control and hope lost, Noel saw the tree and the words NOEL + CIND—he hadn't ever finished the carving and now wouldn't ever get to.

He and the tree would become one.

The coaster, however, never reached the tree. A few feet from impact, the saucer hit a root, stopping instantly and throwing Noel past the big oak into a band of pricker bushes. Kenny, still moving at nearly Mach one an arms-length behind the aluminum projectile, rammed face first into the edge of the saucer, splitting the skin between his lip and nose wide open. With that unbelievable luck that seems in play in so many childhood accidents, the impact point was just low enough not to break his nose and just high enough not to lose any teeth.

Noel had been thrown for what seemed like a hundred feet, though it turned out to be twelve. Shaking out the fog in his head and the prickers in his pants, Noel tried to focus his eyes. When they finally did, he could see Kenny Odorman rising out of the crimson snow like a phoenix from the ashes. He could see the gash under his nose oozing blood. He could see the blood stained grin forming on an unhappy, revenge seeking face.

What he didn't see was the fist.

THWACK!!!

Satan sat straight up in his bed, his heart racing from the jolt of reliving Kenny's punch. A punch that broke the left side of Satan's jaw and bent two molars in. To this day, Satan was convinced his inability to digest certain types of food had something to do with his bicuspids being forcibly altered.

Satan felt the pain of last night's Two-For-One pepperoni and sausage pizza. As he moved, the ball of coagulated cheese that rested on the bottom of his stomach shifted. Reaching over, he grabbed a bottle of Maalox™ from his nightstand and downed four tablets.

It was daylight outside, a few minutes past seven.

Satan threw off the covers and put his feet on the cold floor before remembering it was December. Once he regained the feeling in his toes, he stood and went out from his room, down the hall and into the bathroom.

After relieving himself of what must have been nearly a gallon of liquid, Satan shook himself off and stood in front of the mirror. His pink face had changed little from when he was a kid. There was hardly a trace of stubble even though it had been two days since he last shaved. Wiggling the once broken jaw which still clicked most annoyingly when he ate, Satan made a series of faces into the glass. If there was one enjoyable thing about mornings, it was this: making faces, talking to yourself, farting, scratching, all those things you couldn't do in public. Satan had once asked a friend if she did such things and was immediately branded a disgusting and vile lunatic.

It was as if no one else scratched or farted or made faces or posed in the mirror. The subject, like bad breath, was taboo. But Satan had seen his mother do these things, seen his father, his neighbor, the woman across the street, and once when he was twenty and had a girlfriend—the first and last—he had seen her do them too.

In fact, she left him because of it. Her reasoning was this: how could they ever build a relationship after he had seen her passing gas.

And from Satan's point of view, it might have been for the best. She really stank.

III. THE BIG RED THING

The huge red office building rose above the street like a giant fire hydrant. No one in town was quite sure why the color was chosen or what it meant, but it definitely stood out. Which was great for giving directions. The Hilton? It's just a few blocks away. By that Big Red Thing. You can't miss it.

Kelsey stared up at the building, her body automatically leaning to the right as the clouds passing over the roof gave her the impression that she was about to fall to the left. She loved the feeling of imbalance. Every morning before work, she stood at the front entrance and gazed up at the optical illusion.

It's beautiful, she thought to herself.

"Lady, you wanna move outta the way," came a voice from behind. "I gotta get ta work some time today."

Kelsey stepped out of the way and apologized to the man who grumbled and went inside. Glancing up one last time, she sighed, the wonder leaving her body, then followed the steady stream of suits and skirts into the red enclave.

From Kelsey's office twenty-nine floors over the street, the city looked more majestic, cleaner, somehow more orderly. The dirt and grime and trash that littered certain neighborhoods, from this height, only added shading and depth to their character.

On the desk in front of Kelsey lay the blueprints for a new development just west of The Loop. A mix of retail, residential and office space meant to lure high-tech industries and workers alike with its spacious accommodations and covered skyways. A quick glance at the plans and one might mistake them for the design of a new computer chip—the halls, printed circuits; the open lobbies, resistors and power supplies.

Kelsey stared at the drawing and imagined the people as electrons navigating the tiny corridors.

"What do you think, Kelse?"

A round, red face was smiling at her from across the desk.

"Looks pretty, but what about the increase in traffic?"

The round face connected to a round body scrunched up, wrinkles forming on the forehead. Leo Lincoln thought for a moment. "Hon, let's not get all stressed out. We'll work that out when the time comes. But look at it." He ogled the drawing. "Isn't it great? Pedestrian bridges, glass atriums, cute apartments..." Looking up, "...built-in microwaves."

"Leo, even if we grant a variance on traffic, there's still the little problem of Arnolds Aluminum. They're not going to just sell us their factory because we think it's a convenient place for a parking lot." Kelsey rifled through her desk, searching for a stick of gum or a Lifesaver, something to get rid of the bad taste she knew she was about to get in her mouth. Leo Lincoln (always said as one word when he introduced himself or signed his name—even on cards to his wife—so you couldn't in any way forget his last name) had been appointed city planner simply because of his family's place in history. More than a century later, the Lincolns were still living off the laurels of their one bright light in a tree of not bad, but bland apples. And this Lincoln, Leo Lincoln, had an annoying habit of misquoting his famous ancestor to make the simplest of points.

"As my great, great grandfather used to say: let's cross that bridge once we've built it." Pulling the lid off a brass dish on the desk, he grabbed the remaining piece of candy and popped it in his mouth. "Anyway, Arnolds Aluminum is dead," he said, sucking on what Kelsey realized was her last piece of candy anywhere. She ended her search. "They'll be bankrupt inside a year," Leo added.

"And what if they're not?"

"Hey, I'll wait four score if I have to."

•

"I'd like to buy five hundred and thirty-six stamps."

Marla Jenkins, Postal Worker of the Month, mother of two, glanced up at the source of the voice. The man in front of her was six-one, with icy blue eyes that somehow appeared fake. She couldn't tell because of an oversized jacket, but he seemed a few pounds heavier than he should be, more out of shape than fat. His body bundled up, scarf wrapped around his neck, she had the distinct impression she was staring at a giant kid.

"First Class?" she asked.

Satan looked at the woman behind the counter distrustfully. In her blue-gray uniform she looked like a Confederate soldier still hoping to bring down the Union. Past her, a banner with "Season's Greetings" was strung over an opening that led into the heart of the office. He could see several of the woman's uniformed comrades shuffling envelopes and moving boxes as if time were somehow slowed down once you passed through the doorway.

"How can I guarantee a package be received before the next ice age?"

"Are you trying to be funny," said the woman, glaring at him.

Satan ignored the stare, instead keeping watch on the action behind her. A man with a bunch of mistletoe pinned to the brim of his hat was lifting packages off a conveyor at a speed that made one wonder if the room, the man, and the conveyor weren't completely underwater. Satan saw no air bubbles, so he had to return to his original hypothesis of time distortion.

"The letters I need to send are of the utmost importance," he finally replied, still eyeing the man who, whenever a female employee walked by, pointed to the mistletoe, and said something that was most assuredly tasteless, quite possibly illegal. The man wasn't getting any takers. All the while several hundred packages were speeding off to incorrect destinations. "They are of grave concern to our planet."

"Do you want the stamps or not?"

"Take the Goddamn stamps!" shouted someone waiting in line.

A standoff was at hand. North versus South. Only this time the South was winning. Realizing that the more reliable alternatives to the USPO— FedEx, UPS, etc.—would cost him several thousand dollars and that the someone shouting from in line was nearly seven feet tall and at least three hundred pounds, Satan finally agreed to purchase 536 First Class stamps.

After a few moments of counting, the Confederate woman looked up. "I don't have five hundred and thirty-six. I only have five hundred and four."

"I need five hundred and thirty-six."

"I just told you I don't have that many."

"This is the United States Post Office, am I correct?"

The woman just stared at him.

"I haven't somehow wandered into a Guatemalan Post office, have I?"

Picking at a corner of one sheet, Marla began losing her award-winning cool. "Do you want the stamps?"

"Yes. Five hundred and thirty-six of them."

"Are you deaf," said the big man in line, noticing that a piece of tin foil was hanging out of the back of Satan's cap. "She don't have that many."

Satan glanced at the man, then back to the woman. "Rain sleet snow, you're fine. But run out of stamps and the wheels fall off." He paused. "I don't suppose you could possibly get some more?" Satan pointed to the worker to the woman's left. "This man here has plenty of stamps."

"Don't work that way. You have to buy 'em from him separately."

Satan was about to start screaming when he noticed a security camera pointed directly at him.

"Fine." Satan paid the woman for her entire supply, then saddled over to her co-worker. "I'll need thirty-two, First Class."

"I'm sorry, you'll have to go to the back of the line, Sir."

Marla smiled at him from the adjacent window. "Happy Holidays."

•

Satan's tongue felt like it had been dragged ten miles over asphalt behind a car leaking motor oil. He licked envelope number 535, stuffed in the accompanying letter, then folded over the flap and sealed it. Wetting the second to the last stamp on his tongue, he affixed it to the top right corner. Satan picked up the felt-tip he had bought at Clancy's Drug after the postal debacle. He was sure he would be banned from ever returning to that particular station, especially after the supervisor jumped over the counter and attempted to strangle him.

Satan stared at the bag the pen had been in. "Clancy Wishes You 'Happy Holidays,'" it said over a sketch of a grinning, bespectacled man with his remaining hairs combed over the top of his head.

Clancy, whoever he was, was dead and not wishing anybody anything. Opened in 1896 with what was surely the biggest party in town (an old photograph that commemorated the event showed a rush of eight people— six if you didn't count Clancy and his wife), Clancy's Drugs hadn't changed much. Oh, the displays were modern enough, and the sign out front was only a few years old, but the focus was the same as it had been in those first days. Namely, that two percent of the shop was devoted to "drugs." The other ninety-eight percent was made up of underwear, shampoo, batteries, snow shovels, Christmas lights, greeting cards and, of course, pens and pencils.

The checker, a beautiful woman in her mid-twenties, looking younger than that with creamy, smooth skin and long, silky blonde hair, had watched

Satan from the moment he walked in the store and was blasted by the hot air from the fan over the door. Her stare was not of the usual type given him, which resembled more than anything the way a policeman looks from your driver's license to your face then back when he's pulled you over.

This stare was far more engaging.

"Can I help you?" said a pleasant voice behind him.

Satan had been trying to figure out what color ink to use in addressing his letters. Something that would make the strongest impression. It was down to two. Shocking Pink and Lime Green. When he turned toward the voice, he saw the young woman's visage for the first time. There was a stunningly natural beauty about her. The effortless smile, warm and familiar. The way her cheeks seemed innately rosy. Her eyes were incandescent and appeared deep blue one moment, green the next. She wore little makeup, if any. The nametag that rested on an appropriately proportioned chest said, *Ion*.

Ion stood over the strange man who had been crouching in front of the pens and pencils for nearly ten minutes. The average pen purchase took less than thirty seconds. Blue, black, or highlighter—that was pretty much decided in advance. The half minute was used to weigh the merits of buying just one pen or picking up a pack of say three or five. Most people went for three. Five seemed too much. One…you were always losing pens. For that reason, three-packs were the industry's biggest sellers. Everybody was happy. The customers got a deal, and so did the pen manufacturers, since as soon as that package was opened, pens two and three were as good as gone.

The man in front of her was by far the most interesting person entering Clancy's that day, maybe that month. His face held a sad countenance that was strangely appealing. Ion was a connoisseur of people, and there was something very tasty about this one. Already, this guy's aura spoke volumes, even as she sensed a lack of energy being emitted by his brain. Which bothered her somewhat. Either he was an idiot or a genius. And he could only be a genius if he was consciously deflecting his brainwaves inward.

She had to know which.

"No, thank you. I'm contemplating an esthetic decision," Satan responded.

"Must be important."

"Gravely."

Satan returned to the rack of pens. Fluorescent Yellow was looking good as well. A smooth leg caught the corner of his eye and he forced himself to ignore it.

"What're they for?" Ion asked, more interested in the man's head than in his choice of pens. She reached out toward his skull with an open palm, hoping to pick up some activity. She drew her hand closer to his knit cap and felt not only a lack of energy but also a lack of warmth.

Shifting a bit, Satan sent the back of his head into Ion's fingers, startling both of them and making a crinkling sound.

"What was that?" Ion asked, almost at the same time he said, "What are you doing?"

Ion pulled her hand back, rubbing it as though it had come in contact with acid or nuclear waste. "Your head crinkled."

"My head, Miss…" looking at her name tag again, "…Ion, did not crinkle."

"Just Ion. And I heard it."

Satan lifted the front of his cap, revealing the shiny material, then tucked it back into place.

Ion scrunched up the right side of her face. "You're wearing tin foil on your head."

"It's aluminum. I wish it were tin."

"Aluminum," she whispered to herself. The wheels were turning in her brain. Suddenly, she got excited. "Does it somehow refocus and magnify your thought potential?"

He sighed. "No." He tried to keep his mind on the pens. Maybe if he ignored her she'd go away.

"Does it recycle your body's aura, drastically elevating your emotional state?" she asked, excitedly, still trying to charm him.

He shook his head. He was starting to realize he might have to abort his pen purchase if he was to ever get out of Clancy's.

"Well, it's obviously not a fashion statement," she said, giving up.

He decided ignoring her wasn't working. Confrontation seemed to be the only way out of this. "If you must know, it protects my brain from gamma rays."

Ion cocked her head to one side, peering at Satan and shifting her jaw. "Gamma rays?" she said, one eyebrow rising a bit.

"Yes," Satan sneered. "I really don't have time to explain what they are. Let's just say—they're *bad*." He spoke the last words as if she were a child.

"I know what they are," she said, flatly. "I was just hoping for something a little less—I don't know—stupid."

"Well, have a nice, short life."

Ion was accustomed to men melting under her gaze, following her around, staring, constantly asking her out. It annoyed her that the gender was so easily bewitched, without any effort on her part. The only thing more irritating was someone she couldn't charm.

"And here I was, thinking you might be a genius or something. You're just whacked, is all," she said, irritated.

"You're making a diagnosis of *my* mental health? This from someone who wants to recycle my *aura*," he said, pretending her words hadn't bothered him. "Ion...the name just radiates stability. What are you, some kind of Free Radical?"

Ion gave out a sort of half laugh, half grunt. "Funny," she said without any inflection.

Satan stood up and faced her. She looked even more beautiful close up, tight pores, smooth, high cheekbones. He pretended not to notice.

"I'd like to purchase these." Satan held out the packages of pens. Shocking Pink, Lime Green and Fluorescent Yellow.

She ignored the items. "It came to me in a dream."

"Excuse me?"

"The name, it came to me in a dream."

Jingle Bells was coming over the store's sound system—the Perry Como version or maybe Mitch Miller. Satan couldn't tell. "I'm sure your psychiatrist is very proud of you and thanks you from the bottom of his heart-shaped pool he's now able to afford after helping you figure that out."

Ion was looking over her shoulder at a clock hanging above a Hallmark Gift Angel. The hands of the timepiece displayed a quarter to three.

"I get off in fifteen minutes. Have you had lunch?"

"No," Satan said, his arm still outstretched. "Nor have I paid for these pens."

With a shrug of her shoulders, she said, "Don't worry about it."

Having heard about several sting operations directed at local government officials, Satan apprehensively searched Clancy's for men in mirrored glasses, cameras, any sign of security. He spotted a two-way mirror overlooking the Timex watches.

Seizing the pens, Ion went behind the counter, pulled out a bag and placed them inside. "Here."

"I know my rights protecting me against entrapment," Satan said loudly to someone other than the young woman.

"Wow. You are whacked."

.

"Sixties sensibilities, Y2K technology," Ion said while chewing on a tofu-sprouts sandwich. "That's the future. Club a baby seal, dump toxins in the Lake and you might find yourself the bad guy in a music video or the poster boy for moronofthemonth.com."

A fountain surrounded by beautiful red poinsettias shot water into the air. Several sparrows tiptoed around the shimmering pool, filling the garden with the sounds of spring.

Sitting amongst blooming kaffir lilies, palm trees and ivy, Satan stared out at the bitter cold city beyond the six-story glass atrium of Crystal Gardens. He glanced at the other people scattered about the botanical oasis, eating their lunches and enjoying the warm air and pleasant call of the birds. Several men in suits were eyeing him lewdly, which make him uncomfortable until he realized they were staring at Ion.

She ignored the ogling suits. Men stared at her so often, it had become background noise. "So," she took another bite, "what do you need the pens for?"

"Your pen fetish is becoming quite annoying," he said as he stared at his food. His stomach was grumbling for something to fill it.

"Can you ever just answer a question?" she said.

He glanced up at her, harshly, then back at his meal. She had forced him to purchase a vegetarian sandwich, nixing the half-pound cheeseburger he wanted to order, saying they—he wasn't sure if it was burgers themselves or the cows—destroy the ozone. He hadn't touched a bite. A fly landed on his food, which looked to Satan like a crushed beetle patty. The fly danced around for a moment, then sampled a bit of Satan's lunch. It didn't look very happy. In fact, it seemed to have the same distaste for the food he did. Perhaps it had a relative there in the patty. He could've sworn he saw the fly spit out a chunk of the stuff, before cleaning its feet and taking off.

"I'm personally addressing a letter to the President of the United States," he said, watching the fly buzz off to more appetizing fare. "...demanding the government release information it has about the existence of subterranean intelligent life."

"You really believe people live at the center of the earth?" Her eyes followed two sparrows that were courting each other, circling, diving and twisting.

Satan saw the fly drop dead and crash to the ground, food poisoning no doubt.

"Absolutely. There's no question the government is hiding something. Besides, many great minds throughout history have speculated that the biblical story of Adam and Eve refers to man being cast out from the Inner Earth."

Ion gazed at the birds as the male gently swooped down and gathered a dead insect from the cement and offered it tenderly to his future mate as a gift. "And a lotta people thought the world was flat and leeches were a good idea."

Satan stared in horror as the birds tore at the fly. He pushed the sandwich away, deciding he'd go hungry.

She took another bite. "Besides, it's not like the President reads everything that's sent to him." A thought hit her. "Why don't you cut it to music. Stream it on the Web. Better exposure."

Satan had never actually used the World Wide Web, but he was fairly sure the President wasn't spending a lot of time surfing it.

When Ion didn't get an answer, she shrugged her shoulders. "Just an idea." She went back to her sandwich. "It's all about exposure."

Satan was thinking very much about exposure as he shifted to get a better view of her cleavage. He normally didn't bother with such things, but the tiny hint of her skin was sending tingles through his body. He could see even more if he sat up straight.

His posture was improving, she thought.

But then the feeling began to annoy him. He kept shifting his legs, attempting to find a comfortable place for his erection to land. The lunch-time crowd, he figured, wouldn't appreciate him manually resetting himself. So for now, he had to be content with indirect methods.

There was a long, uncomfortable silence. The conversation was waning.

Then Ion glanced up, a quizzical look on her face. "Tell me why do you call yourself Satan?"

"My *friends* call me Satan."

"What do your enemies call you?"

"Did I make fun of your name?"

"Yes."

He huffed out a bit of air, which only made him feel hungrier. "I told you. It's because of my Netherworlder interest."

"I don't know. Sounds evil."

"I'm not."

Ion studied the man sitting across from her.

"No, you seem harmless. Sorta pathetic, actually."

"Why, thank you."

"Why don't you call yourself something else? Like Hades or Osiris or Pluto."

"Pluto? Who gets to be Mickey Mouse?"

She glared at him, "Prior to his gig at Disney, Pluto worked as God of the Underworld."

"In that case, why don't I just call myself 'Guido' or 'Vinnie' or 'Rocko?'" he said, imposing a thick, Southside accent on the names.

Ion slowly took Satan in—from his shoes to the top of his knit cap. She bobbed her head. "I like that." She seized a huge piece of sandwich between her teeth and tore it off. Some sprouts fell to the ground. "So, Vinnie, let me see this letter."

"My name is not Vinnie…"

Before he could stop her, she snatched a folder resting on the stone wall next to him. She opened the folder and pulled out the neatly typed correspondence printed on thick, gray paper.

"Very nice."

Ion held the paper up to the light. A burgundy logo that resembled the earth with a hole at the center dominated the letterhead. EARTH, INC. was splashed across the top of the page.

"'To Whom It May Concern,'" she read aloud, then stopped to shoot Satan a look. "'Dear Mr. President' might get a better response."

"I'm hoping that if I just ignore him, he will go away," he said, sounding a major theme of Satan's life.

"Change it." Glancing back at the page, she continued. "'To whom… blah, blah, blah.' All right:

> 'We at EARTH, INC. are aware of the fact that our government has been hiding the truth from us—that there are people beneath the surface of the planet, and that the existence of these brothers-in-arms has been kept secret.
>
> 'Be forewarned that we will take any and all steps to reach these beings and reveal the truth. The balance of power will be altered.'

"Sincerely, blah, blah, blah."

Just under Satan's signature was "cc:" and a list of names that went on for seven pages. Ion flipped through them quickly.

"You cc:'d the entire Congress? Both houses?"

"And the Vice President, as well as the Washington Post, New York Times, L.A. Times, and Chicago Sun-Times."

"The letter's only two paragraphs long," Ion said, not quite understanding.

"I'm hoping five percent get through the mail safely."

"If you really want attention, why not cut out letters from newspapers and magazines and paste them together. I mean, what the hell does this mean, Vinnie?"

Satan stared at Ion for a long moment, then did something he never did—he explained.

•

Ion listened to it all.

The letter, the excerpts from books and magazines she had never heard of, the reports he had amassed on gamma rays and other radiation, natural and unnatural. Satan also mentioned his father several times, that he used to come into his room at night and talk of great men and even greater adventures, but she wasn't sure how the bedtime stories fit in.

Satan told her his own story, which should have been saved for bedtime. Not because it got her excited at all, but because it was putting her to sleep. A father who disappeared, a mother who went crazy. Interspersed was a full-blown treatise on the subject of space-borne radiation backed up by quotes from scientists arguing pro and con about the effects this radiation had on aging. And even some evidence—from a science magazine she did recognize—that continual exposure to radiation slowly eroded the genetic coding in DNA until the body could no longer replicate healthy cells, leading eventually to death. This had been the one moment of interest to her, but it was mired in details that only a government bureaucrat would enjoy.

There was, of course, in none of his sources, any mention of putting foil on your head, but for that, Satan said he had his own research.

They were walking in Kronan's on Dearborn, past the lawn furniture and gas grills. *Low, low, low, low prices*, the signs said. It was six degrees outside.

Coyly, Ion reached over and grabbed Satan's hat from atop his head and put it on her own. The action was not received with the playful chiding and mischievous glance she would have expected from any other man. Conduct such as this was usually taken as the opening salvo in the game of chase and capture. Unfortunately, Satan had never taken part in such sport.

"Give me that!" Satan was grabbing at his head. "Do you make a habit of tearing off people's clothing?"

"Sometimes," she said, still hoping for a return volley.

"Well, I am glad to provide for your continued amusement, however, I am not a specimen at the petting zoo, so please restrain yourself."

"Jesus, it's not like you're bald or anything." She looked at him for a moment, then patted down a bit of his hair that was sticking up. "In fact, you look better."

He knocked her hand away. "Stop that."

Snatching the cap from her head, he quickly pulled it back on.

"It was only off for a second," she said, a little irritated "It's not gonna kill you."

"Oh, really? Sit," he pointed to a sofa situated directly in front of fifty yards of microwaves.

"Excuse me?" she said, railing a bit at the apparent order.

He was losing any hint of bravado he had managed to gather for that brief instant.

"Do you want to show me something?"

"Yes." He was growing annoyed by her, but she had some worthy virtues he was enjoying, namely two. One, she was rather attractive, and two, she was still talking to him.

"Then say, 'please.'"

This was one of the main reasons Satan didn't like to commingle with the public. Their incredible need for false courtesies. Along with an array of other fine advancements, Satan was sure the Inner-worlders had done away with such nonsense.

"Sit," he clenched, "Please."

Ion sat, sinking into the cushions until she was almost swallowed up by them. She finally slid over to one end where the effect was not as pronounced.

She watched as Satan headed toward the door, then back into the bitter cold. He disappeared across the street into a small market. In a moment, he emerged with a tiny brown paper bag in his hand. After several honks and at least two profane utterances, Satan reentered Kronan's through the front entrance.

Satan dug into the bag as he approached her and drew out a medium size russet potato, which appeared to be leftover from a harvest in the late 60's. "Those marauders should be convicted of price gouging. I only hope a national grocery chain moves in next door and puts them out of business." He placed the potato on the coffee table in front of her.

Ion glanced at the tuber. She had no idea what he was going to do, but she sincerely hoped it didn't include eating this emaciated fruit of the earth.

Satan reached in the bag once more and pulled out a second potato, which was most likely from two harvests before the first's. "Now, the Earth is constantly being bombarded by an incredible spectrum of radiation. Microwaves, gamma, et cetera." In a moment, he was digging deep in his pockets. When his hands finally emerged, he produced a folded stash of foil. "If we all lived inside, under the surface like we're supposed to, there'd be no problem. Only we don't. So, there is." He tore the foil in half, wrapped one of the russets, the uglier of the two, then returned the unused portion of the metal sheets to his pocket.

He left the other bare.

"What are you doing?"

"Shhh."

He scooped the potatoes off the table and walked over to the bank of microwave ovens.

Satan placed one potato each into two adjacent ovens. It sounded easier than it actually was, because he had to choose which microwaves to use from the lot of them. He picked the two that appeared the most uncomplicated to operate.

"You're not supposed to put foil in—" She stopped when it was apparent the only person listening was the salesmen who'd been checking her out from the moment they walked in. He was smiling at her, leering, raising his brow and generally being a pig. He was so typical. The guy didn't have the guts to come talk to her. He was doing all this on—what? On the off chance she'd give him the nod to approach her. Then he'd saunter over and give her a load of macho b.s. Disgusting. A real man would have cut the shit and said hello in the first place. She wanted to flip him off, but she thought better of it. She'd save that for their exit.

Following several aborted attempts, Satan set the times to seven minutes each, then pressed the START buttons.

For the next six minutes, sparks flew, Satan smiled, and Ion made eye contact with the salesman to keep his attention from the pyrotechnic display taking place in his department.

At about six minutes, fifty seconds the microwave with the foil wrapped potato burst into flames.

A lesser man might have turned tail and run, but Satan knew he didn't have the foot speed to outrun anybody. So, he did the only thing he could do...open the door and grab the potato.

Ten ticks later, at seven minutes exactly, the second microwave beeped, drawing the attention of the enamored salesman. Satan extracted the bare potato. Steam rose off the brown skin and he kept it hopping between his left hand and his right hand like a...well...like a hot potato. Then he tossed it onto the coffee table, just as the second microwave was engulfed by the growing inferno.

"Hey, you! What are you doing?" shouted the salesman. "You can't cook in here!"

Satan didn't have much time and he knew it.

He nervously tore open the foil to reveal a russet that was nearly as crisp as when it went in.

"This is my brain," he said, poking at it to prove his point. With a nod, he invited her to do the same.

Ion nudged it hesitantly. Mostly because the salesman was in full gallop and three more microwaves were burning, as well as a lovely dinette set.

The salesman's breathing was heavy, and the blood was pounding in his head like a jackhammer. He had to catch these people. He hadn't been selling much lately, and his boss was just looking for an excuse to can him.

Ion and Satan looked up and saw the salesmen was only twenty feet away, but to get to them he had to negotiate a tangled labyrinthine maze of sofas, loveseats and matching chairs meant to confuse shoppers into buying something, anything, just to be told the way out.

Satan took the moment to push his finger into the bare potato. It was soft and mushy and his finger went right in.

"This...is *your* brain."

Even with all that was transpiring around her, Ion had to admit, she was impressed. "Cool."

"Don't ever touch my foil."

"Fine," she said as she stood up and grabbed Satan's hand, dragging him toward the door just as the salesman leapt for her on the couch. "Time to go."

Kronan's was becoming polluted with noxious fumes from burning plastic. Satan tried not to breathe it in, but had to give that up when he started getting dizzy from a lack of oxygen.

"Breathe, stupid," Ion shouted over the sounds of alarms and exploding major appliances.

Chaos reigned as people scrambled to get out of the store. Just before the two of them reached the entrance, Ion stopped and turned toward the salesman who was just getting to his feet. She cupped her hands gently under her wonderfully perfect breasts and mouthed "these could have been yours" to him, punctuating it with a little grin.

The salesman began to cry.

Satan was watching the images flashing on the bank of televisions at the back of the store. The last thing he could make out before Ion shoved him through the door was a hundred news bulletins displaying a hundred fire trucks approaching an equal number of blazes.

The trucks all looked very much like the one arriving outside Krogan's.

Satan stood on the landing outside of his apartment with Ion one step below.

"I had fun tonight," she said, her eyes lighting up as if she was surprised by this sudden insight.

"I expect we'll be jailed by morning," he said, fully expecting the police to arrive at any minute with a warrant and a lot of shouting.

Ion didn't react to his words. Instead, she remained silent for a moment, touching his chin, moving his face first to the left, then to the right, surveying him. Finally, she dropped her hand to her side.

"Goodnight, Vinnie."

He was about to say something about the name thing when she quickly turned and descended the steps. As she made her way down the sidewalk without another glance in his direction, Satan decided to keep his objection to himself, since on the one hand he didn't really think it would do any good, and on the other he was enjoying the vision of her departure.

•

Thinking of Ion, Satan put the felt-tip to the envelope and finished addressing the last letter. He held it in front of him and gave it a final look, checking the number, street, and zip: 1600 Pennsylvania Ave., Washington, D.C. 20005, then threw it on the pile with the rest.

He felt the sleepiness that comes with accomplishment, the restfulness of a job well done. Satan switched off the light on the desk and shuffled off to bed to dream of someday reaching the inner world…and, perhaps, of Ion as well.

IV. IONIZATION

Two days after meeting Ion, Satan had his first wet dream. It's true, Ion wasn't actually in the dream—Captain Kirk was, which somewhat troubled Satan. All he could remember was that the Enterprise was going into an ion storm and Kirk had sent someone, Finny his name was, into a pod to take readings. When the storm became a danger to the ship, Kirk had to jettison the pod—and Finny—to save his crew.

That's about where the dream ended, jettisoning the ion pod.

Satan hoped the meaning of his next dream would be clearer.

•

Arnolds Aluminum sprawled along Hauser Avenue in the old industrial district that was once Chicago's largest producer of jobs as well as soot. In the city's plan to attract "cleaner" industries to the area, the plant was the last smudge mark. Its grime-frosted windows were perennially half-open or broken. Even in the arctic cold of winter, the heat escaping from them distorted the top of the building, making the roof waver like a desert mirage. Four white brick stacks, which because of strict legislation spewed much less soot and fumes, still polluted the air enough to leave a faint taste of metal hanging over the area. Locals called it The Foil Factor.

Armand Arnold's office faced the "nice" side of the street—a dormant, hideous looking factory that seemed to have been constructed in stages out of whatever had been lying around at the time. Smooth Deco pillars rose like giant hat feathers before its main entrance, evidently an attempt to distract attention from the blight that was the rest of the structure.

He gazed at the vacant former home of Clark Pipe and Washers. Twenty years ago, in an attempt to streamline operations and eliminate confusion, the company dropped "and Washers" from its name. The sandblasted lettering was still visible between the two tallest hat feathers. Clark Pipe, the country's fifth-largest producer of copper plumbing, had taken a beating when the rising price of copper drove most contractors to switch to plastics. Since Clark Pipe was singularly dedicated to making the best copper pipe, plastics were an abomination, an aberration, and wouldn't be allowed to dilute the company's commitment to quality pipe.

In the end, Clark Pipe was reduced to buying pennies from the public. A dollar for ninety. Armand remembered reading that the company even tried getting its banks to make cash payments to the factory in those copper pieces. Logistics alone caused the banks to turn down the request.

It reminded him of Arnolds Aluminum. So many times, he had begged his father to let him diversify the company. After a while, when Armand realized he was getting nowhere with his dad except perhaps out the door and out of the will, he resigned himself to the fact that his father was going to run the company just like *his* father had, and run it that way until he died.

Who knew he'd live to be ninety-six?

Now, the company finally in his hands, Armand Arnold had to use all his capital just to keep from losing more of the market. His dream was dead. Expanding into resealable storage bags, trash bags, and reusable containers was not to be.

Plastic, Armand realized, was killing this street.

The Clark Pipe factory, as well as the empty Polytronics plant next door, had been purchased by C-City Developers.

Polytronics' claim to shame was that it had invented the 8-track tape player. A uniquely useless device. Amazingly, the company remained in business until 1988. No one has satisfactorily explained who was buying the players since the tapes to put in them hadn't been on sale since the seventies.

C-City planned to demolish the entire block and put up a multi-use village of offices, shops, and apartments. No one from C-City had made contact with Armand or anyone at Arnolds Aluminum regarding plans for the street. Still, it made him nervous. Especially, after he got that unsolicited offer to purchase the land on which the company sat for a parking lot.

Armand's calls to the city planner's office were received with pleasant assurances that Chicago had not turned its back on the blue-collar man, but "won't it be great for the neighborhood?"

Armand Arnold wasn't sure about that, but he *was* sure that his new neighbors in their white-collar townhouses and white-collar offices weren't going to be that thrilled about the blue-collar smells drifting across the street.

Once Renaissance Village was built, it would only be a matter of time before municipal restrictions and resident outrage over pollution would run Arnolds Aluminum out of business.

Armand picked up the phone and dialed a number he hadn't used in months. It was time to fight back. He knew he'd have to release the funds from the small war chest he had originally created to launch new products; now a mere pittance, it was only kept for its symbolic importance. Armand was very bad at letting dreams die quietly.

When the voice on the other end answered, "Brisker, Pendry, and Marks Agency," Armand sat back in his chair, put his feet up, and asked for Peter Marks, whose advertising campaign a little over two years ago halted Arnolds Aluminum's downward market share and had actually increased sales for a time.

"Foil Man," Peter Marks said cheerily as he picked up the line. Thirty-three, tall and handsome, he had a smooth cool approach that was hard not to love, even over the phone. His hair was dark and his eyes a deep Kelly green—testament to his Irish heritage. With one hand, he held the phone, in the other he held up a mock-up of an ad. On the sheet, a huge, overfed head of cattle was eating his way through a cornfield, while a small child starved right next to the animal. A logo for the VEGETARIAN COUNSEL OF AMERICA was set in the lower right-hand corner.

Peter Marks put down the ad and while holding the phone to his ear with his shoulder, grabbed a half-sized basketball off his desk and shot it towards a hoop at the far end of the office. The air ball escaped into the hall, eliciting a loud crash as it landed on his assistant's desk. The ball was picked up and returned by one of the staff.

"What can I do for you?" he said, taking the ball and trying again, missing once more.

"Peter, do you know CPR?"

"The Doctor knows all about your condition, Foil Man. They want to Zone you right outta the neighborhood. Those upwardly mobile folk 'cross the street ain't gonna like smoke very much."

"No. And I think they need a place to park."

"Always said the downfall of America would be the automobile. That and the hamburger." Peter Marks tapped the Vegetarian Council mock-up. "It's worse than I thought."

There was a short pause, then Armand heard Peter yelling out his office to his people.

"Warm up the bull pen, boys and girls," he said. "Arnolds Aluminum has gone Code Blue." He came back to the phone and said in the most reassuring of voices, "Are you taking any prescription medications?"

Armand let out a smile and felt himself relax. The Doctor was on the case.

•

Kirk was just about to jettison another pod as the doorbell rang and woke Satan from a sound sleep.

Satan slowly rose from under his covers and climbed out of bed. He struggled with a robe that he had made a note to wash about six months ago. Slipping it on, he made a further note to burn this one and buy another. By the time he had gotten to his bedroom door, he had decided there was no time like the present. He took off the robe and put on his down jacket instead.

The bell rang again, then two more times before Satan reached the stairs. A few more rings as he avoided empty rolls of foil on his way to the fireplace to toss the robe atop the embers of last night. Another while crossing the living room. All total, a dozen rings give or take by the time he cracked open the door to find Ion standing on the steps.

She was wearing a cute black jacket over a mock turtleneck and jeans with a red scarf wrapped around her neck. This was the fourth morning in a row she had appeared at his doorstep. It wasn't that he didn't want to see her. He just didn't want to see her in person.

"I've been thinking," she said as she bounced purposefully past Satan and into his home.

He stood there, staring out at the morning, surveying the neighborhood for a moment, holding some vapid thought which was wholly unlike him. At first, he had tried to shoo her off with a pageant of poor manners and insolent remarks. "I appreciate that I have somehow enlightened your mundane, pathetic life. However, I do not wish to be your friend and I am not a zoo animal for you to study." He tried that two days ago, but she was there bright and even earlier the next morning. "Do you make a habit of following all of Clancy's customers home? I want my privacy. How much clearer can I be? For all I know, you could be an ax murderer." To which she replied, unfazed, "Oh, we stopped using axes a long time ago. Chainsaws, now. Progress, you know." Every day he tried to get rid of her and every day she came back.

Ion stood in front of a large bookshelf. "I've been thinking about this 'Journey to the Center of the Earth' crap." She pulled down a title: *Nirvana: Discovery Of The Inner Earth* and flipped through a few pages. "I think it's kind of whacked."

"Have I not made this clear to you? I want you to cease and desist!" He glanced over at the clock on the far wall of the living room. "It's 8:30 a.m." He proclaimed the time as if he was saying '4:30 a.m.'

"First of all, it's molten lava. How can anybody live inside molten lava?"

Satan turned and searched the street suspiciously. He had never received a satisfactory answer on how she had gotten his home address. He looked out, wondering how many other people he didn't know knew where he lived.

"Second, how come they don't suffocate?"

A chill ran up his spine as the thought of someone watching his house flashed in his mind. He stepped inside and shut the door, then drew the shades. He was in somewhat of a predicament. He had been thinking a great deal about Ion. Each morning when he finally succeeded in removing her from his home, he felt a tinge of disappointment. As much as he dreaded her appearance, he would be just as saddened if she didn't show up. But she was here, and it was his duty to be annoyed. "What are you talking about?"

Ion had been thinking about Satan from the first moment as well, but her thoughts were more the manner in which a paleontologist contemplates digging up skulls and jaw bones.

"Vinnie, last night I couldn't sleep. I had this incredible vision. It was so vivid and clear. *Foil*," she said, as if the word were sacred and not to be spoken in vain.

It hadn't started out that way. Foil, being sacred, that is. In fact, when Ion woke up from her dream not three hours earlier, the first words out of her mouth were "I'm outta my fucking mind." But slowly, clumsily, the idea took root. Maybe it was the season. Ion always got sentimental around Christmas. It was one of her worst traits, she thought. Maybe it had been too long since her last project. She needed at least one a year, but it had been far longer than that since the actor.

"Now, I've been up since 4 a.m. thinking about this. I've been on the phone all morning and everyone agrees. Drop this Inner Earth crap. It's out there," she said as she glanced at the pictures in the book. "People'll think you're retarded."

He was going to ask who the everyone was she had called, but he didn't really want to know the answer. He was already beginning to get a headache. The only thing keeping him from tossing her out onto the street was that she and the morning had conspired to give him the stiffest erection he could remember ever having. Even stiffer than the one the day before. Satan was still concerned Captain Kirk had something to do with this, but he was very much hoping he didn't. He would work that out later. Right now, any sudden or unconsidered moves and Satan was going to be showing a bit more trimming than he'd like.

Purity of purpose had kept Satan womanless for many years. In fact, in all his life there had been only one. He had mentioned this to Kelsey once, and she had been appalled by the discovery.

"You've only had sex with one person?"

"No, I've only had sex one time."

"One time in thirty years?" Kelsey blinked, trying to fathom it. "What about that girl in college? The one with the…gas problem."

"I never slept with her."

Satan managed to change the subject before Kelsey had the opportunity to reflexively offer her services and embarrass them both.

Satan had to do something, cause some diversion and avoid the unfortunate disclosure of his rock hard shaft in front of Ion. His limited experience in this area revealed that women often reacted quite poorly when being unexpectedly shown a man's penis. Of course, the last time this had happened in his presence he was ten and Kenny Odorman had just flipped out his cock in front of Kathy Collinsworth who screamed at the top of her lungs and nearly closed Kenny's member in one of the huge schoolroom doors in a fit of surprise. You actually couldn't call it a cock at ten years old, it was hardly a penis then, but Kenny didn't care much for decorum or vanity, it was simply a weapon to him.

"But foil…" Ion said, her face glowing as she continued her sermon. "Picture it. People wearing foil hats. Foil lined suits. No longer afraid to stand near microwave ovens…or use cellular phones. Not to mention being nice and warm in the wintertime. And all because of a man with a dream."

Satan looked at Ion, then down at his bare feet and contemplated purposely stubbing his toe on the bookcase, hoping that might deflate the situation. He decided against it when he noticed a downward twitch. Thinking about Kenny Odorman for a few more seconds ought to cure his erection and maybe even prevent another for days.

"I want to offer you my services," Ion said, as she stood with the book at her side. There was a sparkle of excitement in her eye.

Even Kenny Odorman wouldn't be of any help now.

"I refuse to pay you any money for this," he said. Although, if he had any, he might have considered it.

She laughed. "We're going to get other people to pay for it."

Satan winced. This was exactly the sort of sick, unnatural and depraved behavior he had been avoiding all these years. Society was degenerating before his eyes and if he didn't watch out, he would be leading the fall.

Ion knew this would be a tough sell. Her attentiveness, the light touches, the warm smiles, they didn't work with him, although she knew, when she really needed them, they would. In the meantime, she employed subtler means to try and steer Vinnie away from his crusade to get inside the earth, but he was so Goddamn stubborn, and convinced he was right, four days of conditioning had done little to deflect him. He didn't see the value and opportunity his foil hats provided. They were more than fashion; they were the embodiment of life at the dawn of the millennium. Separation, danger, and protection. Sex with condoms, love over the internet, 500 channels. Foil reflected the world as it was.

Under other circumstances in another time, she might have convinced herself the man before her was a raving lunatic. But couched amongst all the nutty prose about super human beings, utopian societies, and molten lava suns, was something truly genius.

"C'mon, get some clothes on. We're going out."

Somehow, Satan got the impression, he and Ion were not conversing on the same subject.

During the walk from his home to her apartment to pick up some warmer clothes, she had cleared up the misunderstanding. "Vinnie, you need exposure," she said, just before explaining the services being offering were for her to be his marketing and PR strategist and not his personal sex toy.

And although he was quite sure he had, at no time, formally accepted her bid, she was dragging him through the city brainstorming ideas on how to promote his beliefs.

"We need to get you out into the community. Start small, clubs, poetry readings, crap like that. Quietly build a base, talking up the risk of radiation and more importantly, the risk of being out of the loop, until...we bring the fear into the mainstream, then offer them a cure."

"Like a snake oil salesman? How noble."

She glanced at him. "This isn't selling. This is coughing on one person and getting everyone sick. It's about being viral."

Chicago was ripe for spreading a virus.

The temperature had dipped below zero, and they walked as fast as they could to keep from becoming ice sculptures. Ion now was wearing an ankle-length coat over three layers of sweaters, a Shetland, a cardigan, and the original turtleneck, and still, the cold was getting through to her skin. Satan wore his standard winter uniform: knit cap, down jacket, mittens.

She was giving him ten days to wean himself of the mittens. He had negotiated it up from a week. The rest would go sooner. A few days maybe. She couldn't throw too much at him at once, else he'd overload.

"I don't understand why I can't keep the mittens."

"Ten days. That's what we agreed."

"I changed my mind."

"Ten days. Not a moment more."

"Why? Is there some local ordinance I am unaware of?"

"Vinnie, let me try to explain something," she said, softly, in a reassuring tone, the best she could manage with her teeth chattering. "I know you don't realize this, but not everybody wears tin foil on their head."

"Aluminum," he said.

"I apologize," she said sweetly, cutting the legs out from under his indignity. She stuck her arm through his and held herself tight to his side as protection against the wind. "And so you know, if you run around preaching to people about putting foil on their heads, you better not look like a wacko. And as strange as it may seem, a thirty-year-old man wearing mittens... looks like a wacko."

Satan had to admit he was the only person he'd ever seen over the age of five wearing mittens.

But that wasn't the point.

"My mother made these."

"Fine, you can frame them and hang them on your wall."

"Would you please, halt," he said as they stood outside Marshall Fields.

He put his hands on his hips and took in a deep breath in anticipation of an important statement, but the arctic draft coming off the Lake crystallized the words in his throat.

After a moment of coughing and having Ion slap him painfully between the shoulder blades, he was able to speak again.

"I am the way I am. I don't want to change. I am comfortable in my consistent unchangingness."

"Vinnie, change will happen regardless of what you want."

He shook his head for no discernible reason. But at that moment he knew he had made a grave mistake—he should have bought the pens at the grocery store.

A little while later as they walked along Division, Satan broke the silence.

"You say, 'Drop the Inner Earth crap,' cause it makes me seem like I'm a wacko."

"No, actually, I said it makes you seem retarded."

"I stand corrected. As if it were that simple, just forget my core beliefs. You've been trying to divorce me from these principles for four days, wanting me instead to focus on superficial and peripheral aspects of my life. I wear foil on my head," he adjusted his hat, "because I haven't found entrance to the Innerworld. Not because it's 'cool.'"

"Listen, Vinnie, whether you like it or not, I'm going to make you into a star. This is your true calling, you understand me? I don't see it as superficial or peripheral. I see it as helping people live longer, healthier, more productive lives. You'll be up there with Pasteur, Salk, Marcus Welby," she said, tenderly fixing his collar. "Now, don't fuck it up 'cause you have a thing for mittens and Jules Verne."

Satan gazed at the fearless intensity in her eyes and wondered if she had ever been a televangelist. As the wind blew frigid air across his cheeks, he looked up at the sun, which was pale and yellow and seemed to lack any desire to battle the winter enveloping the city. He felt akin to the sun at that moment. Her argument was a sound one. Many great discoverers had set their sights on one goal, only to find something more important along the way. He wasn't really giving up his quest for the Netherworld. He would simply put it off until Spring.

If it was good enough for the sun, it was good enough for him.

Ion pulled him closer. She had finally won him over. Foil was his future. Once they got out of the cold, she would write up a plan of action. At last, she had a new project.

As they strolled along the street, she studied Satan, watching his reflection in the passing store windows. It wasn't going to be easy; he was raw talent, an uncut stone—unearthed, to be more precise—but she had seen worse. She figured, with hard work, a little luck, and maybe an arrest or two, come Valentine's Day, he'd be well on his way.

•

Like her name, it came to her in a dream. She saw it purely, clearly, and as soon as she awakened, she knew she was right.

Ion went to the closet in her bedroom and pulled out a sewing kit that her mother had given her many, many years ago. Tomorrow, perhaps the day after, Ion would go to the woman down the street who tailored her clothes whenever they needed it, the woman who had made the ball gown hanging before her—the gift of a man, one she had steered toward *his* dream, playing jazz.

The woman was an artisan, a contriver, and Ion would have to say little for her to understand what she wanted. But here, right now, Ion would use her own hands to fashion the consequence of her dream—what she would later call a Gamma Cap—a beautiful, white cowboy hat lined with four layers of Arnolds Aluminum based on specifications Satan had repeated numerous times. It took her less than an hour to complete her task. The wide brim gave her extra protection as well as looked great.

A woman in Chicago looking like her—chiseled cheeks, square-jawed, curvaceously lissome body—wearing a big white ten-gallon hat would definitely attract attention.

She gazed in the mirror at her handiwork and smiled.

A walking billboard, she thought.

For the next several days, Ion wore her hat and rounded up converts. She had no trouble getting offers of help. Mostly from guys who would do anything for her. She was plugged in to the hip set as well as the rich, society types. But she'd stay away from the moneyed for now. She introduced Satan to Slag, a poet who, as a diversion, produced short avant-garde video essays he called Clips, which he posted on the web. Every day, Ion stopped by Satan's after work and brought him a pilfered felt-tip pen and news of new recruits. "I don't want any more," he would say, referring to both the pens and the recruits, but that didn't seem to be the point of the exercise.

Bringing him pens was Ion's way of showing affection for him. Bringing him recruits, well, that was for her.

Because every night, Ion sat up past two in the morning making notes and jotting down ideas until the first slivers of a plan began to emerge.

•

Slag was pointing a Sony DV camcorder at Satan. "All right, man, move over by the pile of bills." A pale, bony finger pointed at the Chicago skyline done in white envelopes stamped with the logo of Clearwater Sanitarium. "I wanna see your anger when you stare at that symbol of your abandonment," directed Slag. The poet's long, straight, black hair kept getting in the way of the lens.

Satan felt a little strange holding up the latest bill that had arrived today. "Is this absolutely necessary? Who cares about my parents?"

"It's fodder for the masses, man."

"We'll need video if the press picks up on this, Vinnie," Ion said from the kitchen. "Even if they don't we'll stream it on the web."

As Slag zoomed, the camera lens caught a lock of his hair and started to chew it up, making the sound a jet engine makes when it's winding down.

"Are you sure you know what you're doing with that?" Satan asked as the runaway motor started reeling Slag in.

The poet was too busy to answer.

Ion walked in the room sporting her cowboy hat and holding two wrapped Christmas presents. She was also sporting her usual smile until she saw the video camera dangling from Slag's head and still climbing toward his scalp. The noises escaping from Slag reminded her of a PBS special on animal research she had been forced to watch in school.

"Shut it off," Satan was saying.

"Ahhh, ohhh, stop it," were the words coming from Slag's lips, not necessarily in that order.

The poet was beginning to panic. In fact, he was in the middle of panicking. He was jumping up and down wildly, causing the camera to swing violently, finally smacking him in the head, which seemed to temporarily stop the zoom from zooming and Slag from screaming.

Slag slumped to the floor, the Sony hanging in front of his face at about mouth level.

Satan looked at the heap of hair and electronic equipment and saw a large lawsuit in the making involving himself, Sony and Super Cuts.

"Hey...you...Slag, are you all right?" he asked, hoping for a yes.

The poet-turned-director-turned-litigant leaned against the wall motionless, trying to catch what little breath he had left and stuff it back into his deflated lungs. If it was possible, he looked paler than normal. Ion placed the two packages on the floor in a patch she had cleared out of the mess the day before, then disappeared into the bathroom. When she returned a second later, she stepped up to Slag and crouched down in front of him.

"Slag," she said flatly, "You can't break the camera. It's Vinnie's ticket to Fate's door."

"It was like alive."

"Well, seems like it's dead now." Ion reached up and with a pair of scissors cut the camera free, instantly removing a good eighteen months of hair along with it. The poet was too shocked to care, and Satan hoped he wouldn't notice until after he left.

Handing the camera and the attached hair to Satan, Ion picked up the boxes and gave the one wrapped with Santas and reindeer to Slag who burbled a half-hearted "thank you" and plopped the package in his lap. Ion then presented Satan with the other box which was wrapped in black.

"I know you hate the Christmassy shit."

"I hate Christmas," Satan added cheerfully as if to confirm it.

"Well, I happen to like it."

Satan took the box and handed her the camera and the envelope with the logo of the Clearwater Sanitarium on it. She watched as he tore the paper wrap, revealing a hatbox.

"I also happen to think that Santa consumes way too much cholesterol," she said, studying the envelope, suddenly more interested in it than his reaction to her gift. "The guy's gonna drop any second if he doesn't start eating some oat bran or something."

V. THE CORNER POCKET VETO

The envelope lay motionless on the desk, its seams carefully cut open. It was attached by a silver paper clip to a ten-page letter. A bit of powder from a fingerprint check remained on both the letter and envelope.

The President stared at the papers in front of him, seemingly not wanting to touch them, as if they might have cooties or some other vile something or other.

"It's all right, sir, you can handle the letter. We've done all the tests we need to on it," said a man sporting a pair of mirrored glasses. The President wondered to himself why so many of the people surrounding him from day to day wore sunglasses, even indoors. He could never see their eyes or where they were looking. It made him uncomfortable.

"Go ahead, sir," encouraged the head of the National Security Agency.

As the President held the letter and its attachments up, some of the powder fell onto his oak desk. He glanced down at the white flecks, then felt a little tickle in his nose from a few particles that had risen instead of fallen.

"What do you think it means?" he asked, hoping this wouldn't take too long. He wanted to go and hit a few balls on the three-hole course up at Camp David, maybe even get in a little duck hunting before it got dark.

"We're not exactly sure," said the man in the mirrored glasses.

"Is it a threat to, you know, National Security?" he asked, remembering the line from his campaign speeches. The President really wasn't sure what questions he was supposed to ask. No one had ever shown him a letter like this before. Usually the NSA and FBI handled this sort of stuff, and up until now, had done so without his help. He concerned himself with more important things, stately duties, signing the laws his cabinet told him to sign, cutting ribbons, and all the other presidential stuff.

"We're not quite sure, Mr. President," said the NSA head. "But half the members of Congress received the exact same correspondence. As well as several major newspapers."

"Half...really," said the President.

The Secretary of Defense was cleaning the dirt from under his nails with a solid gold letter opener. "It's this damn Communist thing. Ever since the crumbling of the Warsaw Pact and the reunification of Germany, nobody in this country thinks we've got any Goddamn enemies anymore."

The President wrinkled up his forehead. "I don't understand the connection, Bill."

"It's some Goddamn group of anti-nuke radicals," answered the Secretary of Defense. "Listen to this shit. 'We...are aware...that there are people beneath the surface of the planet and that the existence of these...arms has been kept secret. The balance of power will be altered,'" he quoted, leaving out those words that didn't fully support his theory. "Sounds like a threat to me."

The President still didn't understand. The Chief of Staff saw the confusion on the President's face.

"We have reason to believe that these people have somehow gained information regarding the nuclear missiles stock piled in major cities."

The President whispered, "You mean, the ones we moved out of the silos and said we destroyed in accordance with that...ah, pact with the, ah...?"

"—Russians. Yessir."

"Oh, dear."

"Sir, if this is some grassroots movement for disarmament, I'm all for leaving it in the hands of NSA Covert Operations—let them do whatever it is they do to quell this sort of thing. But if this is a terrorist group of lunatic neo-flower children, willing to risk their lives to sabotage our nuclear arsenal, then I think the CIA and Military Intelligence ought to be called in as well."

The President looked around the room. "What do the rest of you think?"

He got fourteen different answers depending on who was talking and what department they covered. Everyone thought they should be the one to handle it, including the Secretaries of State and Education (if only we had educated these people properly, one imagines, this wouldn't have happened.).

The President glanced at his watch. It was getting late. He'd never get to Camp David now. He'd have to settle for billiards in the East Wing with one of the servants. However, if he didn't get this over with soon, he wouldn't even have time for that.

"I think we should stay on top of this," he said, not too forcefully, so that if everyone thought differently and he had to change his mind, it wouldn't be such a big deal. No one said anything, which the President took as meaning it was all right to go on. "You know, seems we could nip this in the bud if we don't really try to decide right here and now what the intent is of these people." Nothing so far, just blank faces. "Let the NSA do its thing, keep an eye on what's going on. But just in case, we shouldn't stop the CIA, MI, FBI, or anyone else from checking these folks out."

"What about Treasury?" asked that department's head.

"Why not. A few Secret Service agents couldn't hurt." Everyone seemed to be shaking their heads in approval. No one was going to get snubbed. Chalk one up for diplomacy. "It's settled then. Well, if you'll excuse me gentlemen," almost forgetting, "...and ladies...I have some important business to tend to."

The President walked out of the room and as soon as he was out of sight, jogged into the East Wing and had Charles, his housemaster, rack up the balls.

VI. THE PERILS OF BENELYN®

Sitting on the floor was the empty hatbox, the insignia of a local shop tastefully laid in gold leaf on the outside. Black wrapping lay shredded on the floor. Voices filtered up from the living room as Satan stood in front of his bedroom mirror, studying himself. He tipped the hat on his head a bit lower on the left side. Not happy, he straightened it again.

"Vinnie, get in here. You got to see this," yelled Ion from the first floor.

The TV blared out Satan's voice saying, "Shut it off, shut it off." Immediately following were several screams—Slag's—for help.

Satan stared at the reflection of the black bowler he wore and marveled at how its rounded top curved smoothly in all directions. He raised his eyebrows up and down, causing the aluminum lining to crinkle. He had never thought of enclosing foil under a second layer of fabric. Ion's improvement not only eliminated the need to reline his hat every day, which she said helped the environment by cutting down on waste, it also made for more comfortable wearing. He'd no longer have those unsightly vertical creases marching across his forehead.

Not that Satan had ever really cared what anybody else thought. It seemed unworthy of the effort. Just when you got yourself to where you fit in, somebody somewhere changed the rules, the hairstyle, the fashions, and you were out again. Cost effectively speaking, instead of always being one step behind the fads, spending money for fleeting recognition, if you just stayed consistent in your clothes and style, in another ten or twenty years, you actually had the chance of setting the trend.

Satan gazed at his visage in the glass. He, quite possibly, found himself on the cutting edge.

He yawned, stretching his arms out and over his head. It had been a long day, and the Benelyn® he'd taken for the near-cold that had been nagging him was making him drowsy. All he wanted to do now was lie down and go to sleep. Pushing back the covers, he sat on the bed, bending over to untie his shoelaces. He took the bowler off his head—it was too nice to sleep in—and grabbed the red and white nightcap that was still at the bottom of the hatbox. Ion had thought of everything.

Pulling on the cap, which felt warm and soft and cozy, Satan laid his head on his pillow and instantly, was fast asleep.

"Are you gonna stay up here all night?" Ion yelled as she ran into the room before realizing.

She studied the sleeping lump of covers and flesh, watching the eyes flicker under Satan's lids like film through a projector. Ion sat on the edge of the bed and stroked his face, gently.

As Ion drew her hand away, she noticed the white envelope she had held earlier—the latest from Clearwater Sanitarium—on the nightstand by his bed where it would stay until next month's arrived to replace it. She wondered what his mother was like, wondered what stories she could tell. Ion quickly put Satan's mom out of her mind. She reached down and pulled up the bed covers, tucking them under his chin. She ran her fingers over the soft fabric and patted it softly.

"Sweet dreams." She bent forward to kiss the tip of his nose.

She stood and moved to the door, stopping briefly to glance back at him before switching off the light and disappearing down the hall.

•

It was like rushing down a raging river, warm water surrounding him, swirling rapids pulling at his limbs. He fell farther and farther, deeper and deeper. His head pressed back into something soft that gently continued to give under his weight—give without end.

Flashes appeared in the blackness before his eyes. Images gathered and blew apart in the void that lay just beyond his reach. After an interval, that seemed like forever, but was only a millisecond, the images settled down and started to take on depth and substance. He could almost touch one. Then finally he did.

Satan ran his fingertips over the petal of a purple daisy, which was strange because the tangerine colored orchids to his left had been the ones asking to be petted.

One of the orchids, apparently the leader, looked up at Satan and said, "Get on with it, will you. Quit jerking around. You've got a long journey ahead of you. If you make it, just remember…" The orchid bent his stem toward Satan and whispered in a conspiratorial tone, "…don't pet the petunias, and never, ever kiss the cactus."

Satan wasn't sure what to say, but he was sure glad for the advice. "Thanks," he said after a moment.

"Don't mention it," bloomed the orchid, just seconds before Satan, starting on his journey, accidentally stepped on the flower and some of his closest relatives.

Ion was waving to Satan from the top of a small hill. Her hair blew wildly in the wind, making her look untamed and very appealing. Then suddenly, the source of the breeze appeared behind her over the ridge. A sort of helicopter-like thing with pink and white bunny ears for blades landed a few yards to her left. She continued to wave to Satan, shouting something that was inaudible above the din of flapping ears.

When Satan reached her, she gave him a kiss and pulled him inside the furry craft.

In seconds, they were airborne and skimming across the landscape at an incredible speed. The ground below turned from green to purple to tangerine to stark white.

It took Satan a moment to realize that the whiteness below him was ice and snow, and not, as he first thought, a huge, overturned diaper truck—which is not to say that coming after a purple daisy, a talking orange orchid, and a flying bunny, an overturned diaper truck would have been a surprise.

Ion glanced over at him, then placed her hand over his. Her fingers were moist and warm, sweaty, but not clammy. It felt reassuring.

Satan was somewhat aware that he was having a dream, yet wasn't totally convinced. Ion seemed the one normal thing to him.

He looked at her and said, flatly, "We're flying in a bunny rabbit."

"Yes, I know."

"You know?"

"Yes."

"Can I ask you a question?"

"Of course," she said, pulling a carrot and a head of lettuce out of her bag and tossing it into what seemed like the helicopter's mouth. He watched the vegetables as they were gnashed at by a large set of white teeth.

"Why," he asked.

"Union rules."

Satan was about to say something when he realized Ion's response would lead to more questions and more answers that led to questions and the whole thing would get very confusing and very boring, and this was a dream and boring dreams were worse than blood clots. He knew one thing for certain, he wasn't going to get the last word here.

It was a short hop to the landing site. The bunny set down on a fluorescent yellow "H" that had been etched into the ice and snow. The bunny's ears drooped as they came to a stop. The furry thing seemed content to sit, wiggle its nose and wait for further instructions.

The sun was bright, reflecting off the white blanket that covered the land. For as far as Satan could see, the terrain was a vast ice plain, interrupted by an occasional formation of crystallized spires. The scene reminded him of something out of Alice in Wonderland. He fully expected to see a giant rabbit hop by when he remembered he'd just flown in on one.

"Can I ask another question?"

Ion stepped out of the rabbit. Her foot sank into the snow up to her knee. "I guess it couldn't hurt," she answered once she was sure she was on solid ground.

"Where are we?"

"How would I know? This's your dream."

Satan thought about this for a moment as he followed her out, then tried another tack.

"All right...do you, at least, know why we're here?"

"Who knows? You're whacked out of your head...stoned, blasted, high on cold medicine." Ion frowned. "You got any more?"

Satan checked his pockets and found he didn't have any...pockets, that is. "No."

"Oh." She seemed disappointed.

"C'mon, you've got to know something. Tell me you at least know something."

"I think it's some sort of sign." Ion nodded her head in a way that made Satan think he should know what she was talking about. Of course, he didn't.

"Well," he paused, knowing now that he was going to have to solve this riddle pretty much on his own, "thanks for the input."

While Satan was busy in his attempt to figure out what was going on, Ion started trudging off through the drifts. She was several meters away before he noticed she was no longer beside him.

"Hey! What are you doing? Don't leave me here!" he yelled after her, desperately trying to catch up. Tripping over one of Ion's footprints, he fell face first, swallowing a mouthful of snow, which burned his lips. It was odd that something so cold could actually burn. After a moment, Satan stood up, gathered himself, then before continuing toward Ion, turned and addressed the helicopter. "Stay," he said.

Out of breath, lips frozen together, Satan finally reached Ion.

"What are you doing?" he asked again.

"What do you mean?"

"I *mean*, I'm trying to figure this thing out and you're off running around like you're in some Jacque Cousteau special." He sucked in a lung full of air. "Now, I've lost my train of thought."

"You really wanna know what's going on?"

"Isn't that what I've been asking you for the past—I don't know—five, six..." He glanced at his watch, which was spinning out of control. "...a hundred and fifty-three minutes," he huffed.

"Then why don't you ask that cactus over there."

Ion pointed ahead.

"What," he said, before following her finger to where it eventually led—a cactus.

The cactus was waving to them. "Hey, guys! Over here. Over here!"

Satan scrunched up his forehead, glancing from the cactus to Ion, then back to the cactus in the middle of the ice plain.

"Over here!"

Satan was staring at the plant, but spoke to Ion. "Is this somehow significant?"

"I would imagine so," she said.

The cactus was swinging his prickly arms as much as was feasibly possible. He wished he could jump up and down, but that wasn't in the nature of things. He was pretty much stuck right where he was, rooted in the middle of nowhere.

Satan wasn't moving.

The cactus was growing impatient.

"C'mon, c'mon. Do you want to get inside the earth or what?" said the seven-foot tall saguaro.

"Excuse me," stammered Satan.

"Inside the Earth. You want in or not?"

Suddenly, it all started to make sense. Satan didn't quite know how he knew—it was a dream you understand—but he realized this was the North Pole, and here was located one of the two fabled entrances to the Inner Earth. He also surmised that he wouldn't be able to just step up to the passageway and strut in. If that were true, anybody could have done it. Surveying the situation in front of him, Satan rationalized that the cactus yelling at him in the middle of the Arctic probably had something to do with gaining entry.

Satan stepped up to the cactus who immediately stopped its yelling.

"Hello," Satan said.

"Hello," said the cactus, putting out its arm to shake Satan's hand.

Satan looked at the arm. "You won't be offended if I don't."

"Oh, I guess not. You're not the first, you know."

Satan wasn't quite sure if the cactus meant he wasn't the first to refuse its hand or attempt to gain access to the passageway.

"Nobody likes me. I don't even know why I try," added the cactus, in a bid for some sympathy. Something it knew it'd never get. Nobody ever thinks plants need love and affection. Dogs, yes. Cats, yes. But cacti, no. "Of course, you'll be dead soon, so it won't really make any difference to you."

Ion perked up at this. "What's that supposed to mean?"

"Oh, you'll be fine," the cactus said, "but him…he's gone."

"What'd I do?" asked Satan, feeling less and less in control of this dream. Maybe it wasn't a dream. This seemed more like his life. Here was a cactus, one he'd never met before, making threatening statements predicting his death.

"It's not what you've done, but what you're about to do."

"And what exactly is that?" said Ion, hoping to find out so she wouldn't unintentionally do the same.

The cactus put both its arms at its side, leaned forward a bit and said, rather sternly, "He's going to try to get inside," then pointed toward a cave that wasn't there a moment ago. "To do that, he's gotta get by me."

"And me," came a voice.

"Us," said another.

"Oh, yes…Us."

A few feet away, two petunias had popped out of the arctic snow and were looking very indignant.

"And them," said the cactus. "But you'll never get that far."

The closest petunia nodded sadly. "No one ever does," it sighed.

Satan had been uncharacteristically quiet, choosing to watch the scene unfold before making any comment that he might later regret. He remembered what the orchid had said.

"I suppose I must pass some sort of test."

"I suppose," said the cactus.

"I'm not going to kiss you," Satan announced, most firmly.

The cactus returned its right arm to an upward position. "Oh, I hope not. It'd be quite painful…for both of us." It was standing in a more natural pose now. If it weren't for the fact that it was talking, you might mistake the cactus for any other giant saguaro growing alongside an Arizona highway. "And besides, who asked you to?"

"No one. I was simply stating I wasn't going to."

The cactus leaned toward Ion and spoke. "Does he do this all the time?"

Ion tried to remember, but it wasn't her dream so she couldn't. "Actually, he's never kissed me."

The cactus studied Ion for a moment, then motioned for Satan to take a step closer.

"Pssst," the cactus hissed, quietly. "WHAT ARE YOU CRAZY!"

"I've been contemplating that very question the last couple of minutes," replied Satan.

"You haven't kissed her?"

"Ahh…no."

Satan glanced at Ion, apologetically. It wasn't as if he didn't want to kiss her. In fact, "I dreamed about doing it."

"Doesn't count," said the cactus.

"Why not?"

The cactus turned to Ion without answering Satan.

"You like him," it asked. "You know…that way?"

"I hadn't really thought about it until now," Ion said before turning to size up Satan. "He's not bad looking. Could use some new clothes, a new razor blade, haircut. But he's not bad."

Satan somehow felt like a slave on the auction block of an Old Southern peanut plantation.

The cactus swung around and nudged the man in the side, sending more than a few needles into his arm. From the look on the man's face, it hadn't been a pleasant experience.

"She's a total *babe*. A knockout. Look at her. She's just waiting for a kiss."

No, she wasn't.

"Kiss her!"

"Ouwww, all right. Jeez, I never saw a plant so worried about my love life before."

"That's cause you never met a plant like me."

"That's cause he's never had a love life," Ion said, shaking her head. "You hear that?" taunted the cactus. "Whatchu gonna do about it?"

A rush of passion and anger raced through Satan's body. He usually had very little of either, so it came as somewhat of a shock to his system. Even before he really meant to, Satan shot out his arms and grabbed Ion with both hands, pulling her body tight against his. He closed his eyes and puckered his lips as he drew her nearer. Ion for her part stared dumbfounded at Satan. The cactus leaned a bit to one side to get a better glimpse of their first kiss. The petunias held their breath.

Satan's lips were about to touch Ion's when he suddenly stopped. Without thinking, he whirled around and planted a big wet smooch on what would have been the cactus' lips had there been any.

The petunias began screaming with glee as the cactus started to wilt.

"Ohhhhhhhhnnoooooooooo, dooonnnnt kiiiiiiiiiii—"

All that was left in the snow was a pile of green matter where the cactus had once stood.

"Ho, ho, ha, ha," the petunias were laughing. They appeared to be dancing.

"You did it," said one of the petunias.

"We finally get our chance," said the other, a bit too gleefully for Satan's taste.

"Now you gotta get by uh-us. Now you gotta get by uh-us," they sang in unison in a most obnoxious tone.

Satan glanced at the two annoying flowers. He felt like punching both of them into the frozen ground. Which is exactly what he did.

The moment he had pounded the second petunia into the arctic plain, the cave disappeared, and in its place, a vast canyon made itself visible. Catching his balance after almost falling into the abyss, Satan stepped back and gaped at the huge hole that seemed to go on forever. It was cylindrical, yet its edges were far from smooth. The passage appeared to have been formed by nature rather than man or machine.

A Chicago Transit Authority bus rose from the black depths and landed on the snow a few feet to the left of Satan and Ion. The door opened.

"Been waiting long?" asked the driver, who appeared, in almost every way, to be human.

Almost.

"Not at all," said Ion, deadpan.

Satan stared at the driver. So far nothing had been as it seemed and he was sure the dream wasn't going to start making sense now.

"I don't have any change," Satan said, watching the driver for his reaction.

"Don't need any," the driver responded with a smile.

"Why not?"

"It's not really a money making venture, this route. Sorta more like a public service than anything else."

"You're going to kill us, aren't you?" said Satan.

Ion nudged Satan to stop giving the driver any ideas.

"That wouldn't be very neighborly of me," the driver said blankly, wondering himself if he was going to kill them.

"You're not my neighbor."

"Put it this way, I don't *think* I'm going to kill you. But then I'm not really in control here, am I?" The driver raised one of his eyebrows in Satan's direction.

Ion stepped onto the bus. She glanced back down from the top at Satan. "That was a sufficiently confusing response that I'm now convinced it doesn't matter what we do."

Begrudgingly, Satan climbed on the bus, which immediately began to free fall into the pit.

"Next stop, the center of the earth," the driver said cheerily.

There was a long time where nothing happened.

Satan was somewhat aware that the bus was still falling, but the blackness that enveloped him was complete and unyielding. He could hear Ion breathing, but could not see her.

Then suddenly, a light appeared ahead. It grew larger as the bus drew nearer to it. A tightness in Satan's chest caused him to hold his fist against his ribs. He was about to make it inside. He was about to get a glimpse of that place which he had so often hoped he'd see, but never thought he would. The light took on shape now as a magnificent brilliance gave way to soft tones of green and yellow. Satan held his breath, reached out and grasped Ion's hand and held that, too. They were almost upon the light when—

Nothing.

The dream stopped.

Not because of a ringing phone, a beeping alarm, a noisy neighbor, no, not for any reason. It just ceased. Satan was back in his room. The silence pounded in his head. He blinked.

The next second he was on the bus, flying into the light. It was glorious. Rolling hills of green and beige, fields of yellow flowers that went on for miles. The horizon, instead of dipping down and disappearing, curved upward and around, eventually meeting itself.

Satan allowed the beauty of this inner world to soak into his heart...

When Satan finally awoke, he was not disappointed. The bus had taken him and Ion on an incredible journey. The people he met, the stories they told...of a better world, unlike our own. Satan saw children playing, people laughing, and green, green, so much green he thought he'd never see the like trekking through a thousand forests.

The revelations were so extraordinary, Satan didn't even mind that the shelf over his head had fallen on him in the middle of the night, didn't seem to care that the baby cactus he had set on the shelf only a few days before had landed on his mouth.

Satan began to mind a few minutes later when he tried to remove the plant and found its needles stuck to his lips.

VII. OLFACTORY SEALED

Satan found himself pacing up and down the linoleum-covered aisles of Clancy's Drug trying to find the drugs among all the brooms, greeting cards and whatnots. He was in a cranky mood, ever since he finally pried the cactus from his face. Now his oncoming cold was beginning to bother him as well. Ion had said to look down aisle six for what he needed. He had rambled from one through nine and hadn't seen a sign of anything that even remotely resembled a drug.

The sinus pressure building up in his head was pushing his brain against the back of his skull. If he didn't find relief soon, his medulla oblongata was going to become an external organ.

Satan's head was foggy, clouded by something more than a cold, he thought, more than the painful cuts on his lips. He had been on edge all day. He had the odd feeling people were watching him. But Ion had told him he was being paranoid. Maybe the waitress at the diner had put something in his hot chocolate. She always hated him—told him so every time he came in.

Maybe it was the half dozen strange looking people he found in his living room this morning. Apparently recruits of Ion, they were installing something they called a "T3 line," bringing in cables and computers and lots of supposed food items wrapped in cellophane.

All to increase his "web presence," or so Ion told him.

Arriving at the section filled with vitamins, Satan stopped and spitefully picked up a bottle that said "B-6" on the front. He sneered at the package and ran his eyes up and down the hundreds of different dietary supplements. Here before him was the bane of the modern man. All a person had to do was down a couple of hundred capsules in the morning and they could spend the rest of the day shoving their face with Gooey Huey's Grease-Burgers, hydrogenated oils, Big Macs, or anything French. Satan had a theory that all the vitamins processed out of prepackaged foods were gathered up at the factory, reconstituted into a powder and formed into pills, and that it was those pills he was staring at.

Marketing wise, it was brilliant.

It was sort of like the way most people paid gardeners to take care of their yards, maids to clean up their homes, teenagers to wash their cars, then spent five hundred bucks to join a gym because they were getting out of shape sitting around all day doing nothing.

Satan's musings were cut short when the bell on Clancy's front door tinkled, signaling the arrival of another possible holdup man. His body always tightened, expecting to hear the words, "Give me all your money," or the sound of gunfire immediately after the jingle of the bell.

He heard neither and relaxed a bit until he felt the floor shake under his feet. It was a metered, consistent boom, boom, boom.

Pulling himself away from the vitamins, Satan tiptoed to a break in the shelving. As the pounding grew nearer, he peered around the end display into the next aisle, revealing only as much of himself as was necessary.

The shelves over his head began to rattle, and a shadow drew itself across the aisle floor. Then he saw them, cat whiskers, fuzzy tufts of hair waggling at about eye level. Fear gripped Satan as he realized it was the grocery store manager/maniac that was approaching.

"Aaahhh!" Satan screamed, without making any noise. Quickly, he turned, heart pounding outside his chest as he collided with Ion who had been standing behind him, observing.

"What are you doing?" she said.

"Aaahhh," he said, even more quietly, before brushing past her and ducking down another aisle which featured feminine products and kids' toys. Satan knocked into the shelving, sending several boxes of spermicidal jelly and a Bert & Ernie puppet set crashing to the floor.

The shock waves continued to rumble through the store for a few seconds more, then stopped, as the manager found what he was looking for. A distinctly different kind of rattling started—the kind of glass against metal.

The manager stood in front of the one area that really was Clancy's Drugs. As the oversized man stood knocking on the glass that separated him from the pharmacist, a tidal wave of fat threatened to overwhelm the retaining wall that was his belt. The pharmacist, a man in his early sixties, glanced up from what he was doing and gazed over the top of his glasses. A small purse of his lips was all that betrayed his annoyance with the large man on the other side of the window. Putting on his best face, the pharmacist pushed up his glasses, walked to the window, and slid it open just a bit.

"May I help you?" he asked, even though he knew who the grocery manager was. He just wanted to annoy him back.

The manager tried to breathe enough air into his lungs to supply his massive body, but fell quite short of his need. He wheezed for several seconds, motioning with his hands before answering.

"I'm...here..." he pulled in some oxygen loudly "...to pick up a prescription.

Anyone could have figured that.

"What's the name?" asked the pharmacist, sadistically. He enjoyed watching the manager flush pink with impatience, raising his already-too-high blood pressure.

"Krieger," wheezed the manager.

"Krieger, Krieger..." mumbled the pharmacist to himself as he absently stared over his glasses at the shelves of bagged prescriptions. He saw the one marked "Krieger," but pretended not to.

The manager shifted his weight from one foot to the other and tapped incessantly on the smooth, white counter as he waited, the pinkishness of his face now fully crimson. Finally, the pharmacist decided the man had had enough.

"Here it is," the older man said as he grabbed the bag. "Krieger. That will be $143.75."

The manager counted out the money one bill at a time much in the same fashion a third grader would. The manager had to dig into his coat pocket to retrieve the last few coins to put him over the amount. The pharmacist slid the money off the counter, and handed the manager the bag of Minoxidil tablets. He stared at the hair sprouting out of the side of the man's head—a side effect of the pills one had to live with.

Satan sat quietly crouching in a corner, waiting for the manager to leave, but he didn't. The man ripped open his bag and popped a pill into his mouth, then took a few steps to a magazine rack and selected a copy of *Muscle and Fitness*. Satan was barricaded with no possible exit and pressed himself against several boxes of cotton swabs, hoping that Fate would be with him in his attempt to elude the manager.

A silence fell over the store, and Satan could hear a strange mumbling as the manager read the articles aloud to himself, followed by several grunts as he looked at the pictures.

From out of nowhere, Ion stepped around the corner.

"Either pick up some cold medicine or leave," she demanded. "You are supposed to be out looking for clothes."

"Shhhhh," Satan hissed, once his heart retreated from his esophagus and returned to its rightful place.

"Why are you acting so retarded?" she said much more quietly.

"I'm…" Satan whispered, "…trying to remain alive."

•

The silver metal dog perched atop the hood of the barge-sized Olds was threatening another crotch, this time a woman's. A whining sound preceded the opening of the driver's power window. The man with the three moles touched the little scar under his nose as he stuck his head out, catching a glimpse of the thin line in the side view mirror. He stared at the woman for a moment, contemplating what he was going to say.

"Hey, Lady…you wanna move your butt outta the way so I can get in the gate," he said to the woman in his path. He grinned slightly at the thought of his Eagle GT radials laying a track across her mid-section.

The sun was bright and near as high as it would get in the winter sky even though it was well before nine.

The woman, in her mid-thirties, had the appearance of someone who had been born a victim. Someone who had never questioned her parents' decisions, who never stopped to explain to her mother that kids in school made fun of you when you didn't wear the correct style of clothes. Someone who thought K-Mart was a pretty neat place.

"Excuse me?" she said, once she realized the man in the car was talking to her.

"I said, could you please move?"

"Oh, was I in your way?"

The man looked past the woman, past the break in the fence that made up the main gate, past the lot full of vehicles toward the large gray building that solemnly sat in the distance. He sighed, wondering if he'd ever make it into work, wondering how someone this dumb—not to know that standing in front of a car might impede its progress—could have survived this long.

"Yes," was all he said, finally.

Her response? "Oh."

He waited a moment.

"Do you have any idea when you might move?" he asked, wondering if it was even worth the effort.

"I don't think I'll be moving soon, Sir," answered the woman. "I'm protesting."

"What for?"

"I got a bad credit rating."

"Do you pay your bills on time?"

"No," said the woman. "But I don't see why that's anyone else's business."

Kenny Odorman looked at his watch, ran a finger over his moles, and wondered if he was having a nightmare.

For her part, the woman was moving back and forth—the way a protester should—across the front of Kenny's car.

Kenny was always a few minutes early to work, so he wasn't worried about being tardy, but the undo delay was annoying just the same. And yet, there was something completely satisfying about seeing the woman pacing in front of him. It was the feeling of pride in one's work. Kenny Odorman took great pleasure in ruining other people's credit much in the same way some people liked sailing or tennis.

"Lady, move outta my way!"

The woman stared at him defiantly. She had seen his kind before, all morning, in fact. It was even possible this was the man that single-handedly ruined her life.

"What are you prepared to do? Run me over?" She sneered at the man behind the wheel and thought of how nice it would be to have a car. Or a home. Or even a DVD player. She couldn't—none of them—bad credit. "Just what are you prepared to do?" she said again, this time a bit nastier.

"Listen, I just want—"

Before he could finish, the woman reached under her skirt, flicked a switch, and exploded.

It took the emergency crews six hours to clean up the mess, get statements from Kenny and the other witnesses. It took them considerably longer to figure out why someone would do such a thing.

The facts, as gathered, painted a picture which looked something like this: Marion Rosemead was thirty-eight years old, Protestant, had a degree in chemical engineering, divorced, no kids. Two years ago, she was laid off by U.S. Plate when, because of NAFTA, the dish manufacturer decided it would be cheaper and far more profitable to make the product in Mexico. Unable to find a job right away, she missed a few payments on her credit card. She finally found work, but when she tried to buy a house several months later, her loan was turned down unless she paid a higher percentage rate which would have made the monthly payments impossible. On January 6th, her car broke down for the fifth and final time. She was unable to finance a new one, forcing her to quit work, because her commute was no longer feasible.

In June, Marion Rosemead went on welfare.

But it was only yesterday, when denied credit while trying to purchase a DVD player at Sears, that she decided to run to the hobby shop around the corner, write a bad check for seventeen Mix & Learn science kits, and blow herself up.

Kenny Odorman was still wearing the heavy cotton shirt and pants the firemen had given him. He had removed all of the personal belongings from his own clothes before the police took them and placed each in a plastic zip-locked bag to be filed away as evidence. He wasn't sure if he would get the clothes back. He hoped so; he liked that shirt. He also wasn't sure why the police had taken them in the first place. Evidence for what, he had asked. There wasn't anything left to prosecute. The woman had done a competent job of incinerating herself; she knew her stuff.

Sitting down at the keyboard of his computer terminal, he glanced at his watch. Three-thirty. Plenty of time to pull up some files.

He leaned back in his chair. It creaked under his weight. He folded his hands behind his head and waited for the system to boot up. A smiling face came on the screen as it logged on to the mainframe.

"Welcome To CreditDat," the screen said.

Kenny Odorman cracked his knuckles and flexed his fingers in anticipation. A moment later, a prompt appeared in a text box beside the words "ENTER NAME:"

Kenny shuffled the papers on his desk. He pulled out the work file and ran his fingers down the crossed out list of names until he came to one that wasn't. He paused and looked at the name for barely an instant. He chuckled to himself, loving his job even more at that moment. Positioning his hands over the keys, he typed:

H-E-N-R-Y D-O-R-O-B-E-K.

•

Satan's leg was beginning to fall asleep and the manager, still in front of the magazine rack, was no closer to leaving the store than before. The manager's grunting had ceased, replaced by something equally annoying: a humming that sounded suspiciously like a grazing cow that grew louder with each turn of the page.

The noise was beginning to pound inside Satan's head like Chinese water torture. Adding to his misery, he was about to lose all feeling in his limb, and if he didn't act soon, there was a good chance it'd have to be amputated. Surveying the area, he searched for an alternate escape, but the only way out was past the manager, surely still peeved about the pickles and sauce.

Ion had given up long ago, going back to work. She said he was being a child.

But then she wasn't wanted for destroying the Food King's bottom line.

Satan contemplated the situation and his options, which were: stay put and lose his leg, or get beaten up.

A picture formed in Satan's brain; a legless man, like some war veteran, wheeling himself along the dark city streets, gathering pity and any spare change he could find, selling pencils and stuffed animals to survive, scooping loose coins off the sidewalk as he rolled by.

Satan chose to get beaten up.

There was really no choice in the matter. Satan would get up, walk by the manager, and pray he was too engrossed in the issue of *Muscle and Fitness* to notice him. Satan waited for the most opportune moment, still hoping he might escape with both his leg and face intact.

Suddenly, the grocery store manager's grunting returned, replacing the humming. Another page, another grunt. This was Satan's big chance. As quietly as he could, he lifted himself out of his crouch and stood. He tried to move slowly, smoothly, surely, but his leg, now fully asleep, no blood in it at all, dragged behind him, making a scraping noise as it trailed the rest of his body.

Satan maneuvered around the manager like the Hunchback of Notre Dame. He was nearly past the man when he made the ill-fated mistake of putting too much weight on his dead foot.

He reached out to grab for something to break his fall.

The overstuffed magazine rack crashed to the floor a second after Satan.

Satan lay motionless and quiet on the remote chance the piercing, shatter-ing sound hadn't penetrated the hair sprouting from the manager's ears.

Unfortunately, that wasn't the case.

Still holding the latest issue of *Muscle and Fitness*, the manager gazed down at the odd man with the worn out old down jacket and a spiffy new bowler atop his head. The man looked familiar to the manager, but he couldn't quite place him.

"You okay?" asked the manager, keeping a finger in the magazine so as not to lose his place.

"Quite. Thank you for asking."

The manager squinted, his eyes forming two slits over which his right brow was pulled up. "Hey, don't I know you?"

Satan remained perfectly still. "I don't believe so."

"You sure?"

"Almost positive."

The cold of the linoleum floor was beginning to force its way past his jacket. Flat on his back, Satan picked up a fallen copy of *Vogue* and pretended to flip through it in a vain, ostrich-like attempt to shield himself.

The manager leaned over and tipped back the top of the magazine. He studied Satan's face for a moment, then let out a little groan.

Sitting up, Satan tried to make a quick get away. "Well, I really must be going."

Adrenaline was pushing Satan's frame to move much more quickly than it was accustomed to. He had crawled only a few feet when he heard the gears in the manager's head seize up as the truth came to him. It must have hurt because the manager let go a wail, sounding once again like a pig under the butcher's knife.

"You! The pickles! The sauce!" The blood pressure in the man's head started to visibly rise, the crimson shade pushing upward like a thermom-eter on a hot, summer's day. Satan was sure this couldn't be healthy for the manager, but he was more concerned at the moment for his own well being.

Crawling past the piles of journals, tabloids and news magazines during his attempted getaway, Satan found himself oddly intrigued by some of the headlines, especially the cover of "WORLD GLOBE"—a name that was sufficiently interesting in itself. SIAMESE TWIN GIRLS CONNECTED AT HEAD, ANXIOUSLY AWAIT BIRTH OF TWO-HEADED BROTHER, the headline read over a blurry picture of two girls riding bikes side by side, their heads joined three-quarters of the way up. This feat alone, captured on film, was incredible enough, but then to think this same family, this very same woman would give birth to a two-headed boy...

Satan tried to calculate the odds of that happening.

And that was his mistake.

The manager had lost all control by now, his blood pressure well above the 200 over 160 range, thinking of losses and shrinkage and revenge. He didn't quite understand why it was so important to smash this man's head in or why he really should care about one jar of pickles or a few bottles of marinara, but that's what the company told him, "control the bottom line," even though he wasn't quite sure which bottom line or where it was. But he was a company man and long ago he remembered his father telling his mother that *he* was a company man, even his brother who he rarely saw said he worked for "The Company" and now a little switch in the man's head flipped and there was no turning back. The manager reached out and picked up a Daffy Duck cookie jar off a nearby shelf and was about to bring it to bear on Satan's head when—

THWACK!!!

The manager reeled from the blow of a Wiffle ball bat to the side of the head.

"All right..." said the female voice. "Drop the Duck."

The manager tried to focus on who or what was ordering him to—

THWACK!!!

—when another blow struck just over the left ear. A few of the hairs coming out of his right ear were knocked from their roots.

"I said, drop the Duck!"

The Daffy Duck jar fell toward the ground and smashed on Satan's leg somewhere between the fibula and the tibia. He let out a muzzled scream of pain. The woman's foot was over his mouth.

The manager was coming back to his senses when he realized he had been hit in the head by a bat, and not a wood one, which would have been a bad thing, but a hollow, plastic tube that really shouldn't have had any effect on a man his size. This was of course before he was hit in the head for the third and final time, and before the world started to go black...

Ion stood over the unconscious manager who had landed on top of Satan. She had hoped the man's momentum would've carried him a bit further to the right, but she was a people person and not an engineer, and he hadn't toppled according to plan and, that was that.

The steel pot she hit the man with had finally done the trick. However, now the item would have to be marked down, or written off as shrinkage because of the large dent in the bottom.

Ion didn't worry much about the bottom line.

"Will you get this heap of flesh off me," said Satan from underneath the belly and arm of the man. "He may be rabid. And I don't wish to undergo horribly painful injections into my stomach if he were to bite me."

"Who is this guy?"

"A grocery worker moonlighting as a hired killer." Satan wanted desperately to be done with this. The fluorescent lights were beginning to annoy him and his hat had been thrown clear of his head. He was clearly in danger of exposure. He liked to limit this kind of thing to bathing and dressing. Two necessary evils that made it possible for others to remain in your presence. At the moment, Satan wasn't sure it was all worth it. "Did you kill him?"

Ion checked the man's pulse before flipping him off Satan.

"No, he's alive." Ion was brushing back the matted hair on Satan's head with her soft, gentle fingers.

"I appreciate the assistance," he said.

"Hey, I'm protecting my investment. I've put too damn much work into you so far to have some nut case ruin it." Ion said something in Spanish to the stockboy who came over after hearing the commotion. With the help of the pharmacist, he dragged the manager out the back door and down the alley. Ion turned to Satan. "You know, at some point, this guy might become a problem."

"He's not already?"

"What did you do?"

"It was the fault of their defective shopping cart," he began. Then he recounted the entire sequence of events to her.

Ion returned to running her fingers in a calming fashion through his hair.

Satan noticed three things at that very moment. One, that he had never really had a need, nor want to use it, but he had another erection, and this time he was positive and gladdened it had nothing to do with Captain Kirk and everything to do with Ion. Two, he had still not found any cold medicine. And three, he was being followed.

•

Armand Arnold climbed out of the cab, grabbed his briefcase off the back seat, then watched as the yellow taxi pulled away from the curb and plunged back into the sea of vehicles. For a moment, he was afraid he might have left something inside. But then he always felt that way. He straightened his tie and turned. Standing on the sidewalk beneath the big red building, he stared up at the toy-like structure. A giant gift box dropped in the middle of downtown. Every kid in the world dreamed of a present this grand under his tree.

But he wasn't here for toys or gifts. This was just the latest battle in an ongoing war against his company. Seemed fitting to have it in a blood red tower.

Armand reread the letter he received two days ago from the deputy director of the Chicago City Development Office. Oh, it was cordial enough, Dear this, Sincerely that, but he knew what it meant. The city planners wanted Arnolds Aluminum out, and fast.

Passing through the revolving doors, Armand Arnold stepped into the Spartan lobby, heading toward a bank of elevators on the far side. He wasn't much for the contraptions, took the stairs to his office every day. Then again, the elevators at the factory were over eighty years old and made strange creaking noises whenever they moved. They sort of reminded Armand of his father who, until his death, also made strange creaking noises whenever he moved, but then if anything on his dad had snapped, it would have been his mind and not a cable. Armand reached out his finger, pressing the up button and waited. His silver Timex told him he was a few minutes early, and he definitely didn't want to appear anxious, so when one of the elevators arrived, he let it go without getting on. Three more came and went. He finally climbed in the fifth and rode it to the twenty-ninth floor.

A pleasant "bing" sounded as the door opened to let him off.

From Kelsey's office, you could see the Lake, its gentle waves lapping against the cement walk that ran along its edge. A shiver went through her that crept up her spine. The thought of Lake Michigan always made her cold, especially this time of year.

She sat back in her chair, breathed in the aroma of fresh leather.

Leo Lincoln was in his office directly across from hers, tapping a pencil on a copper etching of his great, great grandfather that sat on his desk. In fact, there were eight of them, spread out on the glass top. He had just finished emptying all of the change from his pockets, and this was it. Eight cents.

Kelsey could see him playing with the pennies as he talked on the phone to someone, laughing about something. She wondered how many rolls of the copper coins she'd have to stuff in his pockets to sink him in the Lake.

The people from Arnolds would be here soon. She dreaded seeing their faces when Leo lowered the boom and told them that Cook County was revoking its emissions waiver in accordance with Federal guidelines for urban areas. Arnolds Aluminum would have to install new, more efficient scrubbers on all its smokestacks. The company gained the waiver after it acquired sulfur dioxide credits from a power plant in Indiana that had lowered its emissions more than was required. But the EPA allowed local governments in areas of high population density to require that the credits offsetting pollution were from a company within a reasonable distance from the polluter. Arnolds had six months to comply, but work to correct the problem must begin within thirty days or face daily fines. She knew the company didn't have the capital for such an expense, or to pay the penalties of noncompliance. Leo, the weasel, would have his way, perhaps as soon as two months.

Just in time for Lincoln's Birthday.

It was a few minutes later that Armand Arnold walked up to her office and knocked on the doorjamb.

"Hello," he said, quite nicely for someone being forced out of business.

Kelsey glanced up from the blueprints that sat atop her desk for overall redevelopment south of the Loop, including Renaissance Village, saw who it was, and let the plans roll up on themselves.

"Mr. Arnold, how are you?" she said, extending her hand. He was more handsome than she had expected and a bit more weary. He looked tired and beaten and his clothes were not as fine as someone who owned a business the size of his, but he still had a look in his eyes that made her feel warm.

He squeezed her hand for a moment, and she felt better.

"The new Sheriff's tryna run me outta town, but other than that, I'm fine." A sense of humor. She liked that. They parted hands, then sat.

"Kelsey Stuart, Deputy Commissioner. Where's the rest of your people?"

"I'm it," he said, noticing the woman's new leather chair. The kind he had been wanting for a few years now. He had a catalog in his top drawer that had every imaginable kind of chair, wing back, executive, petaled arms. Out of all the choices, he had picked the very style she now sat in. If only his accounting department would let him order one, but they made some lame excuse about first paying the utility bills.

"Mr. Arnold, I'm really sorry about all the trouble we're causing," she said, truly feeling bad for him and for herself for being here.

Armand leaned back and sighed. He tried not to sound defeated, but he couldn't help it. "What is it now?"

"Unfortunately, I have some—"

"Well...hello, Arnold," Leo said, strutting into the room, his round face even redder than normal, showing his excitement and anticipation. He sat his round little body into the chair next to Armand. "Leo *Lincoln*."

They had met a dozen times before, yet Leo would force his family name down your throat any chance he got.

"Have you seen our revitalization project for south of the Loop?"

"No, I haven't."

"Lovely thing," Leo said. "Well. Let's get down to it," he added without pause. "Cook County's revoking the emissions waiver on your stacks."

Armand knew coming in the news would be bad, but when he heard the word "revoke" emanating from the round man's red face, he was most unpleasantly surprised.

"You son-of-a-bitch!" he screamed, losing all the cool he had hoped to maintain. "What kind of time frame are we talking about?"

"Six months to comply. Thirty days to begin the work...or pay fifteen hundred per stack per day."

"You know damn well we can't afford to refit the stacks."

Kelsey watched the man figuring the math in his head and coming up with a very disagreeable sum. Leo for his part was flipping a penny over and over. Heads, heads, tails, heads, tails.

"Then buy credits from within the fifty-mile radius."

"There *are* no clean air credits within a fifty-mile radius. You people have driven them all out of business or out of town. I mean, there's not one Goddamn printer in Printers Row, unless you count Kinko's."

Leo glanced up from his penny flipping. "You could sell out now and still get a good price, before you're...completely over a barrel."

"This is blackmail, Lincoln."

Kelsey had never heard anyone call Leo Lincoln just Lincoln, mostly because no one liked feeding Leo's patrimonial pretensions. However, the name sounded less than distinguished coming from Armand Arnold's lips.

Hearing it, she wondered if the Southerners had spoke of Abe in the same derisive manner.

"There's nothing I can do. Clean air. It's the law."

Now, Armand was beginning to get really angry. Who did this ass think he was? "Since when have you been concerned with the law, Lincoln? I know all about you. How you finally freed up the land for the Sears Tower. You're dirty. And someday, somebody's gonna catch you. And I just hope I'm there to see it."

Leo chuckled in a manner Kelsey thought rather smug. Like a crime boss who had paid off a jury, waiting for the reading of the verdict. He's guilty, but he's going to get away with murder and he knows it.

"This isn't about clean air." A tiny bit of Armand's breakfast came back up near his throat. Leo Lincoln had that effect on people, but Armand wouldn't give him the satisfaction of knowing. "This is about you getting my land for your developer friends and Renaissance Village. Only, that ain't gonna happen, Lincoln."

The man wasn't groveling at Leo's feet as Kelsey had expected. Leo seemed annoyed by this fact.

"I'm not folding under so somebody—especially not your pals—can build a bunch of condos, coffee shops, and nail salons."

"Actually, this is so they can build a parking lot for a bunch of condos, coffee shops and nail salons," Leo said as he stood, went to the desk, and unrolled the plans. He stuck his finger hard on that part of the blueprint where a multi-story garage was drawn.

"You got a lot of Goddamn nerve, trying to threaten me."

Leo moved to the window and pointed a round little finger down toward the street. The sun coming in made him squint his beady little eyes. "See those cars, see the license plates. 'Land of Lincoln.' This is *my* land, this is not *your* land. Land of *Me*. See that?"

Kelsey looked at Leo with disgust.

"I can see all right." Armand was nodding. "And what I see is a tiny little man who uses his name to bully people around. But get this, Lincoln, I'll go Chapter 11, hell, I'll even shut down my plant before I'll ever sell to your buddies. So fuck you."

"You'll have to at some point, you've got debts, stockholders. No bankruptcy judge is going to let you just hold on to that land forever. Especially, if you can't get a permit to operate your factory."

"Fortunately, for me, Lincoln, Arnolds Aluminum leases the land the factory sits on…from me. This is *my* land. Land of *Me*." Armand stuck his finger hard on the plans much in the same way Leo Lincoln had. "And I'll be damned if I'm going to sell it to make room for a fucking parking lot. I'll hold this project up for years."

As Armand said his polite goodbyes to Kelsey and then stormed out the door, Leo Lincoln's face got a little redder.

Looking back on the meeting, Kelsey sat back in her chair and, for the first time in a long time, didn't want to dump Leo's body into the Lake. She wanted him alive to stew in his failure. Arnolds Aluminum might be dead, but without the land for a parking garage, so was the Renaissance Village project.

Like good ol' Honest Abe always said—paraphrased a bit—fuck 'em if they can't take a joke.

•

Satan waited outside of Clancy's for Ion. A group of carolers dressed in long pea coats and wearing various types of hats was singing "Jingle Bells" on the sidewalk just a few yards away, a little too full of the Christmas Spirit. He could smell it on their breaths. Satan tried his best to block out the haunting melody, which he knew he'd hear in his head for the rest of the evening.

"…*sing a sleighing song tonight. Oh! Jingle Bells, Jingle Bells*…"

Unable to stop the sound from penetrating his mittens, his hands, on its way to his eardrum, Satan marched over to the group. One of the women smiled at him, thinking he was going to put a little change in the charity bucket they had placed on the ground. The proceeds of which were going to be given to one of the local homeless shelters after deducting for parking, since everyone drove separately, and for the two pints of rum they had bought to keep warm.

But Satan didn't put any money in the kitty.

Instead, he began to scream at them.

"Isn't there enough violence in the world without you belting out a chorus advocating 'a *slaying* song tonight?' What kind of people are you? 'A *slaying* song?'"

Having clocked out a few moments earlier, Ion observed this event with the helplessness that comes from being a witness to—yet unable to prevent—a tragedy. She rushed over and pulled Satan away from the stunned choir who had lost all harmony and sense of timing after the attack. "What are you doing?"

"You won't let me talk about nice, smart people living inside the planet, but they can promote murder for the holidays?"

"They're talking about Santa's sleigh."

Satan nodded his head. He knew all about Santa and his sleigh. Landing on rooftops, breaking and entering, stealing desserts and dairy products. The guy was a criminal.

"Jesus Christ, Vinnie, you're going to be a star. People are going to be watching your every move. You can't be doing this shit anymore."

"I don't want people watching me."

The mention of people spying on him temporarily put a damper on his recent triumph over the carolers.

They were silent for several minutes as they moved away from the singers who had decided to migrate to safer ground themselves.

"I need you to start focusing. You're gonna make your first public appearance tomorrow night. It's a little blues club on the Southside, no big deal if you blow it, but don't blow it or it'll become a big deal."

"I don't sing the blues."

"You're not singing. You're talking. Introducing yourself to the world."

"You mean in public?"

"Yes, that's why they call it a public appearance."

"I can't."

"Why not?"

"I'm not ready."

"Well, get ready. Because we're gonna agitate the herd, then offer them salvation."

Ion had done a lot of thinking about where and when to bring Vinnie out of his self-imposed obscurity. She had been rounding up people, sending out emails. But one of her greatest talents was timing, knowing the right moment to expose her subject. Another was her ability to maximize someone's strengths and instead of minimizing their weaknesses, turn them into assets. "You're like an artist, man," Slag once said to her after one of her projects got on the cover of Billboard magazine. "Only you compose in people."

Some people work in clay. Some in oils. Some with words. Ion worked in flesh.

"You've been sitting on your ass thinking about this for twenty years.

Time to get off it and start doing something for a change."

"Why can't I just broadcast from the house? You're always going on about that, you know, river thing on the net."

"You mean, streaming?"

"Yeah, why can't we do that?"

"That's just a tool, Vinnie. It can't replace human contact. You're like a match. You have all this potential energy. But a match just sits there until it meets the striking strip. Then it starts a fire."

Satan grumbled at her, although deep down he liked going head to head with Ion. It made him feel alive, more alive than he had felt in…just about forever. At least since his mother was hauled away.

Satan missed his mother, even though he never went to visit her, because the truth is, he missed the woman she was, not the woman she became. But he missed his father most of all.

When Satan was a young boy, very young, a few years old in fact, his father would creep into his bedroom late at night, several hours after he'd been tucked in by his mother. It was their secret time together and he cherished it. His dad was a big man, six-three or six-four, and to little Noel, he seemed to be much, much larger than that. As big as anyone could get. A giant.

Henry Dorobek would kneel by the side of the small, twin bed and stare at his boy under the cover of darkness. He'd lay his hand on Noel's chest and marvel at the miracle of life that made his hand move up and down. His palm covered nearly all of his child's torso, and it felt soft and warm to Henry.

Sometimes, his dad would stay at his perch, staring at his son for hours. And sometimes, Noel would wake up to find his dad watching him. When his dad saw him open his eyes, he always said the same thing. "England! awake! awake! awake! Jerusalem thy Sister calls! Why wilt thou sleep the sleep of death? And close her from thy ancient walls." Years later, Satan realized it was a stanza from a poem by William Blake. But at that time, barely four or five years old, the words "sleep the sleep of death" scared him into thinking falling asleep was somehow a bad thing, something to be avoided at all cost. Thus began a pattern of insomnia that remained with him to this day. From then on, Noel was always awake when his father came creeping in.

"Tell me again, dad."

His father would rearrange the blanket under his son's chin, which was a useless gesture since the boy was completely covered, protected as only a mother can.

Henry Dorobek would sigh, and drop his head, nodding it on the way down.

"I tell you these secret things, Noel, because I want you to know the world isn't always as it seems on the surface." He gently placed his palm over his son's small hand.

"What about my father," Satan asked, his words seemingly coming out of nowhere, catching Ion off guard.

"What about him?"

"He found a way inside. That's why he left us when I was a kid."

"Vinnie, if your dad found a way to get anywhere *near* the center of the earth, he's been spewed out of a volcano by now and the Japanese are playing golf on his ashes.

"I'm telling you, the government is keeping the truth from us. I know it. People have the right to know it. And I'm going to expose the truth."

"The truth!?! People don't want the truth. They want to be lied to. They want to be told their breath won't stink, that they can go to sleep *and* lose weight, that they can be young forever!"

Passing a bus stop ad with a model looking maybe 25, smearing anti-wrinkle cream on her face, Ion pointed at the woman. "I mean look at this. How old is this woman? Twelve? It's a lie. What we're gonna tell people is more truthful than that. Radiation destroys DNA. Damaged DNA causes replication errors, replication errors cause aging. Foil blocks radiation. Your four-alarm fire at Krogan's proved that. So, 'Wear Foil. Live Longer.'"

Satan stopped to look at the ad, which he didn't know was produced by Peter Marks.

"You know, I've got about 70 years of research left before I know whether or not that's really true."

Ion sighed and told him she was going to round up some more help, because if she had to listen to him babble about this shit all day every day, she was going to kill herself. She walked off.

"Okay, I'll see you later?" he said, asking more than making a statement.

All alone in a sea of bodies, Satan stood on the corner, waiting for the light to change. He tried using the power of mind over matter to control the thing within his pants that was still at attention long after Ion's departure, but that didn't work. The more he thought about it, the harder it became.

He attempted not to think about it. That didn't work. You can't forget something you're *trying* to forget. It simply can't be done.

A cold, December wind blew through the street, sending the Christmas decorations jingling and jangling. The sun was almost gone, and the multi-colored lights twinkled in the looming darkness.

It was enough to make you sick.

While he stood there, calculating how much energy was being squandered and comparing that to how many people in Bangladesh could use a good, hot meal, a woman—possibly a former pro hockey player—carrying a bundle of gifts stepped up to the curb and knocked him in the eye with the corner of a box. Satan interrupted his theorizing to check his more-than-likely scratched cornea. He tried to focus his watering eye on the mass of packages and flesh beside him, but couldn't quite figure out which was which. Before he could admonish the woman—or was it the box—for her inattentiveness, the walk signal changed and the woman and her bundles disappeared into the crowd, bludgeoning several others as she crossed State Street.

Satan hated Christmas. The thought of candy canes, little kids, and piles of toys made him nauseous.

He was a few blocks away when he remembered that he had forgotten all about his erection, that was until he remembered he had forgotten. Nevertheless, it seemed to be gone, which was a good thing because all the jingling and jangling had made him have to go to the bathroom and it was more than a little difficult to aim correctly in an erect state.

Satan ducked into a store, pretended to be a customer for a few minutes, then asked for directions to the men's room where he was accosted by Nat King Cole's "Have Yourself A Merry Little Christmas" as he stood in front of the urinal.

It somehow seemed fitting.

•

Kelsey turned the key in the lock, then pushed opened the door of her apartment. Briefcase under her arm, she stepped inside the dimly lit flat that faintly smelled of pine and garlic. Her heels clicked on the hardwood floor, then were muted as she stepped onto the carpet.

Barris was huddled over his writing pad much in the same way he had been when she left him this morning. The only visible difference she could discern was that his Second City T-shirt was replaced, or rather covered, with a thick wool Shetland sweater. An empty bowl, spoon resting on its lip, was set to the left of a rarely thumbed thesaurus. The dish had probably once contained some sort of breakfast or lunch item.

The sight of the back of Barris' head made Kelsey want to wretch. His lack of any drive or motivation further enhanced the feeling until she felt a slight spasm in her abdomen.

Barris turned and gave her a big smile. "Hi, honey. How are you?"

On that, Kelsey ran into the guest bathroom and threw up.

Barris tried tending to Kelsey, but she didn't seem to want any help or sympathy. She instead suggested that he go in the other room and make a fire.

So now, here he was crouched in front of the hearth, reaching a long lighted matchstick toward the Travel section of last Sunday's paper that was crumpled under a pyramid of logs. A section no one ever read. Thousands of trees were killed every day because of Lifestyle sections, Travel sections, Food sections. Barris wondered who the people were that actually read these pages, what they were like, and why they didn't have something better to do.

His musing was interrupted by the sound of Kelsey's footsteps on the floor.

"What happened?" he asked, completely unaware that the sight of him sitting slug-like at his desk had made her sick.

"It must be the flu or something. Stomach virus." Her face was pale and the skin under her eyes was dark.

"Is there anything I could do to make you feel better?"

Move out, get a job, take a bath, clean up after yourself, shave, get a haircut, exercise.

"No, I think I'm okay now."

"Are you sure?"

She stared at him for a moment. The least he could do for her was have some dinner ready when she came home, maybe do the shopping once in a while, offer to pick up her dry cleaning, make the bed, or even, just once, wait until she climaxed before coming, rolling over and going to sleep.

The only tangible proof she had of his existence was the lack of money in her account at the end of the month.

"You know, there is something you—"

The clang of the broken door chime cut Kelsey off. Banlg, clanlg, danlg, clanlg, boinlg.

"I'll get it," said Barris as he stood up, grunted, hands pushing off on his knees like an old man would, then walked to the door.

It was his one talent, answering the door. He had promised to fix the chime, that was a year ago, but he wasn't very good at those sort of things. A great butler he would've made.

Barris revealed Satan standing in the hallway, shifting from one foot to the other trying to stay warm. Barris grimaced when he saw the worn out down coat and the attached round face. He gave Satan a less than friendly look, then glanced over his shoulder.

"It's the King of the Underworld."

Satan never quite recognized the sarcasm in Barris' voice. He sort of liked being introduced that way.

Kelsey shot a dirty look in Barris' direction, a visual scolding, as she walked past him to greet their visitor. She reached up and kissed Satan on the cheek. "Satan, how are you?" A quizzical smile came over her face as she stepped back to take a good look at him. Something was different about her friend. "Come in out of the hall. It's freezing." She put her hand on his elbow and led him inside. With her friend ahead of her, she realized what it was. "The hat. It's new."

Satan touched it gently. "You like it?"

"It's very nice."

"Is that the present fashion trend underground?" Barris asked from his desk. He had already gone back to his notepad and the sentence he was working on when Kelsey had walked in and disturbed him.

To be deaf in a world of sound, how sad it would...

"I don't think so. It's too hot for hats," answered Satan. "Besides I'm not focusing on the Netherworld aspect at the moment."

"What's that supposed to mean? Giving up your quest so soon?" asked Barris before mumbling the sentence scrawled on the pad to himself. He couldn't quite figure how to end it.

"Only temporarily." Satan coughed several times, remembering on the third that it was polite to cover his mouth.

"Satan, is something wrong?"

"Just a cold. Queasy stomach," he said.

Kelsey glanced at the lump huddled over the yellow notepad. "Yeah, I think it's going around."

"I'm sure I'll survive," Satan said, although he was not at all convinced of this. He moved to the sofa and sat, testing the cushions with his hands.

"We haven't seen much of you lately," said Kelsey. "What have you been doing?"

"This and that. Thinking about my future. Do you have any coffee?"

Barris looked up from his pad. Coffee? Satan didn't drink coffee. Something was up.

Kelsey's lips drew up in a smile, but her eyes were cast to the side, her brow pulled down and creased. The last time the word coffee came out of Satan's mouth, it was followed by several expletives and a fairly unsavory portrait of the state of affairs in Central and South America. She glanced back at Satan. "I'll get the Mr. Coffee revved up. Barris, you want a cup?"

Barris was still shocked that Satan wanted a cup and didn't answer.

"Actually, Kelsey, I was wondering if Barris could get it."

Barris perked up on that one. Something very strange indeed was going on, and it looked as though he was going to miss it. He didn't think Satan was trying to make any moves on Kelsey. Still, he didn't like leaving her alone with the guy.

Kelsey gazed into Satan's eyes and saw something there. For his part, Satan screwed up his face and nodded toward Barris.

"Barris, honey, why don't you make us some coffee?"

"Why do I have to make the—"

Kelsey's glare stopped him mid-sentence. Grumbling under his breath, Barris marched off to the kitchen, banging pots and clanking glasses once he got there to punctuate his indignation.

Sitting on the sofa, Kelsey patted her hand on the cushion for Satan to slide closer. After he did, she took his palm and looked at it, ran her fingers over it. It was a big palm with well-defined creases, a long lifeline. It was smooth, not having been forced to do much labor of any kind.

"What's bothering you?" she asked.

The bowler on his head tilted, Satan fidgeted in his seat before making eye contact with Kelsey. His hands were sweaty from her touch.

"Kelsey...you're a woman, right?"

The question was so ridiculous she actually glanced down to check, then answered, "Yes."

"I'm not sure," he paused, lowering his voice a bit more. "But I don't think I know what I'm supposed to do with one."

As soon as the coffee was served, Barris was sent out to pick up a pizza.

VIII. A MIND IS A TERRIBLE THING

The streetlights cast shadows on the floor of Satan's room. Sounds of the city were magnified in the thick night air so that small noises barely audible in day echoed sharply off the near-empty sidewalks and sleeping buildings.

Satan's high school yearbook lay open on the bed, its pages neatly pressed, showing little sign of wear or use. In the dim light, details of the black and white pictures were indistinguishable, hardly more than shades of dark gray.

The talk with Kelsey had inspired Satan to pull the dusty tome from his closet as soon as he had gotten home. Lying on the bedcover, he hadn't bothered to take off his coat and mittens. He sat there, staring at the names and faces.

What Satan figured was most likely the sound of a gunshot and body hitting the ground made its way up from the street below his window, startling him. Seconds later, another noise—surely the dying man's hand rapping on his front door—sounded. Then terrible screaming, definitely a baby…a baby was crying on his front steps beside the dying man.

Satan sat frozen on his bed, wondering what to do. Should he take a look and risk being shot himself? Should he call the police? Should he ignore it and hope it would all be cleaned up by morning?

After thinking about it awhile, curiosity got the best of him. He grabbed a piece of tin foil and stuck it in the yearbook so as not to lose his place. Rising slowly, Satan clung to the wall, barely cocking his head past the sill, just enough to peer down and see two cats fornicating on the concrete steps.

No sign of blood. No baby. No body.

He was a little disappointed.

Another wail from the cats and he remembered why he had taken the yearbook out in the first place. He was trying to remember the name of the first and only female he'd ever had sex with. Obviously a horrifying experience, he had blocked it out of his memory. So traumatic, so ghastly, so gruesomely hideous that he remembered nothing except that it had happened. Who, where, how and under what circumstances was anybody's guess. The bowler still on his head, he sat back on the bed and picked up the volume.

Looking at the glossy pages didn't make Satan wax nostalgic as it did most people. Instead, the pretty photos of cheerleaders, football players, and graduates gave him a rather claustrophobic feeling in his chest as if he couldn't pull in enough air. It was a sensation he recognized well. Because for Satan, from the first graham cracker of Kindergarten to the last Final which he skipped after two and a half wasted years of college, school was nothing less than a superbly crafted form of torture.

•

Think of it this way:

Albert Einstein, the man whose theory of relativity changed how we view time, the world, and ourselves, flunked history.

Christopher Columbus was laughed at by the greatest scholars of his time. He dared to say the world was round. Everyone in their right mind knew it was flat. And Winston Churchill failed almost as many classes as he got beatings from the Headmaster.

History had proven, rather successfully, that in the eyes of educators, intellect was something to be wary of, to be beaten down, to be reformed. The student was the enemy and must be defeated at all cost.

In other words, a mind was a terrible thing.

So in the tradition of so many other great minds, Satan flunked just about every class he took. It didn't really matter what it was. If there was a teacher involved, he was almost assured of an "F."

He comforted himself with the realization that greatness had always been suppressed. That true genius had often been labeled heretic by its peers. In fact, Satan, née Noel Dorobek, was genuinely proud of how much disregard his report cards showed for conventional wisdom and, specifically, the educational process. Education, as practiced in the typical Chicago school, not only closed off a student's mind but also squashed any spark of creativity that student might have once had, leaving behind an empty shell that could regurgitate the capitals of every state and make a really neat magazine holder in wood shop.

"Noel, could you please recite the Preamble of the Constitution," asked the tall, thin man in front of the blackboard that was, in fact, green. The man's fingers were permanently stained yellow from the chalk he held six hours a day. When he realized his pupil wasn't paying attention, he grimaced, revealing a set of pointed teeth.

Sixteen-year-old Noel was staring out the window at the football team practicing behind the school. They were outside enjoying the fresh scents of fall and sweat while every other student was still locked within the bland white walls. Each member on the varsity squad was excused from seventh period Monday, Wednesday, and Friday—Thursday, too, if they had a tough game coming up. Noel had given serious thought to joining just to get out of class. That was, of course, until Coach Dicolio stated in no uncertain terms that if he tried out for the team, he would make Noel run tackle drills with Zak Stankowitz, a solid two-ninety, and the guy who invented the tradition of burning the school name on his head with a branding iron.

Noel decided, smartly, to endure seventh period.

"Mr. Dorobek?"

Noel looked at the teacher, Mr. Eligator (no first name ever given; speculation that Mr. Eligator was actually the half-human offspring of one of those crocodiles brought back from Florida, then flushed down the toilet when it got too big, had been running rampant since he arrived at the beginning of the school year. The controversy finally ended when Mr. Eligator resigned instead of providing the school board with his birth certificate. A few years later at a school in Joliet, one of his students claimed to have been seduced by him. Her story was later splashed across the front page of a supermarket tabloid: CHEERLEADER GIVES BIRTH TO REPTILE).

"You know, progress reports have been sent out. I'm sure your parents will not be pleased with yours." He paused for an instant. "Would you like me to repeat the question, Mr. Dorobek," asked the teacher, flaring his nostrils in a way not wholly human.

Noel's mind wandered. He hoped he could get home in time to get the mail and intercept the progress report before his mother could read it. True, he was proud of his rogue image, but he wasn't stupid. It still hurt when his mom brought out the belt and started swinging.

The girl in front of Noel turned around and started whispering, "We the people..."

"The Preamble. I know it," Noel said without much enthusiasm.

"Can you recite it for us?"

The girl ahead tried to be discreet. "...in order to form a..."

Noel kicked the girl's chair underneath his desk. She fell silent, then a second later started from the beginning again. Noel was about to kick the chair a second time when he felt the pinch of a growing pain in his shins. The feeling shot up through his back, causing him to grab his side. He was in no mood for this school nonsense. "Can you recite it, Mr. Eligator?"

"Yes, I can, Mr. Dorobek. But I'm here to make sure you can," the teacher snapped back.

"The words maybe, sir, but do you know the meaning, the spirit of what the authors meant when they wrote it? Do you have any idea?"

That statement was enough to get Noel a pass to the principal's office. Noel knew the meaning. And that was: *Freedom.*

The main office of Parkinson High (an unfortunate name which has since been changed after three teachers inexplicably came down with that very disease) was about as welcoming and friendly as a hospital emergency ward. And like an emergency room, the walls of the main office were covered with posters urging students not to do drugs, not to get into cars with strangers, not to smoke, not to have sex without protection, not to have sex at all. There wasn't one poster that had something positive to say like "have a nice day" or "the world is a neat place; go and explore it."

It was also ironic that this was the only place in school you could find these posters. Which meant only delinquents and troublemakers got the fullest education offered by Parkinson.

And it was probably no coincidence that the poster showing a pregnant teenager looking grimly into the camera with the words "I didn't think it could happen to me" over her head was hung right outside the principal's office, directly across from his desk as if to remind himself: it could happen to him.

"Noel, how many times have we had this talk?" Mr. McKinney was leaning back in his chair, sucking on his forty-sixth cigarette of the day, which was about half his usual tally by this time; today was the Great American Smoke-Out, and for every cigarette left from the five packs he started the day with, the women in the office were donating a dollar to the Lung Association. "How many times?"

"I don't know."

"Hundreds, Noel. Hundreds." Mr. McKinney's Massachusetts accent robbed his words of most of their authority, and his wound up, nicotine-induced actions made him appear almost unstable.

"I do not recognize your authority over me. Nor do I recognize any sentence you may bestow upon me," Noel said politely, showing his disregard not so much for Mr. McKinney, but his title.

Mr. McKinney took a long drag off his cigarette, holding it in as long as he could, hoping as much of the tar and nicotine as possible would find its way into his bloodstream.

"Noel," he said in a high whisper, so as not to let any of the smoke escape. "You know why I haven't suspended you yet?"

Noel didn't answer; he was too busy checking out the principal's desk, which never seemed to change. It was, as always, cluttered with referrals, detention sheets, book budgets, and the picture of his wife. Strangely, the photo always faced away from Mr. McKinney toward the seat where Noel was sitting. Apparently, Mr. McKinney felt he saw enough of her at home.

He was about the only one to feel that way.

Not only was Mrs. McKinney beautiful, she was also the type of woman most teenage boys dreamed about. Curvy, a bright smile, clingy dresses and, most of all, cleavage. Noel thought back to the last time she visited the school. It was September, a few days after the start of classes, a hot day. The teachers' parking lot was filled to capacity, even the handicap spaces were occupied, so Mrs. McKinney drove around the side of the school and parked in the students' lot which butted up against the tennis courts and practice field. The football team had, as usual, been excused from seventh period and was running drills when she pulled up in her vintage '67 Mustang convertible and got out.

Details of what transpired next were fuzzy and varied according to whom you asked. The official line given by the school was no help, stating that there wasn't any correlation to Mrs. McKinney's presence and "The Incident" as it was now referred to.

As close as anyone can figure, "The Incident" unfolded as follows:

It was a Friday, the day before the Marymount game. No pad practice. Mrs. McKinney was wearing a summer dress, clingy. Her hair was wild, an untamed blonde mane. (These facts are not in dispute.) She was walking toward the back entrance of the school when a tennis ball came flying over the fence, miss-hit by a P.E. student whose class was using the courts because the football team's presence forced them to switch from playing soccer.

As the ball rolled along the asphalt just behind Mrs. McKinney, someone from the courts yelled, "Little help!"—standard tennis jargon for 'will you go out of your way to retrieve our errant ball and return it to us because we're too lazy to get it ourselves.'

"Little help," the person shouted again, this time a bit louder. Mrs. McKinney, who didn't hear the first call, turned toward the voice and saw a young boy pointing at the fuzzy yellow ball that had come to rest atop a drainage grate. Mrs. McKinney smiled at the boy and nodded that she understood his request, then started walking toward the ball.

The boy, realizing whom he'd been shouting at, turned in horror to his partner and whispered loudly, "It's Mrs. McKinney." A murmur began to run through the class.

Meanwhile, several of the defensive backs, having a clear view of the parking lot, glanced over to see what the commotion was about. Seeing the blonde hair, and red dress, they forgot about the wide receivers they were supposed to be covering and began staring openly at the long, bare legs.

The star quarterback, wondering why all his receivers were wide open, looked toward the parking lot. What he saw was Mrs. McKinney bending over to pick up the tennis ball, revealing a bit more than she probably wanted to. What he didn't see was Macon Allen, the nearsighted linebacker—about the only male on the field not gaping at Mrs. McKinney—who blindsided the quarterback, knocking him to the ground and breaking his leg.

The team, which last year came up just one victory short of winning the State Championship and this year was expected to go all the way, was 1-9-0. The "1" coming the week before "The Incident."

Mrs. McKinney was now banned from school property and all sporting events.

Mr. McKinney looked across his desk at Noel. "The only reason I haven't suspended you is that you'd have to stay at home with that loony mother of yours, which is more punishment than anyone deserves." The principal sucked on the last bit of cigarette left between his fingers, getting a lung full of mostly burnt filter, Noel imagined. "What's with her, anyway? Every time I call her to talk about your behavior in class, she starts ranting about 'No fish!' What is that?"

Mr. McKinney was the only person Noel knew who would talk openly about his mother's problem. It wasn't as if no one else knew about it— everyone did—but they all seemed to want to ignore it. His neighbors, his friends, no one would discuss the problem with him. And he needed to discuss it. Noel appreciated these moments with Mr. McKinney, even though he hated the smoke. The principal was like a father figure to Noel. It was comforting, reassuring.

"No meat," Noel mumbled, gently correcting Mr. McKinney. "She's been that way since my father left, sir."

"I know, Noel, but Jesus…" He automatically reached for another ciga- rette, flicked his lighter before realizing, "…Christ! I'm dying here." He threw down the unlit stick and the lighter as well.

One of the secretaries hearing the flint-strike shouted from the other room, "That's one less dollar for some poor child dying inside his mother's womb because she wasn't educated in how bad smoking is for her unborn baby."

"I can't even smoke without someone giving me a guilt trip," Mr. McKinney said, mostly to the voice. He squirmed in his chair, pathetically trying to deal with his withdrawals. Finally, an unfriendly look came over his face. "Screw it!" he shouted toward the outer office. Then reaching into his wallet, he ripped out a dollar. "There. Tell your unborn baby to take that." He tossed the bill on the desk and immediately grabbed the liberated cigarette and lit it. The smoke seemed to give Mr. McKinney an instant high as he sucked it into his lungs. Within seconds, he was calmer. "Noel, you're a good kid." He tilted his head. "Your mother's crazy, but you're a good kid. I'm not telling you what to do, but I think she needs some help."

"She isn't big on doctors."

"Doctors!?! Whose talking doctors? The woman needs a priest! She's possessed," he ranted, the nicotine not taking effect as quickly as Noel had thought.

The principal glanced down at the open folder that held Noel's records. Noel had never actually seen what was inside the folder, but he knew that at some point, it would have to be pilfered, then destroyed. If any of the information contained within were to get into the wrong hands, God only knows what effect that could have on a person's future.

Mr. McKinney stared at the endless extensions he had made in Noel's "probation period." By all rights, the young man across from him should have been given a five-day suspension the last time he had gotten in trouble. Adding today's offense would make this one a seven-day leave. The principal jotted something at the bottom of the page, then closed the folder.

"Give me three days after school," he said. "And this time stay out of—"

A buzz on the intercom interrupted him.

"What is it?"

"Your wife," answered the voice through the box.

"What line?"

"She's not on the phone. She's been spotted in the parking lot."

Moving faster than an adult should, Mr. McKinney shot out of his chair like a solid rocket booster had been strapped to his back and ignited, a projectile speeding toward some unknown destination. "Oh, my God!" came out of the blurry mouth or at least that's what it sounded like.

"It's the last game of the season. She can't do that much damage," Noel heard someone in the other room say before chuckling broke out.

As the door to the main office slammed behind him, what Mr. McKinney shouted said it all: "Basketball tryouts!"

Half an hour later, after the bell to seventh period rang, Noel was cleaning the walls outside the main office with another perennial detainee, Vladamir Gerasimov. Vlady for short.

For the past month, Vlady had broken all records for tardiness, absenteeism, and general tomfoolery. In fact, except for Brian Verdad who blew up the science lab, math lab, and cafeteria simultaneously four years ago, no one had gotten in so much trouble in so little time. Several theories had been going around on why this nice boy had overnight changed into High School Enemy Number One, including one that hypothesized that the boy had suffered some severe side effects from an acid trip. Another thought he might have an inoperable brain tumor that was putting pressure on his centers of higher reasoning.

Both couldn't have been farther from the truth.

Vlady's father had decided after seeing Reagan and Gorbachev shake hands in Geneva in November of 1985 that it was safe to return home to mother Russia. To most kids, seeing Gorbachev on TV meant laughing at the guy with the ink spot on his head. To Vlady, it meant going back to the place he had spent the first six years of his life. A place with no hamburgers, no Doritos, no candy bars, no rock music, no girls in short dresses. Vlady was being shipped to teenager hell.

[Noel received a letter from Vlady a couple of years later, when the ruble was worthless, the economy was crumbling and Afghanistan was becoming the Soviet's Vietnam. His first words after 'Dear Noel' were: 'My father fucked up.' When he wrote the letter, Vlady was serving in the army occupying Afghanistan as a reporter for their version of Stars and Stripes. After the usual pleasantries, he went on about how bad things were, the innocent women and children that were being slaughtered by both the Mujahadeen and the Soviets, how all the soldiers hated their duty there, etc. He told of one commander hanging a rebel from a tree by his hands and feet, then blowing him up to whip up his men for battle. The strangest thing about the letter, besides that Noel had gotten it at all, was that Vladamir (as he signed it) had included one of his articles clipped from the magazine. The flowery prose of an army welcomed with open arms by the people of Afghanistan, of bouquets tossed at the soldiers from peasants in the street was in marked contrast to his personal thoughts. He signed off by saying he wished it would be over soon (at least he was just covering the story and didn't have to kill anyone) and that he missed *I Love Lucy* reruns and *Dallas* on TV.]

For Vlady, who epitomized an American teenager even more than a *real* American teenager, the thought of going back to Russia was like willfully drinking castor oil. Ever since his father had announced the decision at the dinner table three weeks and five days ago, Vlady had been staging a one-man guerrilla campaign aimed at letting his parents—mostly his father—know exactly how he felt.

Noel and Vlady were removing graffiti when they heard the ambulance. Vlady glanced up from his scrubbing to look at Noel, their eyes meeting in unison. They both were thinking the same thing.

It took about three seconds for the two boys to sprint to the gymnasium. It took about four seconds to realize that Mrs. McKinney, or rather her body, had wrecked another season, another sport, and possibly, another budding athletic career.

Principal McKinney's efforts to divert his wife notwithstanding, the leading scorer, rebounder and playmaker in the conference was lying on the floor with a broken nose, sprained knee, and two dislocated fingers.

How these simultaneous injuries came about has never, to this day, been satisfactorily explained. Suffice it to say, it's the stuff of legends.

That night Noel rushed home to try and beat his mother to the mailbox and get his progress report before she could see it.

He didn't.

Coming down the street, Noel saw a red and white ambulance that was almost identical to the one that carried off the star basketball player a few hours earlier. The vehicle, with its lights flashing, was parked silently in front of his home. Three police cars were jumbled up in a distorted triangle blocking the street. Noel picked up the pace. Nearing the house, he watched as two men brought his screaming mother—strapped securely in a white canvas straight jacket—down the front steps of their home.

Within minutes, the ambulance drove off, sirens blaring. The police followed a short time later after shutting and locking the front door. Noel stood by and watched the scene among the crowd. He made no attempt to identify himself as the son of the woman carted off, or that he resided there.

After the crowd had dispersed and he was sure no one was looking, Noel made his way up the steps. Pulling a key from his pocket, he reached for the lock on the door, but stopped when he noticed the open mailbox and the torn envelope inside. The envelope was empty, but the return address said Parkinson High School.

•

Satan closed the yearbook and sat back on his bed. The mating cats had ceased their wailing, and the night was now quiet.

He wondered what his mother was doing at this moment—sleeping most likely. He made a mental note to visit her someday, filing it in the deep recesses of his mind where the same thought had been placed a thousand times since she had been taken away. He knew he'd never do it, never visit, but it comforted him enough just to think about the possibility.

Pushing the yearbook to the edge of the bed with his foot, Satan stared up at the ceiling, his hands folded over his belly like a corpse in a casket. For a moment, a picture of his death shot through his brain. The scene was a simple one, a few people, Mr. McKinney, Kelsey, Barris, Vlady, Ion, a priest, that's all. A tightness grasped at Satan's chest, a nagging claustrophobic sense of what it would be like to never wake, never feel, never breathe again.

To know what nothingness was and not remember.

His heart skipped a beat, then double pumped.

A shadow passed across the bedroom wall from a passing car below. A sound like sizzling meat echoed off the buildings as the tires spun their way over the damp asphalt.

He thought about Kelsey, how she listened without judging, without making him feel embarrassed. Talking with her had been easier than he expected. Now, the memory of her soft words and even softer smell allowed him to relax and forget his fear of death.

The yearbook lay at the end of the bed. He stared at it. He had dusted it off to find the only female he'd ever been to bed with. But he couldn't find her. She, like most of his past, had somehow slipped away and disappeared.

He had never played doctor with a girl, never kissed one in Kindergarten, never promised marriage to a fellow third grader as so many others had done. Satan wasn't sure if he was jealous of missing those things, but he did wish—for the first time in his life—he had been given the chance to fall in love, to reject it on his own accord, not let Fate decide his fate. Love was never around him, not in his home, not in his dreams. The concept was alien; its importance, its purpose lost on him.

But now, in the quiet darkness that surrounded him, Satan wanted more than anything to understand what it meant, what it felt like. He wanted even more than that to experience love.

That was, of course, until he actually did.

IX. PERSISTENT VEGETARIAN STATE

Peter Marks never liked work all that much, wasn't very good at it. He didn't much care for the planet Earth either, but someone or something had put him here without bothering to ask what he thought of the idea.

Nevertheless, Peter Marks figured since he was here, he might as well make the best of it, because he wasn't sure what was coming afterward, but he was pretty convinced it'd be just as big a disappointment.

Starting as a copywriter some eleven years earlier at the behest of a stunning piece of jailbait he'd gotten involved with during his junior year at U of I, Peter Marks had worked his way up through the ranks of the advertising world. He found himself, presently, at the very top of the very bottom. Brisker, Pendry & Marks was known in Chicago as a boutique agency. If you needed something creative, unique, something special, this was the place. Big clients like Sears, John Hancock, they always talked about wanting something special, but really, they wanted more of the same, something that the giant ad firms were only too happy to provide them.

This quirky, creative think tank made him, his partners, and their employees a decent living, and Peter Marks never had to take any job that didn't agree with his sensibilities.

Peter had met earlier in the day with Armand Arnold while some of the creatives walked the factory floor to get the juices flowing. The man looked tired, like he hadn't slept in days, which was probably close to the truth. The city was breathing down his neck, his wife was going through menopause, and another supermarket chain was pulling his brand off their shelves. It was going to be a tough sell, tougher than the last time, but he liked Armand and his company. They were underdogs. Peter Marks loved underdogs.

"Slaughter House Of America," he said to himself under his breath.

"*To* America," corrected one of the staff members, seven of whom were sitting semicircle in front of his red marble desk.

Peter Marks glanced up. "Yes, I know...Thad." He shuttled the sheet of paper he was holding between each of his fingers. Doodlings really. "Did you know that fifty percent of all the water used in the U.S. goes to produce beef?"

The seven faces stared back at him not quite sure how to respond.

"Just beef," he said again, still amazed by the fact. "If Americans cut out meat and poultry from just two meals a week, the amount of wheat, soy, corn and oats saved could feed eight times the number of people who starve in the world every year."

More blank faces.

"Now..." he said without pausing, "The patient's dying on the table. What've you come up with for Arnolds?"

A hand went up as Peter Marks put down the drawing of the continental United States hanging on a meat hook with the words 'SLAUGHTER HOUSE OF AMERICA' scribbled over the top. He placed the sheet beside another with an enormous long horn trampling an outline of the country.

No one had ever raised their hand in his office before, he wasn't sure if he liked it. It reminded him of school, another thing he wasn't too fond of, along with work, and people who ate meat twice a day.

Peter Marks pointed at the owner of the hand. "Go ahead, Rachel."

"I'm a vegetarian."

Peter Marks let the words drift over him like snow blowing in the wind after a heavy fall. "No..." he said, trying to visualize it. "I don't quite get the connection. What else?"

He heard eight different proposals. Four of them were creative. Two were innovative. One, the vegetarian thing, was strange. However, none struck him in any way as particularly effective to do the job. That was, sell more foil.

Peter Marks stood up behind his Italian marble desk and dismissed his troops, sending them back to their cubicles to brainstorm some new ideas with an encouraging word and a warning about the relative instability of their jobs. He was mostly kidding about their jobs, but they got the point. Arnolds Aluminum was going down like a sinking ship, and it wouldn't just tarry on the surface until help arrived.

Throwing himself into his chair once again, he pounded his forehead with his fist, hoping to dislodge something that might be creative *and* effective. Suddenly, Peter Marks had an idea. The freelancer who put together the last Arnolds campaign, maybe he could come up with something.

"Alright, boys and girls, I'm bringing in the big guns now," he yelled out his office door. Several of the staff peered over the tops of their workstations to see what was up. "You interns step aside, the Doctor is calling in the Specialist." He reached for his Rolodex. "Marjorieeee?"

"Yes, sir," said a voice outside his door.

"Get McClane on the phone, pronto."

He glanced one last time at the doodlings he was doing for the Vegetarian Association of America account. All this talk about food and foil had his stomach grumbling.

"Barris!" he said gleefully into the phone when his secretary finally got through.

A few minutes later, Peter Marks found himself seated at Trocadaro's ordering a thick, juicy T-bone.

•

It was that very T-bone, from that particular head of cattle that had eaten sixteen times its weight in grains that were planted in a field that once was part of a rain forest that didn't produce as much oxygen as before that caused global warming that depleted the ozone directly over Satan's head.

He felt the difference. One millirem or so, just enough to put him over the government's recommended daily allowance of radiation. He'd already gotten Ion to increase the thickness in his hat to compensate for a solar flare that erupted a few days earlier. She did a wonderful job resewing the lining so that it looked as if it'd never been touched. Now, she'd have to do it all over again. She wouldn't be pleased.

It was particularly sunny and clear for December and the biting cold almost seemed tolerable because of the warmth of the sun. Satan was walking along the busy State Street sidewalk, doing what he did all day instead of work. Which was:

Not much.

In fact, Ion had asked him about this very thing the night before.

"How do you survive without earning a living?"

Satan had no real answer for her, not because he was hiding anything, but he didn't really know himself. Everything was as it had always been. He didn't know any other way of life. Each month he got a check in the mail from some government agency that pretty much covered his expenses. The rent on the graystone had been paid by Mr. McKinney since he found out Satan's mother had been carted off. The monthly rent controlled payment—$366.00—came entirely from monies Mr. McKinney saved after he stopped buying cigarettes—at that time six packs a day. Mr. McKinney didn't stop smoking cigarettes, he just stopped buying them. After that, much of Mr. McKinney's day was spent mooching butts off of students in detention hall.

Satan made his seventeenth mental note of the day. It was: to pick up the card and present he bought each year for Mr. & Mrs. McKinney in appreciation for their help. With the addition of a black king, he would complete one half of the ebony and ivory chess set this Christmas. Another sixteen years and the two of them would be able to sit down and play.

Just in time for retirement.

•

Ion spent the afternoon planning. Sketching out a strategy.

A few days ago at the newsstand on Madison, she was flipping through one of the European fashion mags, one in Italian. Ion didn't speak a word of the language, even if she had dated plenty of its descendants, but the pictures told the story in these periodicals. And there it was; an up and coming young Italian designer, named Mondria, had clothed his models in aluminum foil to highlight the line of hats he was presenting that day. She showed the article to the owner of her favorite Italian restaurant. He told her that the review of Mondria's hats was less than spectacular, but that the show was garnering a lot of press throughout the Continent over his use of the foil.

Vinnie was definitely onto something. They had to strike now.

Ion found herself standing in front of The Nature of Things Store window, which was displaying "WONDERS OF THE UNDERWORLD." Posters of volcanoes, magma, and deep underground caverns provided the backdrop for a window full of rocks, gems and minerals.

In a moment, she was inside being helped, by a college-aged kid who knocked two other employees out of the way so he could help the stunning blonde. "Can I help you?" he said, trying to act cool.

"I'm looking for a gift for a special friend of mine." She picked through the selection, finding a smooth round stone that seemed to be made out of a mix of substances. "Something sacred. Something with a lot of symbolic or ritualistic importance." The stone had a series of unique shapes carved into it. "What do these markings mean? Are they ancient scrawlings or mystical in any way?"

The kid had to force himself to take his eyes off of her. He was sweating. He glanced at the marks in the stone. "Um, actually, I think that's where the oil drill ripped through the rock."

Ion studied the stone a moment longer, then, handing the rock to him, said, "Wrap it up."

•

Walking along the street, past the decorated shops, the bundled up people balancing bags of gifts, by the uniformed Salvation Army cadets ringing bells beside their red tin pots, Satan found himself thinking not of Christmas, not really, but of Ion, her hair, her face, and he wondered why. This slender, captivating beauty seemed to care for him in a way that no one ever had. And all her crazy attention made him feel—well—*wanted*.

Everything turned out so ideally in books and movies. The bad guys were put away. The heroes lived happily ever after. The couples fell in love.

His mom used to say, everything worked out for the best.

But that was before his father never showed at the station, before she lost her mind and had to be taken off in a straightjacket.

Life didn't give a damn if it worked out or not.

But since Ion had shown up, for the first time in a long time, he didn't feel alone. He decided he'd buy her a gift, not a Christmas present, mind you, just a gift.

Looking in the window of a butcher shop, Satan stared at a white-coated balding man as he sawed a side of beef in half, and concluded he wouldn't find anything for Ion here. Changing his focus to see his reflection, Satan noticed that over his shoulder the man who'd been following him was beginning to get a bit bolder, closing the gap between them. Satan had noticed him the other day in Clancy's. The man was tall, well built, and wore mirrored glasses. A long mohair coat covered what was most likely a blue suit adorned with an Uzi-type weapon. As best as Satan could tell, he was working alone. Which was both true and false. This man was by himself, but he was not the only person following Satan. There were twenty-three others, excluding the three people tapping his phone and the four researchers working in a Washington basement investigating his past.

It was the first time since grammar school that Satan had been followed, back then recess usually ended with him being beaten up and tied to a tetherball post. This time, Satan wasn't sure what to do. It wasn't that he was terrified—although he was—he just wanted to know how these things worked. It'd be terribly embarrassing if he were to do something that wasn't proper followee etiquette.

School never taught you anything that was useful in the real world.

He realized he was on his own in this. He'd have to go on instinct, and since he didn't have any, he decided he'd have to learn by doing. He started walking. The man followed.

Satan sped up. The man kept with him.

Satan slowed down. The man dropped back.

Satan crossed the street against the light. The man got run over by a bus.

•

When Ion was a little girl, she never played with dolls, never pretended to cook dinners in plastic pots. Instead, Ion built roads in the dirt driveway of her parent's brick-front home. Roads, highways, parking lots, you name it, she carved it out of the sandy ground that lay under the loose gravel. Her "cities" were well-planned with accessible downtowns and pleasant suburbs. They had just the right amount of industry, and always a healthy smattering of sports franchises. Football, hockey, basketball, soccer. Baseball was a pussy sport, so if there was a team in town, they were always losers.

But the most amazing element about these cities was the transportation system. In addition to the winding, scenic roads, she constructed subways (empty paper towel rolls she buried), elevated trains, and special bus lanes and terminals.

Most other kids were having water balloon fights, B-B gun wars and bombing cars with dirt at the time.

Ion liked buses.

She loved to watch the people who took buses, loved to study their faces and hands, the personal belongings they carried with them. There were men in suits and women in dresses and sneakers toting high-heeled pumps in Bergdorf bags alongside day laborers and sad-eyed women carting dirty-faced children. She had a theory that if the President and Congress simply rode a bus once a year, there'd be a lot less arguing over whether or not everything was perfect in America and a lot more doing something to make sure it was.

Buses held a special place in Ion's heart. They always made her feel close to her father. Some dads were into trains, others cars, and some even made women their hobby. For Ion's father, it was buses. He was a nut on the subject. He had books and models strewn about the house; volumes dating from the turn of the century, that told you everything you wanted to know and more, from the first buses to the newest: where, why, how.

Ion would sit on his lap, and he'd pull out one of the books and read it to her.

"More," she always said.

"More? Are you sure, Honey?"

"More."

Then he'd go on for hours about buses. She loved every minute of it.

The accident itself wasn't all that horrible. It was that the man following Satan loved buses so much. In fact, in the split second before the huge vehicle struck him, in that one glance as he realized he was going to get pounded, the man discerned the make, model, and year of his demise.

The sound of roaring tires, whining brakes, and screaming people echoed for a few seconds after they ceased.

Smoke spewed from the wheel wells of the blue and orange-striped assassin.

Satan had never seen a dead body before, so when he dashed back into the street to see the man for himself, he didn't know what to expect or how to act. Again, he was acutely aware that he might embarrass himself by touching the wrong thing or not touching something else, or ooowing when he should have ohhhhed. In fact, Satan was so concerned with making an ass of himself that he completely forgot about the man lying in the middle of the street altogether, which was the gravest mistake he could've made.

That's why it came as quite a shock when Satan tripped over the man and landed squarely on top of him, coming to rest across the man's stomach. The two bodies formed a human crucifix that seemed more than a little out of place in the path of the now stationary bus.

"Oooww," Satan heard from the top of the crucifix. An involuntary sound that happened as Satan's weight pushed all the remaining air from the man's lungs.

"Iiieeeee," Satan heard himself say. The voice almost sounded human, and it sent a shiver up through Satan's spine that spread out along his limbs, and finally ended up as goose bumps on his arms and legs.

"Coud you prease ge' off me," said a voice that seemed to come from the dead man's mouth.

"Hhhuuhhhuuh?"

"I sad, cou' y' preas ge' ofme."

Trying to get as far away from the corpse as possible, Satan raised himself on one arm and let out a horrifying scream. So did the cadaver as Satan's hand pressed hard against its injured chest.

Once the blood returned to Satan's brain allowing him to think, he glanced down at the deceased and said, "You're alive."

"I kno tha'."

Satan began yelling to the people that were gathering around. "He's alive. He's alive!"

"Ge' off!"

"Oh, I'm sorry," Satan said calmly before he stood and lost his mind for a split second. "SOMEBODY GET AN AMBULANCE!" he screamed at the very instant one pulled up. "That was fast," he told the paramedic who pushed past him on his way to the injured man. "I believe you'll find him to be alive, which is quite inconsistent with the probability of survival, i.e. a man versus a large mass transit vehicle. I'd say—"

"Hey! Sir! Will you please be quiet and step away from the patient," said the paramedic. He turned to his partner arriving with two large cases. "Looks like we got multiple fractures in the legs, chest, possible internal bleeding, and a definite asshole."

"I don't get the asshole part," Satan said.

"Didn't I ask you to be quiet?" said the paramedic, starting to get edgy. From the looks of his bloodshot orbs, he was dipping into some of the medical supplies a bit too often.

"Yes, but I—"

THWACK!!!

It could have been an anvil or a lead pipe, but it wasn't. It was a pocketbook. One which was attached by a hand and arm to the body of a very old lady.

"He tole a you to shutta up!"

"Excuse me…" Satan started. He was about to say something about his rights, freedoms of speech and self-expression protected under the Constitution, but he wisely chose against it when he noticed the crowd of angry faces staring back at him. These people wanted to witness a death or, at the very least, a near-death, and they didn't want some idiot to ruin it for them.

Satan rubbed the top of his head, fixed his flattened hat, and shut up.

•

"Daddy? Daddy?"

Ion stood in the middle of the antiseptic hospital room, her pale skin blending in against the white walls, white ceiling, almost white sheets. An ancient 19" television suspended over the space between the room's two beds emitted colors from the screen that ranged from blue to red to green—not in random patterns as it should, but in three equal stripes across the picture tube, red sky, green faces, blue grass.

In the far bed, a ten-year-old with a tube of his own, his protruding from his side, was flipping through the fourteen channels the hospital provided. On the sixth pass, he finally found one he liked.

"Daddy...I'm talking to you." Ion's arms were folded in front of her more like a wife than a daughter. There was no response from the man in the bed. Determined to continue the conversation with or without him, she said, "Why were you following Vinnie?"

"They put me in pediatrics," Ion's father said in a low, apathetic tone while he reached for his TV controller and changed the channel, starting a war with the ten-year-old.

"They didn't have any room anywhere else," said Ion. "Budget cut backs because of HMOs and managed care."

"I have Charlie Brown bed sheets."

Ion gave a long sigh, hoping her father wasn't going to insist on bringing the whole Peanuts gang into their argument. "Why were you following Vinnie?"

"I've got Snoopy bed pillows. I hate Snoopy. Just once I'd like to see the Red Baron shoot him down. Just once."

"Daddy, why were you following Vinnie," she said more forcefully.

"He calls himself 'Satan.'"

"It's just a nickname. Don't read too much into it."

"He's crazy," said her father, in a way that made her wonder if he shouldn't have said, "I'm crazy."

Every boy, then later, man, Ion brought home had been a parent's worst nightmare. The rock and roll wannabes, the drug-induced poets, the fifty-year-old professors, each was more terrifying than the one before. She had been such a lovely child, a tomboy who bested the boys at their own games, a student who never had to study to do well.

She questioned everything. What was this? Why was that? How come? Her curiousness never had an end.

Fourteen years after her birth, it all came crashing down.

His little girl was no longer.

He remembered the day as if it had happened a moment ago.

He walked in the front door, hung his coat on the rack at the end of the long, dark foyer, wiped the slush and salt from the soles of his shoes. His daughter's jacket was there, a red thing, not at all his taste, but she seemed to like it, and her friends wore similar somethings in various colors.

Plodding toward the couch, he carried his latest treasure into the living room. He set the book on the coffee table, then pulled off his soggy shoes and socks, and laid them out beside the radiator. The house smelled of food left out too long after a meal; another supper he had missed. Since his wife's death, he had taken to eating by himself in any of a dozen restaurants near his office, unable to face the empty chair across from his, leaving his daughter to cook her own dinner. She seemed to enjoy the time to herself. Tonight's meal out had been unsatisfying, and he thought he might sample some of her leftovers. He loved a home cooked meal, even more, the scrapings that had their own special flavor apart from the original dish. For the moment though, he wanted to put his feet up and rest.

"Kiddo, you upstairs? I got a surprise."

He heard a sound of a flavor and characteristic he hadn't heard for several years. It sent a shiver through him, not a cold one, but a warm, soothing sensation. It was a pleasant reminder of something lost. The noise found its way down the stairs once more, and he no longer was comforted by it. This time it frightened him. His heart skipped a beat, and a dryness formed halfway down his throat. He swallowed hard, trying to calm himself. He felt a shortness of breath.

Standing at the bottom of the steps leading to the bedrooms, he was unable to advance any further. Pain was all that was left in his chest where a heart had once been. He felt like he would cry and he did until he stopped himself. Climbing the first step was almost impossible. Taking the second, unthinkable. By the sixth or seventh, it was almost unbearable. Every step became tougher, more painful.

Another sound.

He made his footsteps louder almost as an announcement of his arrival. He paused outside her door for only an instant, aware that his buddy, his little grimy tomboy was dead. She would no longer care about buses or his silly books. Never again want to listen to stories of cross-country train rides.

He grabbed the handle and pushed open the door. A frigid breeze brushed past him coming in from an open window. Staring at the naked form of his once little girl, he could not believe the alterations time had made to her anatomy. It was as if he was looking at his wife or his first lay. For a moment, she remained frozen atop the covers, alone, no one else present, which startled him all the more. Still not conscious of his presence, her right hand remained between her legs, her fingers between the folds of herself.

He wanted to look away before she saw him, but his shock had deadened his reflexes.

Suddenly, she stopped masturbating and glanced up.

Their eyes met for one painful, horrible moment.

"With all the guys I ever brought home, you never said anything. Never cared who I slept with..." Ion leaned against the wall of the hospital room. She saw her father wince at the mention of her sexuality. "Why now?" she said. "I haven't even slept with this one."

"He's dangerous."

"He's harmless. And in his own odd way, he's a genius."

"That's what you say about all of them," said Ion's father as he began losing the battle with the ten-year-old. If he gave up now, he'd have to endure three hours of cartoons.

"And I'm usually right. You have to admit that."

Her dad raised an eyebrow. "He wears foil on his head."

"It's his best attribute. In fact, I encourage it." She glanced at her dad, then sat on the edge of his bed. "Why're you doing this? Have you been spying on me all these years?" He didn't answer her. "I'm not your little girl anymore."

"I know." He looked away, like he wished he had that day so long, yet not-so-long ago. "I just..."

"I can take care of myself."

"I just want you back. I want it the way it was."

Ion saw the pain in her father's eyes. She was all that was left for him, her mother years ago succumbing to the hateful grip of cancer, when Ion was only twelve. Her father had nearly fallen apart. It was then Ion realized how much help men needed to live. Women don't crumble after the death of their spouses, not the way men do.

Ion took her hand and laid it on his. "Well, you can't."

"Look at you. You look so much like your mother. Stubborn like her. Never listened to anyone." He wanted to reach out and touch her face, but unlike her mother, his daughter never liked that. "Will you at least eat some meat?"

"Meat kills the ozone."

"How does it kill the ozone?"

"We've been over this a thousand times." She paused. "I can't go back to being twelve."

It would have been easier to pretend for him, but she had never done that. Except that time he walked in on her. She had heard him early enough to have covered herself, knew he would barge in. The twenty-year-old she was fucking had sufficient time to slip out the window and make his escape cleanly, but not without first grabbing his shirt, pulling on his jeans and giving her a very appreciative kiss. He was nothing, if not a gentleman, that Peter Marks. It would have been less sordid if she had simply picked up a magazine and climbed under the covers. Her father would have never known; he'd have shown her his new book and everything would be as it always was.

It was harder for her to do what she did, present herself naked to his eyes, but then he'd never again presume to force himself into her space. In all the years that have passed, Ion's father never again set foot in her room.

"And you can't go on pretending she never died."

Ion's father, with his two broken legs, a broken arm, several fractured ribs, could not hold back his tears this time.

The ten-year-old was triumphant as the man to his left began to weep.

•

The graystone was dark and quiet when Ion dragged herself up the stone steps. The building stood out among the others along the street for some reason Ion couldn't quite ever figure. Perhaps it was simply Vinnie's home, that in itself made it unique, or the aluminum foil covering the upper half of the windows, forming heavy lids that made the house seem on the verge of metallic sleep.

Bed, she thought. Seeing her father lying there, helpless, brought back the memory of the day he walked in on her. He did so silently, just by the sadness in his eyes.

All in all, the entire experience made her want to fuck. Nearly a dozen men had given her longing glances on her trek from the hospital, nothing surprising, only she noticed them more in this state. They annoyed her rather than flattered when she was aroused. You couldn't say, "How would you like to lift my dress and slip your cock inside me?" Not to someone on the street, so what was the point of covetous looks.

Ion's sides ached from having run most of the way to Satan's, and just as much from a heedless desire to have someone, something inside her—the vegetarian's hunger for meat, she thought and laughed at herself. So why had she come to this place? Slag's musician friends were much better suited to brief, artful fucks. They were perfect for passionately passionless time-outs. And she indulged in them from time to time. But she promised Vinnie she'd stop by and ease his mind that her father had not put a contract out on his life. For all his zany intelligence, Vinnie was emotionally a sixteen-year-old kid deserted by father and mother. His paranoid delusions were epic in their scope. He had been telling her for days he was being followed. She told him he was hallucinating. Yet, she had to admit, some of his fears were coming to pass in one form or another.

Satan was standing in front of his mirror half-dressed when the doorbell sounded. He walked to the window and struggled to get it open, taking more time and energy than going downstairs to answer the door. Finally, with a last burst of strength that did permanent damage to the sill as well as his lumbosacral, Satan forced the glass and its housing upward. Sliding freely along the smooth track, the window smashed into the top of the frame and shattered. Once the splinters of glass had settled, Satan stuck his head through the breach.

"Who is it?"

Ion stood to the side of the scattered fragments, shaking a few errant shards from her hair.

"Guess."

"Why didn't you use the key I gave you?"

Blowing a blonde lock from the middle of her forehead, she raised two disdainful eyes in his direction, held her keys high in the air dramatically, her middle finger and thumb wrapped around his key, letting the others on the ring hang loosely.

"It doesn't work," she said.

Then one of Satan's mental notes came back to him, the one to make Ion a new set of keys. "I changed the locks."

"Why?" said a very annoyed, sexually distraught individual.

"The hardware store guy. I think he made an extra copy when I had him make you that set."

"He doesn't know where you live," Ion sighed. "And why would he want into your place?"

"I got the feeling he sorta liked me, you know, in a queer sort of way."

Ion didn't know. Satan wasn't normally very aware of his own sexual orientation, let alone that of another. She imagined the shape and proportions of the hardware guy's cock and if he had the slightest idea what to do with it. The last time she had been there for some nails and a hammer, he tried to pick her up.

She needed to be hammered. She needed to get nailed. Fuck, she was hot. She even thought about fucking Vinnie as soon as she walked in the door, if she didn't think it would scare the shit out of him.

Besides, it wasn't the right moment for that.

"How is your father? You tell him I didn't mean it?"

"It wasn't your fault."

"Did he say that?" Satan said, hopefully, glancing at neighboring rooftops for signs of snipers. Someone across the way ducked.

"He's fine."

"I thought someone was following me. I mean, I always *think* people are following me…but to know they actually are… He's not some homicidal maniac or anything, you're sure?"

"Yes," Ion said, then furrowed her brow causing several creases to form on her forehead.

"'Yes' as in 'no' or 'Yes' as in 'Yes?'"

"He is not a homicidal maniac, Vinnie. He was being an ass, checking up on me." Ion noticed Satan wasn't wearing a shirt—she couldn't tell about the pants. His naked chest was more attractive than she had imagined. It was smooth yet, manly. There was a bit of baby fat left, and he was very white, but then, so was she. Her pussy was soaking wet. Could he handle it? she wondered. Would he know what to do with it, if she offered it? She motioned to his body, "What are you doing like that?"

"Like what?"

"Like that!"

He pointed to his chest. "This?" he said, grabbing something to cover himself. "I was getting dressed. We got that thing tonight."

In all the commotion surrounding her father, it had slipped her mind. Christmas Eve at the club. Vinnie's coming out party.

Thoughts of fucking went out the window, replaced by something far more frightening: Vinnie, in front of people, on his own.

She only hoped he was ready.

•

Ion stood outside Satan's bedroom door. "Are you gonna take all night?"

Satan raised his eyes to stare in the direction of the voice. "I thought you wanted me to look presentable," he said, finding himself annoyed that—for the first time since his mother was carted away—he had someone forcing a time schedule on him. And only slightly less annoying was the fact that Slag was standing three feet away videoing him.

"Is this really newsworthy?"

"You never know, man."

The door opened and Ion appeared in the jamb.

"What are you wearing?" she asked, more than a little dismayed.

Slag peered from behind the Handycam. "Kinda out there, huh?"

"Now what's wrong?" Satan said, further put off that he had to answer to someone about style choices.

Ion put her hand in from of the camera lens. "Slag...downstairs."

As Slag left the room, Ion pushed the tip of her tongue into the side of her cheek as she surveyed the fashion damage Satan had inflicted on himself; a powder blue double-knit rayon jacket from a leisure suit now missing the pants (with any luck, they had been recycled into a park bench or a bus stop); white shirt with a clip-on tie, which, from the length, looked to be from his fourth grade wardrobe; brown shoes with gray socks.

"You can't go out looking like that."

"Why not? It's a free country."

"We're going to an underground blues club. It's your debut. Even if it weren't..." she paused to take a second look. She shook her head in disbelief, not so much that he had chosen these things to wear, but that they had ever been made in the first place. Unfortunately, since fashions from the mid-seventies weren't biodegradable, they were going to be around for a long, long time. She realized with horror that six hundred years from now, archeologists digging up landfills would find only clothes like the ones on

Satan, since everything else would have decomposed. She felt a tinge of embarrassment, thinking they might attribute these fashions to the entire twentieth century, and not just to a brief, misdirected decade. "You can never be seen in public with those on. Burn them."

"You said burning garbage is bad for the environment."

"Fuck the environment, Vinnie. Torch those things before I burn them right off your body."

Satan was going to stand firm. He was going to assert himself—tell her he didn't like being told what to do and what to wear, and what to think. That is, until she pulled out her lighter and aimed a can of Lysol at him.

He'd bring those points up some other time.

X. ONE MORE BAD THING ABOUT EXHAUST FUMES

When Kenny Odorman was eight years old, he put his mouth up to the tail pipe of his father's old '63 Chevy Bel-Air.

This may explain much of what has happened since.

•

No Mo' Blues sat on a dirty alley off Gains Avenue. The hand painted letters brushed on the crumbling black-washed brick were hardly visible over the dwarfish entryway. "N Mo' lu" the only things left now. A single incandescent bulb hung from a socket carved into the mortar and illuminated a man standing by the small steel door. Dressed entirely in black, a beard of the same hue covering his face, the bored, affected man held a clipboard and sported a contemptuous gaze for anyone who approached. Around him, the squalid alley was littered with paper, carton boxes, and the damp remains of cigarettes. A dim haze hovered above the passage, and the only clues that Christmas was a few hours away were a brief glimpse of a suspended reindeer hoof at the end of the alley and a red Santa's hat entirely out of place on the doorman's head.

Slag swallowed the last of a McDonald's "eggnog" shake, then popped what was left of a double cheeseburger and fries into his mouth. He gnashed the food with his teeth, much in the way a dinosaur might have sixty-five million years ago, and directed intense concentration toward the concrete ahead as he walked along the sidewalk.

Ion and Satan lagged a few feet behind as Slag led them past the last minute shoppers and under a tremendous banner strung across the street that said: "1 Shopping Days Left." Ion castigated Slag for his choice of food and his inability to "find" a trash can when they had passed twenty. While

Ion railed against America's throwaway culture, Satan watched an old man standing precariously on an even older wooden ladder take the "1" down from the banner and replace it with a pennant imprinted "NO," marking the end of another business day and another holiday season.

Light from the street lamps and Christmas decorations made it difficult to see the stars in the sky, but they were there. Satan nervously gazed at them for awhile, hoping the sight of a few far away worlds might ease his apprehension.

It didn't.

His stomach turned now with every step.

When Ion first brought up the notion of going public to instruct the masses about foil, he thought it was a wonderful idea. It was, of course, one of the main objectives of his mission: spread the word, save as much of mankind as possible and...and...and there was one other thing, oh, buy Arnolds stock. But that he'd keep to himself.

He made a mental note to call a stockbroker in the morning.

Even as recently as this evening, getting dressed in his best clothes, Satan felt excited over the prospect of enlightening others. However, that was then. Now, as the moment approached, he hoped a piano would drop on his head. Anything less, Ion would not accept as an excuse.

He surveyed the windows above the street. No baby grands to be seen.

"I really don't like smoke. Emphysema runs in my family. Is there gonna be smoke in this place because if there is, we might as well just turn around right now. I'm very health conscious," Satan said, giving an extra little wheeze to punctuate his point.

Ion was through yelling at Slag.

"What are you babbling about?"

"Emphysema. I will not enter this establishment if there's gonna be smoke."

"It's a blues club, Vinnie. What'd you think we were going to, a church?"

"I'm allergic, we must return home."

He started to make a move back the way they came when Ion pinched him in the arm.

"First, you didn't like the clothes I found you, now you're allergic to smoke. Next you're gonna tell me you're claustrophobic?"

"I am claustrophobic." He felt the walls closing in a bit.

"Deal with it!" she screamed, startling Satan.

"Huh," grunted Slag as he marched a few paces ahead, his black boots clapping the cement as he stepped, the chains around his ankles jingling like the tiny bells of Santa's sleigh.

"Nothing, Slag. Just keep watching the fucking ground to make sure it doesn't abruptly end and swallow us all," she said to him.

"Okay," the poet answered.

Slag had always been afraid Columbus was wrong and that at some point, the world simply came to a sudden and abrupt end. He had personally mapped out most of Chicago's West and North ends, but here on the Southside he was still a bit skittish. Slag's world grew in increments of three feet.

As they walked in silence, Satan studied the people strolling by, watched their eyes to see if any were staring at him. He caught one woman looking a bit too long and he threw her a silent sneer. Satan *didn't* like the clothes Ion had found. He felt foolish being outfitted in some of Slag's 'digs' or 'threads' or whatever he had called them; oversized black jacket, what-was-once-white shirt, black slacks, mittens (he still had a few days left). Now, the woman's mocking gaze had proved it. He looked ridiculous.

"Sorry, I didn't have no shoes that fit, man," said Slag, giving Satan a reason to wonder how he was able to put together poems when he couldn't put together a sentence.

"It's quite all right." Satan was very happy he hadn't been forced to slide his feet into the footwear of someone with a known aversion to water.

They walked for several minutes more without a word, then Slag came to a break in the buildings, checked to make sure the curb did not drop off into oblivion, and said, "It's safe," before ducking into the alley. A few seconds later, Ion and Satan made the turn themselves, following Slag down the passageway to Jeffrey, that was the doorman, who appeared possessed under the harsh shadows of the bare bulb.

"May I help you?" asked Jeffrey, haughtily.

Having been here a few hundred times, Slag flung his voluminous hair to one side, "It's Slag, man."

"Oh, yes," said Jeffrey, pretending this hardly discernible change in appearance was the only reason he recognized the anorexic poet. "Any guests?"

"Two." Slag pointed to Ion and Satan who were easily visible to anyone caring to look.

Jeffrey pursed his lips and dropped the hand with the clipboard to his side. "You'll have to wait."

"I hate when this happens, man," said Slag to his guests.

"See, it wasn't meant to be. Let's go home," Satan begged.

Ion went up to Jeffrey, grabbed him by the shirt collar, and put her face up to his. "Jeffrey, don't be a dick. You know who we are, we come in here all the time."

"Who's he?" he said, aiming a limp finger at Satan.

"A friend. Now let us in or I'm gonna light your beard on fire."

Ion was in a particularly combustible mood this evening, Satan thought, first with the Lysol and lighter and now with the lighter and Jeffrey's face. Fire seemed to be the operative word for the night. He thought it wise to keep her away from alcohol, just to be safe.

He had no idea she just needed to get laid.

Jeffrey, never being big on flames, stepped aside to let them in.

"Happy Holidays," he said.

After they were gone, he jotted down several rude comebacks on his clipboard, ones he had thought of using, but hadn't. Jeffrey appeared pleased with himself once he finished and sat waiting, scowl on his face, for his next victims.

Inside No Mo' Blues was much like outside, grimy black-painted brick, damp cigarette butts on the floor, hardly any light except for the stage. Yet, unlike its exterior, the club was warm and cozy, and there was a faint smell of rose petals that made it past the cloud of cigarette smoke hanging over the room.

That's what most people thought.

Descending the stairs that brought patrons down from street level, Satan gazed wearily over the men and women populating the establishment. He flared his nostrils, the smell of liquor suddenly filtering through to his olfactory glands. His sinuses were folding in on themselves as the airborne waste of spent tar and nicotine invaded. He made a loud, honking sound in an attempt to clear his stuffed passages. A few people turned to see why a goose was loose in the bar.

Satan had never been in a place like No Mo' Blues, and after studying the drunken revelry, the public displays of affection and bra straps, the faces of different colors and cultures he knew nothing about, he remembered why he had stayed away thus far.

"Isn't this place great?" shouted Ion over the din, finding the club attractive for the very same reasons Satan wanted to leave it.

Music weaved its way through the room like a summer breeze, warm and lazy. At once, Satan's body lost the shiver it had had since leaving his home. And for an instant, he found the club pleasing.

Slag and Ion carved a path in the crowd, Satan followed, heading toward the center of the club where seven or so risers making up the stage formed an oasis. Soft lights, blue, red, orange lit the jazz quartet as they belted out a number.

A tall, black man sporting a trim, well-kept goatee strolled up to Ion, and Satan tightened, not sure what to expect. Satan saw blacks all the time in Chicago; they even had one as Mayor once, but then he choked on a chicken bone or had a heart attack or something like that. Still, he felt uncomfortable around them, the way they spoke and acted.

They were different.

Satan never noticed the difference between blacks and whites or Chicanos and Orientals—Asians now—when he was a kid. In fact, his best friend in Kindergarten was black, Jason Leigh. At least that's what his mother said one day at dinner. Satan was thirteen and they were discussing the time he fell off the front steps, cracking his skull, and had to have thirty-seven stitches above his left brow. Still had the scar. Anyway, Jason and young Noel were playing their seven-year-old games when it happened. Noel lost his balance and came crashing down on his forehead. The blood poured onto the cement steps. Without a word, Jason sprinted six blocks to the shop where his mom worked as a seamstress. In minutes, she came huffing and puffing, and bent to touch the wound. It was a soft touch. She asked him where his mother was. At work, he told her. Okay, she said, pressing her smock to stop the bleeding, everything would be all right. She had Jason hail a cab, and the two of them took Noel to the hospital. Jason had saved his life. Yet, Satan didn't remember Jason as being black, just as being a kid. Even now, he could picture Jason's face, but the pigment of the boy's skin seemed no different than his own. He always found it strange he hadn't realized Jason was black until his mother told him so.

That they were different.

Ion smiled at the man and let out a small squeal. Slag had disappeared into the sea of people. The crush of humanity was beginning to have a claustrophobic effect on Satan. The wall at the far end of the room was rushing straight at him.

"Oh, God, Jason," Ion said, kissing the man on the mouth, "How've you been? Merry Christmas."

"Very merry," he said.

She looked him over. "You look great, really great. What have you been up to?"

Jason held out a trumpet, its perfectly polished brass reflecting the lights coming off the stage. "Just taking it blow by blow." He gave her a great squeeze as he wrapped his solid arms around her frail body. "It's great to see you. God, you look beautiful."

Satan hadn't realized just how thin Ion was until he saw the fabric of her clothes collapse under the man's hug.

"Listen, I want you to meet a friend of mine." Ion whirled around, more giddy than Satan had ever seen her. "Jason, this is Vinnie. He's my latest project."

Jason put out a large, friendly dark hand. "Nice hat."

"I made it," Ion said. "Sort of."

Satan grabbed Jason's hand and shook it. Satan stared at the man's face and tried to imagine what time and a bit of color would've done to the face of his childhood friend. He couldn't make it work. Too many years had passed or maybe it was that this man just didn't look like his friend. Satan wondered what had become of *his* Jason.

"She running your life yet?" Jason asked as he withdrew his hand from Satan's and put it around Ion's waist very comfortably as if it had been there many times before.

"Not really," said Satan, looking at the man's fingers as they appeared on the other side of Ion and rested on her hip.

"She allowed me to see my true calling," he said, then held out the trumpet again, before turning to her. "By the way," he paused for effect. "I signed a contract with Blue Note."

"That's fantastic!" Ion kissed him for the second time in as many minutes. So much affection.

"I know. It's unbelievable. I'm gonna cut an album."

"I knew you'd do it," Ion gushed. "I told you. Thank God. Like the world needs one more fucking lawyer."

"Hey, I was a good lawyer," Jason said before returning his gracious attention to Satan. The blue and orange spots escaping the stage lit a twinkle in his eyes. "What's your habit, Vinnie?"

"Call me Satan."

"All right," he said without a hint of curiosity over the name.

Satan was about to explain his penchant when Ion cut him off.

"Tin foil," she said, tapping the hat on her head.

"Tin foil?"

"Aluminum. It blocks hyper-radiant particles, gamma rays, microwaves, UVA, UVB and the like that are raining down on us," Satan explained.

"For what purpose?"

"Well, as the hole in the ozone—now the size of the continental United States—gets larger—"

"Slows the aging process," interrupted Ion. "Refocuses the brainwaves."

"Hmmm," the black man said, intrigued by her statements rather than his.

Ion stood beside Jason. His hand felt good around her waist. Ion liked the silky texture of black skin. For a long time, she wondered if it was a racial thing, an attraction to forbidden fruit. But she discounted that. It wasn't only men; she often found herself brushing against black women in tank tops as they shopped at Clancy's, just to feel the smoothness of their arms. It had something to do with oil, or the lack of it on the skin surface.

She let the music and Jason's touch soothe her. The band was playing an upbeat tune, and Ion found herself tapping her foot on the floor. She looked across at Vinnie. She was proud of him. So far he was holding his own, not nearly as traumatic an experience for him as she had thought it might be. She was glad she didn't use him to soothe her cunt earlier. He wouldn't have understood, let alone been able to handle the club afterward. She had to take things slow with Vinnie. He seemed more fragile, more childlike than the others. But every toddler had to take his first step at some point, and for the moment, Vinnie was wobbly but still on his feet. As she watched him speak with Jason, she became more and more confident that she could make him a success, as she had done for Jason, as she had done for a guy named Peter Marks with a talent for selling things when she was just in High School, as she had done for a popular television actor whom she referred to now only as The Guy That Turned Out To Be A Jerk.

"Remember that guy that turned out to be a jerk, what's-his-name?" Jason said.

"What about him?"

"His show got canceled."

"I thought it was in the top ten."

"It was. Until he started banging the wife of the network president."

"What an asshole. Where'd you hear this?"

"From a friend of mine in L.A. at the law firm that handles him. The big guy found out and moved the show from Thursday night to Saturday. Type of people who like that crazy-ass show are out partying Saturday night. That's the timeslot shows go to die. Now, it's in the tank. Supposedly your boy's freaking out. Bought some house in Malibu he can't afford now. It's kind of sad, really."

"I'm heartbroken," she said without a trace of sympathy.

As Jason's hand squeezed her flesh, Ion noticed Vinnie watching her watching Jason.

•

Hot chocolate, the smell of it, filled the air. Steam rose from the mug in Kelsey's hand as she lay in bed, reading the latest issue of Modern Architecture. Flipping the page, she glanced at the clock: 11:54. Six minutes and it'd be Christmas.

Barris was in the living room, where he'd been since the day before yesterday. He hadn't said a word to her in a day and a half. He simply kept mumbling "foil, foil, foil" over and over again.

When Barris hung up the phone, he didn't know if he was sitting or standing, but he did know it'd be smart for him to find out which so he wouldn't hurt himself.

Peter Marks had made him a simple offer. Come up with something great for Arnolds Aluminum, *fast*, and get paid an ungodly amount of money.

He was standing.

He sat down.

He glanced over at the work he had done that day on his book. It had been an unusually fruitful day.

> *Before moon and night sky, he gave into the hunger and fed upon her body's feast.*
>
> *"Yes," she proclaimed. "Yes, yes, let your body talk to mine," she begged.*

"Okay...

He tossed the pages on the floor, opened a drawer on the desk and pulled out a fresh yellow notepad.

"Foil, foil, foil." He tapped his head with the end of a pen. "Foil, foil, foil." Barris tried to remember all the ways he had used foil over his lifetime. Lunches, school lunches, spitball fights.....

Childhood stories, that was an idea. A kid—first time making his own lunch—uses Arnolds™ and he's hooked for life.

Too hokey.

He scratched it out, making sure to blacken the letters completely so no one could possibly read it.

Barris then tried conjuring up all the images he associated with foil. Lunches...he had that. Barbecues, leftovers, baked potatoes, TV antenna, better reception, easy to clean up, roast beef, not for microwave use, Satan...

Barris began to chuckle. He had this hilarious picture in his mind of Satan waking every morning, pulling out a roll of foil and wrapping his head. He envisioned the campaign slogan:

Arnolds...the all purpose aluminum.
Wrap your lunch. Wrap your head.
Arnolds...Keeps the gamma rays out...and the freshness in.

Barris was lying on the ground, kicking his feet in the air and holding his stomach, which hurt from laughing too hard, when he suddenly realized if he was going to have any chance of getting this done, he was going to have to get serious.

Catching his breath, he picked himself off the floor and sat back down in his chair.

Thirty-six hours later, he was still pretty much in the same position. His chair had moved a few inches to the right, but that was due more to the vibrations that the 'el' trains caused than any movement on his part.

Kelsey climbed out of bed once the clock changed to 12:00.

"It's Christmas, Barris," she said, bittersweetly, standing in the doorway leading into the hall, remembering their first Christmas together, the passion, the holiday spirit, the sex at the slightest provocation. Kelsey wasn't sure why she was still with Barris, maybe because she thought if she left, he'd end up on the street.

Yet, for all the indifference she'd felt these last few months, she wished more than anything that he would sweep her up in his arms and kiss her. Her insides stirred at the idea of making love to him. She squeezed her legs together to release some of the tension. She actually wanted him inside. Must be the season, she figured.

"Huh," he grumbled.

A small bit of her desire disappeared.

"I said, it's Christmas Eve. I thought maybe—"

"Shit! Already." A day had passed without him noticing.

"—we could…" her voice trailed off without finishing the thought.

"Huh?"

"Nothing." The itch between her legs was fading quickly.

"I'm never going to get this done," he said gathering a stack of loose yellow pages that had been ripped from their pads.

Until now, it hadn't occurred to Kelsey that Barris' day and a half of silence meant anything more than he had nothing new to say to her, that something different might be driving Barris, that the papers in front of him were perhaps not part of his book as she had assumed.

"Are you working on the book?"

He shuttled a sheaf of pages from one side of the desk to the other, then moved another to where the first had been. He seemed to be doing not much more than randomly shuffling the stacks.

"Huh? No, I'm tryna come up with another campaign for Arnolds Aluminum," he said, glancing up from his frantic organizing.

"A job?" she said, happy that she was leaning against the doorjamb.

"Huh? Yeah, maybe, if I can come up with something."

A rush of excitement raced through Kelsey's spine and spread throughout her body. A job. She gazed at Barris proudly. A warm, soothing flush of happiness and contentment washed over her. Not for the reason one might expect.

It meant she could leave him.

Wouldn't that be a nice Christmas present.

•

"So…Satan…how'd you come up with this…" Jason paused for a second. "…whatever you wanna call it?"

Someone from the audience had been pulled up on stage, and there was a screech of feedback from the sound system as a microphone dropped to the ground.

"My father believed in the existence of the Underworld. He was something of a visionary, really. When I got old enough, I began studying legends from around the world. Religious stories with a grain of truth. Compiled all this scientific data," Satan said, as the mic was picked up, sounding another wail. "The people living in the center of the earth either went underground to get away from something...like radiation...or they never left in the first place. I think *we* were the ones kicked out of this province, this Eden, if you will. We are the descendants of—"

A voice blasted from the speakers on stage and exploded in Satan's ear.

"A poem...by me...Slag."

Satan wiggled his finger in the hole above his lobe in an attempt to bring relief to his burst eardrum. His head was throbbing, reminding him of the school trip when he climbed inside the Liberty Bell just seconds before Kenny Odorman threw a brick at it.

Thankfully, someone cut the volume before Slag had a chance to continue.

"This house," the poet began

"This house was neither made of brick nor stone
Had no walls of wood, no roof of thatch,
No cobbled floor
Instead was blood for bricks and spit for mortar
Gathered arrows had the ceiling made
Pages of History stacked for chairs but never used
Sat atop the floor of flesh and bone
But no one ever sat, no one ever knew them there
Had we any love of buffalo or Bull
We may have never built this house
Pulled out those chairs and maybe
We'd have smoked a pipe and known
For hell is where the hate is
And hate is every w'ar
Hell is where the hate is
And on hate is built our home."

There was a moment of hushed meditation in the room. Satan let the words flow over him, leaves falling from an autumned oak. He was thinking, perhaps, he had misjudged Slag's talent when he realized, to his horror, that was a compliment, and he didn't grant praise on surface dwellers. Luckily, someone, somewhere started to clap, and before Satan could wonder whether he'd gone soft, the crowd began its loud applause, and he forgot all about the poem.

"It's your turn," said Ion.

Satan hadn't noticed she was no longer wrapped in Jason's arm and was standing by his side.

"What?"

"This is it." She motioned toward the stage with her arm.

"You have got to be joking. Go up there? What am I supposed to say?"

"Say what you say to me. Tell your story. Tell them about foil. Tell them anything. Just make it interesting."

"I have no idea what you're talking about. Who are you again?"

Ion reached into her bag and pulled out the gift box from The Nature of Things Store and placed it reverently in his hand. He unwrapped the package, revealing the scarred stone, which he held up to the light.

"It's supposed to be sacred. From the Jineuro Eskimos near the Arctic Circle. It's as close to the North Pole as I could get." She pointed at the markings on the stone. "This is for luck. This's for health and happiness. And this last one…that one is for courage."

He looked at it. He looked at it like he was touched, even as he was trying not to be.

"Vinnie," her words were soft and calming, "This is an easy crowd. They're artists and poets and writers and jazz musicians." She paused, contemplating that for a moment. "These people are more whacked than you are. They're gonna love you."

Less than a minute later, Satan found himself in front of a hundred and fifty willing and eager followers.

"I'm…my, my name…my name…is…" He hit his lips on the mic, sending out a squeal that echoed in the silent club. A pin dropped somewhere. "…ah, Noel…Noel Dorobek." He tried to swallow the boulder in his throat. No luck. "But, ah, every, everyone…everyone except her," he pointed a quivering finger at Ion, who, like a parent watching their kid in a school play, was mouthing his next words even before he did. "…calls me Satan."

XI. NO MILK AND COOKIES

Satan was plodding three feet behind Ion, his head dropped, chin against his chest. He had the black bowler pulled down, so the brim hung over his eyes, hiding the bruise under his left one. Slag ranged ahead, surveying their path.

They did not love him.

The artists and poets and writers and jazz musicians started out quietly enough, listening to the few words he could force past his lips, but from there, things had gotten progressively worse. Satan wasn't exactly sure the order of events or how it was that he provoked them, but at some point in the evening, a chair came flying at his head...hurled by Slag. Slag wasn't actually meaning to hit Satan but the guy behind him who was holding a mic stand over his head, about to bring it down on Satan's skull.

But that's not how he got the black eye.

A fist fight ensued with everyone pretty much taking part, except Satan who hid inside the bass drum until the police arrived. While the cops were busy settling things down, somebody recognized the pile of flesh curled up in the bass, then began stepping on the peddle, pounding harder and harder at the drum until its skin burst.

But that's not how he got the black eye.

The fifteen or so CIA, FBI, NSA, MI and Secret Service agents were trying desperately not to stick out in the crowd of bohemians. One of the Chicago cops noticed the heavy hardware these guys were carrying under their coats, and a whole separate rumble began. Terrorists, Satan thought, they're everywhere. Then one of the terrorists screamed something about hijacking a bus or something like that, just before taking a swing at him.

But that's not how he got the black eye.

He got the black eye about two blocks back, when a furious Ion hauled off and punched him in the face.

About the only good thing to come of the night, was that when Jason heard Satan give his real name, he realized the man on stage was his long lost childhood friend.

"You okay," Jason asked Satan, as he walked next to Ion.

"Yeah," Satan mumbled back.

"Hey, it's Christmas Eve, everybody." He glanced at his watch. "Christmas really. Let's all try to cheer up."

Jason looked around to Slag, Ion, and Satan each. No takers.

"Hey, Slag—that poem was fascinating. What was it about?" he asked, hoping talk of poetry might lighten up the mood.

"Indians. How we stole their land and built America on their dead."

"Oh," said Jason, sorry he had brought it up.

He considered singing a Christmas carol. But "Silent Night" was the only one that came to mind. He decided against it. For nearly ten minutes, they walked in silence. Then Ion spoke.

"A riot. A goddamn riot. What were you thinking?"

Satan raised his head for the first time. "What do you mean, what was I thinking? You think I woke up this morning, devising ways to incite a violent riot between rival gangs of peaceniks? This was sheer beginner's luck." His words hung in the air, which was beginning to stir. "And you didn't have to hit me."

"Yes, I did. Everyone else was getting hit. Why shouldn't you, the cause of it all, get popped."

Satan did not offer a comeback and the quiet between them returned. Jason glanced over the rooftops toward the shifting sky, wishing he could find some words to mend the situation.

Finally, reticence began to melt away, and Ion spoke again.

"You leave out the stuff?" she growled at Satan.

"Yeah," he huffed back.

There was a moment of silence for everyone, and confusion for Jason. Slag was off on a mind trip to some place he wouldn't dare go in real life. He wasn't part of the discussion. Rarely was.

"No milk and cookies," Ion said.

"No."

"His cholesterol's gotta be up over three hundred."

More silence. Jason was starting to pick up the scent, milk and cookies, Christmas, cholesterol…Santa.

"So, what'd you leave?" Ion said, still gruff and angry.

"Carrot juice and a coupla tofu bars."

Ion perked up. "Really," she said, sounding a bit more like her cheery self. "Huh. Cool."

She always had a soft spot for ol' Santa.

As the four continued their trek home along the quiet, lonely streets, the sky grew silver, and it began to snow.

•

It was well after one, the offices dark, except for one lamp that shone on Armand Arnold's desk. The factory was quiet, since about nine o'clock, no second or third shift tonight. Everyone had gone home to family and friends to spend the evening in quiet celebration. A chilly draft snuck inside from a crack in the window behind him. He rubbed his neck to rid the kink that lay there.

He felt exalted after the meeting two days ago in the city planner's office, but that shallow victory was wearing thin now. Earlier in the day, he had called the bank and raided the war chest he'd been saving for a final advertising assault, giving it instead to his workers in the form of Christmas bonuses. He had just enough, he calculated, to keep the company afloat for another two weeks, which made him very happy—not the response one might expect.

Armand Arnold could avoid ruining the holidays for his employees, that much he could do. However, he'd have to call Peter Marks in the morning and tell him to give up the battle and send a bill for his efforts so far.

Armand stood up behind his desk and switched off the light. He could see outside now. A light dusting of white covered the giant hat feathers sticking up out of the old Clark Pipe factory across the way. What a waste of a good street, he thought. His grandfather's memory, his father's legacy, was dying. Armand Arnold had made a separate peace with them, and he hoped they understood that he had tried his best.

The hall outside his office was even colder, and a few flakes of snow drifted to the floor from a small hole in the ceiling. He didn't bother closing his door or locking it, nothing to steal. Walking down the lonesome corridor, the years and voices of those who'd done the same echoed in the dark until he regained his thoughts and only heard his footsteps.

•

The computer terminal said: HENRY DOROBEK.

Dark circles had formed in the creases under his eyes. A pen with some yellow cheese on it was snuggled over his ear. Several empty Styrofoam cups were scattered along the desktop, sending the malodorous stench of old coffee into the air. Five or so crumpled brown McDonald's bags and more than a dozen Filet O' Fish, Big Mac and Egg McMuffin wrappers littered the surrounding carpet.

Kenny Odorman hadn't been to bed in three days.

He was sitting in front of the terminal, hunched over a stack of paper, jotting down notes and cross-referencing facts. A Big Mac stuck halfway out his mouth, disappearing slowly as he gnawed at it.

The sight of the woman exploding in front of him was not what kept him sleepless. In fact, except for this morning when a piece of her went swishing across his windshield as he turned on his wipers to wash away some road salt, he had forgotten all about the incident. The chunk flew off once he got up to speed.

Henry Dorobek was keeping him awake, or rather, his son was. Kenny didn't care that he was the only one left at work, didn't care that, in fact, he was the only one who had come in at all today. That didn't matter. All that mattered was locating Henry, which would inevitably lead to his son.

Noel Dorobek had been more than a hobby of Kenny's when he was a boy. The scrawny new kid from some Podunk town in central Illinois had been Kenny's personal whipping post. Every chance he could, Kenny wreaked havoc on Dorobek's life. Spit in his food at lunch, tickle him until he'd pee his pants, punch him in the gut when the teacher wasn't looking. Man, he loved school.

And Dorobek was a perfect chump. You'd hit him in the head, and he'd come right back the next day, thinking you wouldn't do it again, cause you did it yesterday, but Kenny'd hit him again, and the next day, he'd come back again, thinking you did it two days in a row, then THWACK, one more time.

What an idiot.

Then one day, the idiot struck back, holding on to Kenny after Kenny pushed Noel's coaster down the steep side of the hill, the one with the big oaks waiting for you at the bottom.

Kenny touched the scar above his lip.

He'd never really gotten a chance to get back at Dorobek for that, just a pop in the jaw at the scene. A little fracture, nothing to write home about. Dorobek had to have it wired shut, but that wasn't good enough for Kenny. He had something a bit more theatrical in mind for little Noel, like maybe a trip up the flag pole feet first, or a bit of sulfur powder in his egg salad, or perhaps some Nair in his knit cap. Alas, Kenny's father got another job, and they moved before Dorobek had the chance to return to school.

Over the years, it gnawed at Kenny like a parasitic worm, tearing at his insides. No one ever liked Kenny Odorman, he knew that, but at least everyone his age was afraid of him. Dorobek was the only one to ever strike back, draw blood. And for that, he really ought to pay.

Kenny's three moles were swollen and red, and his skin had broken out from the bad food and lack of sleep. His eyes burned as if he had a paper cut in each one, and his skin wreaked like someone locked ten days in a sauna with nothing to eat but garlic and jalepeños.

A wrench had been thrown into his plans.

"Where are you, Noel Dorobek?" he said to the computer screen, which did not answer him. "Where are you, you little fuck?"

He flipped through the information he'd dug up in the archives on Noel's father; birthdate, social security number, last known address, etc. A listing of past due bills, including some from Bergdorf's, Spiegel Catalog, several hotels in Atlantic City, was here; all had been written off as bad debts almost a decade ago. The addresses were out of date, or nonexistent, and they led nowhere. The only open listing in the senior Dorobek's file was from Clearwater Sanitarium in uptown Chicago.

Picking up the computer printout, Kenny looked over the twelve pages of charges—nearly $432,000—that had been run up over the past fifteen years for the patient, Mrs. H. Dorobek.

A few hours earlier, Kenny had contacted Clearwater with a request for the Dorobeks' present whereabouts, but a gravelly voiced woman, who at first he thought was a gravelly voiced man, told him she couldn't release that information and if he really wanted to know, he should write CreditDat for a credit report.

He typed in Henry Dorobek's social security number for probably the two-hundredth time and for the two-hundredth time it came up:

Holder of number is deceased.

According to the records, Noel's father had been dead for twenty-five years, though most of his accounts remained open and active for nearly ten years. The Clearwater bills didn't start until after the tenth anniversary of his death, yet there was Henry Dorobek's signature on file as the guarantor of payment.

All this pleased Kenny Odorman considerably. Now, he would get his revenge. Something was illegitimate here. And if he could just find a little proof, he could make a case for credit fraud.

Then he'd stick little Noel with settling these accounts. And since someone had forged the guarantee of payment signature for his mother's care, maybe a little jail time as well.

•

Jason walked with them to Kings Road, where he split off and continued home. A few blocks later, Ion and Satan left Slag in front of his apartment building. Satan even gave the poet a small acknowledgment for his reading.

Now approaching her doorstep, Ion turned and looked Satan in the eye. She straightened the oversized black jacket, then grabbed his mittened hand.

"Sorry, I punched you."

"Sorry, I was hated and despised by everyone present."

Ion nodded. "You couldn't help it," she said.

Snow was collecting on her shoulders, that part not protected by the white ten-gallon. He wiped it away when it began to remind him of dandruff.

"Good night, Vinnie."

He didn't say anything as she started for the steps then stopped.

"I know you hate this," she bent toward him, "but I'll say it anyway. Merry Christmas." With that, she pressed her lips, gently against his cheek, then swung around and dashed up the stairs, disappearing behind a huge oak door.

Satan eyed the door long after the latch clicked shut. He watched the light go on in her window, then finally decided to go home when his feet began to freeze to the sidewalk.

Satan usually took La Salle to Clark. Sometimes he would bypass Clark and go up Larrabee. He did that whenever he wanted to see trees and birds and people playing instead of elevated tracks and dirty sidewalks. When he was young, before his father never showed, his mother would take him to a park in the town they lived in downstate and let him play around with the other children.

He wasn't afraid of strangers then.

But now, especially at night, he always took the longest route to his house. It was by far the safest path, bringing him by the most donut shops, nearly one every other block. Along the way, he would hear a gunshot or two, and think he was hit, but when he didn't find any blood, he'd continue on, hoping upon hopes he wouldn't be killed because he failed to get a driver's license on account of the fact he couldn't parallel park. It was clearly not his fault that the old lady had been standing in the way.

This night, however, with the blanket of white nearly an inch deep already, prompting him to conclude that the terrorists and murderers had gone to seek warmer climes, Satan took the best way of all. Past Oz Park and its Tin Man statue, past the clock tower that struck the hour of two, past the trees lining the avenues, he traveled. The snow underfoot muffled all sound except the whir of a Northerly wind and the crunch of his shoes sinking into the virgin powder. With the sky a pewter cotton wad, Satan made his way to an unremarkable fence. He climbed through a gap, more suited to a child, and descended a small embankment that led him to an enormous drainpipe. This pipe, which networked with so many others, had been his first gateway into the world below. The summer of his eighth year, he and Jason and Billy Mathers and Tina Hicks and an army of others made this subterraneous maze of adventure and mystery their home.

Satan stepped into the passage and disappeared.

XII. THAT SAVIOR THING

Kelsey woke after only a few hours sleep, the alarm she set for four a.m. beeping in her ear. She rose to find she didn't have anything on, no panties, nothing. If it had been summer instead of Christmas Day, she wouldn't have questioned her nudity. She liked sleeping naked. She was never one to worry about how her body looked, a pound or two this way or that, as some women did, and she enjoyed showing off her shape. But Chicago winters were as cold as Chicago summers were hot, and it wasn't very smart to fight nature. At least in the beginning, she could cuddle her silky skin up to Barris and find warmth and shelter from the cold. Although now that he made her sick, she preferred a T-shirt over vomiting.

That's when she noticed him in bed.

She glanced in the mirror across the room and saw it.

The red nose.

Oh God, she thought. They had *done* it.

In her excitement over finally getting rid of Barris, she had slept with him. A celebration of dubious merit. Still, the event was coming back to her slowly, and it hadn't been all that bad. The red nose was the giveaway.

She had been relieved emotionally; he had been frustrated creatively. It made for great sex, primal, not very romantic, but she liked it that way sometimes.

Naked, she pranced into the kitchen, flipped on the Mr. Coffee, then pranced to the window over the sink, and cracked it slightly. The apartment took in a breath of crisp, morning air which brushed past her. Goosebumps rolled up her arm and her nipples came erect. Reaching outside, she cleared a pillow of snow resting on the sill, then tapped her fingers three times on the wood.

A bundle of fur appeared and pounced from the sill to the sink to the floor. "How're you, you pretty thing," she said.

"Yeowmeow," the kitten replied.

Kelsey poured herself a cup of java, cream for her and the cat, and crossed to the table. Following cautiously at first, the feline advanced to the saucer. The two sat enjoying the quiet morning. Kelsey blew on her drink, sending a steam cloud scurrying for cover. She stroked the cat and pressed the hot mug between her breasts, then slid it down her belly and set the cup on the chair between her legs.

When both the cat and she were done, Kelsey got up and went about defrosting the turkey, preparing the stuffing, and all the other arrangements associated with Christmas dinner.

She was laying down a bed of foil in the large roaster, shooing away the cat who thought it was a new litter box and was batting at the sides with its paws. Giving a gentle push, Kelsey sent the kitten leaping to the floor, its back raised up like an inchworm climbing up a twig.

Kelsey returned her attention to the pan. It was important to make the shape of the foil just so, and there was a trick to it. Her mother had taught her to fold the sides up, allowing the heat to radiate inward, thus browning the meat to perfection without drying it. She bent the aluminum sheet as instructed, adding a twist and a crinkle of her own here and there until it met with her approval. After a moment, she laid the turkey inside.

At six, she slid the bird into the oven, initiating the long, slow process that would transform the white, sickly lump into a beautiful golden brown meal.

At seven-thirty, she went to work on the vegetarian portions for Satan's friend, Eo. Kelsey was curious to see what she looked like. She was even more curious to find out what the woman thought she could gain from Satan.

By nine o'clock, Barris was up and Kelsey was feeling queasy.

•

It had taken nearly an hour for them to position the padded lead aprons in a manner that was acceptable to Satan. During that time, if he sensed that one inch more of his body than necessary was exposed, he'd sit up and the technicians would have to start all over again.

Satan lay under the gargantuan machine, its crosshairs aimed directly between his eyes. Staring into the thing was similar to gazing down the barrel of a gun. At least with a gun, you had the chance it might miss. With

X-rays, like horseshoes and darts, almost definitely counted.

Satan wondered why hospitals seemed to refrigerate everything that came in contact with a patient's skin as he shifted on the steel platform and a new, colder section of metal assaulted him where the gown failed in its coverage.

His arms hurt. His legs and back and stomach ached. But mostly, it was his head that caused his suffering.

It was light outside, he knew, because he saw the sky pinking up as they rolled him into the ambulance. Lucky for him two kids had decided to open their presents early and take their new remote control cars and race 'em in the tunnels. He recalled seeing the headlights of a blue plastic Porsche a second before it smacked him in the eye—the other one, giving him two shiners.

He really couldn't feel it by then, what with the frostbite setting in and everything...

It had been more than twenty years since he and the gang traveled the labyrinth of underground tunnels.

And it was about two minutes after entering them that Satan found himself lost. He yelled and pounded and tried his best at running, but all he did was grow wearier, less confident he'd ever make it out alive. Each tunnel looked like the last and led to another which looked exactly like the one before that. With no exit in sight, it was plainly apparent Satan was going to be exhausted sooner than the supply of tunnels. His heart raced, he barely had enough oxygen to power his legs, and his feet began to go numb. The walls were collapsing around him. Gangrene and claustrophobia were setting in.

He would perish and never, ever be found.

Then, stumbling through the dark, his strength sapped, Satan tripped over something solid and fell on his face, knocking himself unconscious.

When he awoke, and could get his eyes to focus, he saw he had tripped on a metal briefcase, like the ones diplomats carry. He could see this because there was light in the tunnel now. Not light from the sun, but from a fire. Glancing around, Satan noticed neat piles of well-worn clothing stacked alongside several boxes of canned goods. All in all, the encampment had a nice homey feel.

The old man was staring at him through cloudy brown eyes that had once been sharp. It seemed to Satan those eyes held the power to command a great many people, but instead, the old man reigned here in the shadows under the city, commanding rats and roaches.

He ordered one of the rodents away from his food.

"You awake d'ere?" the old man said, a hint of a Southside accent coming through. Italian flavored.

"What happened?"

"You fell." The old man raised some sort of food product out of a pot with a ladle, offering it to Satan. "You wanna eat?"

Satan shook his head as he studied the old man.

The man's white hair was still very thick, slicked back on top and short on the sides. The unevenness suggested a harsh self-cutting process with dull scissors.

"You look familiar," Satan said.

"Ever'body says that."

"Everybody?" Satan glanced down the tunnel, each direction. "You get much pedestrian traffic down here?"

"You don' want none," the old man asked, changing the subject back to food.

"I just want to get out of here."

The man grunted. "I know what you mean." Then, seeing Satan was staring at his metal briefcase, said, "It's nice, huh?"

Satan nodded, not really having anything else to do. Briefcases had no great attraction for him. He could have done with a compass or a map at the moment. "What's in it?"

"Money." The old man slopped some of the food into a bowl and scooped a spoonful into his mouth. "Figure I got 'bout a million two left," the man was saying as a bit of the gruel rolled down his chin.

"Dollars!?"

"No, lira," said the old man, sarcastically.

The briefcase looked secure enough. A combination lock poked out of the top of the metal case. Satan wondered why he was thinking about these trivial things.

"A million?" he said again, more to himself than the man.

"More or less."

"What are you doing down here then? A million isn't what it once was— I'll admit—but you could still manage to purchase a pleasant enough trailer home."

"Can't."

"Why not?"

The man grumbled.

"Listen, I've been here only a few minutes, and already I want to leave," Satan said. "We could both get out of here. You to a nice, modest palace and me to my sad, pathetic life."

"Wish I could help."

"What, exactly, do you mean by that?" Satan asked, suddenly afraid of the answer.

The old man shook his head. "Don't know a way out of this."

"You don't know the way out!? How long have you been here?"

"Pffffft," said the man who looked like he was nearing eighty. "Gotta be at least twenty years. Hard to tell time down here."

The ceiling came rushing toward Satan. The walls closed in. Space and time collided in his brain. And in his paranoia, he saw the man as he would have been.

"Relax…" said the old man, seeing the terror in the younger man's eyes. "I know a way out, just not for me." The old man got up. "You don' mind if I blindfold you?"

"Of course not," Satan said, before thinking what a strange request, and just before realizing: "I know who you are—"

The next time Satan was conscious, the man's stuff was gone, so was Satan's hat—in its place, a large lump—and the blue Porsche was accelerating toward his left cornea.

"Yo' ahh goin ta half do thake of de fooil," said the swarthy-skinned Indian guy probably not licensed in this country to operate anything larger than a pen light, never mind an X-ray machine.

"What?" Satan said, or at least, that's what he meant to say. "Whhnmmmm?" was how it sounded, a lead blanket draped over his lips.

"Yo' ahhhh goang due haaaalf do thake of deee foooooil," said the man, becoming less intelligible the more he tried to be.

The other technician with glassy-eyes, a drawn face, and Albert Einstein's hair, hadn't said much during the hour, although he seemed capable of speech. He came over and tapped on Satan's head where a hastily wrapped roll of foil still had the paper tube attached.

"Foil."

"Yes, I know, but I lost my—"

Before Satan could finish, the man peeled off the metal sheeting, balled it up and shot it toward a wastebasket on the other side of the room. The silver clump arched beautifully over a series of control wires, came down, and smacked the Indian guy, who was seven feet away from the basket, in the ear.

"Damn, missed it," the tech's words slurring lazily out of his mouth.

It looked to Satan as though the man may have skipped class the day they taught about getting behind the lead shielding while the machine was in operation. He was no doubt suffering from radiation sickness, his yellow skin blistering in several places and his hair falling out as he walked, a dead give away. Either that or he was in a methadone program somewhere.

"Awll righd, diss want herd a bid."

Although he was moving as fast as his degenerating muscles would allow, the technician wasn't even close to halfway across the room, and nowhere near being behind the lead wall, when the Indian guy threw the switch.

•

Ion looked at the stocking she had stuffed for herself when she got in late last night. It was a red one, with white fuzzy material around the top. Two bells remained of the four originally on it. Her name, her real name, was stitched down the side in green yarn. Her mother had sewn it for Ion when she was a little girl. It was a keepsake to her mom's memory.

Nothing else in the small, sparse apartment was anything her mother would have allowed in her home.

Ion crossed the petite living room and went to the stocking, which was hung on the back of her couch. Checking its weight, she bounced her hand under the toe. A decent haul, she thought. She was outfitted in a little black dress, elegant and sexy, slim at the waist—far different from her usual non-Clancy's dress of ripped jeans and loose skirts. Her hair this day was brushed straight with a scarf wrapped under and tied on top. She looked stunning.

She hadn't worn these clothes since That Guy That Turned Out To Be A Jerk turned out to be a jerk and left her for L.A. without so much as a phone call.

She had to read about their breakup in one of the tabloids.

It wasn't that Ion expected anything from him or any of the men she helped. The satisfaction she got allowing someone to develop as a person, assisting them on their path to becoming an effective part of society was what she did it for. At least that's what she told herself. But this guy had been different. They all fell in love with her at one point or another, or at least, thought they loved her, but this one, this actor...she had fallen for him.

And when he left, he killed a little piece of her.

Fortunately, it wasn't a very useful piece.

She glanced at the distorted clock on her wall, seemingly the survivor of some nuclear test blast. Satan was late. Late for a lot of things. Ion knew it would eventually happen—it always did—but so far, Satan hadn't fallen in love with her.

But then, nothing had gone normally with this one.

Still, he was very late.

•

The street was unusually empty. No buses. Not many people. A couple wrapped in wool from head to toe hurried across the boulevard, holding hands and carrying gifts of food.

Normally, the street was filled with the money-hungry masses, devouring bag lunches as they raced to pick up dry-cleaning before they had to be back to the purgatory they happily called their jobs.

Then Satan remembered it was that Savior thing today.

Along the entire street, in the gated shop windows, talking dolls and singing bears pleaded for someone, anyone to buy them, but no one could buy today. They were prisoners, hostages all, locked behind the painted plate glass, about to be marked down, or worse, shipped back to the factory and warehoused until next year.

Satan wondered if Jesus had any idea what he was starting.

Probably not.

Jesus was a decent enough guy, but sort of annoying. It frustrated people when they'd ask him "What can we do to be good?" and he'd answer "What do you think you can do to be good?"

Not very smart on his part.

Most people didn't like to think for themselves. They wanted to be led. He probably could have avoided the whole cross incident if he had just told the people what to do and how to do it.

Satan understood this. Whatever came to pass, he'd make sure he didn't get hung on anything.

As he made his way along the icy sidewalk toward Ion's apartment, Satan put saviors and mindless masses out of his head and studied the six-page hospital bill in his hand. A few hundred for this, several hundred for that. A couple hundred for no reason at all. Totaling it up, the little nostalgia trip had cost him sixteen hundred bucks. Not to mention the loss of his hat and a few million brain cells. Which reminded him, he was walking around Chicago unprotected. He reached into the deep, ripped pockets of his down coat, found nothing, then realized he had already used his spare roll. The radiation sick technician had peeled it off in the X-ray room.

He was late. Ion would be furious. And the bruise on the bridge of his nose started pounding.

"Excuse me," said a vagrant, appearing out of nowhere and startling Satan. The man's face was cracked and red from too much sun and gamma exposure. His hair was matted to his head, and his lips were chapped and raw.

"I've been hit in the head with a ladle, irradiated, overcharged, abused and I'm late. I have no change and no time for this. Please, get away." That's what Satan would have said had he not been scared to death and white with fear. It came out more like: "Hhhhuuhha?"

"Do you happen to know," said the vagrant in a very aristocratic voice, "…where I may find the theaters—they do not show movies—they just emit radiation."

"Pardon me?"

"I'm looking for theaters that don't play films, they emit radiation."

There was a moment of silence in which Satan was thinking how many weirdoes there were running loose in Chicago.

"I don't know what you're talking about."

The vagrant studied Satan from head to toe to head again. "No…" he paused, "I don't suppose you do."

With a disdainful look, the vagrant started past Satan and weaved his way down the sidewalk. Satan wasn't sure, but he felt he'd just been insulted by someone who lived in a cardboard box.

Which, more or less, was in line with the theme this day had taken on over the past ten or fifteen years. For Satan, Christmas was a lot like Friday the 13th, only everyone was much more cheery as they wreaked their havoc on him. He turned the corner onto Grant, and tried not to think about what happened last year. At least, so far, he hadn't been attacked by any midgets.

•

Barris was staring at the piles of notes he'd made over the last two days. There was no real order to them even though the pages were stacked in neat sheaves. There were, in front of him, a hundred thousand words or more, he calculated, on how to use, abuse, and sell foil. In all that, there was nothing to lead the buyer to Arnolds™ over any other brand. Foil was, pretty much, foil.

The processes and ingredients were the same from one brand to the next. The store brand was cheaper because it paid out little in advertising and promotion. The national brands, like Reynolds, cost slightly more, but were industry leaders with a great deal of name recognition and customer loyalty.

Arnolds, on the other hand, was nearly as expensive as the nationals because of its outdated, inefficient factory, and nearly as anonymous as the store brands because of its lack of advertising.

Barris couldn't come up with one reason to buy Arnolds Aluminum.

Which was exactly why no one did.

"Barris," said Kelsey, calling from the kitchen. "It's getting late, do you think we should phone Satan?"

"Huh?"

"I said, should we call Satan?"

"I thought we weren't eating until one-thirty?"

"It's past two o'clock."

"Oh."

Barris' conception of time was, at best, limited. Kelsey leaned on the counter that separated the two rooms. The cat purred and rubbed up against her leg as a few butterflies flew around in her stomach. The cold breeze coming in the window over the sink brushed past her. She felt comfortably warm in her long sweater and skirt. Yet, Kelsey was nervous. Most of the morning, she had ignored it, but now, with Satan and Eo a half an hour late, the feeling grew inside her gut. Satan had never brought a girl to meet them, never spoke of them at all other than a few sexist remarks, which she dismissed as ignorance about the subject.

Growing with every minute, the uneasiness crept up toward her chest. In an attempt to forget it, she went about rearranging the meal that lay in the oven, in the refrigerator, and on the counter.

Ion wouldn't speak to Satan.

"Listen, you don't understand. I was hit in the head with a ladle," he said, pointing to the bandage. "Look for yourself."

"You know how embarrassing it is—how *rude* it is to be late the first time you meet someone?"

"I've known Kelsey and Barris for years."

"Me, Vinnie! I'm talking about me!"

"I told you why I was late."

"Yes, Vinnie, you told me. And I'm going to forget you ever said it. In fact, I don't want to hear you utter one word about this at dinner. You hear me? Not one word."

"But it's true. That's got to count for something."

They were walking across Wenet Park, the new snow crunching under their feet.

"Jimmy Hoffa?" she said, shaking her head. "Jimmy Hoffa."

"I'm telling you, it was him."

"How do you know that?" She wanted to hit him in the head, but he already had a mild concussion.

"It looked like him."

"That'd stand up in court." Her voice was a knife in his gut.

"He had over a million in cash with him. And the metal briefcase had his initials on it."

"Oh, that's right, nobody else in the world has the initials 'J.H.' C'mon." She was beginning to wonder again whether she had made a mistake with this one. "Did you see the money?"

"No," he answered, knowing he should have lied.

"You just believed some old guy living in the sewer that he had a million dollars in a metal case without looking at it?"

"Well—"

"I don't *believe* you. 'Sorry, we're late, but Vinnie here had some business to clear up with Jimmy Hoffa.' 'That's right, the ex-Teamster president—'" She hit him in the arm. "'—knocked off by the mob twenty-five years ago.'"

"Everyone *thinks* he's dead, but they never found a body."

"So, what's he doing in the sewer, hanging out with Elvis and Jim Morrison? They form a band down there?"

Satan thought Ion would have understood. She listened to his lectures on the Inner Earth, and, even though she wasn't a true believer, had never ridiculed him for his views. Not really.

Then again, the nurse at the hospital hadn't believed him either. The murderous scowl on the bloated woman reminded him of the manager/maniac and that he'd have to hunt for a new place to shop. He scanned the woman's uniform, searching for a name among the folds of skin, wondering if it might be the man's sister. After a moment, he found it, or most of it, but then he realized he didn't know the maniac/murderer's name.

"He only hit me after I said I knew who he was."

"Vinnie," said Ion, tight-jawed. "Don't tell them we were late because you saw Jimmy Hoffa, okay? Blame it on me. I'll tell them I had to change my clothes twenty times."

"Why?"

"It'll make me happy."

•

When Jesus was a young child, his mother told him that God had a special plan for him. This seemed to be a good thing. Everyone else spent most of their lives trying to figure out what they wanted to do and what their purpose on Earth was, which caused more than a little stress and had been the impetus for more than a few wars.

But not him. He knew that at some point a sign, a marker, would appear to guide him toward his destiny.

"Heh-sues," the man said.

"Geez-us," replied Jesus.

"Since when you become Geez-us, *Heh*-sues?"

"I've always been Geez-us, you've just always pronounced it wrong." Jesus stood over the man who had been his employer for three years now.

"Well, *Geez*-us, hand me the socket wrench."

Jesus del Veccio reached for the tool and picked it up. It was cold. The heat in the Jiffy Quick Tune-up Meisters' shop was turned off since it was Christmas and the place was closed. Jesus had offered to help his boss fix his '81 Coupe De Ville, just in case this had been the sign. He glanced around the greasy quarters, but saw nothing resembling a sign, only a few nude pictures hanging on the wall.

As he gave the wrench to his boss, Jesus gazed at the car, which was possibly the largest vehicle he had ever seen. "I gotta get going," he said.

"Whataya mean?"

"I mean, I quit."

"What?" the boss said, hitting his head as he pulled it out from under the huge hood too fast. "It's Christmas. You can't quit on Christmas."

"I shouldn't be *working* on Christmas."

Before the man could say anything more, Jesus walked out of the shop. The wind outside chilled Jesus' thin frame, and he wished he hadn't left so quickly without his coat. He glanced at the dirt under his nails and wondered if he'd see the sign today.

He had thought he had seen it when he saw television for the first time. But his mother explained it had been around for awhile. Recently, he was convinced the sign was Lotto. Soon he was playing every week. A dollar, two dollars, then ten, then twenty. Before long he was spending most of his free cash at the machine in Clancy's Drug around the corner from his apartment. He watched the drawings on TV, sitting in front of the tube with a cold can of Campbell's Pork 'n Beans as they picked the numbers, hoping, praying they would be his.

Then finally, it happened. He won.

Forty-six million dollars.

It was unbelievable. His hands trembling, he checked the numbers twenty-three times before jumping up and screaming. The entire trip down to the claim center, he clutched the winning receipt between his fingers, not trusting his pants pockets. Jesus decided to take all the money at once. He'd only get half the amount doing that, but he didn't have to wait for his yearly check. He could quit his job, invest the money and live the rest of his life on the interest, looking for the sign.

Once in the Lotto claim center, which was nothing more than an old unemployment office with a kindergarten paint job, they made him fill out a stack of forms, pose for six rolls of photos, and give nineteen interviews. It worked out to about 6.5 million an hour. Finally, after the IRS figured out how much he owed, Jesus was cut a check for $12.6 million—

"Excuse me," said a vagrant, who was old and wrinkled from the sun. "Do you happen to know where I might find the theaters that emit radiation?"

"Why do you wish to find them?" asked Jesus.

The vagrant had never been asked that question before.

"I don't know."

"Perhaps, when you find out, you may find *them*."

"Hmmm," the old man said. "Thank you."

The vagrant turned and went back the way he came, thinking he'd have to find something new to do with his life now that his search for the theaters had been rendered meaningless. He decided he might get a job after the holidays were over.

Jesus watched the man disappear down an alley. He returned his thoughts to a subject he had grown fond of lately. Namely, Fate.

Fate, luck, and pure chance seemed to play into so many events in the world, it was hard to imagine such a thing as free will existed. Take his situation:

Was it fate that led him to choose the winning Lotto combination? Or was it luck that the numbers he chose came up? Was it pure chance that he happened to deposit the $12.6 million dollar check in a Savings & Loan? Or Fate that it went belly up the next day?

Who knew?

.

Satan trudged up the stairs toward Barris and Kelsey's apartment, each step pounding in his head. He could see Ion waiting at the top, giving him an unsympathetic look. The doorman, a fat little man who secretly plotted the deaths of each tenant, had begrudgingly let them in as if put out by the request. Satan often wondered what the man thought his job was if not opening the door.

Perhaps, the man thought it was to harass the mail carrier, which Satan had witnessed on several occasions. Satan had no love for the U.S. Postal Service, but the doorman had a personal vendetta against the entire outfit because they once returned a love letter he sent out. It had come back to his house with postage due. This, in itself, would not have been such a big deal, except the doorman's wife was the one who picked up the mail.

Satan could never quite figure out how someone could be so stupid to put a return address on a letter to a mistress. Then again, he'd never been in love, and didn't understand anything about its effect on people.

Milking it for all the sympathy he wouldn't get, Satan struggled to the top of the stairs holding his head.

Kelsey opened the door, revealing her tardy dinner guests.

"Satan…Eo, how are you? I was starting to worry. Are you both okay?" she said, staring at Satan's head which besides being black and blue and bandaged was uncovered. She couldn't remember ever seeing his hair, which was a surprisingly attractive sandy brown laced with hues of blonde as the hall light shone on it.

"I was beat—"

Ion kicked Satan in the back of the foot without anyone else noticing. He decided Jimmy Hoffa would have to remain dead awhile longer.

"Come in, come in. It's so nice to meet you Eo."

"It's Ion."

"Ion. Sorry," Kelsey said, a bit embarrassed. "It's such an unusual name…" She stopped before she dug herself any deeper.

"It is, isn't it? Actually, *I'm* sorry. It's really all my fault that Vinnie and I are late. I went through everything in my closest. I have a punctuality problem. I was two weeks overdue at birth."

"Vinnie?" asked Kelsey, looking past them for more guests.

He wasn't in the mood to explain the historical origin of the name. He was tired and hungry and the more he tried to forget about Jimmy Hoffa, the more he obsessed on him. "It's her pet name for me."

"I see." Kelsey motioned inside. "Well, come in, come in. Merry Christmas," she said, giving Ion a friendly cheek to cheek greeting. "Good afternoon, Satan."

"Good afternoon."

Satan took off his coat and glanced around. The holiday decorations were kept to a minimum, a sickly tree in the corner covered with brambles and the last remains of last years tinsel. Stretching out his arms, he breathed in the scent of turkey and stuffing. Immediately his head began to hurt some more, so he sat down to stop the room from rocking, hoping he could dry dock the building if he just kept still. When he dared to reopen his eyes, he saw Barris crouched over his desk, mumbling to himself.

"Barris…how's the book coming?" Satan said from the couch, wondering if it were possible to get motion sickness even if you weren't moving.

"Huh? Fine, fine. Merry Christmas," he muttered, not lifting his head from his work.

"Barris has a job," Kelsey whispered.

Satan raised an eyebrow. He hoped his friend's novelistic endeavor had not been abandoned in the name of commerce before it had a chance to fully develop. Barris seemed so creative, it'd be a shame.

"C'mon, let's eat. The food's all ready."

Satan was all for that.

A clinking of glasses, the usual holiday toasts, and the meal had begun.

The air in the room was a mosaic of smells that forced the nose to continually sample the fragrances. Although the apartment was cool, the dining area was comfortable; heat rising from the food warmed the table.

Ion took a cautious bite at the potato, eggplant & tofu dish on her plate.

The woman had called her "Eo" twice more since sitting down to dinner. A guarded feline dance was taking place, with both watchful of the other. The kitten was off to the side, wondering when someone would let it play.

Satan was too interested in his food to notice anything. The colors and the smells rising from the table were overloading his senses. Kelsey's holiday feasts were extremely tasty, and he looked forward to them. It was true, he had no point of reference since his mother couldn't cook even before she started up with the fish thing.

It was also true that Satan hated Christmas, but he was, after all, a realist in the classic sense of the word and Christmas dinner was entirely too delicious to dismiss solely because he had a slight problem with the *reason* for the dinner. He enjoyed it, as long as you kept the "ho-ho"ing to a minimum. To clarify, it wasn't that Satan had something against Jesus Christ, the man—in fact, with the exception that he never gave a straight answer, Christ was one of the greatest men in history. Satan simply had a problem with his "birth" day. The truth of the matter was that the week from December 17-24, the winter solstice, had been the pagan festival Saturnalia long before anybody had ever heard of this guy Christ, and way before the emergence of the Church bearing his name, which formed *five hundred years* after their savior was nailed to a cross. Obviously, there had been some organizational problems. It *was* a time of peace on earth and good will toward men—mainly because by Roman law no war could begin during the Saturnalia. At the end of the Saturnalia, on the 25th, there was another holiday, the "Birthday of the Unconquered Sun," celebrating the sun's rebirth as the days became longer. The powers that be in the fledgling religion had no idea when their "unconquered son" was actually born (sometime in August or September) and besides, they wanted to make it easy for pagans to convert. Thus, December 25th. It was sort of like Christ's Birthday (Observed). Add to this the tinsel and Santa and singing and "Happy Holidays" from people who wouldn't talk to you 364 days out of the year, and it made for a sanctimoniously annoying time, salvaged only by the promise of a really good meal.

Chewing on a piece of juicy meat dipped in a bit of mashed potatoes, Satan glanced over at the syrupy green and beige abomination on Ion's plate. Ion made sense a lot of the time, but when it came to food, he'd just as soon listen to a car mechanic.

Slipping the food off her fork, Ion tried the dish and tasted a sweetly sour flavor in her mouth. Pleasantly surprised, she went for another forkful.

"This's quite good," Ion said, glancing at Kelsey and smiling at her for the first time.

"I'm glad you like it. An old boyfriend I had was a vegetarian."

"Really?" There weren't that many in Slaughter Town.

"He was into health and fitness," she said, nodding. "He was quite remarkable actually."

Kelsey glanced at Barris who didn't notice the remark. He was staring at the foil the turkey sat in, thinking *who cared what brand of foil you used.*

Disappointed she couldn't get a rise out of him, Kelsey curled up the sides of her mouth as she ate some stuffing. Ion gave her another smile, and the two women exchanged glances.

"A toast," Ion raised her glass. "To old boyfriends and remarkable sex."

Satan wasn't sure what was going on, but he was sure he wasn't part of it. He decided to stick to the matter at hand—his nutriment.

"Here, here," said Barris who had only heard the word 'toast.'

Ion and Kelsey began to laugh.

"I was hit in the head by Jimmy Hoffa," Satan said with a mouthful, not wanting to be left out of the fun.

Ion stabbed a chunk of eggplant with her fork, mortally wounding it. "Vinnie," she said, sternly, "What did I tell you?"

"I don't understand why I can't disseminate this information. I happen to think this is an incredible story. I may even sell it to the National Enquirer." He glanced at Kelsey. "Listen...Ion didn't make us late. I was at the hospital this morning—"

Ion took the meatless forkful and smacked him in the head with it.

Barris looked up. "Who's in the hospital?"

"Hospital? What happened?" Kelsey asked, waving Barris off.

Satan explained every excruciating detail—including the Indian guy, the bloated nurse, the vagrant, and the midgets...until he realized midgets was last year's Christmas debacle.

•

Satan was lying on the couch, staring at the ceiling, thinking he'd eaten too much, and that somewhere in Somalia two hundred and fourteen kids could've been satisfied with the amount of food he just forced down. The bump on the bridge of his nose thumped with the beat of his pulse, annoying him in the same manner eating ice cream too quickly did.

Barris was at his post, writing.

Ion and Kelsey were in the bedroom, looking over a photo album.

"I'd have left him a year ago," Ion said.

"I should've. I just worry he'll end up on the street." Kelsey slipped out of her dress, revealing an attractive figure, curvier than Ion's, but not as awe-inspiring. She grabbed a pair of sweats. "But this job might just be my ticket out. You want to change into something more comfortable?"

"No, thanks. I kinda like this outfit. Haven't worn it in a long time." Ion flipped through the album, half of which were pictures of the weekend Kelsey and Barris met; the other half of Barris at his desk. "What's the job?"

"Advertising. Freelance. Maybe he'll get some direction in his life."

"I don't know, Kelsey. Men aren't very good at making a life for themselves...without our help." She closed the album. "Then again, women aren't very good at enjoying it without theirs."

Kelsey looked at the thin, striking woman a few years younger than herself. "You know," she said, thinking 'You're not so bad.' "I like you." They both smiled at each other. "Let's be best friends."

Ion nodded. "I'd like that. I don't usually connect well with women."

Kelsey could see why. Ion threatened most females. Her looks. Her poise. Her attitude. Without her even trying, most men would fall for Ion the instant they met her.

"Satan is a very special person to me. He's like family."

"Vinnie? Oh, yeah, he's *special*. Unrivaled is another good word."

Kelsey picked the photo album up off the bed and put it on a shelf that also held her high school and college diplomas, a picture of her family, and a faded, dried bouquet she'd caught at a wedding earlier in the year. She ran her fingers over the brittle petals. Several tiny flecks crumbled and broke off.

"He likes you, I think."

"I pay attention to him. And we have similar interests. We worry about a lot of the same things. Like the ozone. Only I plant trees. He wears foil on his head."

"Are you two...you know..."

Ion smiled sweetly. She felt genuine warmth toward Kelsey. Maybe they *could* be friends, although, right now, Ion knew that she was being interrogated. It was candy-coated, yes, but it was still a grilling. "Not yet. I'm trying to focus him right now. I think actually touching my body might be too much of a distraction for him at this point."

Kelsey glanced over Ion's body, that was, indeed, distracting. The fact that Barris hardly noticed it—accept for a moment during dessert when a bit of cream slipped off Ion's fork and landed on the skin between her breasts—concerned her.

"You're very beautiful. I would imagine a lot of men feel that way about you."

"It gets annoying after awhile. It's very hard having men adore you just because of how you look. I know that's gotta sound just so," Ion laughed, "ridiculous. 'How to make another woman hate you in two seconds.' But most of them see me and fall in love with a package. They don't try to find out who I am or what's special about me. They just see this." She motioned to her body. "And they turn into puppies. I don't want a puppy. I want a man. At least with Vinnie, he doesn't lose it when I flash him a smile or give him a flip of the hair. Who knows, maybe he's too terrified, but he makes me work for it."

"You know, when you get past his posturing, he's really very vulnerable. I think he's only been with one woman."

"Really, I would have said less." Ion played with a loose string on the bedspread, then glanced in the direction of the living room. "Speaking of puppies, what are you going to do?"

It was a very good question. If Barris didn't notice Ion, especially dressed the way she was today, he certainly wasn't deserving of the designation 'male.' Like Ion, what Kelsey needed in her life was a man.

"We've been going on inertia for awhile now. I think it might be time to move on."

Ion gave her a nod. "I wouldn't put up with it."

Kelsey agreed, bowing her head slowly. No, Ion wouldn't, she thought. As much as Kelsey wanted someone strong and confident, she knew Ion would want that even more. And despite the fact that Satan didn't become a lapdog every time she batted her eyes, what was she doing with him? He may not be a puppy, but he certainly wasn't a man either. Kelsey considered all the possible ways to be subtle and indirect, but there just didn't seem to be any. Ion obviously liked him, but it still didn't make any sense. In the end, it came out: "Ion, what the hell are you doing with him?"

From his perch on the sofa, Satan watched Barris at work. The veins beneath the skin of his friend's forehead pounded, the oxygen feeding the cells as each new thought came to him. He was writing furiously. Satan couldn't tell if he was happy with his work, angry, or just plain committed. Watching such dedication gave him a headache after awhile. Satan reached a hand up and rubbed his head, then suddenly sat up. No foil. All this time, the walk over, the dinner, the couch, since the X-ray technician had made him take it off—he had been exposed. Jumping to his feet, Satan raced toward the bedroom.

He came barging into the bedroom just as Ion was about to explain to Kelsey her vision of Satan's future.

"Foil," he and Ion said in unison, only for different reasons.

Satan continued, "I need some right away."

Kelsey raised her hand and pointed. "In the kitchen, by the stove."

He grunted, then disappeared.

Satan rushed into the kitchen, his hands arriving a few seconds before the rest of his body. Reaching the stove, he found the blue, silver and pink box. He grabbed it, shaking it frantically in his fist.

"Is this the only box?" he screamed into the air. Like a cornered rabbit, he began pulling out drawers and opening cupboards.

Hearing the commotion, Kelsey and Ion stepped out of the bedroom.

"There's none left?" said Kelsey. "I didn't use it all."

"It's Reynolds," Satan shrieked with alarm.

"So?"

"So…I can't use Reynolds. I will only allow Arnolds Aluminum to touch this scalp."

Pacing the small kitchen, about two steps long, Satan tried to figure where he could go on Christmas to buy foil.

"I will only allow Arnolds Aluminum to touch this scalp," echoed Barris from his desk, thinking he had just thought it up. He wrote the sentence down, then furrowed his brow. What a strange thought, he remarked to himself.

Kelsey glanced over at Barris.

"There's gotta be something open today," Satan mumbled under his breath as he abandoned his search.

"There's a 7-Eleven around the corner," said Kelsey, still looking at Barris.

Satan looked at her, looking at Barris. "They don't carry Arnolds. Isn't there some place else? Don't Jews need to shop?"

"Everything's closed."

"Fine." He gave out a disgusted sigh. "I'm sorry everyone, but I must return home."

Ion wasn't paying attention to Satan anymore. She was watching Kelsey's face. "Is something wrong," she asked.

Kelsey shook her head as she moved toward her soon-to-be former lover. "Barris," she said. "Isn't the campaign you're doing for Arnolds?"

"Arnolds?" Ion said.

"Only Arnolds!" shouted Satan, going for his coat and the door.

Barris nodded, annoyed that he was being distracted. "Yeah, yeah, yeah, Arnolds."

Ion stepped up to Kelsey. "Stay!" she said to Satan who didn't know how to react to the demand except to stop.

The two women looked at each other.

"You think?" they said in unison.

•

The trouble with collaboration is that no matter who comes up with an idea, it's almost assured that someone else will get the credit for it. A corollary to this is that everyone present at the conception of an idea will think their contribution is the one that made it all work.

Barris—who had neither come up with the idea of using Satan as a spokesman for Arnolds (Kelsey), nor the plan of using gamma ray deflection as the point of promotion (Ion)—was going to be the one paid a very large sum of money...if they could convince him.

"That is the stupidest thing I've ever heard of." Barris had his hands on his hips and was trying to stand as erect as possible, a sign of strength, he thought. Actually, it made him look ridiculous more than anything else.

"It's brilliant," said Ion.

"Brilliant? Can you imagine—*him* pitching foil on TV." Barris pointed toward Satan.

Satan was still standing by the open door waiting for someone to give him the okay to leave so he could get some of the very same foil everyone was discussing. For the moment, though, he was happy to remain where he was and listen to the conversation from a safe distance. He wasn't positive, but he had read somewhere that most murders occurred during domestic quarrels. This had the makings of front-page material.

"You thought I was crazy the last time," Kelsey said to Barris.

"That was different."

"How?"

"It was a good idea."

"*You* didn't think so."

Ion stepped between them, which pleased Satan.

"Who are you working for, Arnolds or an agency?" she asked.

"Brisker, Pendry, and Marks."

"Peter Marks?" Ion started to laugh.

"You know him?" asked Kelsey.

"Know him. I've had sex with him. I helped him get his first advertising job," she said, before turning to Barris. "I'll take it to him myself, if you don't."

Barris was dense, but he had enough brains to know when he was outmatched.

"I'll call him."

As Barris went to the phone and picked it up, Ion walked over to Satan.

"Vinnie, how'd you like to be a star?"

"What does this entail exactly?" he asked, recalling the failed experiment at the blues club. He wasn't cut out to be a star. Too much pressure. That was another great thing about living inside the planet…no stars. He thought maybe now might be a good time to go back to his original plan and continue the search for a passage to the Inner Earth.

A moment later, Barris was on the phone with Ion listening in on the cordless. "Peter…I think I've got something for you."

Satan was fidgeting by the door, like a kid who had to go to the bathroom. "Can I go get some foil now?"

XIII. THIRTEEN

In Russia, they have a saying about superstitiousness. It's not easily translated into English, but it goes something like this:

Don't fuck with shit you don't know dick about.

Vlady was standing on the corner of State and Calhoun. He was tired and hungry and not very happy. The cab he'd taken from the airport was numbered 1313. His flight from Moscow had lasted just over thirteen hours, and all he had left in his pocket was a wallet and thirteen American dollars.

Vlady wasn't all that superstitious—at least, *he* didn't think so—but he figured too many thirteens couldn't be a good sign. To break the pattern, he decided to give one of the dollars away to the first vagrant he saw.

Not much traffic, pedestrian or vehicular. No beggars in sight.

Vlady glanced up and down the block. His hair was longish on top, short in back and waved like a flag in the wind coming off the Lake. Folding his arms, he tried to keep out the cold, but his Soviet bomber jacket, made for Siberia, didn't seem to be enough here in Chicago. He wore the leather coat as sort of a joke to remind himself of the absurdity he had seen in covering the Afghanistan "action."

Two green eyes searched for someone to give the thirteenth dollar.

Finally, he caught a glimpse of a poor soul across the street.

Vlady was in a hurry to rid himself of his unlucky buck. Not waiting for the light, he left his bags behind and ran into the street. A huge Oldsmobile screeched its tires and fish tailed on the icy roadway. Siding sideways, it was heading straight for the Russian.

The driver's door came to rest a foot from Vlady's knee. He stood frozen in the middle of the intersection.

"You wanna move outta my way, asshole," said Kenny, about eleven inches from the man's face.

Without a word, Vlady regained control of his legs and continued to the far curb.

Kenny Odorman glanced at the man, his jacket, and shook his head, "Communists," then hit the accelerator, his wheels spinning across the snowy pavement on his way to stakeout Clearwater Sanitarium.

Vlady stepped onto the sidewalk. He wasn't paying attention to the fact that a diseased, food-starved rat the size of a small dog was stalking him. He was intent on giving the dollar away.

That car back there had almost done him in, he thought a second later.

The diseased rat scurried several feet behind its prey. A nice chunk out of the tall thing's leg and it'd be set for a couple of days. By that time, the weather might break.

Rats didn't understand seasons.

A large truck with an eggnog intoxicated driver was heading down the alley, forcing the vagrant to move out of its way.

Seeing the homeless man flee the passageway, Vlady shouted, "*Da,*" before remembering he was back in America. He gave chase after the man. The rat was clicking his teeth in anticipation. The truck was bearing down. It wasn't quite clear which one would get him first, but it *was* clear that if the rat were victorious, Vlady wouldn't have to wait for the slow painful death of rabies. The truck would put an end to that.

Vlady slipped and fell on the icy sidewalk, sliding past the alleyway, just out of the truck's path. The rat following close behind Vlady opened its mouth and bit into—a tire, which squashed it on the second revolution.

As the driver steered the truck onto the street, a little red blotch on the right front wheel, Vlady picked himself up, and brushed off. After a moment, he finally caught up with the homeless man.

"Here," said Vlady as he handed the man the dollar.

"Merry Christmas," said the man.

Vlady had forgotten. "Oh, yes, it is."

Vlady turned and walked away satisfied.

Now that he had only twelve dollars left.

Problem was, Vlady had not only forgotten Christmas, he had also forgotten the emergency bank note stuffed in the bottom of his shoe. With thirteen dollars to his name, his luck was about to change.

XIV. SEX AND ADVERTISING

Satan was sitting in his home staring at the ceiling. He wished Niro, his landlord, had let him put in the lead panels. Then there'd be at least a slight chance they might cave in and kill him and put him out of his misery. He searched the room for something dangerous enough to inflict bodily harm. The fireplace poker had potential, but he was too squeamish to injure himself. An accident, he'd welcome.

Dreaming of fame or pretending to lead the masses in the privacy of one's own home was one thing. Actually going out and doing it was a lot less fun.

He'd been happy preaching to the walls about the perils of irradiation; enjoyed informing the sofa on the proper use of foil; looked forward to his nightly sermons in the shower on the Netherworld, fighting off every challenge to his beliefs with a saber-like wit.

All that was gone.

In the five days since Christmas, Ion had made it clear his life was no longer his own, that he had a greater calling. She had revised her earlier calculations on his prospects, believing even more emphatically that he was destined to break through the clutter and make it onto the radar screens of America, maybe even the television screens. She was preparing him for life under the microscope. She forced him to get a haircut, have his teeth cleaned, and purchase a new set of clothes. She was merciless. Out was the old down jacket that had been his companion for the past nine years, tossed in the trash like an empty carton of milk—and with less ceremony. Out were the mittens. Although he was allowed to keep those only because his mother had made them. Out were his shoes, his socks, his underwear, all had been close to him for a very long time.

In were a navy peacoat, black leather gloves, twill slacks, and a new bowler.

Of all the new things, only the bowler pleased him. When Jimmy Hoffa stole the first hat, he didn't think he'd ever love a piece of headgear as much. But this bowler stood taller and made a slightly better impression. Ion picked it out and Jason's mom refurbished it. For the past few days, Ion had been trying to convince Jason's mom to quit her seamstress job and do hats exclusively. For now, she did Ion's relining work on the side.

Removing his gaze from the ceiling, Satan studied the seven plastic bags his new clothes had been carried home in. He spent the better part of two days weaving through the crazed sale-seekers and exchange-mongers that populated the stores in the weeks following Christmas. Ion had wanted to accompany him, but one of the other cashiers at Clancy's had unexpectedly given birth—no one, including the overweight woman herself, knew she was pregnant—forcing Ion to work double shifts until a replacement could be hired.

Looking in the mirror at Scaridd's department store earlier in the day, Satan saw someone else reflected in the glass. The man in the mirror had similar features, but there was something different about him. Satan was oddly shaken that he no longer recognized himself.

"It perfeckkt," said the small Lithuanian man, chalk in hand, ribbon tape measure around his neck hanging almost to the floor. "You like, no?"

"No."

"Good, good, I make for you."

Satan searched the men's department for an employee that might speak English.

"Do—you—understand—English?"

"Eglish, yes, yes, good," said the man, rechalking the pant cuffs at a more British length.

A woman that seemed to be in upper management passed by the cosmetics island about twenty yards away. He assumed the big-haired woman's position by the fact that she did no work of her own, just ordered others in her path to do it for her. Presently, she was pointing to a huge, phallic display for men's cologne that took up most of the counter space, making some comment about it. The sales girl standing behind the giant thing could only see customers indirectly in a bank of mirrors that lined the side counters.

The big-haired woman obviously appreciated the large object—she kept running her hand along its side—however, she recognized an obstacle to sales when she saw one. Collaring a passing stockboy, she ordered him to remove the display and, handing the young man a set of keys, Satan assumed, had him put it in her car.

Satan made a noise to gather her attention after the display was well out of sight. The woman turned to find him waving her over.

"May I help you?" she asked, once she reached him, in a tone that made it clear she hoped the answer was 'no.'

"This employee of yours does not speak English."

Standing now, the man smiled and shook his head, thinking he was being commended.

"Explain yourself," the woman said, doing her best android impression.

"He doesn't speak the language we are now using, which wouldn't be a problem if we were in whatever country he comes from."

"Lithuania," said the woman.

Satan tried another tact. "I don't want this suit. He doesn't understand that. He wants to make five for me. I put up my hand to say 'stop' and he starts writing up five orders."

The man held up his open palm, smiling. He had never had someone order five suits from him.

Satan was getting nowhere. He abandoned his practical argument and decided a philosophical approach might jog something in the woman's head. He grabbed two pairs of pants he had tried on. "Answer me this. How come a size 36 waist from this company," he raised one higher, "is not the same as a 36 from this one? I mean, we're talking inches, right? Tell me there's more than one way to measure an inch and I'll understand."

A few minutes later, security was escorting Satan out the front door, one of the size 36 pants still wrapped around his neck.

Ion strutted into the room, lifting Satan from his daydream.

"C'mon, c'mon, c'mon, let's move. Let me see."

She grabbed him and stood him up. Circling him with a hand to her mouth, the three middle fingers across her lips, Ion checked Satan out.

Ion puckered her face and drew up her shoulders. "Yiiiiccck."

"What."

"You look normal," she said. "I told you to get some *new* clothes, not turn into a lawyer.

"I am normal."

"No, Vinnie, you are *not* normal. You're a genius. Listen, let me explain something. Einstein couldn't match his socks. He didn't have fashion sense. He had no concept what a comb was." She put her hand on his shoulder. "You follow me?"

"Not really."

"That's why you need me." She grabbed his hand. "Let's go."

•

It was New Year's Eve. The air was beginning to be charged with the excitement of the upcoming celebrations.

Peter Marks glanced at his watch, three-thirty. He hoped he could make the party at Brisker's home this evening. Taking his head in his hands, he smoothed back his hair, then grabbed the ends above the nape of his neck and pulled. A long sigh escaped his lips, puffing out his cheeks slightly. Screaming, a Tarzan yell, he pushed his chair across the rug, rolling over a stack of toys and crushing a Talking Tammy™ doll, causing it to cry. He'd been working every day since Christmas on the Arnolds' campaign, and from all the sighing and shouting, it seemed to be going well. Normally, the agency was closed between the two holidays, and it was, for the most part. Only a handful of "volunteers" were in the office, scripting the TV spots and running copy for the print work. Several others were in the basement studios herding talent and building sets. Still more worked on creating a presence on the web for Arnolds, ads, info, etc.

"Marjorieeeee," he shouted out his office door, "Get me—" then he remembered that his secretary was at the Club Med in Martinique probably burning her tits at the moment. Not that he thought about her breasts a lot, once or twice a day—more since his last relationship ended—but a nice run on a *topless* white sand beach was definitely something to consider.

He decided it was in his best interest to put her breasts out of his mind and get back to the job at hand. He pressed a button on his phone and when the dial tone sounded, he punched in a number.

The female voice answered, sounding as though it was coming through a tomato, endive and sprouts sandwich, which it was.

"Yweah?"

"Hey, sport, it's Peter. How's the transformation going? Do I have a star?"

"You ever read Kafka," asked Ion.

"Only the Cliff notes."

"I think we've reached the pupa stage."

Her voice echoed in his office. Without a face, the words coming over the speaker were somehow more intense, less friendly than talking to her in person. He tried to picture Ion's face and body, but every time he did, her father's footsteps would echo in his mind, along with a picture of himself hanging by his fingertips from the windowsill.

"What do you want?" she asked, crunching into her sandwich again which sounded like a car accident over the phone.

"I was wondering if you wanted to join me at a party tonight?" He glanced out his office door, seeing several of his staff racing back and forth at various distances like ducks in a carnival shooting gallery. "It'll be a chance to talk about something other than business."

He stared at the phone, waiting.

There was a long pause.

"You're hoping I'll get drunk and let you take me back to your place."

"Well…"

"You just wanna get laid, Marks."

"That is so rude."

"I have other engagements this evening, Peter, but it's the dirty thought that counts. Speak to you in the morning."

"I…"

Ion hung up the phone.

"What do you think?" said Satan, dressed in a mishmash of clothes he and Ion had gathered from a tour of several thrift shops and Goodwill outlets.

"Perfect."

"I almost like it," he said, sounding extremely cheery for Satan.

"You know," Ion began, swallowing the last of her sandwich, trying to sound nonchalant about it. "I think the woman at the Salvation Army store kinda liked you."

It was possible Ion was right. The quiet, mousy woman had followed him around the entire store. He made a little game of it, turning quickly, doubling back, just to see if she'd continue to shadow him. She did.

"I can't shake her," he told Ion as he passed by.

The girl giggled shyly as he tried on each piece of clothing. "I think that looks good," she'd say and smile, squinting through thick glasses and keeping her head tilted down. She made him wonder what Ion might look like if she was more shy and had less than 20/20 vision.

"You think so?" he said.

"Most definitely," Ion replied.

Ion had no trouble enlisting the girl into the fold, especially after she told the girl Vinnie was eligible. Ion traded for the clothes by donating several Gamma Caps for sale in the store. As they were leaving, Ion noticed the girl try one on.

"I bet she's there tonight."

That bit of information didn't make Satan happy. "Really? I hope not. What was her name? Pollywog. Lillypad?"

"Lilly."

"Oh."

"It's a pretty name, don't you think?"

"No."

•

Brisker, Pendry, & Marks sat on a little street overlooking a duck pond. The building was old brown brick, six stories tall, with large modern smoked windows. The agency took up the top two floors, the ground floor photo studios, and the cavernous basement, which housed soundstages.

Perched on the roof of the refurbished edifice, a gigantic rooster standing ten feet high welcomed visitors and clients alike.

Armand Arnold stood in the hall outside the penthouse offices. He pulled in a breath of air before reaching for a doorknob in the shape of a hen.

His heart raced, his palms were sweating. It was as if he were about to ring the doorbell of a blind date. Actually, it was very much the same. He didn't know why he was here, or what he was going to say. Phoning Peter Marks Christmas Day, Armand felt he'd been clear. Arnolds Aluminum could no longer afford a massive advertising blitz.

"Just come by," Peter had said, "the Doctor gonna fix you up."

Armand twisted the tail of the chicken. Pushing open the door, he revealed the hip, high-tech decor of Brisker, Pendry & Marks: open ceilings, painted heating ducts hanging from the rafters, staggered workstations on multilevel tiers. Roosters every few feet. Armand felt a little out of touch—a bit old—whenever he came here, but after a few minutes with the people, he inevitably loosened up. And after a while, the place did something that even science has yet to do. Made you feel young.

Peter Marks came hurriedly out of his office, wearing a short-brimmed hat, which reminded Armand of someone in a 1950's press corp.

"Foil Man," he said, jovially.

"Peter," Armand responded, the tone of the single word saying so much; what are you doing, I can't afford this, why am I here?

"Oh, c'mon, don't be so glum. The Doctor got your cure, Foil Man."

Armand glanced across the room. Back in the far corner, several copywriters were busy covering their walls with aluminum and pacing back and forth, shouting out strings of words. Armand turned his focus out one of the large windows. The view was breathtaking, a park under a blanket of snow, trees, the frozen duck pond, the Lake in the distance. He sighed.

"We can't afford it, Peter, I told you."

Peter Marks placed his arm around the solemn figure and drew him closer.

"I'll tell you, Foil Man," he said, walking him closer to the window for a better look at the scenery. "I know what you said on the phone, but you've got to hear me out, okay? It won't cost you a cent to listen."

Only my pride when I have to say no, Armand thought. But he owed it to Peter. "Okay."

"The best thing about this campaign, Foil Man...is we don't do anything...nothing...until *after* it starts working."

Armand was silent for a moment. Nothing for nothing, his father always said.

"I don't understand."

Peter took off his hat and threw it on a drafting table a few feet to the left of them.

"There is your answer. What do you think that is?"

"A hat?" said Armand, sounding not quite sure, even though he knew it was a hat.

"A very special hat, Foil Man. Pick it up, put it on your head."

Armand reached for the hat. He turned it over and studied the inside. It seemed well made, sturdy. The fabric was of above average quality. Along with chairs, he was something of a hat connoisseur. He ran his fingers over the soft silk lining, and...and it crinkled.

"What..."

"Foil, my friend," said Peter. "Arnolds Aluminum foil."

"I still don't understand."

Peter tilted the flat-panel computer display so it faced them. "Have you checked your orders the past week?" He punched in a few numbers and letters as he spoke.

"Yes. They were pretty average."

Peter found what he was looking for and pointed to it on the screen. "This is a breakdown of local stores that carry your product. These six," he circled his finger around several bolded store names, which included Clancy's and five others. "...have been selling out of Arnolds every day this week. Every day. They get a new supply, and it's gone in hours. And the best part is, their customers won't settle for any other brand. It has to be Arnolds."

Peter had piqued Armand's interest.

"And you're saying you know why?"

"Yes. Because, for the past few weeks, a nutty old friend of mine has been parading her newest project around town. Namely, a guy who claims wearing foil on your head will protect you from gamma rays and maybe even slow the aging process."

Armand sighed. Arnolds Aluminum had stooped to pandering to the lunatic fringe.

"And I know what you're thinking," Peter said, reading his client like any good ad man worth his weight. "This isn't just the weirdoes. It's got some funky residual effect I haven't quite figured out. It's so bizarre, people are into it, even if they don't put it on their heads, even if they don't buy into the gamma ray thing, they are buying your product. Because it's hip."

"Do you buy into it?"

"The gamma rays?" He got a nod from Armand. "We've got a couple of physicists from the University of Chicago working on it. But it looks promising. All the stuff's got to do is stop a micron of radiation and we can sell it that way. Besides, we're gonna play it up tongue in cheek. Make it fun. Make it snap."

Armand pulled out a chair and sat. He had given up on his grandfather's company, resigned himself to defeat. But could it be? A tiny breath of life breathed back into it, and him.

"I don't know, Peter."

"What's to know?"

"What do we do?"

"Well, first thing we do, is we take your rollers..." he twirled his hands around each other, "...the ones you use to make the Gatorback, and get an engraver to cut you a new pattern."

"What pattern?"

Peter Marks loved his job at times like this. He leaned in close to Armand.

"A mystique is being created around Arnolds as we speak. You want to punish those who don't buy your brand. So you have to have a way to let everyone know who is and isn't buying it."

Peter handed Armand a set of artwork. With 'Arnolds Aluminum' drafted in the style of the 1940's. Retro-hip.

"What's this?"

"Your new logo. Have the engravers set you a repeater plate with the logo on it. That way everybody will know who's cool and who's using Reynolds." He put his arm around Armand again. "Once we build some momentum through the Internet and people on the ground, and get you some capital, we go get it with TV and radio."

"TV?"

"Come with me, Foil Man. Let me show you what I have in mind."

•

It was a bit after four-thirty when Satan sat on the front steps outside his home and lifted his eyes toward the sky. Looking at the pink light disappearing over the buildings on his street, he thought, what a ridiculous time for the sun to set.

He hated Winter.

As the street lamp over him flickered on, slowly growing in intensity, Satan kicked at a doll that one of the neighborhood kids had left on the steps. The blonde thing bounced and rolled onto the sidewalk, coming to rest on its side, its arms and legs in a running position. The snow had melted off the sidewalks and streets, leaving in its wake dry white salt stains. Once when he was a kid, he had dabbed his finger in the powder and tapped a bit on his tongue. It tasted very little like salt, more like doctor-prescribed nose drops that drain into your throat by accident.

On the way back from the thrift shop tour, he and Ion had passed by Wrigley Field. There was still snow there. However, on any piece of land that was paved, which was just about every piece of land, the wet flakes were just a memory.

A jingling sound preceded the arrival of three of the street's most notorious hoodlums. A bike tire ran over Satan's new shoes.

"What's up, Mr. Satin," said one of the little deviants, named Bobby. The boy had a box of crayons sticking out of his pocket, obviously just back from a graffiti session. "Like my new bike?"

"Who'd you steal it from?" said Satan to the grubby nine-year-old as his friends skidded next to him.

"Nobody. I got it from Santa."

"Really," Satan said, studying the tilted caps covering various colors of stringy hair and the inside out jackets the kids wore. "I would have thought you'd be a prime candidate for some sort of fossil fuel. Large quantities, I'd guess."

"He gotted it from Santa," said one of the other future delinquents, a blond kid who looked a little like the doll's brother.

"I didn't get no present from you, Mr. *Satin*," said Bobby.

Satan smiled at the boy. What he wanted to do was spank him.

"Som'in wrong?" Bobby asked.

"I'm wondering if it's a mental deficiency that causes you to misspeak my name."

"Nah, just my momma don't like me saying the devil's name's all."

"Just doing his work," Satan added with a little sneer.

These three terrorists struck fear in the hearts of old ladies and young children alike. An entire four-block radius was their domain. Two months ago, on Halloween, they splattered his windows, his door, and his stoop—everything—with eggs. Satan didn't actually witness the act, but he was positive it was the three in front of him. Bobby had left his calling card on one of the eggshells—a little crayon drawing. A few years from now, he'd move up from Crayolas to spray paint once he was old enough to drive to Skokie. It was okay for people to buy cigarettes in Chicago, but they couldn't buy, sell, or even possess spray paint under penalty of law.

Showed where the priorities lied.

"Shouldn't you three be heading home or something?"

"My mom don't get home till six-thirty," said the last kid, pointing to a fairly nice men's watch dangling on his wrist because it didn't fit.

It looked new. Satan wondered if they were the ones who knocked over the local jewelry store several weeks ago. He wouldn't put it past them.

"What about you, Mr. Satin?"

"My mom don't come home no more," he said, mimicking their speech.

"That's right, she crazy," said Bobby, his sunburned face and bad grammar indicating he spent very little time in school.

Satan stared at them and tried to recall what it was like to be nine. Memories came rushing back, but the past is usually seen through the eyes of today, making it difficult to remember how one truly felt then.

Some moments, however, are tamper-proof.

When Satan was nine, there was an old house down the street, nestled in among the row of houses. It had a gray picket fence in front that ran along the sidewalk. At one time the fence had been white, but the years and the weather had conspired against it. There was a dirt path lined with pink and beige rocks leading up to the house, which was set back a ways and not visible from the street because it was shielded by a canopy of green from several drooping trees. In the winter, when the leaves fell, the gray and rotting slats of the house could be seen through the branches. The yard for as long as anyone could remember had been overgrown with wheatgrass and wildflowers.

There were kids like Bobby then, there always are.

In the beginning, the neighborhood bad boys knocked on the fence, trying to draw out the occupants, whom they planned to run from at the first sound of a creaking door—but no one came. As the weeks past, they grew more daring, opening the gate and taking a few steps onto the property before turning and sprinting off.

Still, no one came.

Later, the boys challenged each other to go kick a few rocks out of place. They even urged Noel to do it once, but when he got inside the gate, he chickened out, and the boys closed the gate on him. He was so nervous, he couldn't get the latch to work and had to climb over the fence, snapping off the top of two rotting boards and ripping his shirt in the process.

But even then, no one came.

No one went out for the mail, which arrived sporadically. A few weeks worth was less than an average home's daily take. The mail seemed to disappear every once in a while. They didn't know if someone came out late at night and picked it up, if it was stolen, or if the mailman took it back after a time.

Just after Satan's ninth birthday, several of the boys on the block made a pact that they'd go up to the door and ring the bell. Anyone who chickened out was a fag and a homo and wouldn't be cool anymore.

Nine kids entered the gate, about six made it to the end of the path. It was a hot summer night and the whole kid block was there. All the neighborhood girls—and the boys who hadn't made the pact, including Noel—were standing outside the fence looking through the spaces, or sitting perched on top. Two of the boys actually had the guts to step onto the porch. The trees hung low that summer so no one except the other four that had made it to the end of the path could see anything.

From what the four said, the two boys stood on the porch several minutes arguing in whispers over who had the balls to ring the bell, and whether they had to stay and wait for someone to answer the door to prove their fearlessness.

Finally, they both rang the bell, the eerie, rusted sound giving everyone a jolt. Noel was crouched on the outside of the picket, next to the gate, his right eye poked as far into the fence space as possible. His fingers were wrapped around the wood boards for stability.

Everyone waited.

A creaking sound came from the house, and everyone inside the gate but the two on the porch drew back toward the path's halfway point. By then, no one but the two bravest could give witness to what was going on. The house creaked again and a window broke on the second floor. And suddenly, all the boys inside the yard came sprinting down the path, save one.

Noel watched with a terrified fascination.

"Boooo!!!" Kenny Odorman screamed in his ear, sending Noel's face into the fence.

His heart started up after a minute or two.

Kenny threw another rock, missing glass and hitting only house this time. Several of the older boys, who didn't find Kenny or his pranks funny, chased after him. A couple of days later, Noel spotted Kenny near his house sporting a black eye.

Everyone had panicked except for one of the two on the porch. He stayed long after everyone else had run away screaming. He said it showed true guts.

Some of the others said he had crapped in his pants and didn't want anyone to know about it.

Which was probably more to the truth.

It was a few months later, just as school was about to start that the mystery of the strange house was revealed. A determined real estate agent, who had tried for months to get the owners to answer, got so frustrated that he broke the front door down.

The old man and old woman he found inside were dead. Her, about four years. Him, a little more than three. The skeletons were lying next to each other in the upstairs bedroom. The man had gone to sleep for almost a year with his late bride until his death.

When they finally tore down the old house and put up a brightly painted apartment complex, Noel's childhood came to an end. His age of innocence and wonder were never quite the same. Brick and concrete were no match, imagination-wise, to wood clapboard, rotting fences, and slouching trees.

"See ya, Mr. Satin," Bobby said as he and his compadrés rode off into the sunset, on their way to wreak some havoc.

Satan heard a woman scream just after the boys turned the corner.

Night was approaching and Satan leaned back on the cold cement steps, thinking of the old house, and the old neighborhood. He suddenly realized something he never had before. Lost in a past that seemed just outside his reach was the knowledge that he had been normal once. Picked on, taunted, beat up—yes—but normal. Satan had always figured it was his father's leaving that ruined his life; that for as long as he was cognitive, he had been strange.

This recovered tidbit of his childhood forced on him another view. And it surprised him to recognize that his mother's growing madness and ultimate departure had created what he was today.

Now, Ion was creating someone entirely new. She had come along and knocked him off his steady tracks. Although being considered odd hadn't always been pleasant for Satan, its unchangingness had a sort of comfort to it.

But now, he was nowhere. Not odd, not normal. Just in a state of limbo.

He wanted his red mittens back, and his old down jacket with all the stuffing at the bottom. He wanted back the safety that came from years of keeping everything exactly the same.

•

Satan was still on the stoop at eight o'clock. The cold didn't seem to bother him. In the clear night, he could see past the city's reflective glow in the sky and gaze at the stars.

There was a noise overhead.

"Vinnie?"

He tipped his head back and saw an upside down Ion leaning out the broken window, her hands resting on the sill.

"C'mon inside," she said softly. "It's too cold out there. And you've got to get ready for tonight."

He nodded his head, "One moment," and returned his gaze toward the spotted black canvas.

She wanted to make him a star. And although stars burned bright, they ultimately exploded and collapsed in on themselves and generally made a big deal about dying. He'd just as soon go quietly into that dark night.

Slowly climbing the stairs, he made his way toward his bedroom to dress for the night's festivities. He was a little nervous, returning only a week later to the very spot at which he had been accused of starting a riot. But Ion insisted. And there was very little he could do to resist her. She held him in her powers and wouldn't let go. Not that he wanted her to.

Reaching the bedroom door, he found the lights off. A candle flickered somewhere in the room. Incense burned as well. It smelled like someplace sacred, someplace mystical, someplace he didn't want to go.

Ion was there, waiting for him under the covers of his bed. After a moment, she pulled back the comforter, revealing her naked beauty. She patted on the sheet for him to climb in with her.

"Come to bed, Vinnie," she said, quietly. "It's time to complete the metamorphosis. Time for the caterpillar to become the butterfly."

He silently undressed and slipped under the covers, pressing against her warm, smooth flesh that was scented vanilla. Her skin was hot to the touch, hotter still near the center.

She took his hand and gently led it over her body. Trailing it between her breasts, across one of the nipples, past her stomach, down further to the trimmed patch of curly hair that sat above the most heated place of all. His fingers hesitated there, unable to move for the longest time, but finally, slowly at first, they began to roam amid the fleecy wool until by accident or chance he came upon the softest wetness. An area unobstructed and unfettered by any spindly locks.

"Yes," she said, raising herself into his hand.

He let the tips of his fingers smooth over the wetness. The burning folds were drenched with moisture, dripping with pools of warm, slippery fluid. His breathing quickened and he felt a thousand warm pins prick his body.

"Yes," she said again.

He could hardly see her in the dark, but he looked toward her face anyway. "I...I think I..."

She put a finger to his lips. "Shhhh. No promises."

XV. F.F.L.

A primal scream emanated from the graystone at around 9:15. The federal agents bugging the place anonymously phoned the police who arrived on the scene six minutes later with eight cars and a helicopter. They came prepared. After all, this was the address of the guy responsible for the riot at No Mo' Blues.

•

The alleyway outside the club was brighter than usual. A new, more powerful light had been screwed into the socket over the doorman's head, and the grime had been mysteriously washed away from the passage.

Jeffrey stood, with his clipboard at his side, looking very happy.

A line of people—two hundred by his estimate—had queued up behind a red velvet rope hanging between two silver stanchions set on the cracked pavement. Inside, the club was already near capacity, with a number about the same as those waiting in the alley. Since New Year's Eve was not an 'in and out' night—once someone got in and paid the cover, they usually stayed until after midnight—ninety percent of these people in line would be ringing in the New Year in a cold and dreary alley, which was why Jeffrey was smiling.

Misery loves company.

It was just after eleven-twenty when Ion and Satan turned the corner into the alley. She looked sweet, sexy and stunning as was normal for Ion. Her hair was pushed over one ear, and the ten-gallon was tilted to show that. Satan, on the other hand, was sporting his thrift shop acquisitions and moving his head from side to side slightly as he bounced down the alleyway. His lips could hardly keep his teeth from showing. A few blocks back, he had given up trying.

He definitely had a serious case of F.F.L.

The term F.F.L. originated in Southern California—Newport Beach specifically. It then passed from person to person, making the move east into Phoenix and Denver, and north to San Francisco and Seattle. It was from the City by the Bay that F.F.L. made its meteoric jump into Chicago on the back of a transplanted commodities trader.

Its introduction into local vernacular occurred on June 7th, 1981 on the floor of the Chicago Mercantile Exchange, when the San Francisco trader noticed a rosy-cheeked grin on his partner's face and remarked, "You got some serious F.F.L." to which the partner said, "What?" which in turn was answered, "The Freshly Fucked Look."

"Wipe that grin off your face," Ion said, coyly.

"Sorry," was his reply after a momentary pause, during which the words had to fight their way into his thought pattern.

"You handled the police very well, I have to say."

"They were pretty accommodating once you came prancing downstairs naked." He took a moment to replay the stunning vision in his mind. "Asking to borrow the handcuffs was a nice touch."

"I thought so," she said. "You ready?"

He nodded. "I think so," he said, no hint of hesitation in his voice. It had the tone of a late-night DJ on a soft hits station. "You know, I still wish you would let me wear my mittens. This night would be perfect then."

"I like holding your hand better like this."

Subject closed.

Ion led Satan past the waiting wannabe revelers. About halfway to the door, she noticed Slag's long straight hair among the crowd.

"Slag?"

"Hey," he said, with a generic nod until he realized who she was. "Whoa. I didn't think you'd make it. Saved you a place."

"Slag, we're on the guest list. You didn't have to wait."

"Really?"

"We've been on the list for a year, Slag."

"Right," he said, nodding continuously now. "I keep forgetting."

Ion grabbed the sleeve of the poet's jacket and pulled him to the door. The three of them stood in front of Jeffrey who immediately lost his smile.

"Can I help you?" His tone was prissy at best.

"Jeffrey, we're going in."

"You'll have to wait in line."

Ion still had her F.F.L. so she just smiled at him. "Jeffrey," she said, sweetly. "We go through this every time. We know the owner." She said the last sentence as if speaking to a cute little baby.

"Last time you were here you almost tore up the place."

"We did tear up the place, Jeffrey. But that's the beauty of this club, it doesn't look any different."

Jeffrey pretended not to notice them.

That didn't work.

Ion put her hand gently on his shoulder. "Jeffrey, let us in, or I'll have Slag breathe on you. I don't think he knows what a toothbrush is, so factor that into your decision."

Jeffrey never liked plaque or gingivitis, especially not up close.

He let them pass.

Once the door closed behind them, his smile returned to his face. He did, after all, enjoy abuse.

•

The President was about to shoot the eleven ball into the side pocket, his mouth wide in concentration, when his Chief of Staff knocked on the door. For a second, he hesitated and looked up. Lowering his head again, he went back to aiming the cue through his fingers, hoping the man might go away if he ignored him.

Another knock.

The President stood straight up and thought for a moment. He started to put down the stick, then stopped. He was the leader of the Free World. "Just a minute," he said.

Finally set, he pulled back to fire—the Chief of Staff banged on the door once more.

"Sir?"

The eleven hit the side bumper, bounced and tapped the eight ball into the corner pocket.

"That's game, sir," said the small black man the President was playing.

"How much do I owe you, Charles?"

"Greenland, Panama, and Indonesia."

"I'm good for it," said the President as he ambled to the door and opened it to find his Chief of Staff about to knock again.

"I'm sorry to bother you, Mr. President."

"Is there something wrong?" The President looked at his watch. It was nearly 11:40. He hoped there was no national crisis, nothing that needed immediate attention anyway; he was due to play a game of cards with the Misses at midnight to ring in the new year.

"I think we should go into your office, sir."

"Okay," sighed the President.

Entering the Oval Office, the President walked to the desk and flicked on the light. "...the Middle East? Korean Peninsula? NATO? Drug Lords?" He'd been trying to guess the entire way from the living quarters.

"It's this 'Earth, Inc.' thing, Sir. I've been monitoring the situation, reading the daily reports."

"Ah-huh."

"Last week, one of our agents was run over by a bus."

The President had never taken a bus, but had seen enough of them to know he'd never want to be hit by one. He winced.

"Is he, you know...is he...dead?"

"Hospitalized."

"I see." It was a quarter till. "I don't understand why you're telling me this."

"Then a few days later, a bar room brawl broke out and several of our agents were injured."

"Oh, my."

"Several more were arrested after they beat up the local police."

The President scrunched up his face. "I..."

"It's been straightened out." The Chief of Staff threw down a packet of photos.

Gingerly, the President spilled the envelope's contents onto his desk. He used a pencil to pick at them.

"You can touch them, sir."

"Okay," he whispered as if someone had told him to raid the cookie jar with his mother in the next room.

The President looked over the pictures that seemed to feature a man, thirtyish, in a black bowler hat. "I don't..."

The Chief of Staff pointed to one photo of the man and a few others entering a building. "An ad agency. They're going public with the information about the missiles."

Five to midnight. The President was exasperated. "Who are *they*?"

Four minutes later, the President was seated across from his wife with a deck of cards and a bottle of Dom Perignon.

It had all been straightened out.

•

There was a brief second after Jeffrey closed the door where the sounds outside had been cut off and the music from the club hadn't made its way up the stairs yet. In this instant of silence, Satan found a certain peace.

Descending the steps, the mix of music and talking rose up and grew louder as if the lid were being pulled off a can of partygoers. Below, Satan saw the backs of a dozen people swaying to the rhythms put out by the band. At first, he saw only the feet of the performers, then their knees, then hips. As the noises built and intertwined, the entire club became visible, and he could finally see the faces of the musicians.

The club appeared different to Satan, and not because of the damage done during the ruckus a week ago. No, it was his perception that had changed. Nothing was ever the same as the first time you saw it. Things and people and places were altered by familiarity. This place would never again be new to him, and that thought saddened Satan. Which surprised him. He liked things the same.

Maybe not everything. His lips were still swollen, his senses heightened, and the warm aftermath of sex languished through his insides.

A faint whiff of sweat and marijuana passed under his nose, tickling his nostrils and causing him to blow out a snort. The room was overcrowded with dressy outfits and grinning, two-fisted drinkers. Bottles of champagne were being handed out. It took Satan a moment to notice, but the people, most of them anyway, were wearing hats. Not party hats, but *real* hats, like his and Ion's and Slag's foil-lined leather cap. Many of them had Arnolds logos stitched into them.

People were actually *listening* to him. He wasn't sure he was comforted by that.

Ion had dragged Slag over to where Jason was standing. A darkly handsome woman donning a colorful wrap had her arm through his. Satan joined them after evading a cluster of recruits who were waving to him.

"Satan, I want you to meet, Talia," Jason said, offering his date. "Talia, this is someone I hadn't seen in twenty years."

"Hello," said the woman, quietly, gently.

Satan greeted Talia, and the two shook hands. Some other introductions were made, which he didn't pay attention to.

"Where did you get that?" he asked, feeling the fabric of the woman's dress. She seemed vaguely familiar to him. "It's beautiful."

"The Shop-At-Home Network," she said, rather proudly.

There are moments in life when one is truly surprised. At these times, there is a simple rule of thumb: say nothing, nod a great deal. However, human nature being what it is, people invariably find the silence too unbearable, and end up blurting out something which they wish, as soon as it's said, they hadn't.

This was one of those moments.

"You actually purchased something from those charlatans?"

The Shop-At-Home Network was one of Satan's pet peeves, along with Christmas(Observed), Visa cards, and CreditDat—even more so, once he realized they were all in conspiracy with one another. His neighbor, Mrs. Strom, had the inane buy-a-thon beamed directly into her home twenty of the twenty-four hours that normally made up a day. Under the guise of guilt by proximity, the buying spree was forced upon Satan for much of his waking hours. For the first few years, he flipped his TV to the same channel before going to bed, hoping to confuse the sound waves into thinking they didn't have to blast his home. However, after he unwittingly purchased twenty-nine gold-over-silver serpentine neck chains, a patio set (he had no patio) and a 64-speed blender, Satan figured another tact was in order. Never mind that when he called the Shop-At-Home Network to get his money back and for them to cease transmission, saying he placed the orders while in a video-induced dream and would sue for invasion of privacy and deprivation of civil rights, they told him the blender was bought at 3 p.m., the furniture at noon, and the neck chains, over a one month period, usually between the hours of ten and two. While he was berating the customer service rep on the phone, he saw an enchanting candle set he just had to have.

Jason forced a smile at his former childhood friend.

"I'm one of the hosts of the show," said Talia through a set of beautifully clenched teeth.

In a second, it hit Satan. "I've bought every unnecessary item in my home from you," he bellowed.

"You don't *have* to buy."

"Explain that to a drug addict."

"Change the channel."

Ion was losing her warm feeling and decided to pop Satan in the gut rather than let it erode any further. "Vinnie, I suggest you shut up and apologize," she said, under her breath.

"Why? I was just—"

Another love nudge. "Do it."

Satan turned to Talia and her color wheel dress. "Although, that's not necessarily a bad thing."

•

Leo Lincoln's round face was redder than usual. His grin was wide, drawn back, showing the best teeth his dental plan could buy. Scattered throughout his home were a hundred people, donning paper hats and blowing paper horns.

But that wasn't why he was smiling.

Most of the guests milling about his garish five-bedroom were either employees from his department or big-time Chicago developers. Hidden in the corner were the two, and only two, representatives from the city's forty-three neighborhood associations. These two had been chosen to receive invites particularly because of their lack of social skills and inherently shy natures.

One of the developers' dates was up on a table doing a very seductive version of "Auld Lang Syne."

But that wasn't why he was smiling.

Leo Lincoln was smiling because he had a foolproof way to destroy Arnolds Aluminum.

Barris stood by the buffet—which he hadn't been more than an arms-length away from all night—stuffing his face with chicken divan and an eggroll as he watched the woman gyrating atop the table.

"Barris..." said Kelsey.

"Yes, dear?"

"Let's go home. I've got a headache."

"You want to leave?" he said, taking his eyes off the woman only a millisecond.

"I have to put up with Leo two hundred and thirty days a year. Another year of that is not something I want to celebrate, especially not *with* him."

"But Kelse, it's almost midnight. We could leave right after." He piled some pizza slices on his plate, then slopped on a helping of beluga.

Looking at his culinary nightmare, she said. "We should have followed Satan."

"Lower your voice, Kelse, the Christians are beginning to stare."

•

Thirty minutes and a few swigs later, everyone had forgotten about the Shop-At-Home confrontation. They were more concerned with the approaching New Year and who they might get to make out with.

"It's time," Ion said, as she danced with Satan, slow. Her breath brushed against his cheek, wistfully. Aside from the brim of her hat, which kept poking him in the eye, it was very romantic.

"It's ten till," he said, feeling a stirring in his pants. It was harder, more engorged, than the one earlier this evening. Because of Satan's limited knowledge, he didn't know that was the way it was supposed to be. He found the pain a tad frightening. He made a mental note to call a doctor in the morning, wondering if this was a precursor to some dreaded sexually transmitted disease. Right after that, he was wondering if they would do it again when they got home.

"Not New Year's. It's time for you to go up on stage."

Satan drew back from her and stared into her azure eyes. He knew this was coming, but he had hoped in all the celebration and confusion and sex, she'd forget.

"I don't think it's such a good thing. These people seem to be having a good time. I wouldn't want to spoil it with a riot."

She ran her hand along his shoulder and down his arm. "You were dying until the riot started, remember that. It saved you." She was pointing around the room. "Look around you, Vinnie. They're wearing foil on their heads."

Satan glanced at the patrons, stared at the hats.

"If I do everything you ask, then will you let me try and get inside?"

She stared at him for a moment. "It would be too much to hope that you were talking about trying to get inside *me*."

From the surprised look on his face, she knew it was.

Ion stroked her hair back over her ear, in deep thought. "I'll see what I can do. But not until this is over."

"Then lead me hither," he told her.

Jason was holding his date close to him while watching Ion. He had never quite gotten over her, but he knew it was for his own good that she had pushed him away. She made it possible for him to be a success. Still, it was always hard leaving the nest.

"Ladies and gents, listen here," a man said after the band hit their last note, and the crowd's applause had died down. The man was the owner of the club. He stood several inches shorter than six feet, his balding crown covered by a hat. "We'd like to welcome back to No Mo' Blues…a man of some distinction. He gave us quite a time last week, babies, and livened up our little Christmas Eve…"

Satan still had no idea how he had caused the mayhem seven days ago… which bothered him since he didn't know what not to do this time to cause it again.

"…let's give a cool, funky welcome to none other than…Satan."

The crowd threw up its hands and started screaming. In the back, they began stamping their feet and shouting his name. Not the reaction he had expected—which was somewhere between stone silence, airborne vegetables, and just plain stones.

Satan stepped to the mic.

"Hello, my name's—"

"SATAN," screamed the crowd.

"Right, right." He gave a nervous laugh. "I see a lot of you wearing our hats." He smiled, looking around. Several people were waving their hats in the air. "I'm, I'm glad. But this is just the beginning…here. You're the genesis of a new way of thinking. A new way of living. Protecting ourselves from space-borne radiation is only the first step. Television, computers, radios, credit checks. These are our next targets. From there, we make our quest to find—"

There was some clapping that grew into enthusiastic applause. Ion took this moment and stepped up to the foot of the stage. Tugging on Satan's pants, she got his attention.

"Cut it."

"But it's going well."

"All the more reason. Mention the publicity tour, then cut it." She drew her hand across her throat.

With a sigh, he shook his head and went back to the mic. He ended by saying several thank yous and telling the crowd to watch for his upcoming talk show dates.

As Satan was stepping off the stage, the owner grabbed the mic.

"Hey, man, that's cool. Let's give Satan a hand."

The crowd acknowledged Satan with a rowdy round of applause. Several of the guys slapped him on the back as he made his way through the mass of bodies. A few women smiled as he passed. For a moment, a tingle rushed up from his toes through his body to the front of his forehead. Entering Ion's warmth had given him almost the identical sensation, and although being overwhelmingly accepted by the mob that had nearly stoned him to death exactly one week ago was a wonderful and triumphant moment for him, this feeling was nowhere as intense as the one Ion had given.

Satan wanted to feel her again.

•

Barris was having trouble finding Kelsey's coat. He had come back twice already. "Did you wear the blue coat?" "Black," Kelsey answered the first time. "You sure you didn't come with the blue coat?" he asked the second. "My coat is black, Barris."

Unfortunately, with Barris gone, Kelsey had become the target of a couple of the developers hoping to score a little midnight cheer. She was almost glad when Leo came over to save her.

"Ah…my, my. Very nice." Leo looked her over.

"Listen, Leo, I showed up. I've fulfilled my obligation. Now, leave me alone."

"You know when you talk like that, I almost want to get on my hands and knees and be your slave."

"Unless you'd like to see me vomit all over the creme de mint, I'd go bother some other female."

"Just making sure my favorite subordinate is happy," he said, giving a wink to one of the developers who passed behind Kelsey.

"Leo, how many sexual harassment complaints have been filed against you?"

Twelve was the answer, but he decided to ease up. Thirteen was a very unlucky number. "I saw that you checked out the Renaissance Village plans," Leo said.

"I'm suggesting changes."

"What for?"

"Maybe you should spend less time in the closet with Miss Venizio and more time in your office reading memos." She looked at his red little face. The pleasure she got from saying the next few sentences was nearly sinful.

"Arnolds Aluminum is raising capital to refit their stacks. They filed for permits on Tuesday. That means the plans have to be revised to put all the parking underground. That means your friends will have to go really deep." She accented the last word to tease Leo, but he wasn't thinking about sex. He was thinking that being unable to obtain the Arnolds land would double the cost for the parking structure. Plus, having Arnolds there…

"What are you talking about?" Leo was beginning to sweat. The developers were waving him over.

"All those nice folks are going to look out and have to see that ugly factory from their bedroom windows."

Barris came out of the back hall with a blue coat in his arms and a stupid look on his face. Kelsey knew when to make a perfect exit. She snatched the coat, whose ever it was, then grabbed Barris, and marched them both out the door.

•

"Well, it's almost that time, babies. One more minute and this year is *history,*" said the club's owner.

The crowd screamed its approval, which it did every year. It seemed most people were happy enough to let the old year slip away, hoping the next would be better. Only by the end of next year, everyone would be doing the same thing, which made one wonder if life wasn't just a maze and people the rats chasing cheese that someone kept moving farther and farther away. There was a theory Albert Einstein had been fooling around with at a party in New Jersey in 1956; that if just one person in the world were sad to see the old year go, maybe time wouldn't be so quick to do so. But he had a bit too much to drink that night and got his picture taken with Marilyn Monroe, and he forgot to tell anybody.

"You did great, Vinnie." Ion pulled him close, their bodies warm against each other.

"Eleven, ten, nine…" the crowd was chanting.

"I'm really proud of you."

"…seven, six, five…"

"Ion, I…I really want you to know…"

Their lips were moving closer, closer toward Satan's first New Year's Kiss.

"…three, two…"

"I love…"

"…one…"

"…you."

At the exact second that the old year was about to give way to the new year, and his lips were to touch her lips, Peter Marks and his exhausted creative team were just pulling into the driveway of the Brisker home, Barris was standing in Leo Lincoln's driveway about to get his *last* New Year's Kiss from Kelsey, Kenny Odorman was squatting outside Clearwater Sanitarium, wondering if he should check himself in to get closer to Dorobek's mother, Vlady was wondering why he was having so much bad luck, Jimmy Hoffa was downing a pint in the sewer wearing his newly acquired hat, Armand Arnold was getting his first goodnight's sleep in six months, although if he only knew what Leo was planning…and the Food King manager/maniac was thinking about cleaning the wax out of his ears.

It just so happens it was also the very second that Lilly from the Salvation Army store decided to show up, and throw a monkey wrench—a used one—into the works, ruining Satan and Ion's kiss.

"Hi," she squeaked, pushing her Coke-bottle glasses up higher on her nose. "I thought I might find you here."

Satan was staring at Lilly, trying to come up with some way to get rid of her, hoping that the shoddy ceiling of No Mo' Blues might give way and crush her, when Ion pulled away from him and began kissing men in the crowd at random.

Lilly stood on her toes and planted a wet smooch on Satan's lips.

"Happy New Year," she said, glancing down at the champagne-and-beer-moist floor, shyly.

When Lilly Anne Rose first laid eyes on the tall, odd-looking man in her shop, she had fallen madly in love. Never mind that she didn't know the first thing about him. He just seemed like the kind of man she could spend the rest of her life with.

Lilly was twenty-four and given to such flights of fancy on the average of one a week. Only, the men she normally pined after always turned out to be gay. Not many straight men came into the thrift shop—mostly women and gay men. Straight men always seemed to buy their clothes at full price, she reasoned.

The man had entered her shop a little after three in the afternoon. She was going to close up early because of the holiday, but several of her fag regulars had convinced her to stay open. New Year's was a big bash and tons of people would wait to the last minute to pick up something funky to wear for the evening, they hissed at her.

And they had been right.

But by two, Lilly was growing tired and wanted to get home and eat, and maybe settle down with a nice romance novel for the rest of the afternoon and evening.

Although she thought about men all the time, and re-read the nastiest sections of her novels over and over wishing someone would do those things to her, Lilly was, without a doubt, a virgin. And a lonely and frustrated, yet imaginative virgin at that.

Once, she had been naked with a boy, the paperboy, back in eighth grade, but he was too nervous to do anything and kept saying he had to get back to his route. Since moving on her own after graduating magna cum laude from Smith College—no boys there—she had opened the door of her Chicago flat several times without clothes on, but the mailman, the Federal Express man, and the UPS man always seemed to have a time constraint, and ran off before she could invite them inside…so to speak.

But this one—Satan, the woman called him—he was attainable. As soon as she saw Satan and the woman he'd come in with, she knew they weren't boyfriend and girlfriend. The tone the woman used was more like a teacher to her pupil.

"Try this one," she said. "Try that…no, not that, how about this. Hmmm. More something like the first thing with the feel of the second," the woman said.

Lilly went up to them and asked if she could help. After that, she followed him around the store, thinking how wonderful he'd look in a suit and tie, and how great he'd be in bed.

Satan sneered at the squeaking woman. Not six days into the plan, and already he had groupies. He had tried to imagine what Wayne Newton would do in this situation, then decided that was too disgusting. That's when he came up with the idea of sneering in her direction.

She thought he was smiling at her.

"It's Lilly, from the thrift store," she said to remind him.

"I know who you are."

"Really?" He remembered her.

The sneer wasn't working. He tried a scoff.

"What are you doing here?" he scoffed.

A gay man whirled by her. "Lilllllieee…I luuuv thissss thang," he said, pirouetting with his foil-lined hat outstretched.

"I wanted to see you," Lilly said to Satan, ignoring the man doing Evita to her left. "You look great in that outfit. Definitely better with the black pants."

"Do you mind?" Satan said, wishing he could twinkle his nose and make her disappear.

Out of view, Ion watched from a raised area of the club. Every few moments, she saw Vinnie looking around, presumably for her. She had taken off her hat to be a little less visible. At this distance, with all these people even someone like Ion would be hard to spot.

Jason came up behind her. Talia was across the room talking with some friends she had spotted while making the rounds at midnight. Jason silently observed Ion as she watched her latest project. It was a cool gaze, he thought. Finally, he looked past her to observe Satan himself.

"Does he know your presence is only temporary?"

Ion didn't turn around. She was silent for a long moment.

"Did you?" she said.

Jason shook his head. "Never saw it coming."

"You understand why I do it." Ion turned to face Jason. "If I stayed, he'd always believe the success was because of me. This way, if he makes it, it's his success."

"I'm living proof." There was a hint of acrimony in Jason's voice. "Don't get me wrong…I'm grateful for everything you did. You taught me to maximize my strengths, minimize my weaknesses. You set me on the right path. I owe…everything to you. But I think you leave so you don't have to feel something you can't control."

He stared directly into her eyes. Her face was blank. If she had a reaction to his words he had missed it by blinking. After a moment, Ion returned her gaze to the club below and Satan, who was now frantically attempting to rid himself of the girl.

"I better go get him," she said, reaching out and running her hand along the center of Jason's chest. She allowed her hand to linger a moment, then descended into the crowd.

Jason watched her navigate the mass of humanity, concentrating on the way she walked, the manner in which she swayed. Even now she possessed him, haunted his thoughts, his dreams. Ion was an extraordinary woman.

Beautiful in a way that defied description. As if all the parts, the slender nose, the lithe body, the creamy skin, the perfect ass, the aquatic eyes, the full lips, didn't add up correctly. Added up to something more. With Ion, 1+1+1 equaled 111. She was also smart and sexy and tough. She rescued men and made them into stars. But who would rescue Ion? Who would save her? For eleven remarkable months, he thought it might be him. But as the months turned into a year, he came to realize, it wasn't. She left him for that actor from the Steppenwolf, telling him right before he was about to play the biggest gig of his life—sitting in and blowing the horn with Wynton Marsalis.

Jason had loved her. And sometimes, sometimes like now, he knew he still did.

Jason caught Talia's eyes, and he wondered if his face betrayed any guilt because her smile from across the club became bittersweet.

Satan couldn't shake Lilly no matter how hard he tried. "I am in the midst of a project of great concern to the planet. Please, stand clear."

"Tell me what I can do to help, and I'll do it."

"Scram."

She liked the sound of that. "I'd love to."

"Ion!"

•

As with all things, the night, the year, and the freshly fucked feeling faded into the blackness of the past.

XVI. ALL THAT SIBERIAN JAZZ

The first sun of the new year came in through the broken window and shone on Satan's face. The brilliant light illuminated his bed, casting an eerie shadow on the far wall that strangely enough took on the shape of a man in mirrored sunglasses.

A pigeon escaping the cold flew in and perched itself on the sill, making it appear that the shadow man was lifting a camera and aiming it at Satan. He was about to reach over and tap Ion to wake her up so she could witness this phenomenon, when the shadow moved toward him and whacked him on the head.

.

The four smokestacks rose out of the asphalt on either end of the factory, bedposts for a giant mattress. Ten feet off the ground a pipe drove itself into each of the brick spires, connecting them to the furnaces. A door was located at the foot of the stacks. Once a week the entry was breached, sending tiny clouds of white dust into the atmosphere. Next, a large square truck with a giant hose like some oversized Hoover would back up to the door and vacuum out the soot from seven days worth of foil making.

The trucks came less often since the Safeway chain decided to no longer carry Arnolds products. The stacks were quiet now, idled for the holiday.

Leo Lincoln stood beneath one of the two hundred foot stacks. His shirt was torn after catching on a barb as he climbed over the fence. A slight wound was bleeding red onto his jersey. His coat was undamaged. He had taken it off and thrown it over, knowing the long trench would make it difficult to surmount the obstacle.

Leo held in his hand a simple device. A timer was attached to a battery, which was strapped to a blasting cap. The bomb was identical to the three he had hidden at the foot of the other stacks. Like felling a tree, it would take only one properly placed strike to topple the immense chimneys.

Arnolds Aluminum was dead already, but Leo Lincoln liked to be thorough. He also wanted to send his stubborn friend Armand a message not to stand in the path of progress lest he be run over.

Leo attached the explosives to the base of the smokestack, setting the timer accordingly. Stepping back to look at his handiwork, he was quite pleased, happy in the knowledge he would be successful once more in freeing up land for development as he had for the Sears Tower, the Hancock Center, and the big red office building his department called home.

Ah, the Chicago way.

•

Satan woke up about two hours later to find the pigeon sitting on his nose, cooing at him much in the same way Lilly had last night. The bird didn't seem to notice that it was clawing a human with its feet. It just liked the warmth rising off its perch. For forty-two minutes, Satan stared at the bird and did not move. He was afraid the thing might scratch his eyes out if he were to make any sudden gestures, so he just lay there motionless.

The pigeon's feathers reminded him of the old Irishman who used to live in the house next door, in the Before Time, prior to the Shop-At-Home-A-Thon of Mrs. Strom. The man's gray-white hair appeared soft and fluffy. Once, old McGinty let young Noel touch his head and feel the fleecy strands that stuck to his scalp.

Resting on his nose, the bird's downy feathers looked like McGinty, and smelled almost as bad.

The old man would stink of liquor by nine in the morning. And Noel, who caught a whiff every day on his way to school, was never sure if the Irishman had gone to bed in this state, or was just getting an early start on the day.

Satan noticed a tag halfway down the pigeon's leg. The metal was crimped around the rubbery orange skin just above the joint. Focusing his eyes, he read the queer letters etched in the ribbon. Although he couldn't understand the meaning, the Slavic writing told Satan that the bird on his face had somehow traveled all the way from Russia and survived.

Ion stirred in her sleep, causing the startled pigeon to jolt and fly away. Unfortunately for the bird, it had no idea how broken glass worked in America. On its escape from the room, it flew into a jagged pane, piercing its head, and dropped lifelessly to the pavement, making a faint *thwat*.

A gooey white liquid dripped down the side of Satan's nose.
He passed out at the sight of it.
It was the start of another banner year.

•

Vlady was fiddling around in his bags. They were strewn about Lincoln Park at random as if they had been dropped from the belly of a plane. Clothes and shoes littered the disappearing snow, and a pair of jockey shorts clung to a tree branch.

Ever since giving the dollar away, Lady Luck had bid him *adieu*. Searching for the last six hours, Vlady had come up with nothing. No pigeon, no lucky rock, no autographed Communist Party memorabilia. He knew the pigeon wasn't too happy when he stuffed it in the travel bag just before entering the airport in Moscow, but the rock and the memorabilia weren't as discerning. He stuck his hand through the hole the bird had pecked at the bottom of the valise.

Vlady sat hard on the park bench, getting a pant seat of melting snow. As the cold liquid soaked through his garments to his briefs, he hurled the bag into the air, its contents spilling upon impact.

That rock meant a lot to him. Stupid bird.

He acquired the rock in 1991, early in the year, just a few months before hard-liners kidnapped Gorbachev, attempted a coup d'etat, which lead to the disintegration of the USSR in December 1991. Vlady was in the frozen wasteland above the Arctic Circle in Verkhoyansk—a place where for some unknown reason people actually chose to live—in the midst of hopping military planes on his way to do a story about the dismantling of the Kamchatka listening post on the far eastern coast, when an eight-piece Siberian jazz band hijacked the plane he was on and demanded safe passage to New Orleans.

It was cold.

The military jet sat like a shivering bird in the plummeting temperatures while several bundles of fur attempted to refuel it. It wouldn't be ready to fly for another twenty minutes, if everything went smoothly, which it never did. An Aeroflot ostrich had its nose stuck halfway inside the hanger as it prepared for passenger boarding.

Vlady crouched in the corner of the tiny, drafty terminal, if you could call it that, wrapped tightly in his bomber jacket, smoking an American cigarette he'd bummed off one of the passengers, a Korean doctor on his way to Kiev and the Chernobyl plant for soil testing. Vlady took in a long drag and glanced around the crumbling cement and rusted metal that formed the hanger/terminal. A flock of sheep was milling around on the far end of the building, right next to three head of cattle—probably meant for the local Communist Party chief. There were no ticketing agents or skycaps like he'd seen in O'Hare and Heathrow. In fact, only he and the several soldiers policing the area were in uniform. A set of cafeteria tables greeted the thirty or so travelers, most of whom were dragging boxes and chickens and sacks of belongings.

He checked his watch. Six hours late and counting. He was about to walk out onto the tarmac to ask the bundles of fur when the plane might be leaving, when a soldier came over to him and told him the bad news.

Engine trouble.

The plane wouldn't be fixed for three, maybe four days, and this was the only military flight scheduled out of Verkhoyansk till next week.

Thanking the soldier, Vlady snuffed out his cigarette and stood. He ambled over to the Aeroflot and got the attention of the pilot.

"What is it?" the man said, leaning out his cockpit window annoyed until he saw Vlady's uniform.

"Would it be possible to catch a ride with you? My plane has been delayed for at least three days."

"Of course," said the former fighter pilot. "Climb aboard."

Vlady gave a half-wave half-salute, then walked back to the corner where he'd been sitting and grabbed his dufflebag. That's when he saw the jazz band, eight people, carrying instruments and dragging drum and bass and trumpet cases. No one realized at the time that the reason the group had their instruments out wasn't because they had been practicing on the way over, but that the instrument cases were packed with sawed-off shotguns and dynamite.

Dragging his worn khaki bag up the icy steps, Vlady gave a last look at the scattered house lights of those brave enough, or foolish enough to think they could tame this barren waste. Stepping onto the plane, he caught a whiff of something from the galley. He glanced around the interior at all the faces, then sat next to a young woman, seemingly alone. Lowering himself onto the cushion, he was surprised by the comfort of his chair, in stark contrast to the jump seat provided by the military jet. Even the Spartan, outdated technology of the Aeroflot was a welcomed relief.

The woman, named Sasha, was a brunette, with light brown eyes and smooth white skin. Her lips were full, and pouted slightly when she spoke. During their talk she explained that she was a nurse, here to help pregnant mothers in the area, teaching them what to eat and how to care for themselves, and educating them that they shouldn't not smoke or drink until after the birth of the child, as well as other prenatal tips.

None of which was an easy job. There was nothing to do in Verkhoyansk, *but* smoke and drink and drink and drink.

They spoke for several minutes as the jet doors were closed and the rest of the passengers were seated.

Because Vlady was not a "soldier" soldier, he came in contact with women on a daily basis, unlike the men on the lines whose only female companionship was a local whore, if there were any to be found.

All kinds of women, he met—tall ones, short ones, blondes, brunettes. Mostly, they were secretaries, a couple were radio personalities. Vlady knew them all.

So when he looked at Sasha, he was not looking through the eyes of a man deprived of female companionship, or the feminine touch. Instead, he gazed upon her with the eyes of a man who had never seen such softness. It wasn't necessarily her beauty he was taken with, although she was strikingly handsome, it was more the way her face and eyes and mouth made you feel at ease, comforted somehow.

"So, why are you here with us?" she asked. "And not on your soldiers' plane."

"The engine. Some malfunction. I don't really know, actually." He was watching how her mouth moved when she made the "w" sound and how her tongue flicked when she came across an "l" as in "plane." He hoped they would speak a great deal during the flight.

"Well, I am glad for the company." She had turned away four other men attempting to sit down, for reasons ranging from the way they smelled to the way they leered at her.

"Me, too. Much nicer seats as well."

The jet was taxiing out to the strip of frozen snow and ice that would be the runway. Suddenly, the deafening thrust of the engines shot them back into their chairs as the craft shook and bounced along the airstrip, kicking up a small snow storm. In a moment, the nose of the plane rose up, and the wheels lifted off the tundra. A mechanical whine sounded, then a thunderous creak as the landing gear returned to the safety of the jet's belly.

Five minutes later, he was sure he was in love.

Less than a minute after that, Vlady watched the members of the jazz band open their cases—to play something lively and romantic, he hoped—and pull out six automatic rifles and a dozen sticks of dynamite.

•

Looking up at the four brick and mortar stacks that towered over the factory, Armand Arnold honked the horn to wake the guard at the front gate. He pressed the heel of his hand to the steering wheel until the guard finally stirred. Coming out of his Technicolor dream, into the almost black and white—gray and white was more appropriate—reality of Chicago in winter, the guard was shocked to find anyone needing his assistance. The day workers were off, and the second shift wouldn't arrive till five, an hour later than normal.

"Yes," said the bleary-eyed ex-police officer, who was almost as effective now as then.

"It's me," Armand said. "Mr. Arnold."

The man seemed to register this. "Didn't expect no one to be coming so early. It's jus' bout ten. Somethin' wrong?"

"I wanted to get a head start," said Armand, feeling much more alive than he had in months, and not in the least bit upset by his employee's lack of dedication. Peter Marks and his crazy idea had won him over. So sure was Peter that he guaranteed Arnolds a drastic improvement in sales or he wouldn't charge the company a penny. The only thing that saddened Armand was that now he wouldn't get to fire his good-for-nothing relatives sitting on the board. Worse, they'd try to take all the credit for Arnolds' resurgence.

Armand made his way up the stairs and into his office. He clicked on his desk lamp even though it was bright outside. He went to the side window, the one looking out over the plant, and stared at the massise chimney that rose from the ground just a few feet away.

Down at the base of that chimney, although Armand couldn't see it, a timer moved closer to its destination.

•

Vlady was sitting on the park bench, thinking how a single moment could change the course of an entire life.

"Hey, everybody be cool," said the bass player, standing in the middle of the plane, brandishing what looked to Vlady like a grenade launcher. "We don't want to hurt nobody, man."

"Just be real mellow like, and no one will get pumped full of holes," said the drummer.

Vlady found the speech patterns unusually annoying, especially since the jazz band/terrorists were using American slang poorly translated into Russian.

"What do you want!?!" shrieked one of the stewardesses, obviously absent during the lecture about keeping calm during a crisis so as not to alarm the passengers, but then again, Vlady thought, Aeroflot probably never gave such a class. A tall Slav wearing tiny-lensed wire glasses—the lead singer and piano player—pulled out a piece of paper from which he read:

"We are the members of the band, The Kosaks. We demand that this aircraft be diverted to New Orleans, America, so that we may attend the New Orleans Jazz Fest, and that there be a big white limousine and a thousand screaming fans waiting for us at the airport."

Vlady squeezed Sasha's hand, then pried his fingers loose from her grip.

"Where are you going?" she whispered as he went to stand. "They're hijackers. They will kill you."

The lead singer continued, "And we will kill everyone on board and blow up the plane if these demands are not met."

"See," she said.

"Oh, and we need eight hotel rooms, each with its own toilet—if possible," the singer added.

"These are a bunch of musicians," Vlady whispered back. He thought about that for a moment. "They have no idea what they're doing—look at their shirts, they don't even know how to spell Cossacks—which makes them more dangerous than hijackers. They're gonna get us *all* killed."

He stood, which immediately was taken as a threatening gesture. A grenade launcher, Chinese-made, was stuck in his rib cage.

These guys were more than dangerous, they were stupid.

"Do you realize, that if you fire that at me…you, me, and anyone within ten meters will be blown to bits?"

"Hey, Daddy-O, I know what I'm doing. I used to pop off guns all the time, shooting caribou when I was a kid. No one ever got blown up."

"That's not a gun, that's a grenade launcher."

The bass player, several inches shorter than Vlady and boyish, pulled the weapon toward him, scanning it. "I can't read this."

"It's Chinese."

"Cool."

Vlady glanced past the bass player toward the piano man/singer. "You really want to hijack this jet?" he said, incredulously.

"We don't look serious to you?" said the drummer, looking ridiculous with his bohemian threads and machine gun. A goatee, under his nonexistent lower lip, topped the whole thing off.

"Very serious," lied Vlady. "I just don't think you've thought this thing out, that's all."

"Let *us* worry about the details, man."

Vlady took in a breath and held it for a second. "There's nothing to be gained by scaring the passengers. Have you informed the pilot of any of your wishes?"

"I was getting to that," said the piano man. "Don't rush me, guy."

The piano man sent the lead guitarist to inform the cockpit.

"You gotta gun, soldier boy?"

"I'm a *reporter*, Military Information Office. We don't carry firearms." Another lie. Vlady had a 9mm pistol in his duffle bag, but he figured it was best not to mention that.

"Check him," said the man to his bass player.

"Leave him alone," scolded an old woman. "He's a veteran. You people should be ashamed of yourselves."

"We are doing this," the piano player explained to her, "because nobody in Siberia wants to hear jazz. Russian folk, yes—maybe some Beatles if you can find a bootleg copy. But jazz, no one wants it!"

"We'll listen to some now," offered a middle-aged coal worker hoping to return home safely after a visit to see his mother.

"Too late," sniped the piano man. "You had your chance."

"He's clean, man," said the bass player, more than a little afraid of his weapon at the moment, especially since he had loaded a bunch of bullets into the clip, which, as he recalled, didn't seem to fit all that well. He was somewhat curious what would happen if he tugged on the trigger, would've been even more so if someone else was holding the device.

"What is *jazz*?" asked a woman coddling a chicken in her lap.

"Enough! I want silence."

The guitarist reemerged from the cockpit. "I just told them of our demands."

"And what did they say?"

"They laughed."

The piano man was looking around for someone to kill as an example of his seriousness. Vlady concluded this was a good time to change the subject.

"What kind of jazz do you guys play? American? R&B? Latin?"

"What do you know of jazz?"

"I grew up in Chicago," said Vlady.

The man looked at him mistrustfully.

"We moved there when I was six. Moved back when I was sixteen," he explained.

"Chicago," sighed the guitarist, "That's a great Blues city."

The piano man leered at his guitarist, then sniffed. "There is only one jazz...American."

"I would like to hear some," said the coal miner, optimistically.

"Quiet!"

The bass player stopped for a second as he passed by the coal miner's seat. "Maybe later. Ivan...ah, I mean, ah...*he's* under a lot of stress at the moment, man."

An instant later, Ivan's hand slapped the bass player in the back of the head. "Nice job, *Boris*."

"Sorry."

Vlady had gone back to his seat and was sitting on the arm, his feet dangling in the aisle. He gazed at Sasha for a moment, watching her eyes dart back and forth as they watched his. "Has anyone ever told you, you have the most lovely eyes?"

"Not while being held hostage by terrorists," she said, curling up the sides of her mouth ever so slightly.

His white teeth were revealed when he let a much-needed smile escape. He pushed out his jaw, more square now than when he was a boy, as he held back a chuckle.

The plane hit a small air pocket and dropped for a quick instant, reminding Vlady of the situation and ending his brief interlude of happiness. He turned toward the hijackers.

"Are you aware," he said to Ivan, the singer/pianist-turned-terrorist, "that this plane doesn't hold enough fuel to make it to New Orleans? I doubt with fuel so scarce because of the strikes we've got enough to go much further than our scheduled stopover in Yakutsk, let alone make it outside the USSR. We are going to have to land sometime, somewhere, and wherever that is, we're never going to get more fuel from the Soviets. You probably should have waited to tell the pilots until after we left Yakutsk."

"We probably should have waited to tell the pilots until after we left Yakutsk," the bass player agreed.

Ivan began to see that his foolproof plan was more "fool" than "proof."

"Dammit! And we've been working on some really great tunes," he whined.

•

Armand Arnold was walking through the factory, glancing around at the machinery lying idle. In a little more than six hours, all this would change, the workers would arrive and the switches would be switched and the furnaces would heat up and the foil would be rolled.

But for now, he was alone with only his company to comfort him. He strolled aimlessly around the plant unaware that soon one of the gigantic chimneys would crash through the ceiling directly above him.

•

Vlady was back holding hands with Sasha. The jazz band had settled into a routine: threaten passengers, play a few tunes, then threaten a bit more. Right now, the eight were in the midst of a jam session, filling the compartment with a lively version of an old Louie Armstrong song.

"I'm glad your plane was delayed…but sorry, too," Sasha said, caressing his hand.

"They don't want to hurt anyone. They want a record contract."

He looked past her, out the window and saw the two MIG fighters that had been shadowing them for over an hour. Normally, the sight of rescuers would instill hope, but Vlady knew the military too well; they'd just as soon shoot down a planeload of innocent people as let one hijacker get across the border.

"We'll be fine," he said as reassuringly as possible.

Sasha reached down between her legs and beneath the seat. She opened the top of her bag that lay on the floor, and produced a piece of rock. It was about the size of his fist, a shimmering purple and gold and cobalt blue, completely unlike the gray and white land it had come from.

"Isn't it beautiful?" she said.

Vlady took the rock in his palm. Its weight was heavier than he imagined, reminding him of lead. Only the colorful patterns in the stone appeared to be mineral. Although quite simple in their structure—a few large swatches of purple and gold and blue—the patterns were nevertheless fascinating.

"What is it? It's very odd. Heavy."

"I don't know," she said, in a haunting tone, as if wondering herself. "An old woman gave it to me after I helped deliver her daughter's baby. She kept trying to tell me something about the rock, she was Asiatic and didn't speak Russian."

Vlady placed the stone on the seat arm between them.

"Let's have dinner once we get out of this," he said to her.

"All right, let's," she said a little breathlessly.

Just then a jolt rocked the jet, and the band abruptly ended the tune, dropping their instruments and replacing them with weapons. The co-pilot ran out of the cockpit and up to Ivan.

"We're running out of fuel. We have to land."

"Ahhhhhh," he grunted. "Where are we?"

"Twenty miles from the Chinese border."

Several minutes passed, during which the plane nosedived and the passengers screamed. Finally, the pilots touched down the out-of-gas jet, and brought it to a shaking, shuddering, perilous stop at the end of a short runway located on the edge of a tiny military outpost about sixty meters from the Chinese border. The two fighter planes touched down immediately afterward, and joined the jet at the far end of the strip, boxing it in.

Several thousand Chinese soldiers watched the scene in amusement. They were in a good mood, relatively certain they would get to shoot at someone sooner or later.

"We are the members of the band, The Kosaks. We demand that this aircraft be refueled and allowed safe passage to New Orleans, America, so that we may attend the New Orleans Jazz Fest," Ivan was shouting into a radio mic, once the dust had settled, apparently abandoning his insistence on there being a limo and fans and bathrooms awaiting their arrival…for the moment at least.

"Release the hostages or die," was the response, more or less.

A couple of bursts of gunfire shot over the top of the plane made the point a bit clearer. It had been over an hour since touchdown and Vlady could see several troop transports arriving on the scene, probably from the army base thirty-five miles east of the airstrip. The soldiers climbing out from the trucks looked conventional enough, but Vlady knew they were Special Forces—counterterrorist, he figured. What flagged him were their movements, how they deployed themselves, spreading out smoothly, gracefully like a Russian ballet, without anyone ever giving an order.

"Stay here," he said to Sasha. He stood and went up to Ivan, grabbing the singer's shirt collar. Several guns were pointed at Vlady's throat, but he ignored them. "Don't you get it? They aren't going to give us any fuel or let us take off. No one's going to ever *know* about this. It's not going to be in the paper or on the television, so it doesn't matter how many of us get killed. They're just going to storm the plane and blow *everyone* up."

"Hey, man," said the bass player. "They wouldn't do that, would they?"

Ivan shook his head, indicating that, of course, they wouldn't. He pointed out several sticks of dynamite taped to various parts of the jet. "They try and we all go boom."

"Would you play that one song again," asked the woman with the chicken on her lap. She had grown to enjoy jazz over the duration of the hijacking.

Suddenly, gunfire sprayed the windows of the plane and Vlady found himself diving for the floor. A second later, the exits were blown, releasing the inflatable slides. Screaming passengers clawed their way to the doors trying to escape while three dozen soldiers made it onto the aircraft, sending bullets into the bodies of anything that appeared threatening. The bass player was the first to die, then the drummer, the guitarist, and the rest. The last was the piano man.

Vlady lay still on the floor, the rock a few inches in front of his eyes. A small circle of blood was dripping from his chin onto the carpet. He raised his hand to his face to see where he was bleeding from; he felt no pain, but had heard frontline soldiers tell similar tales as they lost legs and eyes and fingers. Vlady's hand came back with a fair amount of crimson on it. Still, he felt nothing. That's when a drop hit his face from above. Lifting his eyes slowly, he saw Sasha's bloody hand hanging over the arm of the seat. Shattered pieces of a blown out window lay beside her. He looked away, not wanting to see what the exploding glass had done to her pretty face.

In looking away, what Vlady saw was the dying hand of Ivan reaching for the crude detonator under his jacket. Screaming a warning to those still inside, Vlady fled to the nearest exit and leaped through it, sliding down the ramp, several soldiers and a few straggling passengers right behind him. Seconds later, the plane exploded, shattering like Waterford crystal smashing against a marble floor, sending a brilliant plume of fire forty meters into the air.

•

The timer was moving methodically toward its final tick.

Armand Arnold stood beneath the smokestack nearest to the employee parking lot. He was staring at the door at the base of the chimney when he exploded.

"I told you people a thousand times, these things have to be emptied once a week!" Armand screamed at two of his men, who had come in early to get the furnaces started for the nightshift. He was livid. The filter catch was clogged with soot and looked as if it hadn't been cleaned in two weeks. "Do you realize how dangerous it'd be if the vents were to get completely blocked? This place would go up like the Hindenberg."

"The what?" said the younger of the two.

"The Hindenberg," encouraged the older one, "that German rocket ship."

"That's a V-2! I'm talking about the *Zeppelin*," Armand said.

"I wish I woulda been around to've seen *them* in concert."

Armand Arnold stared at the two men and wondered if saving Arnolds was such a good idea after all.

"Get the stacks cleaned before firing up the furnaces."

"Yessir."

•

Forcing himself up from the park bench, Vlady stood and let a moment of dizziness pass. His joints were sore from the cold. Grinding his teeth together to regain control of his emotions, he gathered his clothes off the snow covered ground. With his bags in hand, and a valise slung over his shoulder, he began the aimless roaming which had characterized his first week back in America.

He spat on the ground. A tiny ribbon of steam rose up from the spot where the phlegm contacted the snow, and he wondered what might have been if he'd been able to have dinner with Sasha, wondered how his life could have turned out.

He cursed the sky, and then the pigeon.

His only hope now was that the bird would flap around the city for a week, *then* find its way to the top of the John Hancock building before any of the other homing pigeons winging their way from Moscow did. If the bird went directly to the Hancock, which was a distinct possibility, the organizers of the race would get suspicious, and he'd never get the $2500 prize. He thought he had a sure-fire plan, taking the bird on the plane, but obviously the pigeon had plans of its own.

Vlady wasn't particularly proud that he had tried to cheat. In fact, he felt guilty. He figured God was punishing him with the bird's escape. But the truth was, Vlady needed a break. He needed to find a decent place to live. Twenty-five hundred would go a long way to getting him back on his feet.

The years since the hijacking had not been good ones for Vlady. The crumbling of the Iron Curtain, the dismantling of the Soviet Union, and the political unrest in the reborn Russia made soldiers, even liberal ones, an unwanted commodity. He tried writing for *Pravda* but his tendency for self-censorship didn't fit in with the emerging "free" press, and he was "let go" after two years. Economic anarchy and the unforeseen emergence of ultra-nationalists a few years later only made things worse. Since then he had gone from place to place—too radical for some, not enough for others—until a few weeks ago when he decided to return to that wonderfully free and vibrant place he knew as Chicago, Illinois, America…with its elevated trains and its elevated way of thinking.

Many things had affected his life—his childhood in America, his time in Afghanistan—but he still couldn't help thinking about that day so long, yet not so long ago. The day his life took a left turn at Verkhoyansk. A turn for the worse.

It was an incredible day, one of excitement and fear and courage and sadness…and love. Nineteen people died on the Aeroflot jet that day. The eight members of the Siberian jazz band, ten unnamed passengers…and Sasha Krolnachev.

He was right, no one ever heard of the incident. It never made the papers. In fact, it was six years before he learned Sasha's last name when some old Soviet files were made public by the new Russian government.

And yet, everyone on that plane, and many others who weren't, were victims of that day. Fear and heartbreak spread like wildfire through a drought-stricken plain, and each death had a rippling effect, emanating outward from the moment and the place—a raindrop in a stagnant pool—changing the future forever.

Changing his future.

Vlady trudged across the park, staring down at the grass that peeked through the patches of melted snow, grieving the loss of that rock.

XVII. NEW YEAR'S RESOLUTION

Kafka said every revolution eventually evaporates and leaves behind only the slime of a new bureaucracy.

The Foil Thing hadn't started any mass revolt, yet Ion could sense the slime already queuing up outside the door. Talk shows and tabloid news programs desperate for something—*anything*—different had been calling since Peter Marks issued a press release on the 27th. Talent coordinators on the other end of the line loved the fact that this guy called himself "Satan," which annoyed Ion to no end. And just this morning—New Year's Day, mind you—the Chicago *Sun-Times* phoned to find out what all the hoopla was about. Of course, she hung up on *them*.

The "legitimate" press had a condescending way of making the out-of-the-ordinary seem on the verge of being downright dull.

She had coughed on one person. And now, the virus was spreading like a wildfire. She would have little control over it, if any.

A frigid wind slipped in through the broken pane and slapped her in the face. The breeze made a faint noise like the tinkle of bells, sending a shiver up her spine. It didn't seem cold, although she knew it was. Satan was asleep, his arms wrapped around her, keeping her body warm. Slowly she turned to look at him. His face. He looked so innocent and sweet, his breathing shallow and warm. His left arm that went underneath and around her touched his own face so that the back of his hand rested on his lips.

She stared at him for a long time. Nearly twenty minutes. There was a welt on his forehead and his nose had some scratches on it, and a tiny bit of white mucus had dripped out during the night. She wondered how he had gotten the abrasions and the lump, but she forgot about them after awhile. There was something she felt which she couldn't quite understand. It was warm and melancholy and it sat in her chest like a mug of hot spiced cider pressed against her on a winter day. She had the urge to reach out and touch his face, but it meant leaving the cocoon of his arms…and she didn't want to do that, not now, not just yet.

Instead, she tilted her head and placed her lips softly on his arm, kissing his skin tenderly.

She almost felt like crying. And maybe she did. She was alone. It was her moment. No one else would ever know, would ever see the tears, so maybe it never happened.

She pulled her pretty lips away from his bicep and turned her head so that it lay on her pillow again. She smiled because she was happy. She cried because she had never experience happiness like it before.

So warm and so protected. A simple touch. Not from any man, not from her father, not from Peter or Jason or any of a hundred others. And there had been hundreds.

Not even from that guy that turned out to be a jerk who touched her more than most.

She nuzzled deeper into his grasp and pulled the covers higher.

Just before closing her eyes, the wind whispered through the room, making the noise again. She turned toward the sound to see the foil taped to the top of the window had come loose. She glanced at the nightcap on Satan's head, foil just barely visible through the weave.

An icy look washed over her, and the room seemed somehow colder.

With all the self-discipline she had, and she had a great deal, she blanked out the last few moments. She could not, and would not, give up control, could not give herself over to any man.

Especially not one with foil on his head.

Even if she wanted to.

•

Ion was sitting on the edge of the bed staring at Satan who was still sleeping six hours later. The welt on his forehead had gotten a bit larger and the mucus had dried white. It looked quite sickly, so she wiped it away with the corner of the sheet.

Just having come back from seeing her father in the hospital, Ion was thinking about sex and wondering if a romp with Vinnie might relieve her. Once upon a time it, made her uncomfortable, the thoughts her father sparked, as if it was some sort of sick fascination or repressed incestuous tendency, but now, the years having passed, she understood her passions better. Her dad unleashed these desires mainly because he was such a passionless man, at least about physical things. His work, which she had never quite figured out, seemed to occupy most of his thoughts and time, especially after her mother died. Yet, even before that, he showed only guarded affection, never lust.

After a brief talk with the doctors, where she learned nothing except that they had absolutely nothing to report, she went in to see him. Her father could sit up on his own now, and his physical therapy was coming along quite nicely, although he was giving the nurses hell about still being in the Pediatrics Ward. The ten-year-old in the next bed had been replaced two days ago by a six-year-old who felt the need to scream "Migey Mouuze!" every time any animated creature came on the television screen, which seemed to Ion's father to happen a lot more than he ever imagined.

Once he regained control of the TV remote, he flipped it to CNN, the news channel having very few animated creatures. Of course, he was still worried about Ion's involvement with "That Satan Character," as he had taken to calling Dorobek.

The Bureau had asked him to find out what he could about Dorobek from his daughter, but the screeching six-year-old was paramount for him at the moment. After prevailing over the kid, he turned his attention to her affiliation with Dorobek.

Ion tried to ignore her dad at first, but after the fiftieth mention of "That Satan Character," she told her dad that if he didn't drop the subject, she would leave and never come back. Calling her bluff, he mentioned it a fifty-first and fifty-second time. It was only after she commandeered the controller and threatened to turn on the Disney Channel that he finally gave up.

After that, the conversation went something like this:

"When are they letting you out?"

"Soon."

"I'll have Anna Marie clean up the house for you."

"Why won't you eat red meat?"

"C'mon, Vinnie, let's get up." Ion tugged at his shoulder. "We've got to brush up for the interviews and practice the commercials. C'mon." As he let out a sigh of indignation, she smelled his breath. "Whoa. But first, we're gonna brush our teeth."

"Just five minutes," he mumbled, rolling over and pulling the covers above his chin.

She let out a tiny sigh of her own, then reached down toward the floor.

"Let's go!" she said, after lifting to her lips a bullhorn she had picked up the day before as an impulse buy.

Satan sat up straight in the bed. "Is there a particular reason you have chosen to completely destroy my hearing?"

She moved herself and the device closer. "GET...UP," the words came screaming out of the speaker.

Satan's head gave off a pleasant tone as it vibrated.

"Is this a post-coital ritual you like to perform? Some sort of pain/pleasure thing?"

Ion put the bullhorn on the bed and smiled at him with such mock innocence, he couldn't stay mad at her.

"I've been trying to wake you for forty-five minutes."

"That's because I was smacked in the head by a shadow, further aggravating my concussion."

"I've never seen a bigger complainer in my life. You need to mellow out."

"I am mellow," he said, a little uptight. "I had a pigeon fly in my bedroom and relieve himself on me," he added as if to lend some insight to his behavior.

"You'd complain there was too much happiness in the world."

"Happiness is overrated."

"It's one o'clock. Get over it."

She pushed aside the bullhorn and caressed his head.

It felt good to him, which only momentarily interrupted his worrying.

Satan pushed the two bed pillows against the wall and sat back. The cold January air was passing through the room like a polar wind. He had fired off several angry notes to Niro, his landlord. So far, he had only gotten one response.

> *I receive your note. So sorry, window broken. Cannot replace till weather warmer. Too cold to handle glass.*
>
> Sincerely Your Best Regards,
> *Niromshi Nagasikima*

Satan gazed down at the covers and folded them over a few times. When next he spoke, he didn't look up at her.

"I don't know if I want to go through with this."

"Don't start this. It's a new year. A new beginning. You were a hit last night. They loved you."

"See, that's my point. I have no understanding, for instance, of why they all of a sudden liked me last night, yet rioted the week before? This is a question I need answered."

"They always *liked* you, Vinnie, they just didn't *love* you. People need to warm up to someone like you," she said. "I hated you at first."

"Thank you."

"No thanks necessary. It didn't take any effort on my part."

Satan wondered how the No Mo' Blues' crowd might treat someone they didn't like, then shuddered at the thought.

"This stuff with Arnolds, you're not telling me everything."

In fact, she had told him almost nothing. "You're going to be a star" was about the extent of the specifics divulged to him so far.

"Vinnie, there's not much to tell." Ion kept her eyes lowered. There was a great deal to tell, but she had made the decision to tell him only what he needed to know when he needed to know it and not any more or any sooner.

Satan put his hand on her thigh. It felt warm against his skin. She thought his touch a bit tentative, as if he expected her to push him away. She had to keep reminding herself that he was a sixteen-year-old in this regard. He needed some encouragement, something to build his confidence.

"You were great last night," she said.

"So you've told me."

"No, I mean..." She motioned toward the bed with her eyes.

Satan's heart skipped a beat. He tried to smile and make the most of the moment, but his body rebelled against his will. His muscles tensed up and his pulse quickened until he was dizzy and lightheaded. Just that little glance at the bed sent him into a tailspin. He was not completely surprised by this reaction, but he expected a bit more from himself. Because last night, he didn't feel this way. He performed as well as he could have hoped. Perhaps better. He was nervous, yes, but he wasn't afraid. Maybe not afraid, maybe that was too harsh a word for what he felt now. It was more like apprehension. He looked into her eyes. Her beautiful eyes. No, it *was* fear. He felt fear. Paralyzing, agonizing fear. What was wrong with him? He did it last night. Did it well enough, he thought. But then he had no fears of failing last night because he *knew* he would fail. Failure was not something he needed to worry about. It was bound to happen, so why care about it? But since he succeeded last night, now he cared. He had tasted victory's sweetness. Defeat would seem only that much more bitter now.

So, in the end, he decided to punt.

"I feel lost. I still wish you'd let me continue my search for the Inner Earth."

Ion was thinking about sitting on his cock when the words hit her brain. She exploded. "Vinnie, there is no Inner Earth! Do you understand!?!"

Failure had been averted. Only now that the chance of being in bed with her again was gone, he was thinking how nice it would feel.

She tried to calm herself. She brushed his hair with her fingers unconsciously. "Vinnie, you do this, do everything I say…and you'll be able to seek your Holy Grail. You'll have the money and the resources to go to both poles if you want and see for yourself. But you have to listen to me. And you have to be the person I've seen when you're alone with me. Strong, clear, intelligent." She paused. "You can say anything you want, as long as you sound credible."

Satan put his hands behind his head and glanced out the broken window toward the north. What Ion didn't seem to understand was that he didn't mind all the things that were happening so much as he minded them happening to *him*. If there were a way to lead everyone without actually having to give his name, he would be all for her schemes. But it didn't seem to work that way. Satan could wait a while longer and postpone his search for his father and the way Inside, but he couldn't take much more of this being on display.

A small stone came hurling through the window, bouncing on the floor and coming to rest against the wall behind the creaking door.

"Hey, man, anybody home?" said the voice belonging to Slag.

Seconds later, a large rock landed in the middle of the floor with a THUD.

"Hey, yo, anybody there?"

Satan glanced at the small boulder, then at Ion. "I really need to get Niro to fix that window."

Ion got up, walked to the window, and was nearly pegged by another rock. She ducked, letting it fly past, then leaned out.

Slag's covered head was tilted upward, the videocam tucked under his arm.

"It's open, Slag."

"You keep your doors unlocked?" he said, informing the whole neighborhood. "Cool."

"You left my door open?" Satan asked, wondering what had been stolen in the interim.

Pulling her head back in, "You won't let me make a Goddamn key, remember?"

"I told you...I don't trust that guy at the hardware store."

"Well, now you gotta trust your whole neighborhood."

Downstairs, the door opened and closed. Heavy footsteps made their way to the second floor. Finally, Slag appeared in the doorway, the Sony aimed at Satan.

The poet was mumbling something. "...about to begin his quest for longer life and better foil," Slag told the camera's microphone.

"I think we need to discuss this lock problem," Satan said to Ion. She glared at him hard, so he turned his attention toward Slag. "Turn that damn thing off before you need a crew cut."

•

After showering and getting ready, Satan went downstairs to the living room. As he was descending the steps, he found that the room housed not only Slag, Ion, and several recruits, but two new people he'd never seen before. One was a thin, spindly man Satan vaguely remembered seeing on the wall in the Post Office, but introduced himself as someone from "the *agency*."

"Before you get all fucking daft, that's the *ad* agency," Ion whispered in his ear, allaying only some of his fears about government spies.

Wearing horn-rimmed glasses that he kept adjusting, the agency man was dressed in expensive clothes from the finest shops. But the fabrics were slightly wrinkled and he accessorized them with Nike sneakers.

Someone had moved Satan's pile of bills. The massive stack no longer looked like the Chicago skyline. Actually, it reminded Satan of the Liberty Bell, which immediately gave him a headache as he remembered Kenny Odorman tossing a brick at the national monument while young Noel was secretly exploring inside it.

He heard the chewing of gum and glanced to see a woman he did not know sitting in the lotus position in front of the idle fireplace. As she poured over a pile of papers, she was droning on about liability insurance and signing this and initialing that.

Ion was staring at the woman, thinking:

The Slime had arrived and was drinking tea in Vinnie's living room.

"Vinnie, these two are gonna brief you on what you need to know. And how you should handle the interviews," Ion said as calmly as possible under the circumstances. She hated the mundane, bureaucratic side of success. She stood and straightened out the rips in her jeans. "I'll be back in a few hours."

"What do you mean, you'll be back in a few hours?" he said. "Where are you going?"

"See ya," she said, waving to everyone in the room. Quickly seizing the door handle, she was outside in a flash, leaving the window curtains to billow as she swiftly slammed the door behind her.

Satan glared at the faces staring hungrily back at him. He understood what Christians must have felt like in Rome.

•

The television screen flickered its blue light in the room. A second of darkness was replaced by the smiling face of a woman as she stood in her perfectly manicured kitchen, meticulously preparing several school lunches.

"If you're like me..." the housewife said, her eyes directed past the boundaries of the screen toward her unseen audience of millions. "...you worry a lot about your kids. You want only the best for them."

A young blond-headed boy came into frame and pirated one of the cookies laying out on the counter. The woman chuckled and mussed her son's hair.

"That's why I not only want my family to have the freshest lunches possible..." She folded a length of aluminum foil over one of the sandwiches, then released a longer sheet from the Arnolds Aluminum box. "...I want them to enjoy a long and healthy life." The housewife wrapped the giggling towhead in a metal turban.

Like a tornado, her husband rushed into the kitchen, his head covered with the shiny metal, gave her a quick kiss, then grabbed his lunch and left for work.

"That's why I trust Arnolds," said the woman.

The smiling boy pulled a winter hat over the foil as his mom dropped a sandwich in his lunch bag. Then, showing her pearly whites, she dropped a couple of extra cookies into the bag.

"Arnolds..." she said, sending her son on his way. "...the All-Purpose Aluminum. I can protect their lunches from getting stale and their heads from getting fried—"

There was a scream very much like a baby being tortured.

"No, no, no, no!" howled Peter Marks as he came out of his crouch and walked in front of the camera.

A collective sigh was heard from the crew; it was the sixty-fourth time Peter had cut into the commercial. The key lights were dimmed and the camera assistant removed the spent High-Definition tape magazine from the top of the VTR and set in another.

"...getting *fried*?" Peter said, not at all pleased. "What is *that*? We're not talking about eggs here. Did you read this thing?" He pointed at the script. "Tell me where it says that. I want to see it."

The woman's smile disappeared. "I was using dramatic license."

"I'm not paying you for dramatic license. If I had *wanted* a dramatic interpretation, I would have hired Meryl Fucking Streep!"

The towheaded boy came pouting to Peter. "She hurt me."

"What?" he snapped.

"She hurt me when she put on the foil."

Peter Marks bent down to the kid's level.

"For the last time, Billy...Shut your little trap! You're getting paid more than all of your teachers, so quit your whining."

"I'm gonna tell the union," he said.

"Go ahead...and you'll be washed up in this business before you get out of the third grade."

The boy's mother stopped flirting with one of the lighting guys long enough to come to her son's defense, albeit too late.

Peter Marks put up his hand as she was about to say something. "I don't want to hear it, lady. Like I told your meal ticket here, shut up, or I'll get ten other kids in here who'd be happy to replace him...for half the price."

Billy was looking a little pale, having devoured more than five dozen cookies over the three hours of trying to nail down this scene.

Peter Marks blew out a lung full of air. "All right. Shall we try it again?" He glanced at the housewife, who was getting her makeup retouched. "'...keeps the gamma rays out...and the *freshness* in.' Spreiken zie Inglesh?"

Twenty-five takes, two dozen cookies, and one pail of vomit later, Peter Marks had his commercial.

•

The Clearwater Sanitarium was situated along an unusually quiet street in the far north end of the city, in the poorer, extremely diverse section known as Uptown. The streets were littered with papers and Styrofoam fast food containers much like leaves cluttering suburban streets in fall. The debris sprinted across the street as the wind kicked up, slowing and accelerating as the cars broke the breeze as if the litter were intelligent creatures worried about self-preservation.

On a set of low stone steps, suffering from a mild case of exposure, his teeth clattering in the near zero degree temperature sat Kenny Odorman, the source of most of the fast food litter. For a week and a day, he had spent all his spare time staking out Clearwater in the hopes of finding some information on the whereabouts of his old nemesis, Noel Dorobek. So far, all he had gotten was a lousy cold.

He sneezed.

"God Bless you," said Father Leery reflexively, knowing immediately, he had made a mistake.

Kenny searched the area around the stoop on which he sat. The sound seemed to come from right next to his ear, but no one was anywhere near him. A couple of Hispanic children were playing down the street, much too far to have offered the blessing. There was a small band of Irish thugs a block away stealing his hubcaps and car stereo that, unfortunately, he couldn't see.

Kenny faked a sneeze. "Ah-chew."

Father Leery bit his lip and didn't say a word. He tried not to breathe or move, but he could only hold his breath a few seconds before turning red, then blue, and had to let it out.

Kenny studied his surroundings more closely and realized to his surprise that for the past week he had been perched on the steps of a church. A white marble Jesus stood directly behind him and he wondered if he was going mad or if the stone figure had wished him well. He came to the conclusion that it hadn't simply because if it had, the statue would have said something more like "*I* Bless you."

Father Leery could see the man through one of the decorative keyholes in the church doors. He'd been watchful of the stranger for nearly a week now. Every day at five-thirty five, the man would appear and set himself down on the steps of the church with a bundle of papers and a half-dozen bags of fast food. Father Leery knew the deterioration of the neighborhood which had miraculously skipped this block could no longer be kept at bay with prayers and the sight of a cross overhead. Although he hadn't seen any transactions actually taking place, the Father feared this man was a lookout for drug dealers.

Father Leery's eyeball was beginning to freeze up as the frosty Lake air rushed through the keyhole. He had been praying the last five days for guidance in this most grave matter. Each night as part of his evening prayers, he asked God for an answer to this problem. A line had to be drawn; a line made across this street. He had to make a stand for his neighbors—a simple "No" to the pushers and addicts, a safe haven, a small act of faith.

He knew…a journey of a thousand miles begins with just one step.

When last night God finally answered his prayers, Father Leery was somewhat startled by His wisdom.

While Kenny Odorman was contemplating whether or not to stake out the Clearwater any further, Father Leery crept up behind him. Kenny was thinking, maybe it was time to give up his childish ways and let bygones be bygones. It was at about this time that the Father clubbed him in the side of the head with a solid brass staff topped off by a gold cross.

Father Leery stood over the man that lay motionless on his steps. He felt a pang of guilt and a rush of excitement all in the same instant. God had never given him so important a task; the power was surging through his veins. Like an old pro, the Father nodded to the two altar boys standing in the open doorway. The boys dutifully jumped into action and dragged the man down into the church basement.

•

Satan sat in the chair trying not to slip off and tumble to the carpet, which he found was more like gravel in its properties than anything else. Peter Marks was standing behind a bank of monitors watching him. A woman seated next to Satan was pretending to be any one of a dozen talk show hosts. Right now, she was doing her best Oprah impression.

"We're gonna run through this a few times, so don't get nervous if you screw up at first." The voice was unmistakably Peter Marks', but it came off somewhat ominous because he could only be heard, not seen. "Now, look into the camera."

Satan tipped the chair to the left farther than it was designed to until he could see a sliver of Peter Marks behind a bank of monitors. Peter had retreated there in the hopes that if Satan couldn't see him, he might, just might, look into the camera. Instead, all that was visible was the side of Satan's head.

Where is Ion?" Satan asked.

With a heavy sigh, Peter Marks emerged from behind the monitors, walked up to Satan and kneeled in front of the man.

"I know this is difficult for you, but you must understand. The camera is your friend. It is your lover."

Satan glanced up at the camera, thinking 'what a sick thought.'

"You want an answer. You have to talk to me, the audience. Here." Peter Marks twisted to the camera, his faced becoming very pleasant. "Where is Ion?" he said, with a warm smile.

Peter stood and made his way back behind the monitors. "Now, you try it. Into the camera."

Satan looked deep into the single eye of the lens as if it were Peter Marks. "Where is Ion?"

"I have no idea," said the disembodied voice.

•

In the middle of Grant Park, between the Field Museum and Soldier Field, a pool of frozen water had been created for the purpose of ice skating. The huge Lake rarely froze and when it did, it was hardly safe for skaters, even though there were always those who would attempt it. One year, after two young boys were lost in the icy deep, the city decided to set up this rink in the park to give Downtown folks a place to skate for free.

The hundred or so people on the ice when Ion arrived were a mix of all ages, sizes, and shapes. Older couples, young lovers, bands of kids slaloming in and around the more conservative, tiny children slipping and sliding and looking very much like they were learning to walk all over again.

Slung over her shoulder were the pair of white skates Ion bought her last year in college. The blades clanked together noisily as she strolled toward the rink. The skates hadn't been used all that much since school, but she kept the blades well-oiled when she packed them up each Spring in a box with her winter jacket and ski pants.

Ion seated herself on a chilly wooden bench beside a man and woman in their late 70's who were taking a break. The man smiled at Ion sweetly as she undid the laces on her shoes, pulled up her drooping socks and slipped into the skates. Once she had tied them up, Ion smiled back at the couple and made the short, wobbly walk from the bench to the ice.

The first few passes she was rusty, this being her first skate of the season, but after a while, her old form came back and soon she was gliding across the frozen surface as gracefully as a bird in flight. A sharp, biting wind blew over the ice, sending the last little bits of snow scattering for cover. Green patches were more prominent than white in the park, but the air had grown colder so that yesterday's damp ground crystallized and crunched under the weight of human steps.

It didn't take long for Ion to spot the thick glasses and bowed head of the person she had come to meet.

Lilly made her way across the brittle grass, taking only a minute to change into her skates after reaching the rink. As soon as she was finished, she stood and jumped on the ice.

"Hi," she said, coming up to Ion who was skating backwards.

"Lilly, stand up straight. Your posture is horrible. You look like the poster child for osteoporosis. If you were sixty, I'd be giving you a fucking calcium tablet every six minutes."

"Okay," Lilly said, pushing her glasses higher on her nose.

"And stop fucking with your glasses! It's annoying."

"Sorry."

Lilly's skeletal and optical imperfections had been harassing Ion for nearly twenty-four of her twenty-six years, ever since her mother's brother's wife gave birth to the girl.

"I told you I thought you might like to meet this guy. I didn't say *rape* him."

Lilly glanced at her cousin as she pushed up the glasses once again, thinking about something that had been puzzling her for two days. "Have you slept with him?" she asked.

The answer was always "yes" to that question. Lilly had never heard Ion answer anything but yes when faced with a query on any aspect of the subject of sex. Either Lilly was incredibly observant, or her cousin was incredibly loose.

"What kind of question is that?"

"A simple one, I think," Lilly said, watching a group of guys bothering a pretty co-ed wearing a U of I, Chicago sweater, wishing some guys would bother her sometime. The co-ed, who seemed annoyed by all the attention, was younger than Lilly, although it appeared the opposite was true.

"That's not an issue here," said Ion.

"So you did have sex with him then."

A little kid went skating through Ion's legs as she gave Lilly an exasperated sigh.

Lilly had never witnessed Ion being this evasive before. It was something to see. "Did you have sex with him or not?"

Ion sucked in a breath of air, the cold burning her lungs. "Yes! Are you happy, now?"

"Not really. It's not my first choice to have one of your hand-me-downs," Lilly said, adjusting her frames, "but I guess I'm desperate." She was pondering whether or not to "accidentally" expose her breasts to the guys hassling the co-ed. Maybe they'd bother her if she did. Unfortunately, Lilly couldn't figure out how to make taking off four layers of clothing look like an accident.

"Just you..." Ion wasn't sure why she had started the sentence or where the original thought was going, but she covered for the gaffe. "Just you treat him right."

"I will. I told you...I like him." Lilly's tone was sincere. She shifted from one blade to the other as she came around the outside of a figure 8 she was forming. "I liked him the moment you brought him into the store." She scrunched up the right side of her face. "Does he have Major Medical?"

Ion shot a hard glance at Lilly as she skated by, but most of her mental attention was focused on the near future, making sure everything went smoothly. She didn't have time for her cousin's stupid questions. Vinnie was on the verge of a major leap in terms of personal achievement. In less than a month, she had helped bring to flower what was once a paranoid, social outcast. In its place, a living, breathing, somewhat functional human had emerged. A misfit had become a person.

"Lilly...shut the fuck up."

"I was just asking. I don't want him dying on me."

Ion always left an escape route for herself. When the time came, she introduced her project to another woman. It made her departure less painful for them. Less complicated for her. These women didn't replace her, no one could do that. Sometimes her projects resisted at first, but it was amazing to witness how quickly a properly chosen surrogate could soothe the male ego and divert the masculine mind.

With all the change she induced in others, Ion remained constant. Even with all her beauty and charm, Ion was a misfit herself. A misfit who was unwilling or unable to share in her own successes.

She didn't enjoy being a bitch, but it was the only way she knew to inoculate herself, especially the closer she got to leaving. She tried to keep acting the playful ingenue, but like a star swirling downward toward a black hole, unable to escape its grasp, she was powerless to do so.

Skating with her hands on her knees, Ion moved in closer to her cousin who was staring down at the ice as she began tracing a new pattern.

"I want you to understand...I'm trusting you with something very special."

"Is he good in bed?"

"Lilly..." Ion forced the word through a clenched jaw. "You can fuck him all night and day, on the fridge, under the table, in the sink if you want, as long as you understand one thing." She paused until she was sure she had Lilly's attention. "The thing that makes him a genius is that he's whacked out of his head."

The girl stared blankly at Ion.

"Do you understand?"

Lilly didn't really, but she nodded anyway.

"He starts thinking he's *normal*, and he's done for," Ion added with finality.

She raised out of her tuck and pushed off on the sides of her blades, skating quickly around the outer edge of the rink. Her legs churned and her arms swung across her chest. There was a dull pain in her heart like the kind you get when your dog dies or you leave something valuable in a hotel room a thousand miles away. It was the enveloping feeling of claustrophobia when you hear of someone very much like yourself passing the Bar, earning their Masters, climbing to the top of a mountain, or purchasing a bigger home, knowing the more that time passed, the less likely you'd ever do any of these things.

That was how it felt in Ion's chest. The feeling of loss.

It would only grow stronger, more painful the closer it got to quitting time—the day she would have to leave Vinnie and let him fly on his own.

A tear escaped from her right eye and nearly froze halfway down her cheek.

XVIII. OF PAINTED HORSES AND EXPLODING CIGARS

Armand Arnold was sitting at his desk when the news came in: orders in the Chicago metro area were up nearly sixty percent. That wasn't all that much foil, sixty percent in such a limited area, but the astonishing thing was that the numbers were going up rather than down. For years, he had gotten used to watching the numbers get smaller and smaller to where he sometimes wondered if it was worth all the trouble of dealing with people like Leo Lincoln and his half-witted relatives. But here it was, in black and white, a sliver of good news for a change. Some of the stores were even reporting a three hundred percent jump in Arnolds' sales.

Sonofabitch, he thought to himself, Peter Marks was right.

A copy of the order requests sat on Armand's desk. He didn't seem to want to touch the pages for fear that they might crumble and disintegrate. His shipping foreman stood on the other side of the desk and assured him this wasn't a joke. The burly German told him that filling these new requests would reduce the stockpile the company had built up when sales were sluggish enough that they might even have to increase production if the trend continued. Armand was so happy that he grabbed the man and kissed him on the bridge of his nose, which immediately made the foreman wish he hadn't personally brought the good news. He dreaded telling him the even better news.

The foreman took several steps back toward the door. "Oh, and Safeway decided to stock us again."

Armand Arnold burst into song, something from Rogers and Hammerstein, and the foreman was glad he'd moved away.

After the foreman had left, Armand sat back in his old worn out chair, elbowing one of the broken springs back into place, then put his feet on the desk and his hands behind his head. With the heel of his shoe, he expertly hit the switch on his intercom and summoned his secretary.

"Tina," he said once she answered, "make out an order for a new chair."

"Right away, Mr. Arnold," said the woman over the speaker. "But you know what they're gonna say."

"I've got a feeling this time, Tina. A wonderful feeling."

"Of course, Mr. Arnold," the woman's tone indicating she was convinced this time would be no different from the previous ten. "I'll get it out today."

"And get me Peter Marks on the phone. I think we should celebrate."

"Yessir."

Armand spun his chair around and gazed at the giant stack outside his window, which reminded him of a cigar. He flipped open the lid of his empty cigar case. His mouth watered a little, thinking about biting off the tip of a nice fat Cuban and lighting up.

·

"Excuse me..." said the man on the street below, "what're you doing up there?"

"Contemplating my future," bellowed Satan. He stuck the bottle of Caffeine-Free Diet Cherry Coke under his nose and took a sniff. Raising the glass, he drank noisily, making the sound of a plugged drain after a few minutes alone with Liquid Plumber. "Go away."

"Are you all right, Mister?" asked a woman who had stopped after noticing the man on the sidewalk gazing toward the heavens.

"If you would leave me alone, I would be."

"He don't look fine," the woman said to the man on the sidewalk.

"No, he doesn't," agreed the man.

"You alright, Mister?"

"Do I appear to be all right? I think it's safe to assume that anyone sitting atop a billboard in the middle of Chicago in January cannot be considered *all right*."

Satan was leaning against a billboard that touted the benefits of smoking on ninety-three percent of its surface area while warning of the dangers to life, lung, and unborn baby on the remaining seven percent. He had climbed up here to escape, but these horribly good Samaritans were obviously not about to let him.

"Would you people just leave me alone!" he shouted at them both, in much the same way he had yelled those words at the people on the soundstage.

Peter Marks and his merry band were appropriately shocked. They were even more surprised when he then stood and rushed off the stage. They had invaded his home, then dragged him down to the agency. For more than three hours, communication specialists and ad whiz kids had been drilling him on questions and answers, how to look into the camera, what to say if someone challenged his beliefs, et cetera, et cetera, et cetera. This was not what he had in mind when he agreed to promote Arnolds Aluminum. He *did* have something to say, but he wanted it to be *his* words, not some moronic drivel thought up in committee in the dark hollows of an ad agency cellar—responses based on market research and consumer testing.

Wandering the streets, he realized he couldn't go home, some recruits were "upgrading his server." And even if they weren't, that would be the first place Peter Marks would look. There was something very strange about having to flee your own home. He was a refugee. An American refugee. He wondered if Canada would grant him asylum.

And yet it was not just the indignation of being told what to do and what to say. There was something else at work here. An emptiness as deep as space, an uncontrollable tenseness that ran throughout his body. He knew what it was, but refused to recognize its presence until it all but paralyzed him. In the beginning, he thought it was fear. He *was* afraid…of many things, not the least of which was sitting on stage while the likes of Oprah and Sally and Montel and Jerry and Jenny pounded him with questions. But that wasn't it. It had to do with the thin, pale blonde that he'd fatefully bumped into in the pen and pencil section of Clancy's Drugs.

He was in love with Ion. He knew that, even though he didn't quite know what that meant, exactly. An odd thought crossed his mind: It hurt. It hurt dreadfully to love her. There was a sharp, formless pain just below his ribs that wouldn't go away and only got worse the more he accepted his feelings. It didn't make any sense, no one had warned him about this. Love was *supposed* to be a good thing. So why did he feel so awful?

"He gonna jump?" asked a second man, hopefully. A friend of his had witnessed somebody jumping from the top of the Wrigley Building a few years back. His friend said it was a horrible sight. Still, the man, smoking hard on the very same brand of cigarette being hawked on the billboard above, had never seen anything horrible—except his wife of thirty years after a few drinks and not enough sleep—and he hoped he'd see something of it now.

"You think so?" said the woman. "Oh, dear Lord."

"Maybe I should call the *police*," the first man said, half to the woman and half into his lapel.

"I guess," said the second, a little disappointed he might not get to see the conclusion of this situation. He was a black man, and black men and police didn't mix very well, even old ones like himself. Seemed like the police were always finding black folks doing something wrong, even if they were just trying to see something horrible happen.

Satan watched as the three people below were joined by a fourth, a cabby who pulled over to the littered curb after seeing the three staring toward the sky. Satan had come up here to think. He always did his best thinking alone. There weren't many places left in the city where a person could be by himself. When Satan was younger, he liked to wind his way through the residential streets in his neighborhood—just in the daylight hours of course—but it only took a few people passing by to distract his thoughts and make it difficult to concentrate on whatever it was he wanted to concentrate on.

Walking no longer did it.

The giant tunnels under the city were out. Although the chances of meeting up with Jimmy Hoffa in the sewer again were slim, the old man's prowess with a ladle made such a meeting undesirable and not worth the risk.

So, he came here. Only to be harassed by the insatiable curiosity of human beings.

"That man has got woman trouble, I can tell," said the woman to the men. Then she shouted, "You wanna talk about it, darlin'? Love's a hard row to hoe sometimes."

"Isn't there something you people could be doing instead of bothering me? Censoring pop music and picketing abortion clinics are two that come to mind. Either is infinitely more interesting than watching me sit here in quiet thought."

"We won't let you kill yourself," shouted the woman, drawing the attention of nearly a half-dozen more people.

"What?" The thought of jumping hadn't entered his mind, but he felt he had to defend his privilege to do so all the same. "I think, madam, that I am guaranteed that right by the Constitution of the United States."

"I don't think that's true," said the man, hoping his lapel mic was still working. He was looking around, discreetly, watchful for anything that might be dangerous. Ever since that FBI agent had been hit by the bus, all of the teams following Dorobek had become much more cautious, much more vigilant. The President had given the word: Use any means necessary to neutralize this threat. If the police would only arrive in time, they could finally get this guy off the street and behind bars where he belonged. It would make the President happy.

"You a Supreme Court justice?" asked Satan.

"No."

"Then stay out of this."

Suddenly, the thought struck Satan that he had seen this man before, saw him on the street several times, in fact. This wasn't unusual, he was always seeing familiar faces in the crowd. Still, it felt odd to recognize someone you didn't actually know. Last March, when he had taken to spending his days in the Art Institute, he ran into the same woman every day for nearly a month. He had retreated to the museum to escape Mrs. Strom's television, which had become increasingly louder each day until after three weeks she finally realized her hearing aid batteries had gone dead. Satan and the woman in the museum never spoke, only nodded to each other after passing glances for more than a week. She was always parked in the same section every time he saw her, staring for hours on end at an oil painting of horses ranging the French countryside. It was hung in the gallery housing the works of several Renaissance artists. Every once in a while, she would jot down a note or two about the dark rendition. Sometimes, Satan would come back to the museum just before closing and study the painting when she wasn't around. When one day he finally decided to say hello to her, and maybe speak for a moment about the painting's attributes, he discovered she wasn't there. To his surprise, the painted horses were gone as well. For several days, he convinced himself that the woman had spirited the canvas away, stealing it like some thief in a bad thriller. After returning to the Institute for a week and finding no sign of her or the painting, he asked one of the curators about the piece and was told that it had been on loan from the Met in New York and had been returned. Satan often dreamed at night of riding the train to Manhattan—planes flew much too far off the ground for his taste—and finding the woman standing in front of the painting. But he never went.

"There's so much to live for," the woman shouted.

Satan glared down at the woman. These people wouldn't let him alone, which was all he really wanted. "I have a rash that started as a tiny little dot and now encompasses one-third of my body. My hair has been falling out in huge clumps whenever I take a shower. Yesterday, I thought there was a dead rat swirling about the drain."

"That's no reason to commit suicide."

"I'm...*not*..." he said to the woman, forcing the words through his teeth and clenching his hand in a fist. Looking at the fist, Satan noticed that the rash, which really only covered a few inches on his right arm, was making a run for his fingertips. There was nothing sinister about the skin irritation. He had similar bouts before, whenever he felt stressed. His hair, too, could be attributed to his increased level of anxiety. It was moments like this he wished he had never mentioned foil to Ion.

"Look who we got here," said a new voice in a deep Southside accent.

Satan peered over the edge of the landing and saw one of the policemen that had come to the house New Year's Eve.

"Hello," Satan said, feebly.

"What's it today? Riot? No, that was last week. Sexual perversities? No, that was the other night." The cop rubbed his fingers across his chin as if he was really thinking about something. "I got it. You're protesting cigarette ads, is that it?"

"Actually, I was just trying to get some peace and quiet. Is that illegal?"

"Not yet. But doin' it on a billboard thirty feet up is." The cop pulled out a set of cuffs from the back of his belt. "I got some place you could get away from it all. Course, it ain't too quiet, and not real peaceful, neither."

"Don't pressure him," the woman said. "He's likely to jump."

"Jump?" said the cop.

"Yes. *He* said so." She pointed to the black man who was shaking his head nervously and looking for an escape.

"I didn't say nothin, ma'am."

The policeman eyed the black man. "You know this character?"

"Never saw him befo'e ten minutes ago, Officer."

"Hrrrrmmm," the cop said in a low growl.

The black man saw that the policeman had been thwarted for the moment, and decided that as soon as the cop turned his head, he'd slip out and get on his merry way.

The cop was twirling the cuffs now. "Why don't ya come down here and we cain disguss this."

Looking out over the crowd that had grown to nearly a hundred people, Satan was confident he was witnessing his demise. Another police car came screeching to a halt, nearly hitting the black man who had gotten past the core of the crowd by that time.

"Where you off to so fast?" asked the cop driving the car.

The old man was in no mood to put up a fight. He knew when he was beaten. He extended his arms out to make it easy for the cop to cuff him.

Meanwhile, the first policeman's partner was making his way up the ladder beneath the huge billboard. He hated being so far off the ground and was afraid of heights, terrified in fact, but because of his small stature, he almost always drew this type of duty. Keeping his eyes from looking down toward the hard, ungiving pavement that seemed several football fields below, the cop on the ladder gripped one rung at a time, squeezing most of the blood out of his fingers with each successive move up the ladder.

Satan was sitting passively on the wood landing, resigned to the fact that Authority was going to win this one. Leaning against the billboard, just below a gigantic cigarette filter, he could see the top of the policeman's head rising above the landing's horizon. A few seconds later, an arm appeared and flung itself over the edge, searching madly for something to grab onto. When the fingers finally found a crevasse in the wood, they clawed at it until they were secure enough to pull the rest of the body onto the landing.

It was about this time that Ion rushed onto the scene, pushing through the crowd, dragging with her Slag and a television news crew.

"Leave him alone," she shouted at the policemen on the street who didn't know what to make of the beautiful blonde wearing a cowboy hat and dangling ice skates over her shoulder.

"Ah...he's...ah...not supposed to be—"

"I'm doing an interview with him up on the billboard," she said, lifting her hat and shaking out her hair so that it brushed across the cops face. "How do I look?"

"I...ah...don't have...ah...any knowledge of—you look nice."

"Thanks. You think you can help me get—" She was cut off by the "oowing" of the crowd.

Spread out on the wood walkway like a sunbather, his breathing heavy, the small, frightened cop drew his gun, laying it on the pine to support its weight.

"You're...you're under..."

Before he could actually place Satan under arrest, the cop accidentally glanced at the ground through a crack in the wood and fainted. His hand holding the gun slipped off the edge of the landing, and the weight of the pistol was enough to pull him over the side.

The camera crew caught it all.

The policeman fell off the walkway on his way to the hard, ungiving pavement.

Satan snatched the man's arm as it was disappearing over the side. He wasn't sure why he did it. It just seemed natural. Instinct had taken over his body. The pull of the dangling man dragged Satan across the wood landing, sending splinters into his stomach, chest, and arms, which acted like Velcro stopping him from sliding any further.

"This is going to hurt at some later point," he whispered, mostly to himself and the puffy white clouds above.

●

"I think a party's a great idea," said Peter Marks.

"Just a little something to thank everyone," said Armand.

"No, no, no, no. It's gotta be a big, wondrous event. You gotta put up a gigantic tent in the parking lot and fill it with food, a band, and lots of people."

"You think?"

Peter was watching a live newscast on the TV in his office which was replaying video of Satan saving the cop. "Foil Man, you got to take advantage of this. We'll invite the press. Your distributors. Some Wall Street types. Who knows what could happen."

Armand, who didn't have a TV in his office, was thinking this was going a bit overboard. I mean, it was just Safeway.

"Listen, I'll take care of everything," Peter said.

Of course, Peter Marks wasn't a party planner. He wasn't a caterer. He wasn't a music coordinator. His last attempt at party giving was New Year's 1992. It was a horrendous affair that began with too little liquor and ended with him toasting the New Year on his way back from a beer run with an Illinois State Policeman.

Marcey knew all this as she sat outside his office, listening to the conversation coming from Peter Marks' speaker phone, still tanned and rested from her holiday in Martinique, which had been wonderful, except for her nipples, which were sore from a nasty burn she'd gotten on the second day.

She knew that she was about to become all of these things, party planner, caterer, music coordinator, and much, much more.

Peter Marks hung up the phone. "Marceeeeeeey!"

At the very moment her name rang in her ear, she hated her boss. She hated her job. She hated America. And most of all, she hated having to wear a top.

•

Satan found himself seated in a lime green Naugahyde chair facing a lighted mirror. The place smelled like mothballs, talc, and thirty-year-old cigarette smoke. His naked torso kept sticking to the seat back. He was in pain, but he took some comfort in knowing that the wood splinters had kept him from tumbling off the billboard. Which, the more he thought about it, might have been less painful, certainly less humiliating than being paraded on a nationally syndicated talk show…which was what he was about to be. At the moment, a gruff-looking Teamster-type was powdering his cheeks, the tan dust getting up into his nostril and tickling the insides of his nose.

The man's name was Nelson. Said so, the moment the guest coordinator led Satan into the makeup room.

"Okay, whadda we got here," Nelson said, sizing up Satan—whose scratched body was still bleeding in places. The man raised a concerned brow. "Well, we gotta do something to make you presentable." His voice was a pile of gravel thrown at a high-speed metal fan. He nodded at the scratches. "What happen to you, Satan, you fall on your pitchfork?" He laughed at his joke.

Since then Nelson had used his name in at least a dozen sentences.

"So I said to the fuckin purducer, Nelson Pinkerton don't do animals," he proclaimed one of the twelve times. Then glaring at the effeminate, dark-skinned man working the woman's makeup chair, Nelson said, "Although, I know a few who do." He returned his attention to Satan. "Purse your lips."

For the next few minutes, Nelson silently went about his business, dabbing and shaping and stroking almost every part of Satan's face. Satan watched intently at his refection as the contours of his chin, nose, and cheeks were altered by the pen of this seemingly out of place man.

"I'm not a fag," explained Nelson, paying special attention to the last word.

Satan wasn't sure what brought on the statement, or how he should respond to it. He chose avoidance.

"I just happen to like doing makeup. That don't make me a homo."

"No. Why should it?"

"Exactly. It's a talent." The man made a sound—"Pfffft. Who the hell knows? I'm working a show a coupla years ago—transportation," he said, tightening up his free arm in a pose that said 'Teamster.' "Purducers were in a bind. I help out, found out I like it." Nelson dabbed a bit of color under the eye. "Better than luggin crap all day."

"I'm sure." Satan picked a few last splinters from out of his navel. He lifted one up to the light and studied it. The pin-sized tip had a tiny prick of blood on it. Satan let out a small sigh. Somehow, some way, Ion had managed to turn the whole incident around, and instead of him getting arrested, he was going to get a commendation. In fact, the only person to get arrested was the old black man, who had absolutely nothing to do with him being up on the billboard. Ion immediately called the ACLU and NAACP. The lawyers from those groups would most likely be filing a lawsuit on behalf of the man against the city for discrimination and false arrest very soon.

Unfortunately, being dragged across the wood landing had ripped Satan's clothes to shreds. He looked down and stared at the red and white polka dot pants he wore, which someone had dug out of a closet somewhere. They were left over from the days when Bozo the Clown used to tape his show in this studio. Apparently, the pants had been kept for just such an occasion as this, although they were a bit dusty from a quarter century of waiting for one to come up.

"Wardrobe's trying to find something more appropriate for you," said the effeminate man, as if reading Satan's mind.

A few minutes ago, a small, grayish man had come in and measured Satan. It all happened so fast, he couldn't understand how the man could get the sizes right, never mind remember them in his head.

"Somehow, I find them sadly appropriate," Satan sighed, gazing down at the pants.

Nelson stepped back and stared at his handiwork. Finding something not quite to his liking, he picked up an eyebrow pencil and darkened up the hairs on Satan's sideburns.

"She's very nice. Tough lady, but nice. You'll like her. "

"Like who?" asked Satan.

"Marsha Kirkland," said Nelson with a sudden hint of haughtiness. He gave a last look at his work. "Perfect."

The anorexic brunette in the slim, tailored dress looked into the camera, holding a microphone close to her painted lips.

"Foil…you've wrapped your food in it. Now, will you wrap yourself in it? Can foil add years to your life…?" She paused dramatically. "…on the next Marsha Kirkland Show."

•

Marsha Kirkland stared into the camera with a sincerity that can only come from great practice. "Our guest today is a man causing quite a stir in Chicagoland. He extols the health benefits of wearing foil on your head, claiming it can extend your life. And for one Chicago cop, it did just that."

As she continued talking into the lens, Satan sat in the guest chair, trying desperately to keep from tipping over onto his face. Peter Marks mock interviews had at least gotten the chairs right. The backs, he said, were past vertical to keep guests sitting up straight.

Ion crouched in front of Satan as Nelson gave his face one last dab of powder.

Satan gave her a hard look. "This is all your fault. I never would have been on that billboard if you hadn't left me alone with that Peter guy and his people. What were they, trained by former Gestapo members?"

"Yes, Vinnie, I'm sure you were so easy to work with. And absolutely no reason for them to get tough with you."

"You still haven't told me where you were." Satan coughed after sucking in a bit too much powder.

"Close your mouth," ordered Nelson.

"For the thousandth time. I was taking care of some things." Ion had grown tired of this. She should have just given him a good lie the first time he asked. Should have said she had gone to visit her dad, but she hadn't. Now, it was the principle of the matter.

"What things?"

"Things."

"Great. Meanwhile, I'm nearly dragged over the side of a billboard. And now this. Marsha Kirkland. Apparently, millions of people are going to be watching." He said these words as if he had said, 'millions of people are going to be murdered.'

"That's the idea."

"Four point six million," chimed in Nelson.

"Four…poi…" Satan nearly bolted, but Nelson was in his way. "Ion, if you have any care for me in your heart, any at all, please, please, please, end this nightmare."

"Vinnie, I do care. But you've got to trust me. You can do this."

"But I don't want to."

"You're just nervous. I'm proud of you. And I want you to know, saving that cop's life was brilliant. We've gotten incredible PR off of that. It was a great idea."

Satan stared at her for a moment. "There is something chemically wrong with you, are you aware of that?"

"It doesn't make me any less proud. Mention the aging thing and the website. Remember, this is TV. Say anything, do anything, just don't be boring."

Nelson finished and got up. "Good luck."

Ion started to crawl back out of the way. "You do well today, and tonight, we'll have a nice, long bath together and then we'll..." She leaned forward and whispered something in his ear.

Pulling back, she smiled at him, hoping the promise of sex would ease his mind. Instead, it only made matters worse. Performance anxiety, both on and off the stage, rattled in his skull.

Marsha was winding up. "...here he is, Noel "Satan" Dorobek."

Applause erupted as the camera zoomed in on the terrified face of Satan.

•

Armed with the latest sales figures, an invite to his party, and a tape of Satan saving the life of one of Chicago's finest, Armand Arnold marched into his bank to once again try and secure a line of credit to begin retrofitting the stacks before the thirty days was up.

The bank manager wasn't moved by the jump in sales. "I'm sorry, Mr. Arnold." Nor the invite. "I'm busy that night." Nor were his purse strings loosened by Satan's act of bravery. "Yes, that is a wonderful thing, Mr. Arnold. If only it had been my district manager..."

It was the threat that Armand would unleash Satan on every syndicated talk show on the continent to announce that the Bank of North America had heartlessly turned down a bona fide hero's attempt to clean the air.

Work on Stack No. 4 began two days later.

•

The elevated train clicked and swayed as it made its way along the track above Wells Street. The gentle motion of the car was hypnotic, punctuated by a swirling cacophony of sound. Even the metallic clang of rough track that started ahead and quickly moved underneath, then behind, had become, for Satan, a comforting noise.

Satan pushed away a malodorous vagrant sitting in the seat beside him. The rotting man had fallen asleep, his head coming to rest on Satan's shoulder, knocking the bowler off kilter. Satan's shove sent the man's limp body tilting toward the aisle. The only thing keeping him from crashing to the floor was the large, skirted buttocks of a secretary on her way to work. The man's nose was stuck right between the woman's cheeks as she stood in the aisle, and either she didn't notice or didn't mind.

At the next station, an ad for Marsha Kirkland stopped right in front of his window. She was smiling at him in the same manner she had on the set. Only then her mouth wasn't as big as his head—it only seemed that way.

"The Chicago media has nicknamed you 'Saint Satan,'" Marsha said, "after you heroically saved Officer Petrie's life. That was a very courageous act, wasn't it?" Marsha turned toward the audience, which erupted in applause.

"It was just…reflex."

Marsha smiled again and felt his arm, ooowing to the crowd. "And fine reflexes they are, girls."

Satan grabbed his bicep after she let go and rubbed it.

Getting back on point, she leaned forward, tilted her head and said, "How did you get the name Satan in the first place? You're not a devil worshiper."

Ion watched from the side, just off stage. This was the make or break moment. The moment people would get beyond his idiotic name or crucify him for it.

"No, no, not at all. I'm glad you asked me that," he said, finding it peculiar that he was parroting the exact words the ad people had drilled into him. He was too terrified to think for himself. "It has nothing to do with the devil. It's just a pet name a friend of mine gave me because I have a fascination with people who live…" He paused. Ion winced. The audience waited. "…underground."

Satan heard an audible sigh of relief come from somewhere offstage.

Immediately, Marsha Kirkland got excited. "You believe radiation is what makes us age."

"That's part of it." Satan could feel the sweat pouring down the side of his chest.

"All this money we've been spending on anti-wrinkle creams and plastic surgery and you're telling me I should have been living in a cave and wearing Arnolds Aluminum all this time?"

The audience laughed.

"It would be a start," he said, thinking she and all the other babble show hosts should be sent to live in caves where they couldn't foist insipid drivel on the already-too-vapid masses ever again. "Although, it's not only about wearing foil." Satan looked offstage to see Ion glaring at him, mouthing, 'don't do it.' He hesitated for a moment, then looked back toward the audience. "I believe people want to live in a world that is safe. Where everyone is happy and everyone is nice. Where it's always warm and bright."

"Amen to that" Marsha said, mugging to the crowd, rubbing her arms and pretending to shiver.

Satan shifted in his chair and tried not to focus on the moisture draining out of his body. He had to express himself truthfully. He didn't care if he incurred the wrath of Ion. His beliefs were too strong, held for too long to simply eschew them. "All I am saying is that there has to be something more than what's on the surface. We have to dig deeper inside to find it. My mission is to get to that place. True happiness can only be found within."

Everyone in the crowd nodded.

"Not bad, Vinnie," Ion uttered under her breath.

"Well said, Satan." Marsha Kirkland turned and gazed into the camera. "We'll be right back...with a special surprise for Saint Satan...the cop whose life he saved. Don't go away."

In the weeks that followed, Satan went from television studio to radio booth to newspaper office on a well-planned, calculated public relations campaign. It didn't hurt that Piggly Wiggly's, Ralph's, and even Williams-Sonoma had announced they would begin stocking Arnolds and that Macy's would carry an exclusive line of Gamma Caps in its Flagship New York store. The hats, in various styles, would be fashioned out of a mylar/Goretex blend which made their finish appear like flexible foil. The insides would be six layers of Arnolds, the new standard, and lined.

Peter Marks and Ion personally went over Satan's itinerary and deleted anyone or anything that could be hazardous and continued to prep him exhaustively.

Things were going well, or so they said. He was definitely being exposed, but to what end. Several nuns had taken up residence outside his house carrying signs that said things like "Foil Satan's Plan."

After guiding Satan through the first few interviews, Ion no longer accompanied him. She said she couldn't take any further time off from Clancy's and she needed to visit her father who was continuing to improve.

Arnolds Aluminum offered to hire a driver for Satan, but Ion turned them down, saying it was in the best interest of all concerned for Satan to remain a "regular" oddball instead of a pampered one for awhile longer.

So here he was, gazing out the window, staring into people's homes, into their lives. Sometimes he would see wonderful meals being set out on white linen tablecloths. Other times he'd see someone alone, their eyes glued to the blue-white light of a television screen. Sometimes he would look out past the glass and see beautifully manicured parks and bustling streets lined with shops. Other times he'd glimpse nothing but squalor, hardship, and hopelessness; children playing on the skeletons of old, abandoned automobiles; thin, frail men, who should be in their prime, leaning against rundown buildings because they had nothing better to do but drugs and loitering.

These trips distressed Satan because they made him realize that all the terrible, terrible things that had happened to him during his life, well, they weren't all that unusual. He had competition. Lots of it.

The train screeched to a halt and the voice of someone, possibly a human, came over the speaker above Satan's head. As the doors opened, the voice bellowed out a group of jumbled utterances sounding more like the grown-ups in a Peanuts cartoon than any language known to man. From the intonation and pattern, Satan knew this was his stop. Pulling the sleeping man's face from out of the secretary's buttocks, Satan struggled past the bodies. The man fell back against the window, and was shoved over as one of the boarding passengers sat down.

Stepping onto the platform, the doors closed behind Satan, and the train eked away from the Fullerton station. The late January air was still, as if the cold had frozen the molecules in place. This was the coldest time of year in the Windy City. December was tropical compared to the weeks following Martin Luther King's Birthday.

A mass of people carried Satan down the stairs to the street.

A few blocks away, as he waited at the corner for the light to change, he noticed the city crews had removed most of the more offensive signs of Christmas. A few strands of garland clung to several light posts, and a reindeer that stubbornly refused to be taken down remained prancing atop the awning of Thompson-McCabe, but that was about it. The local stores had disowned Christmas like a poor relative and were already onto new game. Disgusting pink hearts were springing up in shop windows across the city. Displays of boxed candy were paraded out for all to see, a chocoholic's dream/nightmare.

Satan had succumbed to the unrelenting promotions, buying two boxes of assorted nuts and chews for himself, which he immediately devoured on the ride home the night before.

The light changed, and whether he wanted to or not, Satan was forced across the street. The mad, money-hungry mob, obviously late for work, thankfully deposited him in front of the very place he had to be.

Putting a hand up to the glass to cut the glare, Satan peered inside Frances' Deli. It was crowded, but Satan saw Slag seated near the window at the end. The poet was alone, his hair hanging in the way of his pen. Every once in a while, he had to shake his head to move the strands out of the path of the ink.

"Hey, man," Slag said, glancing up from his latest verse as Satan walked up to the table. "Didn't know if you'd show. Saved you a seat."

Slag was always saving a place for someone, and always unsure his friends would show to make saving the place worthwhile. He had good reason not to trust in his friends. He couldn't remember exactly why that was, but he knew it to be fact. With the exception of Ion, and now maybe Satan, no one had ever shown up after he had gone to all the trouble to save the ungrateful souls a place.

It was lost on Slag that other than Ion, and now maybe Satan, he had no friends. Oh, everyone knew him; he was quite famous in the Chicago underground scene. Once, the *Sun-Times* did a story on local artists and a poem of Slag's was part of the article. But when it came to actually having friends, Slag wasn't very good at it.

"You want somethin to eat, man?" Slag asked, motioning for the waitress.

"Pancakes. Blueberry," Satan told the older woman who studied him curiously for a moment as she wrote the order.

"Blueberry? Not potato?"

"Why would I want potato in my pancakes?"

Slag pointed to his plate that had the remnants of kosher sausage and potato pancakes. "Can I have some more latkes…and an order of braised short ribs," he said to the waitress.

"We don't serve short ribs till after eleven," said the woman, a little disgusted at the thought of ribs this time of day.

"Oh." Slag furrowed his brow. "Gimme two eggs and some corned beef instead."

"So, skip the latkes then?"

"No, bring them too."

Satan peered around the edge of the table to get a better look at Slag's bony frame. He wondered how it was possible for the poet to eat the way he did and not be a Weight Watchers test subject. Maybe Slag was bulimic.

A man across the room was having his leftover food wrapped in foil by one of the counter guys. After paying his check, the man twisted the metal into a swan, set the foil bird on his head, conformed the base of it to the shape of his skull, then went outside. Satan watched the man as he passed in front of the window before disappearing around the corner.

"Where's that pale, skinny chick with the hat?" Slag asked Satan. This was the main reason Slag had no friends; he couldn't remember their names.

"Ion?"

"Yeah, her."

"I don't know. She stayed at her apartment last night." Satan took a sip of water. "Said something about getting into work early."

"Oh." Slag scribbled a note to himself on the pad. "Ion," it said. "You know that one with the glasses?"

"Lilly?" Satan suggested.

"Yeah, that's it."

"What about her?"

For the past twenty-six days, since New Year's Eve, Satan had been avoiding Lilly like one avoids a mental patient in a knife shop. But she was persistent. Relentless. Several nights he was forced to climb up the back wall so she wouldn't see him coming home. The answering machine Ion had hooked up—over his protestations—now came in handy, allowing him to screen his calls, eighty percent of which were from Lilly, fifteen percent from bill collectors, and the remaining five percent were split between Peter Marks and Ion, who almost always were calling for each other, either him for her, or her seeing if he had called her.

"I told her we'd be here," Slag said, remembering this piece of trivia after seeing a girl with thick glasses entering the deli.

"You what?!"

"Hi," giggled Lilly as she pulled up a chair and sat down. "What're you guys up to?" She pushed her glasses as high as they would go on her nose, which wasn't very far.

"What are you doing here?"

"I'm having...EGGS AND HASH BROWNS," she shouted to the waitress who was just putting in the boys' order with the cook.

"Why aren't you selling moldy clothing?"

"Day off," she said. "So...when are you gonna take me to dinner?"

"Hey, you two should eat right here, right now, man. It's cool."

Satan shot a quick glance at Slag, then turned to Lilly. "What do you mean, take you to dinner? I'm not taking you anywhere."

Lilly was busy rearranging the table to accommodate herself.

"I bought a new dress. Very short." She slid her legs out from under the table, marking with her hand where the hem would fall. "I also got a garter belt. So, when I don't wear underwear, there won't be any pantyhose in the way. Easier access."

Satan clicked his teeth together, chattering them to alleviate his pent up frustration. Ion had been absent from his bed for the last four nights, and whenever he did see her, she was distant and businesslike.

"I could care less about your easy access," he said, thinking about it the more he tried not to.

Slag found the subject of Lilly's lingerie curious, but was writing about slavery at present and didn't want to spoil his somber mood.

"Take me tonight," she said, leaving her precise meaning in doubt.

Satan squirmed in his chair as the food was served. "No. Now, would you please leave us alone?"

"I've already ordered," she replied as her food arrived.

Satan let out a groan, which was followed by a long sigh.

"Hey, haven't I seen you on a Soap or something?" asked the waitress, not looking where she was placing the hot plate and scalding Satan.

"I don't think so," he replied, painfully, as he spread some butter over what looked to him to be a second-degree burn.

"Butter's not good for burns, man," Slag said through his forest of hair.

"Yeah, I seen you somewhere on TV." The woman was nodding her head and nearly spilled a plate of hash browns down Lilly's shirt.

"Maybe you saw him on the news the other day," Lilly said, gently pushing the fried potatoes in the general direction of the table. She turned to Satan. "You were great."

"Don't watch news," the waitress said.

"He's been on all the talk shows…Oprah, Good Morning Chicago, Marsha Kirkland."

The waitress's eyes lit up. "Marsha Kirkland! That's it. You're the guy with the tin foil, ain't I right?" The woman was smiling, and yelling something to the cooks in the kitchen. Then suddenly, she became serious when a giant box of Arnolds Aluminum was tossed to her. "Can I have your autograph?"

•

Vlady walked along Clark Street, struggling with his bag that was dragging on the sidewalk, too heavy for him to lift in his weakened state. He hadn't eaten a decent meal in days, hadn't showered since the one he took in Moscow a month ago, and now, he was being hounded by several dogs who smelled the half-eaten cheeseburger he found in the garbage, then hid in his carry-on. The small valise and the one other piece of luggage he had left were worn, with tiny tears in the fabric, especially on the sides. The rest of the baggage had been lost or stolen or just plain abandoned because he was too tired to lug it around anymore.

He was searching for somewhere to eat in peace when he passed Frances' Deli. He didn't know his old friend Noel was sitting at one of the tables in the window, although he saw him. Perhaps, Vlady didn't recognize him because he was staring at the food on his plate more closely than his face.

Even if he had noticed, he wouldn't have known what to say.

Vlady cut down an alley and lost the dogs in a crowd of people. He climbed up a set of rungs leading to a fire escape and ate the leftover cheeseburger huddled in the corner like a rat with some cheese. For some reason, Noel Dorobek came to mind. He wondered what had become of the boy. Vlady chuckled to himself, realizing his friend was no longer a boy. Noel was forever in Vlady's head as an awkward sixteen-year-old, curious about girls, but more curious about why his mom was so weird.

Finishing the last of the burger, and the two fries that had stuck to the cheese on the wrapping paper, Vlady climbed down onto the slick asphalt. He made for the end of the alley, walking briskly into the crowd traveling the sidewalk on his way to Noel's house.

If it was still there. If he was still there.

If Vlady could remember where there was.

•

The party had started out as a simple idea. A small celebration. That's what Armand wanted.

But Peter Marks had turned it into something much more than that. A sales tool. Actually, his secretary, Marcey had done all the hard work. Peter Marks was, as he had always been, an idea man.

Satan and Ion were walking along State. She was talking on her phone. Every once in a while he tried to say something to her, but she'd put up her hand to quiet him. So, now, he just kept to himself, trying to avoid the onslaught of people on the sidewalk.

Passersby, he noticed, seemed to have a look of recognition in their eyes. They would whisper to each other and look back over their shoulders, point their fingers at him even.

Instead of basking in his newfound celebrity, he was more than a little unnerved by it. The idea of everyone looking at him, well, it was spooky.

At first, it was somewhat cute and only mildly annoying. But now, only two days from February, with his—or rather Ion's—legion of sycophants growing, a new book of poems—"Ode to an Aluminum Hat" by Slag—at the local bookstores, and the media blitz only getting more intense, Satan found the attention debilitating. There was nowhere left for him to hide.

Ion turned to Satan after hanging up her cell phone. He was several yards behind her, something he always made sure of whenever she was using the irradiating device. "Okay, the party's Friday night. They'll send a limo to take us to it," she said.

"This Friday?"

"Yes."

"The 2nd?"

"Yes."

"Groundhog Day? We're going to share the spotlight with a woodchuck. Sounds like a catastrophe in the making. It's bad luck."

"What's bad luck? A cute furry little groundhog?"

"I'm telling you, bad luck."

"You're always saying you don't believe in superstitious crap." The wisps of hair not covered by Ion's cowboy hat blew in the cold breeze.

"That's because I'm too superstitious to admit it."

Ion let out a lungful of air. "Sometimes…you make me crazy."

"Shouldn't you be taking something for that?"

A passel of young girls walked by them, several wearing hats. One of the girls, the prettiest, followed Satan with her eyes as she passed. A ripple began to spread through the group until, a moment later, they were standing in front of him, out of their minds with excitement.

"I told you it was him," the pretty one said to the others. The sixteen-year-old lifted up her hat to reveal several layers of foil underneath. "My boyfriend says I look younger already."

Satan stared at the girl.

"That's wonderful," Ion said. "We really appreciate your support."

Suddenly, like a bomb had exploded in her head, one of the girls got an idea. "Can I have your autograph?"

Instantly, they all went nuclear.

"Me too."

"Me too!"

Affecting a somber tone, Satan gazed at the girls. "Sadly, no. Carpal tunnel syndrome." He stuck his fingers out stiffly, like Frankenstein calling a runner safe at the plate.

But the girls pressed in, pleading with him to scribble his name in their notebooks. Sensing trouble, Ion reached into Vinnie's pocket and pulled out the "emergency stash" of foil, tossing it into the air. The girls scrambled for the silver sheet, ripping it to shreds, giving Ion and Satan time to escape.

Once they were around the corner, Satan leaned against the wall to catch his breath. "It's a nightmare. Yesterday, I went to the Food King and had to sign three hundred boxes of foil."

Ion muttered an acknowledgment as she glanced up at the wall behind Vinnie, trying very hard not to betray any reaction. "C'mon, they might still be following us." She grabbed his arm and peeled him away from a thirty-foot likeness of himself, holding a sheet of foil in front of his otherwise naked body under the tag, STOP EXPOSING YOURSELF.

As they ran down the alley, he turned to her, "Did you know the Catholic Church is picketing my house?"

Ion nodded. "It's the name thing. I told you."

•

"I'm leaving, Barris."

Kelsey stood at the door, looking back at the man she'd spent the last two years of her life with. He sat at the desk that had been his residence for most of that time. But it was different now. The yellow notepads were neatly stacked in the corner, not having been touched in several days.

Barris finished tying his sneakers and stood up.

"Did you hear me? I'm leaving." Kelsey said it this time like she would when she left him for good.

"Huh? Oh, yeah, honey. I was just thinking," he said, going into the kitchen and grabbing several bowls, a spoon, and five boxes of cereal that were placed on the counter. "Have a nice day."

Kelsey lingered in the doorway watching as Barris poured cereal into the bowls, then soaked them with milk. He tasted each of the sugar-coated breakfasts, jotting down notes on a white pad as he went along. Barris was dressed in a new pair of sweats emblazoned with the emblem of the Chicago Bulls. His hair was freshly cut, less than three days old.

Peter Marks was so pleased with the progress of the Arnolds Aluminum campaign, he not only paid the handsome sum he had promised, but he came by two nights ago with an offer of permanent employment for Barris. Kelsey was staring at the first assignment: Come up with something new and different to sell kids' cereal. Peter said that with the trend toward healthier foods, they had to get more creative in pushing sugar on moms.

Kelsey was oddly jealous that Barris had come out of this so well. After all, it had been *her* idea. Ion and Satan, both, had done more than Barris. Yet, it was Barris being paid to sample pre-sweetened breakfast cereals. He didn't even have to go into the office. He could sit in his pajamas all day and get a check every week.

She had prayed for Barris' success for two years, but now that it had arrived, she was very depressed about it. Especially when she had nothing to look forward to every day but Leo Lincoln's red little face.

Watching Barris shove a spoonful of sugar-frosted flakes into his mouth, Kelsey's mind shifted away from her annoying boss and her ungrateful lover and toward the handsome face of Peter Marks. It was a nice face, one that she had definitely been attracted to. He was tall, with deep green eyes that were never still. When he looked at her, they moved back and forth from eye to eye as if he was studying each pupil for the deeper meaning of her words. She even liked the way he sipped at his drink, double tipping the glass every time he drank. It was unfortunate that Barris had to be there, otherwise the evening would have been wonderful.

"I'll see you later," she sighed. "We've got that dinner tonight. We're supposed to be ready by six-thirty. Make sure you can still fit into your suit."

"Hmmm?" he said with a mouthful. "Yeah, sure. I'll be ready."

Kelsey made her way downstairs, once again grateful for Barris' success.

At least he wouldn't starve to death when she left.

•

Ion stood in Vinnie's room staring at the open closet when she saw them—hiding innocently in the corner, trying desperately not to be noticed. Leisure suits, polyester "silk" shirts, that whole non-biodegradable look Vinnie loved so much before she met him.

A shiver climbed up her spine as if ten people had scraped their nails across a chalkboard simultaneously. She just couldn't get nostalgic for polyester.

One of the recruits came into the room with a garment bag.

"Where do you want this?"

"Just put it on the bed," Ion told the girl, without looking.

The girl laid on the comforter the new jacket and pants that Jason's mother had tailored for Satan, then left the room.

Ion went into the closet to find a pair of socks to match and there, on the floor, stuck halfway out from under a pile of dirty laundry, was the nightstick the cop had given Satan for saving his life. It was scratched up pretty good from the fall off the billboard landing, and several grooves were burned into the wood when the thing fell onto a power transformer, blacking out the surrounding neighborhood.

Behind the pile of clothes, an old chest of drawers sat quietly filling one corner. A faded and yellowed doily rested on top of the dresser. Ion pulled open the top drawer of the oak chest. It was filled with scraps of paper and pieces of things that had no meaning or purpose on their own. There were parts of toy cars, scattered Lego blocks, a plastic orange horse with its own flimsy plastic base. Pushing back the first layer, she found among the trinkets an electronic calculator and an invitation to a fifth, then tenth-year high school reunion, the return envelopes still inside, never having been sent off.

She sifted through the debris left from Satan's past, the flotsam of a life strangely devoid of anything but fragmented memories. A number of times, she tried to explain to Vinnie that everyone forgets most of the events in his or her life, remembering only the odd, the triumphant, or the tragic. Everyday occurrences were as quickly forgotten as what you had for lunch last Tuesday.

He didn't buy it, saying his life was different. And perhaps, it was.

Ion was about to close the drawer—she had to get home and shower and change for the dinner tonight—when she noticed the crumpled up bag

stuffed way in the back of the drawer. Unfolding it, she stared at the lettering: "Clancy Wishes You 'Happy Holidays.'" A date, month-day-year, was
handwritten below the grinning face of Clancy. The date she and Satan met.

A little heart was drawn, then scribbled out.

She crumpled up the bag and put it back where she had found it. Closing
the drawer slowly, she gave the room one last look before heading out.

●

Leo Lincoln was pacing in her office when Kelsey arrived a half an hour
after leaving Barris.

He was rubbing his hands together, happily, which meant that someone,
somewhere was being screwed out of something.

"Ah, there you are," he said.

"What is it, Leo? I'm in a really shitty mood. Barris is getting paid ungodly
sums of money to sit at home and taste Chocolate-coated Super Sugar
Smacks while I have to brave gale force winds to spend eight grueling hours
with you."

He ignored her comments, chalking them up to menstrual irregularity,
although it seemed that recently her periods were coming closer and closer
together and lasting longer and longer.

"Drop everything," he said. "We're going to be moving on Renaissance
Village today. I've taken the liberty of clearing your desk and handing over
all your work to Gina and Bobby."

"I was in the middle of some very important negotiations, Leo."

"Not anymore," he said, pursing his lips and tapping on them in the
manner an Indian on the warpath would get beaten up and called a squaw
for. He glanced at his watch. Only a few more hours.

Kelsey sat back hard in her chair. "Your friends haven't filed the revised
plans yet. They're not moving a piece of dirt until they do."

"There's going to be no revisions."

"Leo, the ratio of parking spaces per square foot for that kind of—"

"Arnolds is gonna sell."

"What?" Her voice was full of shock and disappointment. She couldn't
believe it. She and Barris were attending a dinner with Armand Arnold that
evening. A show of appreciation for everything Barris had done. She liked
Armand, even though he kept congratulating Barris over and over and over
for coming up with all these great ideas. And Barris, that prick, just nodded
and humbly told him it was nothing.

But then that wasn't Armand's fault. He seemed kind and gentle. Attractive, too.

Kelsey played with a pencil on her desk.

She was beginning to find more and more men attractive, she realized. Except, of course, her boss and her boyfriend, the two men with whom she had to spend most of her time. There was something very sad about that.

"When did this happen?"

"The details are not important," Leo huffed as he picked a dried chunk of mucus from his nostril. He flicked it out the office door and watched as it landed on the desk of one of his employees. He smiled. Soon, the explosives would destroy the stacks at Arnolds Aluminum and that awful Armand Arnold would be begging to unload his useless property.

•

The drip, drip, drip of a leaky pipe was what Kenny Odorman awoke to. It was annoying sounds very much like this that had influenced more than a few murders, he thought. The metered plop of the water hitting the puddle on the cement floor of the church basement was wearing on him before ten minutes of consciousness was up.

Kenny's head hurt, just above the neck, but his hands were tied which didn't allow him to feel out the bump and determine its severity. After awhile, he wasn't sure if the pounding in his ear was from the dripping water or the blood flowing to the wound.

It was dark, damp, and very musty in the cellar and the floor was extremely cold. A window above spilled frozen air into the already chilly room. Kenny attempted to focus on his surroundings, but all the darkness would reveal was more of itself.

Suddenly, there was a click, and a bright light temporarily blinded him. When his eyes adjusted themselves, he gazed upon the silhouette of a robed man that seemed ten feet tall.

"You're the Devil, aren't ya?" asked the five-foot-nine Father Leery.

"What?"

"Don't be coy with me. God revealed himself to me last night."

"That's very interesting. Who hit me?" asked Kenny after the silhouette moved from in front of the hanging bulb, allowing him to see that he was speaking with a middle-aged priest.

"I did."

"I don't understand. You're a priest. Why would you hit me?" Kenny was worried he might get an answer he wouldn't like. He hadn't been to church in nearly two decades, and had heard about nuns beating unruly students, but nothing about clergy accosting the fallen.

Father Leery glared at the criminal scum in front of him. "Why're you playing the lookout for drug dealers? This is a fine neighborhood. I won't be letting it go to pot for the likes of you."

"Drug dealers?" said Kenny, a bit testy. "I'm trying to find a guy who owes a half million dollars."

This was drastically worse than Father Leery had imagined. A half million dollars. It was hard to believe that many drugs could be sold in such a fine neighborhood. And right in the shadow of a church. What was the world coming to?

"Aye, a million dollars."

"Half a million."

"It's lucky I caught you when I did. Tell me what your friends look like so I can catch them, too."

"I don't have any *friends*." Kenny was being as patient as he could. It was obvious the clergyman had been into the sacramental wines.

Kenny didn't like being in church. He liked being in the basement of one tied up like a calf marked for the slaughterhouse even less.

"Harrghhh," the priest grunted. This was going to be much more difficult than he imagined. He had hoped in some way the robes and collar would scare the criminal into a confessional tone, but alas, it hadn't happened. "Here, eat this."

"What is it?" said the criminal. "It smells awful."

"It's all the food you'll be getting so's you might as well take it. You're going to need it to build your strength."

"And why is that?" Kenny asked, sampling the gruel that tasted worse than it smelled.

That was a month ago.

Since then, the priest had left him alone in the dark for the most part. Every two days he'd show up with a glass of water and ask the same question. "Who are your friends, boy?" He'd hold out the water for Kenny to take. "You'll not be getting out of here till you tell me that for sure."

Kenny heard the door open. A moment later, the priest appeared. But this time a young boy dressed in white robes and black sneakers came down the creaking steps while Kenny was sipping at the water. The dust the boy kicked up filtered through a beam of light cutting across the room and shined on a puddle in the middle of the floor.

"It's ready, Father," said the boy as if talking about a guillotine or a hanging noose.

"Good, good," Father Leery answered. "Now we can fulfill God's Word, my boy." He turned to the man. "Since you won't be telling me what I want to know being stuck down here near these forty days and forty nights, we'll be trying something new."

After the man finished drinking the water, and after gagging the kicking and screaming criminal, Father Leery and the altar boy dragged him up to the bell tower.

•

Later that evening, as the moon was rising over the tops of the buildings, and the street dogs began their nightly howling at it, a limousine came to rest by the curb in front of Satan's graystone. The house looked like all the houses on its block; it was slender, built of masonry—overpainted brick or ashen stones—and imperfectly vertical. Satan's was skewed slightly to the right, tilting toward the east and the Lake. The car was a big black thing with darkened windows so you couldn't see in, and a body that looked too long to make a proper turn.

Ion sipped at a glass of Cabernet and looked past the smoked glass, watching Satan descend the stairs very deliberately, watching him take each step in the same manner as a beauty queen in high heels. The street lamp cast a pink-orange light on him, and even in this artificial glow, Ion could make out the details of his wardrobe, his hair. A look of surprise washed over her face, and she nearly spilled the wine on herself. She put her hand on Jason's knee for a bit of support. "Hmph," she whispered to herself.

The driver got out, walked stiffly around the front of the car, and held open the back door for Satan, who ducked his head and stuck it halfway inside. Satan glanced around to see Ion and Jason facing forward, and Slag, Kelsey and Barris facing back. Everyone was staring at him strangely, and he wondered if he hadn't missed a bit of toothpaste on the corner of his mouth or forgotten to zip his fly.

"You look great, Vinnie," Ion said. There was a general nodding of heads in agreement. "C'mon in, babe." She patted the empty space next to her.

Satan sat as best he could, leaning back against the seat like a monarch easing into his throne. The others mistook this for grace. The fact was the little rash that had begun on his arm encompassed nearly a quarter of his body and was spreading faster than gossip at a family picnic.

"Let me take a look at you." Ion shook her head. "Unbelievable. Who would've figured you could look this good. Kelsey, what do you think?"

Resting her chin in the palm of her hand, Kelsey looked him up and down. She was silent for a moment, contemplating her answer. She had known Satan for several years and had never found him attractive—until now. There was something about a man in a double-breasted jacket that made even the worst of them look respectable. Satan wasn't nearly the worst of them—wasn't the best either, but that wasn't the point. The jacket wrapped around his waist and hugged attractively on his hips. Complimenting the black-tie attire, his hair, which had been cut for a second time in a month—as many times as he usually had it cut in a year—was loosely combed back over his head.

"You do look handsome," Kelsey finally said.

Slag was staring out the side window, a little apprehensive about the driver's ability to avoid the end of the world if they were to come upon it. No one knew exactly where this dinner was taking place, which made him suspicious to begin with, and more than a little nervous.

"Slag?" said Ion. "What do you think?"

"Huh?" said Slag and Barris both at the same time.

Barris was staring at Satan much in the way a man lost in the desert stared at a pool of water in the sand, unconvinced that what he was gazing at was actually what he was gazing at. The man Barris was studying could not have been hidden under the old, down jacket with all the feathers at the bottom, he thought to himself. And where was the hat? No knit cap, no bowler, nothing.

"Where's your hat?" Barris said when he was convinced the man across from him was not a mirage.

A look of horror flashed across Satan's face as he reached up and felt around. In his excitement, he had completely forgotten about the one thing that had brought him to this point.

"Stop the car!" he screamed to the driver, who didn't hear the order.

Before anyone could stop him, Satan lunged forward, reaching his body over Kelsey's to get the attention of the obviously deaf driver, when he THWACK! smashed his face into the tempered glass that separated the man at the wheel from the passengers at Ion's request.

Hearing the muffled THUD, the driver pulled the limousine over to see what had happened.

•

"Foil Man," declared a beaming Peter Marks as he strutted into Armand's office, dressed smartly in a gabardine suit and looking very sophisticated. He held his hand out awaiting a strong handshake from Armand. It was like Christmas all over again for Peter. He hadn't felt this good since one of the women at his gym asked him over for drinks, then asked him to unwrap her in front of a roaring fire. Of course, this was business and that was simply cheap, meaningless sex, but it was sort of the same. He had received the latest sales figures from Arnolds on the drive over. Arnolds Aluminum was shipping more stock than they had in eight years, and it had even rehired several hundred workers that were furloughed last spring.

All of which made him incredibly happy. That he was the talk of the advertising trades didn't hurt either. Everyone was talking about how Brisker, Pendry & Marks had miraculously resuscitated Arnolds Aluminum, almost overnight.

Yet, when Peter finally got a hold of Armand's hand, it was cold and moist and not very firm.

"Hey, what's wrong?" Peter said.

Armand was sitting behind his desk, quietly. He appeared a bit apprehensive, not at all what Peter expected to see tonight.

"I just saw the figures. You're looking good, Armand, better than I expected. There's nothing to worry about anymore."

There was an uncomfortable moment, a stillness, a slightly dead feeling to the room.

Armand Arnold glanced across the desk at the ad man. He wanted to say something, thank you perhaps, but his mouth was unable to open. He was a man unaccustomed to having nothing to worry about, which made him more worried than worrying did. At least prior to this he *knew* his company was in the toilet and that nothing could be done about it. There wasn't any pressure in that. No dishonor. He was a decent businessman, a competent leader, but he'd inherited a dying company, one that no one expected him to save. Therefore, if Arnolds had gone under, everyone would've simply said, "I told you so."

Only now something *had* been done about Arnolds, and it was no longer on its way to the corporate cemetery. Not only that, but the television spots running in the Midwest markets were building a kind of momentum that, if it continued, could make Armand the head of the number three producer of aluminum foil in the country.

The higher the company soared, the farther he had to plummet.

"I'd gotten used to the idea of running a lame duck," he said to Peter Marks, serenely. "It's harder now. Things go wrong, I can't blame my dad's stubbornness anymore." He paused, looking out the window at the brick chimney rising outside his window. "I'm not sure whether I'm happy about this."

"You're welcome," the ad man said. "I got a little surprise for you." Reaching into his satchel, Peter pulled out a box of cigars, selected a thick Cuban for himself, then tossed one to Armand.

"I was wondering if this would ever be used again," Armand said as he flipped open the wooden case on his desk and emptied the contents of the box into it. "Thank you."

Peter Marks bit off the tip of his cigar and spit it into his hand. "You're worried you can't pull it off, that's all."

That's all.

"I had settled on retiring to a tropical island."

"Well, I guess you got yourself a problem now," Peter said, remembering how tan his secretary was after returning from Martinique and that he should give her a—no he couldn't mix business and pleasure.

"Yeah, I have to keep working, thanks to you."

"Ain't success a bitch," said Peter Marks, lighting the tip of the stogie and filling his cheeks with a deep drag.

After a moment, Armand lit his cigar and offered it up in a salute. "Thanks," he said, sincerely, nestling himself into the supple glove leather of his brand new chair and taking a pull on the tobacco. Along with the smoke, he got a good whiff of fresh leather.

Peter Marks waved him off with his hand. "It was nothing. Sometimes Fate drops a gift in your lap. I chock it all up to statutory rape, my friend," he confided, not making sense to anyone but himself.

Armand perked up at the comment. He had just been about to invite the ad man over to dinner at his house, but decided his sixteen-year-old daughter was already making his life difficult enough. "Really?"

There was something to Peter Marks' statement. It was true, perhaps, that if, as an aimless, sex-crazed twenty-year-old college kid, he hadn't met the then fourteen-year-old Ion and almost gotten caught in her bed by her daddy, none of this might have happened. Not only this particular business with Arnolds, but any of it: his graduation from college near the top of his class, his graduation from college at all, his career in advertising, his success.

"Look, I'm just an ad schmuck. I don't know diddly about running a real business. That's why I have partners. One schmoozes the clients, the other takes care of the details. Me, I concentrate on throwing shit against a wall and seeing what sticks."

The air was thick with smoke, and a comforting haze hung near the ceiling. Armand rose from his new chair and stood behind it, resting his elbows on the back. He was starting to feel a lot better since Peter Marks arrived. A few minutes in this man's ad agency, with the exposed air ducts and the giant rooster perched on the roof, had the same affect, Armand thought, making him feel younger, more alive. He was smiling, on the verge of a chuckle. "What're you saying?" He had no idea what Peter Marks was talking about, but he was enjoying the conversation anyway.

"I don't know. Maybe, nothing," said Peter, grinning. The smiles were contagious. "Just enjoy it while it lasts."

"You know what upsets me the most."

"What?"

"That I can't tell my good-for-nothing relatives on the board that they're out of a fucking job."

Both men had a good laugh at that.

•

Leo Lincoln made the decision to follow Kelsey not more than two seconds after she informed him she was leaving the office early to accompany Barris to dinner with Armand Arnold. This good fortune was almost more than he could take. He'd get to see for himself what Ol' Armand did when he heard his factory had been murdered.

Within ten minutes, Leo canceled his appointments for the rest of the day, called his wife to tell her he'd be working late, and snuck down to his car. It was a Lincoln, a big white Towncar with personalized plates that said, "4 SCORE."

When Kelsey emerged from the elevator and stepped out into the parking garage, he slid himself down in his seat. Limited on how far he could go by his round little body, Leo was only halfway out of sight. As she pulled out and headed for home, he tried to sit back up, but was stuck. Finally extracting himself from beneath the steering wheel, he followed after her.

It wasn't hard; he knew the way fairly well, having made the trip several times before in a vain attempt to catch a glimpse of her undressing in the window. Loitering outside her apartment, he had tried to come up with an excuse good enough to knock on her door in the middle of the night and maybe see her in her robe or T-shirt and panties. That was, until he found out she lived with a guy.

Jealous boyfriends often shot at unwanted voyeurs.

At least, that was Leo's experience.

Nevertheless, Leo's fascination with Kelsey didn't die, it simply had a change of venue.

Kelsey was hired because she was the most qualified person to apply, not because of her appearance—which was attractive to most men, but more so to Leo. She, of course, had not been hired by Leo—he was on vacation at the time—otherwise, looks would have been the sole criteria for her getting the position. His standards differed somewhat from the city's.

And yet, upon returning from the Caribbean, he didn't even notice her right away. At the time, he was in the midst of an affair with one of the secretaries in the County Registrar's Office, a bright woman with bright red hair, bright clothes and a dim taste in men. Aleeta Parks was her name, and for a while, she was enough to draw his lecherous attention away from the other women in the office.

But eventually his infatuation waned.

It took a good two months before he noticed Kelsey. During that time, memos from him came across her desk addressed to the former holder of her job, Gary Kinsley. She didn't look very much like Gary Kinsley, who was short and balding and had teeth the size of most people's fingers. When Leo finally realized she wasn't a man, it was quite a shock. It was a Thursday, a hot one in June and his flush with Aleeta was wearing thin. He barged into Kelsey's office expecting to see Gary so he could chew him out over some memo he'd received about the women's restroom. Leo had no idea what Gary was doing in the women's restroom. All he knew was that that was *his* territory. Busting through the door, he caught a glimpse of Kelsey leaning over a set of plans, hair draping her face, her blouse puckering just enough to let him see a few inches further than she might have liked. His red little face paled at the sight of her and he nearly swallowed a penny he was flipping into the air.

From that moment, he had a new target. This was the Land of Lincoln. And in the land of his ancestors, he usually got what he wanted, even if he had to blow something up to get it.

Kelsey didn't want to be a target—especially not of Leo.

Only problem was, the more she refused him, the more he had to have her.

It was after nearly a year of repeated harassment, bouquets of flowers, and offers of gifts that she finally had enough and threatened to report him for sexual harassment to the police and the District Attorney's office if he didn't let up. The D.A. was Steven Douglas, a man whose family was known to have a chip on their shoulders regarding Lincolns in general. He'd enjoy a chance to drag a Lincoln through the mud to avenge his great-great grandfather's humiliation at the hands of Honest Abe.

Fear of scandal and Douglases caused Leo to cool his jets, as well as disconnect the bomb he'd planted under Kelsey's car. This mandated suppression of his desire gave rise to his present attitude of forced contempt, which masked an even greater need to bed her down, if only to save face.

Leo watched as the limousine driver got back behind the wheel after stopping for some mysterious reason. The man had gone around to the rear door, stuck his head inside for a few seconds, then re-emerged. The well-dressed man, who had just been picked up a block back, jumped out of the back seat and disappeared. A minute later, he returned with a bowler atop his head.

How odd, Leo thought. But then seeing Kelsey and Barris get picked up by a stretch limo wasn't what he expected either. This whole evening wasn't turning out like he thought it would.

The limousine was moving now, and Leo pulled his car out from the curb and continued to follow.

Several other cars, unmarked federal ones, pursued a moment later.

As the big black thing navigated toward its final destination, Leo got a bad feeling in his stomach. As the limousine pulled up in front of the huge white tent that had been erected in the parking lot of Arnolds Aluminum, Leo Lincoln got a bad feeling in his testicles.

He had the horrible feeling he was going to lose them tonight.

•

There were about twenty tables, seating eight people each. Most of the chairs continued to remain empty. A dance floor occupying the center of the tent seemingly held most of the guests hostage. The crowded parquet floor was sandwiched between an eight-piece band producing unobtrusive background music and a buffet that spread out for almost sixty feet. Jason was talking to some people over by the band and Slag was leaning over a few of the items on the buffet, studying them, trying to figure out what they were and why someone might want to eat them. He was a considerable hindrance to the line of folks wanting to get some of whatever it was he was looking at. Most ended their frustration by giving up and going around him.

Meanwhile, Satan stood by the entrance of the tent flanked by Ion and Peter Marks. Ion had her arm through his. And he wasn't sure who was comforting whom.

"You look hot," Peter whispered toward Ion.

"Keep it in your pants, Marks. We're here to sell foil."

Oblivious to the exchange, Satan could feel the rash spreading over his body. He wanted to itch, but he was afraid his entire insides might ooze out if he did.

"Did I ever tell you I used to have nightmares as a child about being squashed by an enormous elephant in a tent very much like this one?" Satan said to Ion.

"Shhhh," she said, quietly.

"Well, I did."

She clenched her teeth in a forced smile. "I don't see anything in here resembling an elephant, Vinnie." Ion glanced around the room. "Except maybe that woman by Slag, and I don't see a trunk on her."

Ion always got nasty and mean-spirited when she was nervous. She had the feeling she was going to be mean a lot tonight.

"The elephant would ask me if it could sit down, and being polite, I would say, 'Sure, have a seat.' That's when it happened," Satan said in a loud whisper directed at her ear.

"I'm going to brain you with that thing sticking out of the leg of lamb, if you don't drop the fucking elephant." Ion was pointing toward the buffet table. Her nervousness was dissolving into something more like bitchiness. Her period had started about a half an hour ago on the way over and she didn't have time to go to the ladies' Port-O-Pottie. Add to that the fact she was famished.

She glanced over at Slag and the food he was researching. It was a vegetarian's nightmare. About the only good thing the spread offered was that the tools used to hack away sides of beef and racks of veal were a lot more dangerous than the stuff used to dice carrots and celery.

"Would you two shut up," chimed in Peter Marks. He was also feigning a smile as several crews from the local television stations had their cameras continually panning the room, hoping they'd catch something they could use. Most likely none of the footage they were shooting would ever make it on the air, but just in case Peter wanted everyone looking happy.

"Why didn't you tell me Armand was going to do something this big," Ion said to Peter. "I should've been consulted."

He was about to say he didn't know when—

"And don't give me any of that shit saying you didn't know," she added before he could. "You did this. It's got your fingerprints all over it," she said, glaring at him.

That wasn't exactly true, but Ion wasn't one of those you could fend off with a flurry of semantics. He had tried many times, and even back in the early days when she was barely fourteen, she wouldn't buy it.

"The Event Planner did this," he said, leaving out the fact that his secretary was the Event Planner. He raised his eyebrow, trying once more in the hope his luck with her would change; it didn't.

"And who would that be? The woman over there talking to the caterer who looks remarkably like your secretary? Don't give me that crap, Peter."

"Smile," he said, as a cameraman made a pass over the room.

"Don't tell me to fuckin smile. I'll sit here and look pissed off whenever I damn please," she said with a big, phony grin slapped across her face.

•

Sweat poured down Leo Lincoln's forehead. His round, red cheeks were swollen with worry; his lips were white with fear, and he'd been biting his tongue for an hour and wasn't sure it would ever work properly again.

A month ago, synchronizing the timers to go off during tonight's second shift dinner break seemed like a brilliant idea. The plant had been deserted for the holiday, which gave him free rein of the grounds, and the long advance gave Armand plenty of time to change his mind. Of course, that was seven hundred and ninety-two hours ago, and now with that number down to one, the idea didn't seem so fabulous.

The cold January had frozen the explosives to the ground and cloaked them under a blanket of white. Brushing aside the drifted snow, Leo gently revealed the device on the stack closest to the tent. He had acquainted himself over the years with the who, what, wheres of bomb making. He was expert in getting the material to set a building on fire, or blow it up. Knew who built the best devices and how to get in touch with those people while keeping his identity a secret. All of which had gotten him to where he was today. He could even assemble an explosive device himself; he had seen enough of them. But in all that time, Leo had never thought to ask anyone how to *deactivate* a bomb.

Huddled beside the base of the stack, less than an hour to go, he was making his first and possibly last attempt to do exactly that.

•

Armand paused at the glass doors that led from the relatively plush corporate offices into the sweltering heat and soot covered floors of the factory. He took in a deep breath and let it out, took in another and held it as he adjusted his tie. Walking through the doors, he was greeted by a warm cheer from the workers, which surprised him. They usually nodded as he passed, said hello occasionally and then only if the Union was being kept happy. Agreeing to a modest wage increase several weeks ago, all he got was a belated Christmas card.

Embarrassed by the display of adulation, Armand Arnold smiled at the men as he passed on his way toward the far door, and ultimately, the tent.

Reaching the huge door, which one of the men working the rollers opened so his boss wouldn't get his hands and clothes dirty, Armand stopped. He glanced down at the ground, at his shoes that were polished so brilliantly, then peered over at the roller's well-worn boots. There was a smell in the air. A metallic scent that reminded him of the first time he set foot in the factory when he was only six. Nothing had changed very much since then, except the size. The place seemed to shrink as he got older. What was once so enormous was merely adequate for what had to get done.

Swinging himself around, Armand turned toward his workers.

"How would you all like to get some free food?" he said.

The place erupted in a gigantic cheer.

When Armand arrived at the entrance of the tent with his army of workers behind him, the TV crews went nuts, scrabbling to get a shot of the scene; the legion of grimy, dust-covered crew, standing as one with their tuxedo-clad leader.

The two hundred or so well-dressed guests inside the tent were openly shocked at the sight of over a hundred men, and a few dozen women, who were eyeing the buffet as much as they were the cleavage popping out of the low-cut dresses several women were wearing.

Peter Marks' fake smile turned into a real one.

"Perfect," he said. "I love a man with style."

Barris watched the men pour into the tent and immediately head for the buffet. They heaped spoonfuls of food onto plates, grabbing as much as they could carry.

"What are they doing here?" Barris said, disdainfully as he shoved two miniature ham and cheese croissants into his mouth.

Kelsey didn't answer him. She was busy studying Armand Arnold in the distance.

Armand walked up to Satan and put out his hand. It was not a forced gesture like someone posing for the cameras; it was genuine.

Staring into the man's eyes, Satan acknowledged for the first time the effect of his "stupid little idea." People were putting foil on their heads. They were lining their ceilings, their hats, their clothes. It had become a fashion in the inner cities. Suburban kids were buying t-shirts and gear with Arnolds Aluminum logos on them. It was joked about on the late night talk shows. A pair of research scientists had even written a paper that said, if someone were to wear foil on his head at all times, there was evidence, he might live a year or two longer.

However, all that seemed removed, hardly real or substantial.

What was undeniable was the powerful glimmer in Mr. Arnold's eyes, something not there the first time they met only a few weeks ago. The distinguished-looking man didn't say anything to Satan. But his eyes spoke volumes.

Moving past Satan, Armand shook hands with Peter Marks, then he kissed Ion on both cheeks.

If all he ever did in life was spark this change, Satan would be satisfied he had served a noble purpose.

•

A bead of sweat rolled down Leo's arm and along the knuckles of his index finger. The drop of perspiration hung stealthily on the underside of his fingertip, only making itself known once he touched the battery and had twelve volts pass through him. It wasn't enough to hurt, really, but the surprise caused his heart to skip a beat.

For the better part of sixty minutes, Leo had done nothing but stare at the bomb in front of him, maybe clean away a bit of snow, and have horrible visions of what would happen if he didn't stop the devices from going off.

He had eight minutes left to disarm four explosive devices, and he hadn't yet made an effort at the first one.

•

The broad, flexible pipes that continually poured heated air into the tent ran down the slope of the canvas roof. The two umbilical cords were hooked to a massive generator truck that vibrated as it churned out the warm, dry wind that was keeping everyone inside comfortable.

Armand stood under one of the openings in the ceiling. A soft flow of tepid air brushed past him as he gazed out at the crowd of men and women, wealthy and blue-collar that were gathered under the protection of the tent.

He glanced at a set of cards displaying his scribbled notes, then cleared his throat.

"I want to thank each and every one of you for coming this evening." He nodded as if to each of them. "Just a few short weeks ago, I was convinced Arnolds Aluminum was dead. I had given up on my grandfather's dream, my father's obsession."

The gathering was quiet.

"But it can be a fine line between making a business profitable and going under. And so much has happened in those weeks. An odd mixture of luck and people and implausible events have come together to make possible this incredible comeback. It proves once again the miraculous rejuvenating power an idea can have."

Leo was shivering, more from fear than cold. He could hear the muffled echoes of someone speaking inside the tent, hear a smattering of applause every so often. Whatever delight he had taken in watching his targets burst into flames in the past was tempered by this moment. All he tasted now was dread. Lifting his eyes toward the white-brick spire that towered over him, Leo calculated where it might land. Dead center of the big top was his best guess. Leo knew there weren't any booby-traps on the four devices. All he had to do was cut the wires. But plastic explosives were temperamental things, and he liked his arms and face enough not to want to lose them. He'd given up on the other three stacks, but he still had to sever the wires on this one or kill a few hundred people. For maybe the first time in his life, Leo Lincoln thought about somebody else.

He snipped the blue wire, then the red.

Armand looked at Satan, Peter, and then his employees. His throat began to tighten, and it was hard to swallow. He sniffed back a set of tears that wanted desperately to roll down his cheek.

"This is only the beginning. It is up to us to maintain and build upon this tiny first step. For the moment, it's enough to save Arnolds from bankruptcy, but there is much to be done to ensure the long-term stability of this company. That's why, as we continue to regain our past glory, we will also reinvest in our future, moving into new markets, increasing the value of this company, as well as offering a wider selection of food storage products. Not just for my benefit, but for all the men and women who have toiled to make this day a reality."

There was a brief bit of applause that almost muffled the three tiny pops.

However, the thunderous crashes that followed could be heard for several miles.

•

Three of the four huge cigars sticking out of the earth around the Arnolds factory exploded, sending bits of masonry whizzing in every direction. The white-brick towers crumbled and smashed to the ground sending a shock wave that rocked the neighborhood and shattered every remaining window in the abandoned Clark Pipe building across the street. The tinkling of broken glass raining down filled the air.

One of the stacks fell on Armand's office, crushing his new chair. Another bisected the factory, destroying the rollers, the presses and most of the lesser equipment. The third demolished the generator truck and took with it the air tubes, which pulled down the tent, collapsing the canvas roof on the band, the food, and the people.

At the base of the fourth smokestack, a shaken and quivering Leo Lincoln crouched in the corner, the wires of this device cut. He warily glanced down to find that his hands and arms were intact. His gaze rose the length of the chimney.

Seeing that he and the chimney were still whole, Leo Lincoln got religion.

"Thank you, thank you, thank you, Jesus, thank you!"

•

Jesus was sitting on a bench outside the Shedd Aquarium. Most people gazed out from this point toward the Lake, or Chicago harbor, but not Jesus.

He was staring back at the city, watching how the lights flickered in the heat waves formed when warmth thrown off downtown structures collided with cold air encroaching from the Lake.

It was from this vantage point that Jesus saw three flashes of light emanating from the area south of the Loop. He directed his eyes toward the spot and witnessed a ball of black smoke rising past the buildings in the foreground.

It was strange, but Jesus didn't realize this was the sign he'd been waiting for until nearly an hour afterward. Walking along the shore of the Lake and thinking about the miracle of life and how the ocean and land and air coexisted, it hit him like a sucker punch, and his head made an involuntary start.

Within minutes, Jesus was standing before the entrance gate to Arnolds Aluminum, surveying the destruction, surveying the odd beauty that an explosion wreaked.

XIX. THE PRINCIPAL OF SURVIVAL

The canvas was covering Satan's face, making it difficult to take in a full breath of air. The claustrophobia that normally kicked in unrestrained at times like this had failed to materialize so far. Instead, he felt far away, as if his mind was protecting him from himself.

His nightmares about the elephant never included the tent being dragged down on top of him, although he was sure they would in the future. Still, the feeling was very much the same—suffocation—only the elephant's butt was wrinkled and smelled far worse than the canvas.

The elephant aside, Satan could think of nothing more demoralizing than being smothered by a giant piece of cloth. That was, until Lilly crawled up to him from under the rubble, carrying a skewer of lamb and vegetables between her teeth.

"Hi," she said without unclenching her jaw. She looked as if she was having a good time.

Satan wasn't, and the sight of her jogged his mind and brought him back from that far away place, depositing him into the nightmare that was his life.

He screamed, shattering a few glasses somewhere.

As the fear rose in his breast, he began to hyperventilate, sucking in large quantities of air. Strangely enough, the stink of the explosion's aftermath reminded him of high school chemistry.

Then he really started screaming.

•

Noel was teetering on one of the stools in the chemistry lab, stools obviously not designed for use by humans. His feet hung off the floor, and the lip of the seat pressed into his thigh, slowing circulation to everything below. Every few minutes he'd shake out his legs in a vain attempt to get some blood down there. It didn't seem to be doing much, other than garnering him a few disdainful glances from the girl sitting across the lab station from him.

One of the greatest minds alive was being kept a physical and mental hostage, he thought, in a room with slow-witted females in painted faces and morons with their football numbers burned into their shaved heads. If that weren't enough, he was about to lose the feeling in his legs. He wondered how many other geniuses in the world had never come to bear fruit because of the intolerant, prison-like atmosphere of public education throughout the ages.

Ten-thirteen. Only three minutes into the period and already Noel was watching the clock.

Ms. Lugar was staring at the students much in the way *Gestapo* officers stared at Jews during the Second World War. She methodically slapped a wooden pointer in her palm and waited an excruciatingly long moment before addressing the class.

"Clazz…" she said, her thick Bavarian accent making it nearly impossible for anyone to understand even her simplest demands. "Todey, vee vill takes a looks at zee combo-nation of elemints zat vill produze a zmall eggsplosion."

Noel's head hurt whenever he tried to decipher what Lugar was saying. So, instead, he ignored her. He'd nod his head every once in a while as if he was listening, but he never heard a word. This was reflected in his test scores, which were hovering around the 30 mark. Last test, he randomly chose the answers, doing no worse than on any of the previous exams where he had tried.

The fact that his grades were sub-par didn't faze Noel. He knew he was smart. He didn't have to prove it like some circus animal. Yet, that's exactly where he found himself—in a circus that only the Romans, and possibly Barnum, could have envisioned.

He used to pass the time sending notes back and forth to Vlady, but he was gone, somewhere in Russia by now. They had made their brief goodbyes on the way home from school two days ago, no ceremony, no tears. Although, every once in a while, Noel would think about his friend, his only friend, and feel a sob rising within him. He fought it, but not well enough at times.

Ms. Lugar slapped the pointer hard on the counter in front of Noel, making a noise as startling as suddenly finding a nuclear bomb in your shorts.

"Vhat our yous doang…Mista Dorobekkkk?"

"Nothing."

This was true. However, what he was supposed to be doing was mixing chemicals. Ms. Lugar re-acquainted him with this fact, with a few unintelligible words and a poke in the stomach with the tip of the pointer.

Noel glared at the woman, who glared back at him.

"Vhat'z on your tinzy brrrain?"

He wanted to tell her that she should've been hung at Nuremberg, but instead, he said, "I'd like to know when I'm ever going to need to know how to blow up something in the real world?"

"If effer yous meets me in zee dark alley," she said, sounding more threatening than a teacher should.

"Can't you see that I'm very distraught at the moment. I'd appreciate it if you did not interrupt my grief."

"Silenze!" she bellowed.

Ms. Lugar was too young to have been born when the War broke out in Europe. However, that didn't stop Noel from imagining her in an SS uniform, exacting new and inventive forms of torture on her prisoners.

"Outzide," she said, pointing toward the door. She turned to the class and slapped the pointer in her hand a few times for good measure. "Vile vee our outzide, continuez vid zee eggsperamint."

Once in the hall, Ms. Lugar slammed the solid oak door behind her. He had done several tours in the hall before, knew the rules. Stand up, no sitting, don't move, no gum. He only followed these guidelines for a few minutes, just in case Ms. Lugar came out to check. After that you were pretty much on your own until the end of the period. During his various stays, he had read every notice and poster within twenty paces in either direction—straying any further and he'd be courting trouble. One time, he surmised the exact number of floor tiles in the hallway. The time after that, he calculated how long it took to lay them.

Doing his time in the hall, Noel used more math, language, and problem-solving skills in one period than he would in a whole day of classes. He had once tried to figure out a way to get Mr. McKinney to count these hours as work-study, but the principal hadn't gone for it, although he admitted it was a creative approach to the problem.

Noel was so completely lost in his thoughts that he didn't realize Ms. Lugar had not gone back into the classroom. He was jolted by a hand to the ribs as she forced him hard against the wall, then thrust her pointed chest toward him menacingly.

"All right, Dorobek. I've had just about enough of your shit. I've let you get away with murder around here. But this is it. I've had enough. I'm drawing the line."

Ms. Lugar went on for another minute or so, but Noel stopped listening after only a few sentences. Not because he didn't want to get a headache from trying to understand her, but because her words were penetrating his mind too clearly. Like a sharp blade piercing the skin without drawing any blood, this wound was painless, but the damage was, nonetheless, extensive. There was absolutely no trace of an accent in her voice. He stood against the wall, dumbfounded. Only once before, when his cat, Freckles, died, had he felt as dumbstruck. Kenny Odorman had dropped Freckles off the roof of his house to see if she would land on her feet.

She did.

Even his mom telling him his dad wasn't ever coming home again, didn't strike him as profoundly as Ms. Lugar—the last of the *Nazis*—without her threatening guttural tone.

He gazed at her like a man looking upon God. Stripped of her menacing voice, she was actually quite pretty. Her hair was soft, her face, creamy. And her lips quivered and shook, a tiny earthquake whenever she spoke.

Ms. Lugar was quiet. She stood up after finishing, retracting her finger that for the last few minutes had been pointed alternately at his head and the floor. He didn't answer. He hadn't heard a word she'd said. Well, she thought, she knew something he'd listen to.

Noel was thinking how nice her breasts were when she cracked the pointer over his head.

•

Mr. McKinney was sucking on a cigarette, his sixty-seventh since breakfast, the Great American Smoke-out only a horrible footnote in his memory. He seemed to be savoring the nicotine and tar in the stick as if it were a gourmet dish. He pulled his hand away from his lips and gazed at the cigarette. It was a beautiful woman to him.

"You smoke, Noel?" Mr. McKinney asked.

Noel was still concerned that his skull had been cracked and wasn't listening very closely to the principal. Feeling around his head, Noel searched for fractures. Luckily, the pointer had snapped in half, diffusing the force of impact. It took some time for the question to reach his centers of thought.

"Ah...no, sir."

The principal stared longingly at the wrapped tobacco between his fingers. "It's a rare and wondrous thing," he said.

"Excuse me?"

Mr. McKinney took a final drag on his cigarette, his last, and snuffed it out unceremoniously. "What's this I hear about Lugar clubbing you over the head with a pointer?"

"What part are you curious about? The fact that it was a completely unjustified attack? Or the possible cerebral damage?" Noel asked.

The principal stared at Noel for a moment. "Where did you learn how to talk like that? Obviously, not public school."

"*Elements of Style*, third edition. We have several copies in the library, although I've never actually seen them used by anyone but me."

"Alright, give me the skinny. I mean, Lugar's a *Nazi*, but she's never actually tried to murder anyone before." He was holding to his desk like he thought the earth was going to suddenly begin quaking. It didn't. The empty cigarette pack stared back at him, mockingly. "What'd you do?"

"Nothing."

"Nothing?" he said, in a tone that was less than believing.

"Not really. All I did was question why I'd ever need to know how to blow something up."

"Ask Brian Verdad."

Noel was surprised to hear Mr. McKinney utter the name. It was well known by everyone in school that the name was not to be mentioned in public, especially in the principal's presence. Mr. McKinney's body shook for an instant. This happened whenever he thought of Brian Verdad. The boy had used the knowledge he gained in chemistry class to destroy the science lab, math lab, and cafeteria simultaneously. The kid was an overachiever as well as a juvenile delinquent.

"That's all there is to the story?" he said.

"Basically," Noel answered.

"Doesn't sound like it deserved a stick across the skull."

"Something happened to her. I think she flipped out or something. She even lost her accent for a while. It was weird."

Mr. McKinney raised his brows. He could never just raise one, although he always wanted to—he found it so debonair—but he couldn't get his muscles to work that way. Whenever he tried, he ended up looking like someone surprised to find a snake in his pants.

Mr. McKinney was raising his brows because Brian Verdad had said the very same thing four years ago about Lugar's missing accent.

"Really?" the principal said, his hands still involuntarily gripping the desk, waiting for the Big One. The Midwest didn't get very many earthquakes, but every century and a half an extremely powerful one would hit. He had the feeling this was it. Kicking the habit cold turkey was going to be more difficult than he thought. It was only two minutes, forty-seven seconds since quitting and already the withdrawals were setting in.

"Is something wrong?" asked Noel, noticing Mr. McKinney's stranger-than-normal behavior. Noel glanced outside to see if the man's wife was somewhere nearby. Mr. McKinney never seemed comfortable around Mrs. McKinney. Of course, she *had* destroyed the football season, and now basketball, which you'd think would make her unpopular with the fathers, but it hadn't. They all loved her. In fact, they were upset with Mr. McKinney for banning her from sporting events. Now they had nothing interesting to watch.

Noel studied the man across the desk. Being so uneasy in his wife's presence Noel wondered how the principal ever had sex with her. He realized it was entirely possible they had never consummated their marriage since they didn't have any children, although Noel couldn't quite imagine anyone passing up the chance to sleep with Mrs. McKinney.

In fact, he would jump at the chance.

Mr. McKinney was staring at his lighter and surveying the desk for something to light. "I've been thinking."

"Yes?" Noel didn't like the sound of this.

"What about your house?" said Mr. McKinney, wondering if he could smoke the dittos piled in front of him.

"What about my house?"

Frustrated, the principal gave up and decided to just come to the point. "Noel, if I'm not mistaken, a bunch of guys in white suits came and dragged your whacked out mother off to the funny farm a few days ago."

"Yeah?"

"So, where are you gonna live?" he said, annoyed.

"With my aunt."

"You don't have an aunt."

"How do you know I don't have an aunt?" Noel asked.

"I checked."

Noel had been wondering about this very subject, housing, for the past few days. His mother wrote a check every month to a well-dressed Japanese man to cover the rent. It was almost time to write the check again. And Noel knew that little piece of paper had to be backed up by money, something he had very little of.

Once he realized his mother was not returning anytime soon, Noel set out a plan to survive. He searched the house and found his mother's bank accounts, taking out enough money to buy food and a few things he thought he should have gotten for his birthday but didn't. There wasn't much in the bank, and Noel knew he'd have to do something about that soon. "I'm going to quit smoking," announced the principal. Actually, the only thing he quit doing was *buying* cigarettes.

"Excuse me?"

"The money I save, I'm going to give to you for rent. There's no need to tell anybody about this. Anyone finds out and they'll want to put you in a foster home till you're eighteen. That's almost as bad as having your mother back living with you."

"What's the catch?"

"Whattaya mean, what's the catch?"

Noel was watching as Mr. McKinney's knuckles became white, the blood being squeezed out of his digits as he held onto the desk. "What do you expect from me?"

"Nothing."

"Nothing?" said Noel much in the same disbelieving way the principal had earlier.

"Not really. Just keep a 'C' average."

"WHAT ARE YOU OUT OF YOUR MIND!?!" screamed Noel.

"I don't think that's too much to ask."

"These teachers hate me. They hate everything I stand for. They have a total disregard for all things academic and creative. Not one of them would give me a 'C' if they had a gun to their head."

Mr. McKinney was staring at his hands when he decided he should let go before any permanent damage occurred.

"They don't hate you, Noel," he said.

"Oh, no." Noel pulled out a light blue essay booklet from his bag and held it up. The words "You'll burn in Hell" were scribbled on the cover right over a gigantic "F" in the recognizable scrawl of Mrs. Reilly, an ancient woman who taught U.S. history and spoke of Thomas Jefferson and Ben Franklin as if she knew them personally.

Mr. McKinney leaned over to get a better look at the booklet. "I wouldn't call it hate. They just don't like the way you treat them...disrespectfully."

Noel took a deep breath. "How can I respect someone who thinks I need an exorcist? Reilly keeps making references to the Salem witch hunts."

Mr. McKinney sat back in his chair thinking how nice it'd be to have a smoke right about now. "Well, she'd know. She was there," he said.

It always amazed Noel how often Mr. McKinney said things that echoed the conventional wisdom of the students he supervised. This led Noel to wonder if the man sitting across from him was unfit to hold his position. It was the sworn duty of principals everywhere to crush the hopes and dreams and beliefs of the pupil, no matter how "right" they may be. A green slate was not a green slate, it was a blackboard. The virtues of freedom of expression were extolled in the classroom, yet denied there as well. It was a wonder anybody learned anything.

But Mr. McKinney was different. Noel could defy the title, but not the man. Which made it difficult to live by his guiding axiom:

Question Authority.

"Why are you doing this to me?" Noel asked.

"Because, Noel..." The principal paused. "I like you."

Noel glanced at the floor. No one, but Vlady ever said that to him.

"*And* I don't want you growing up to be some mass murderer. How'd that look on our record? We've already got credit for Brian Verdad, we don't need a Charlie Manson running around killing people and screaming he went to Parkinson."

"I wouldn't do that," Noel said.

"Oh, you'd be surprised at the things people shout out when they're on a killing spree."

"I mean, I wouldn't kill anybody."

Mr. McKinney took a deep breath. The air was too clear. He needed some nicotine.

"Well, I bet if you asked your mom when she was sixteen, seventeen if she thought she'd go fucking bonkers, I'd venture to say her answer would've been 'No.'"

"That's different. She's crazy."

"Yeah, well, you know, I like you and all, Noel, but insanity has a funny way of rubbing off on people. Kind of like yawning."

Noel started to yawn just at the mention of the word. Then the principal yawned. This went back and forth for a minute or so.

Mr. McKinney stared at Noel through the long moment of silence. "So?"

"So, what?"

"So, are you going to take my offer?"

Noel gazed out the window past the principal and saw Mrs. McKinney walking up the steps. She was gracefully climbing the cement stairs. Her hair was blowing in the December wind—

•

Satan quickly sat up, grating his face along the fallen roof of the tent. His head pounded and the pain caused his right eye to twitch. It was Truth that pounded in his head, and it bore down on him like a lead pipe, like a ton of bricks, like the smokestack would have if Leo Lincoln hadn't snipped the wires. He sat there, silent, trembling, finally realizing why it was he couldn't remember such an important detail of his life, finally recalling the first and only girl he ever slept with.

The fact that it wasn't really a girl but a woman didn't distress him as much as who her husband was.

XX. ASK NOT FOR WHOM THE BELLS TOLL

Once the echoes of the explosions and falling debris had settled, Ion sat up as best she could and coughed out a lungful of dust. A small white cloud came bursting forth. There was a chalky taste in her mouth and she spat to get rid of it. Everything had happened so quickly. One minute she was watching Armand Arnold standing proudly in front of the gathering, a tiny twinkle of hope in his eyes, and the next, she was draped in a canvas shroud.

A few painful moans filtered past her, although she was unable to see anything because her eyes were still closed. Ion had so far refused to open them, convinced the same dust that had gotten in her lungs would love the chance to get in her eyes.

Blindly, she felt around for Peter Marks. He had been next to her when the sky came tumbling down, maybe he'd know what was going on. Searching the surrounding area, she put her hand into something so disgusting she nearly vomited. It was warm and wet, and it squished as she removed her hand from it.

She was feeling Peter's entrails smeared on the ground.

"Peter," she whimpered. "Oh, God."

"Yes?" God answered.

"Am I dead?" she asked the voice which seemed so kind and familiar.

"I don't think so," He replied.

Ion reasoned it would be best to meet God with her eyes wide open, so she lifted her lids slowly, trying to keep the dust out. But this was Heaven and the dust had obviously been left on earth along with the rest of her body. She stared in the direction of the voice and found that God looked very much like Peter Marks.

"Are you all right?" Peter said to her.

She peered around and saw no puffy white clouds only a huge ham bone and a side of beef. She glanced down and saw that what she had thought were Peter's guts was actually just a crumbled Jell-O mold that had been doused with a huge pot of coffee.

"I thought you were dead," she whispered, softly. She wrapped her arms around him and he squeezed her tight. "What happened?" she asked after a quiet moment.

"I think I've been fired," he said.

Peter Marks rarely made sense to her. He always seemed to be talking in some advertising patois, some dialect that mimicked English and yet mocked it as well. Back when Ion was just a teenager, he would explain an idea he had for an ad campaign, and she'd stare back at him blankly, thinking how in the hell could what he was saying possibly work. But there was always something in the way he said things that made her believe in him.

When, after a little help from her, he got his first job as a copywriter, he created one of those ads that she hadn't understood and sales jumped. She still didn't understand it, but she had to admit it worked.

"Fired?" she said, hoping to get a further explanation.

Peter Marks pointed toward the front flaps of the tent. The entryway was about the only thing left standing and she had a clear view of the outside. Past his finger, past the opening, Ion could see the destruction that the three falling stacks had exacted on the factory. The administrative offices were nearly leveled with little more than a wall here or there left standing. The factory building itself was less damaged, but the stack that had fallen across it had destroyed most of the primary equipment inside. Even if the machinery could be repaired, rebuilding the smokestacks would take time. Simply replacing them was out. The company would have to go through the entire permitting process all over again.

Arnolds Aluminum was dead. In a last gasp, one of the furnaces belched out a thick cloud of unfiltered smoke, then made a noise like a dying dinosaur, and itself became extinct.

Hidden in the shadows, Leo Lincoln clenched his fist triumphantly, while Ion lowered her head in defeat.

A quiet sadness enveloped her and she sunk deeper into it.

"It's over," she said.

"Looks that way," Peter sighed, putting his hand on her shoulder to comfort her. "I really thought we were going to pull it off. Just a bad break, I guess."

He shook his head and lowered his eyes to the green outdoor rug that had been thrown over the parking lot. The covering looked much less elegant up close, and reminded him more than anything else of a miniature golf course. And he always hated miniature golf.

•

Arnolds Aluminum was several structures—built at various times over the years—which were fused into one haphazard unit. Very little was left intact from the early days, it had all been rebuilt or added on to. The piece-meal way the factory had been constructed had given rise to several unique characteristics. A stroll down any hall and you could tell by the color of the floor when the section was built. Green from the thirties, black from the fifties, yellow from the sixties, and white from everything after '72. The main hall not only contained all of these colors, it also changed widths several times. The plumbing and electrical systems put in at different times didn't function properly with each other. When the factory was in full production, it might take ten minutes to flush a toilet in the administration building.

Of course, that was all academic now. You couldn't flush anything at Arnolds Aluminum at the moment, except maybe the hope of ever doing business again.

Armand Arnold crawled out of the tent and got to his feet. He surveyed the factory grounds, the plant his father and his father's father had built, and, immediately, he burst into tears.

He cried for forty-five minutes without stopping—twenty-two seconds of which made it on the eleven o'clock news right after footage of Punxsutawney Phil seeing his shadow, predicting six more weeks of winter.

Jesus watched from the gate. He wanted to do something to comfort the man, but the police and fire crews wouldn't let anyone in. And besides, he was just a mechanic and wasn't sure he'd say the right thing.

Ion and Peter Marks climbed out from under the canvas with the help of two firemen, one of which asked Ion for her phone number.

She put her arm through Peter's, and held him close. As the sirens of police cars and fire trucks arriving filled the air, the two of them stood tightly pressed together in the cold, staring at Armand Arnold, unable to do anything for him, unable to ease his pain, except, finally, to get the news crews to stop filming.

•

"This is unbelievable," Satan said as the limousine drove them back to their respective homes. Their clothes were muddied and wrinkled and some were even torn. "How could this happen to me?"

The seating was cramped since Lilly forced her way into the limo at the factory. She did this despite Ion's objection to her being there, and her presence made a tight situation that much more uncomfortable both physically and emotionally. Kelsey reached around Lilly who was sitting on the floor where everyone's feet were supposed to be. Finally overcoming the obstacle, Kelsey rubbed Satan's forehead to try and ease the tension in his face. Lilly watched with a thin tolerance, thinking she could, and should, be doing whatever rubbing was going to be done to Satan.

Barris stared out the car window thinking about how to sell more sneakers and humming to himself. He was the only one not in a foul mood, and he was pretty much ignoring everyone else so it could stay that way. Lucky for him, he'd already been paid for his work on the Arnolds campaign, so tonight didn't effect him in the least. Although, he was annoyed the explosions had interrupted the party before he got to eat anything. The food looked incredible.

"I don't know how," Kelsey said quietly, still soothing Satan's temples. "But Leo Lincoln's involved in this somehow. I know it."

"Lincoln?" said Satan, not understanding how Lincoln could have been involved in his having sex with his principal's wife.

"It all works out just a little too damn nice for him."

Satan stared at her for a moment once he moved out of the way of Lilly's head and could see her. "*What* are you talking about? I'm sitting here reliving two of the most horrific moments of my life, which, up until about two hours ago, one I didn't even remember, the other hadn't happened, and you're driveling on about the 16th President of the United States! The man's been dead for a hundred and forty years. Give up the torch, woman!"

"Not Abe...*Leo*," Kelsey said.

Ion glanced up from her fingernails, which she had been playing with constantly since climbing in the limousine after the police finished questioning everyone. "This doesn't have anything to do with that *fucking* elephant sitting on you, does it?"

"No...it doesn't. However, I did warn you about the groundhog."

"Clamp it, Vinnie."

Jason patted Ion on the knee. "Hey, everybody, let's cool it. We're all a little jumpy. We got a scare tonight."

Ion picked his hand off of her leg and threw it aside. There was no emotion in her voice. Except maybe a touch of anger.

"I didn't get a *scare*, thank you, Jason. Everything we've been working for, literally, went up in smoke tonight. Weeks of planning, Weeks of strategizing—for what!?! Nothing! So, don't try to be Mr. Smooth n' Unruffled. Stick to playing horn and let me worry about handling people."

"You're real good at handling people. You just don't know shit about caring for them."

"Yeah, it was all about me me me when I was helping you. You'd be just another lawyer stuck in a job he hates without me."

Jason's round eyes tightened up and he pulled his lips in so that they looked like two dried prunes. "Fuck you, Ion," he said. Then he reached past Slag and banged on the glass separating them from the driver. He had to pound several times before getting the man's attention. "Stop the fucking car!"

With a look of surprise, even more surprise than when he witnessed the three smokestacks crashing to the ground, the startled driver nodded his head, and then, at the first available spot, pulled the limousine over to the side of the road.

"Jason, don't do this, she's just upset," pleaded Kelsey.

"I know she is," he said. "So, are a lot of people."

Ion made no move to stop him, and in an instant, Jason flung open the door, climbed over Lilly, and disappeared down the street.

In a minute, the sound of Jason's dress shoes clapping the cement faded away.

"I'm composing a poem," said Slag as if asked what he was doing.

Everyone looked at him except Barris, who instead went, "Huh?"

"What an asshole," Ion said. "Shut the door, Vinnie, and let's get out of here."

Satan reached out for the door when Lilly stopped him.

"Why don't you get the door yourself?" she said, glaring at Ion.

"Lilly, shut up before I break your glasses. Then where will you be? Lost, I imagine, since you can't see ten feet without them."

Satan glanced back and forth between Ion and Lilly as they squared off. He was hit in the upper arm by Ion, which startled him.

"Close the door."

"Don't hit him!" Lilly shouted, pushing Ion back into her seat.

"I'll hit him whenever I damn please." Ion took another shot at Satan.

"Hey," he said, holding his arm.

"Would you two cut it out!" screamed Kelsey as Lilly and Ion began rolling around on the floor of the limousine, pulling hair and throwing punches to the midsection like two seasoned professional female wrestlers.

Kelsey started to try and break them up, when Barris put his arm out and stopped her.

"Let 'em fight it out," he said, hoping to see some underwear if it got rough.

However, having the fight take place in such cramped quarters was causing everyone in the limo—except Barris—to flinch at every punch, every thrown elbow. One nearly hit Kelsey in the jaw and she gave the two a kick in the ribs to show her displeasure. A shoe flew by, followed by the foot it belonged to, one just missing Satan's head, the other connecting with his chest.

"Can't you two see that I'm in the middle of a near nervous breakdown," he wheezed, trying to catch his breath. "I've just recently realized I had sex with my high school principal's wife."

"Who cares?" said Ion as she mashed Lilly's face into the carpet.

"I do," Lilly mumbled, spitting out a few fibers. "Was she pretty?"

"That's not the point," yelled Satan. "Don't you get it?"

Slag raised his head from the one inch squared Post-it pad he was writing on and parted his hair. "How do you spell *conflagration*?"

"Just like it sounds," sneered Ion.

An earring went whizzing by, then another shoe.

Satan had had just about enough of this. He decided to put his foot down. "Somebody's gonna get hurt."

"What're you, my mother?"

"Did you hear me? I said, stop it," Satan shouted, stomping his foot on the ground by way of Ion's hand.

She yelped and shook out the pain. "I'm going to crack your head open, and we're gonna finally find out what's really in there," she said.

"Depends what side you crack," he said defiantly, even though, or perhaps because, she wasn't listening anymore and was now trying to crack Lilly's head on the curb. He continued anyway. "Hit me on the left and all the useless mathematical equations I ever learned'll come pouring out."

"What about the right?" asked Kelsey, suddenly curious.

"Big cuddly stuffed animals."

By this time, it was clear that Ion was winning the battle, having Lilly pinned with her head halfway out the open door. Passersby were beginning to stop and congregate outside the black limousine. A few moved on when Ion sneered at them. After it had become painfully certain there was no way for her to prevail fairly, Lilly decided to bring out her secret weapon and drop it like a bomb.

"That's it, Cousin!" she said, smiling, her eyeglass frames twisted on her face.

Immediately, a calm washed over the car. Ion let go of Lilly and blew out a little "Hmmff." The softness returned to Ion's face, even as she bit down hard on her lower lip.

"Very good," she said.

Satan looked confused. "Cousin?"

There was no answer from either of them.

When it finally hit Satan, it was like having a safe drop on him from three floors up.

"All along, you knew who she was?"

Ion was silent.

"All this time, you let me act like an idiot, having *you* help me in keeping her away?"

Ion was about to say something when he cut her off.

"And don't you tell me to shut up or you'll knock me in the head or something like that. I'm not afraid of you!"

He flinched as she raised her hand to point at his face.

"Vinnie, I don't tell you how to wear your foil. You don't tell me how to run your life."

He stared at her for a moment, his eyes blinking more often than they normally did, the right side of his mouth turned up in contempt. Her statement was completely illogical, but then logic was never a priority for Ion.

"Can somebody please tell me what's going on?" asked Kelsey.

Satan glanced at her. "I really don't know, Kelsey. Which is pretty much how my whole life has been. Only now I don't know for a reason. Isn't that right?" he said to Ion.

Lilly cleared her throat, still unable to move with Ion on top of her. "I think we should discuss this at a later time," she said, clearing her throat again, a little louder this time.

Ion shot her a look. "Who asked you?"

"What seems to be the problem here?" asked a policeman as he bent down to get a better look inside the limousine. He was a big man with mahogany skin and a thick mustache.

Ion tilted her head, throwing her mane of blonde to one side, giving the cop a big smile. "Family dispute, Officer."

"I see. You know, you're parked in front of a fire hydrant?"

"Really?" Ion said, trying to sound surprised. Of course, she knew it was there. She had thought about wrapping Lilly's head against it, but the fight ended before she could put her plan into action.

For her part, Lilly was trying to smile while her head hung out the door. The uniformed man had wonderfully strong legs, and she wanted to reach out and touch them. "Nice night, isn't it?" she said, looking up at the sky.

Ion dragged Lilly inside the car.

"We'll be on our way, Officer," Ion confided to the cop, giving him a knowing smile and a charming, apologetic nod of her head. "Sorry to trouble you."

"Not at all." The cop returned the volley with an admonishing gaze that was more playful than condemning. "You have a good evening."

"We'll sure try and do that," added Satan in a fake Southern accent just as the car began pulling away from the curb.

Cops always seemed to let rednecks and pretty woman off the hook.

•

After dropping off Slag, then Kelsey and Barris, the limousine pulled up in front of the graystone house on Grace and out stepped Satan, followed by Ion and Lilly. The night air was crisp and it burned Satan's lungs as he took a deep breath. He was thinking about Lilly and Ion and how angry he was at both of them, when he glanced down at his feet and saw the body lying across the steps. There was a torn piece of luggage dragged halfway up the stoop, and a small valise that was set under the head of the man as a pillow. Satan was sure the man was dead, but then he had been sure Ion's dad was fatally wounded by the bus. Still, he thought it best, having no interest in touching a dead person, to sort of jab the body with his toe. The body shook, then rolled like a Slinky down the steps.

Lilly screamed as the body came to rest on her right shoe. The only one she had been able to find after the fight.

At the piercing sound from Lilly's throat, the corpse opened its eyes and lifted its head as if awakened too early by an alarm clock.

"He's alive!" yelled Lilly as if she was yelling, "He's dead!"

Ion shoved Lilly out of the way, then gently lifted the man's head with her left hand while patting his chest with her right. "Are you all right?" Ion gingerly cradled the man, using her body to warm him.

"All...right?" Vlady said, a bit deliriously. His throat was tight, and he tried to swallow. "I am..."

"Good."

"...looking...for...Noel," he added after a moment.

Crouching down for a closer look, Satan kneeled over the man, pushing the hair away from his face. The weather and sun had done battle with the man's skin. It was cracked and red. Tiny lines were etched into the surface, making him appear much older than he actually was. Yet something about the man's eyes was familiar to Satan.

"Vlady?" he said, softly.

Vlady wanted to say something back, but he was too weak, his head becoming slack in Ion's hand as he fainted.

"He's burning up," she said, touching his cheek. "We should get him inside and call a doctor."

Satan handed the keys to Lilly, and while she got the door opened, he and Ion lifted Vlady off the cold stone steps and carried him into the house. A moment later, Lilly gathered up the two pieces of luggage and brought them inside as well.

•

Ion was lying on the vinyl couch in the emergency room waiting area when Satan emerged from behind the ER doors.

"The doctor said he'll live."

"Great." She yawned and rubbed her eyes. "Who the fuck is he?"

"A guy I knew from high school. His folks moved back to Russia in 1985."

"Why would anyone move *back* to Russia?"

Satan sat down, balancing himself on the edge of the cushion since Ion was taking up most of the couch. "I don't know."

She was staring at the ceiling tiles, which were all different shades of white on their way to yellow.

"So...that's it?" he said.

"What's it?" she asked without taking her eyes off the ceiling.

"Arnolds Aluminum blows up, and I find out I am Oedipus, I am Hamlet, having sex with my surrogate father's wife. And now we all live unhappily ever after? Is that how it goes?"

Ion glanced down from the tiles. "What are you talking about, Vinnie?"

"I'm talking about life, my life, what am I going to do for the rest of it?"

"What does fucking some principal have to do with life?"

"I didn't have *sex* with my principal. I had sex with his wife."

"All the more reason to be happy," she said without much enthusiasm.

Satan stared at Ion, studying her. He has seen her upset, cranky, annoyed, frustrated, but never defeated.

"I'm confused," he said. "One minute I'm doing talk shows, filming commercials...I'm the talk of the town. The next, I'm sitting in a hospital, the proud owner of five thousand shares of Arnolds stock, which this morning were worth about two hundred thousand dollars, and tomorrow will be worth $47.50."

"Keep your voice down."

"I don't want to keep my voice down. I like SHOUTING AT THE TOP OF MY LUNGS!"

"It's a hospital. Can't you read?" She pointed at one of several signs that shouted 'Quiet Please!' with the exclamation mark ironically inappropriate.

"Yes, I can read. What do you take me for, the average American?"

A few of the average Americans in the waiting area began glaring at him over copies of People and the National Enquirer.

"I wanna know what's next?" he said.

"There is no next, Vinnie. That was it. Tough break. Better luck next time."

"Whattaya mean? Where's your pal, Peter Marks?"

"Taking care of Armand. Making sure he doesn't try to slit his wrists, not that I'd blame him."

Just then Lilly entered the room, returning from the cafeteria with two bagels, a turkey sandwich, and a Planter's roasted nut bar.

"Hi, guys. This was all they had left."

Satan tapped the sandwich. From the timbre, it sounded like it was made of wood. "I'll take a bagel."

Lilly sat down right beside Satan, pressing her body against his and moving more often than she needed to.

"What are you doing?" He was attempting to spread some cream cheese on his bagel, finding it difficult with all her jiggling.

282 | IDIOTS IN THE MACHINE

"I told you I wasn't gonna wear anything underneath my new dress." Lilly began to expose more and more of herself until Ion whipped the sandwich at Lilly's head.

It made a sound—THWACK.

"Ouw. That hurt."

"Lilly, pull your skirt down. Christ." Ion ripped off a chunk of the nut bar. "You can't go around flashing genitalia in public just cause you haven't gotten laid in twenty-four years," she said with a mouthful.

Prying himself from Lilly, Satan stood up and paced the room a few times, then stopped in front of Ion.

"What about the never quit, never-say-die woman who would put a bull-horn to my head and bark orders at me all day and night, what happened to her?"

"She just said 'die.'"

•

Like most bell towers, the one rising above St. Augustine's was a pretty drafty place. The wind passing through the Gothic arches often sent the clappers against the sides of the thick metal for no apparent reason. The fact that the church was located in the windiest of all cities didn't help matters.

Kenny Odorman found the bells most annoying. He spent much of his day staring at the three odd-sized castings as they hung overhead, wondering as they swayed in the wind, how he could cut them down without crushing himself in the process. The oversized chimes seemed determined to ruin any moment of peace, any moment of rest he tried to achieve.

What the bells didn't wreck, Father Leery did.

The priest had changed tactics since bringing him up to the bell tower. Instead of leaving Kenny alone and hungry, now, he never seemed to sleep. Three in the morning, six in the evening, the crack of dawn—all hours of the day—he would appear in front of Kenny with a few strange words—mostly clipped passages from the Bible—and sometimes with a bowl of soup or a piece of bread.

Kenny ate the food, not because he was hungry—he had given up on life and no longer needed such things as nourishment. He ate because it was the only way to make the priest leave. The man would stand there in his black frock and hover over him like a mother over a baby until every crumb, every drop of broth was finished.

"Waste not, want not," Father Leery always said.

But Kenny Odorman didn't want anything anymore, except to be left alone. He would gladly die of starvation if only he could have a few hours of peace. Even the bells, which he despised, would be tolerable if the priest just stopped coming to visit.

It was late afternoon and the winter sun hung over the tops of the buildings to the west like a big, bright billboard for some new diet soda. The wind was picking up and the bells were beginning to hum. Out of habit, Kenny stared east toward the Lake, and the Clearwater Sanitarium.

The Clearwater building was white with heavily painted sills surrounding frosted windows that had tiny wires crisscrossing through the glass. Only on the fourth floor could you see inside. The windows there were clear, Kenny supposed, because no one from the street or neighboring buildings could see into that level. The surrounding buildings were mostly low two and three story structures. He figured the sanitarium's designers never took into account the church tower—who'd be watching from there?

Unfortunately for Kenny Odorman, doing exactly that had been his only source of entertainment.

Only nothing eventful ever seemed to happen in the sanitarium. The patients would shuffle from one door to the next, stopping slowly to stick their head in each room as they passed, hoping to catch a glimpse of something. Kenny wasn't quite sure what these folks expected to see, but whatever it was, they never saw it. They just went on their way to the next room where they'd find the very same nothingness as the room before.

At some point during this daily ritual, his attention eventually focused on one woman, a frail black-haired wispy thing who did nothing but sit in bed watching television from dawn until well past ten in the evening. She laughed often at the programs, hitting her bony fist into the mattress and throwing back her tiny head in hysterics. What she was watching Kenny could never tell for the TV was just out of sight, but she seemed to enjoy every second of it.

He was observing the woman now.

She and the other patients of Clearwater appeared to him to have a very limited existence—not that when he thought about it his wasn't, stuck in a freezing cold, drafty bell tower with a maniac priest tossing him bread and soup at all hours of the day and night. But somehow, the condition of these people's lives touched him in a way his own plight did not. Perhaps, it was because he had given up on himself. He had never been very tough in a pinch. As long as he was bullying someone or trashing somebody's credit rating, he could forget about how empty he felt inside, but up here, with no one to bully, no one to push around, all Kenny Odorman did was think about what little there was inside him.

It would have been very easy for him to just cut the ropes of the bells and let them fall where they may, which was most likely right on top of him. Still, somewhere deep within him, Kenny Odorman cared, just a little. He tried to keep it out of his mind—it depressed him more than the emptiness. He was much happier not feeling anything—but that tiny bit of care surfaced from time to time, whenever he thought about what he had given up.

Kenny Odorman had lost a great deal during his obsessive search for Noel Dorobek. He had lost much more than just his freedom. He had most likely lost the only job he ever enjoyed. Three weeks unexcused absence was like not paying your bills for a decade. But that wasn't all; he had lost his will to live, and now, he was losing his mind.

"What is it you'd be thinking about, lad?" asked Father Leery as he crawled through the narrow opening that led down into the steeple, wondering what was inside the mind of this criminal, any criminal, curious as to how they could do the horrible things they did and live with themselves?

Kenny didn't answer. Instead, he continued to watch the woman laugh and pound the bed.

"Something devious for sure, I'll bet," remarked the priest as he smoothed and straightened his frock. "Who are your friends, boy?"

Kenny Odorman turned and looked at the man and sighed. He felt tired, used up. He could sense that the life was seeping out of his body as if an open wound was leaking blood onto the stone floor.

"Why are you doing this to me?" Kenny asked, not really caring what the answer was, his voice rough and cracked from underuse.

"God told me to."

"Hmph," Kenny nodded, looking out again. There was a long pause as the bells hummed in the wind, then finally he returned his gaze to the priest. "Did he happen to tell you *why*?"

Father Leery stood with his head directly under the smallest bell, making him look like the pope with a thyroid problem. The priest put his hand to his chin and rubbed it a moment. He hadn't thought to question God's Word to him regarding the young man. He simply took it as a test of his will to do what it took to save his Parish. He hadn't really considered the man's feelings at all.

"And what are you meaning by that?" he asked the man. It had been the first time the man had spoken in two weeks, so he took it as an important question.

"I mean, what did I do that would justify this? I'm asking for informational purposes only," Kenny said, in an almost polite tone. Gone was the menacing sneer, the nasty delivery. Gone was the crude, condescending language. Kenny Odorman was nearly a perfect gentleman. As he closed on his impending death, he reverted to the goodness and innocence he had been born with.

"Are you wanting to confess your sins, boy?"

"I never put very much stock in sins or confessions. I guess I figured if there was a God, he'd know everything already, so why'd I have to go through all the pain of reliving them over again?"

Kenny leaned back against the cold stone and stared out over the city. Nothing very interesting. Just your average view of rooftops and TV antennas. Maybe a few hundred years ago when people lived their lives mainly on the ground and not above it, this panorama might have been a sight, but after being up in the Hancock and the Sears, this was ho-hum. Still, a few days ago—his first night in the tower—he had seen a terrible burst of smoke rising from the riverfront on the Southside. He couldn't see much else, the office buildings in the Loop blocked his view. The smoke didn't last long, less than an hour, but it was spectacular while it lasted.

Kenny Odorman was about to tell the priest to stop coming by, to stop bringing him food, when he happened to notice the woman pounding her fists into the mattress again. There was someone else there, a man, and he was fixing the drapes. As the man pulled open the curtains to let more of the dying sunlight into the room, Kenny got a glimpse of the TV for the first time. Models strutting down a runway wrapped in foil. Then a man was surrounded by the starlets. Immediately, Kenny recognized the face on the screen. Over and over and over again, the thirty second ad repeated itself on the television. Over and over and over again, the face of Noel Dorobek filled the tube. It was unmistakably him, older, yes, but it was definitely him.

And then another thought hit Kenny: He had seen this face recently, on the street awhile back. A few weeks before Christmas, to be exact. Only he didn't look like that. He had on a big down jacket with all the feathers at the bottom, big red mittens, and a knit cap.

In that moment of recognition, in that brief instant of cognitive realization, Kenny Odorman became rejuvenated. A slight, but definitive brightness came into his eyes. A sneer began to form below the tiny scar under his nose. Kenny Odorman was born again. "It's him!"

"Yes, son, yes, it is," screamed the priest joyfully as he saw the light of God enter the man.

Like the Phoenix rising from the ashes, Kenny rose to his feet, and after a moment of unsteadiness where he tried to get his legs to work after weeks of disuse, he pushed past Father Leery, made his way to the passage door, and stumbled down the one hundred and thirteen tower steps, cracking three ribs, and rendering himself unconscious.

XXI. PRE-PARTUM DEPRESSION

It was a day later that the weather broke. It came without warning, a quick February thaw. So quickly, in fact, Satan wondered how the glass buildings in the Loop hadn't cracked from the strain.

As cold and unbearable as it had been since the middle of November, Indian Summer melted away the remaining ice and snow that hid in the shadows, and melted away the sullen disposition of the people passing each other on the streets. A big pink heart sitting atop the See's Candy store on Michigan that looked ridiculous in the freezing cold, somehow seemed inviting in the warmer weather.

Satan weaved a path down the sidewalk, his head slumped forward, thinking how depressed he was and how much he'd rather be in bed with a vaporizer on. The lightweight baseball-style Gamma Cap Ion had originally sewn for Spring was resting on top of his head. A large red "C" was emblazoned across the front, the Arnolds logo in back.

"What's the 'C' for?" he had asked her.

She gave him a look. "Are you kidding me?" She paused for a moment before realizing he wasn't. "The Cubs…Chicago Cubs…"

He stared back at her blankly.

"…Cubbies…baseball…does any of this sound the least bit familiar to you?" she said.

More blankness.

"…Wrigley Field…it's like ten blocks away."

"Wrigley. The gum guy," said Satan, enthusiastically.

"Yes, the 'gum guy.' He also invented the game," she said with a very sad sigh.

"What game?"

"BASEBALL! You idiot!"

So, here he was navigating the streets of Chicago wearing his Cubbies' hat, severely depressed. Depression was often seen on the faces of those donning Cub's hats, but that was because the team hadn't won a World Series since 1908. Satan's despair had to do with exploding aluminum foil factories and the snipping of an umbilical cord.

When Satan was a boy, his mother had her own way of lifting him out of his doldrums. She would bring him a glass of hot spiced cider, sit him in a big comfortable chair, then slap him across the face three or four times and tell him to snap out of it.

Maybe that's why he never visited her, punishment for hitting him. Only every once in a while, when he was alone and really calm, he realized that she *had* made him forget about what was upsetting him, which usually was that his father wasn't there anymore.

It wasn't that he forgave her at these times, he just understood.

Crossing the intersection, Satan glanced over a couple of blocks, and he could just catch a glimpse of the Wrigley Building. It was white and intricately detailed, and for many years had been the city's trademark.

The gum guy made him think of Ion, her golden hair, the tiny beads of sweat forming on her upper lip as the temperature outside climbed. Then everything made him think of her. He thought about her constantly, the way she moved, the way she spoke—the way she looked at the hospital when she told him there was no next step, that she didn't have a plan. Even then.

Ion was taking the explosion at Arnolds harder than anyone, including Armand Arnold. She discontinued the phone calls to reporters, stopped making hats, and reduced her visits to his house until they were almost nonexistent. Her father was out of the hospital and at home recuperating—that was the excuse she gave—but according to Lilly, she hadn't visited him in days.

Ion had come into his life and turned it upside down. She forced him to see the world as a place where reality was not always what you wanted it to be. But mostly, she stirred in him feelings he never thought possible.

And he hated her for it, almost as much as he hated his mother and father for leaving. Almost as much as he loved her.

Feeling dejected and unloved and unlucky and thinking maybe he'd been right all along that the only place on Earth he'd find happiness was in the center of it, Satan trudged through the crowds, gripping a letter from the

Archdiocese of Chicago saying it would stop picketing his house since he had gotten what he deserved and they now felt sorry for him. Satan always hated when people felt sorry for him. They never did things because they liked him; they did them out of pity. He wasn't complaining—not really—he just didn't like it. Niro, his landlord, wouldn't be so understanding about the overdue rent. The problem was Vlady's hospital visit cost twenty-two hundred bucks for them to poke and prod and tell him he needed to stay in bed and drink a lot of liquids. What a shocker. Luckily, Satan had gotten the hospital to bill them for it. He could put it off until Vlady could take care of it himself. Not so easy to put off was the hundred and sixty dollars worth of prescriptions the doctor wrote. Those needed to be filled immediately. Then there was food—another two hundred. Vlady wasn't eating yet, but the doc said in a couple of days he'd be up and around and ravaging the refrigerator.

The fridge was so packed with liquid, every time anyone opened it, the thing seemed to slosh to one side, then back again, like his stomach after drinking too much.

Add it all up, the pills, the food, the electric and oil bills—very important during Winter in Chicago—and Satan was out of money.

Unfortunately, the mysterious government check that came every month from parts unknown was late because of a budget dispute between Congress and the President. *He* was busy golfing and playing pool, and *they* were in the middle of prime fundraising season. Both were too preoccupied to realize that—just like their campaigns—the country needed money to run. Who knew when the check would get sent out? Satan only hoped it came before his death benefits were paid.

On top of all that, Mr. McKinney's rent allowance, which normally arrived the first of every month, had yet to appear, putting Satan in a complete financial quandary.

The rent was already six days late. And Niromshi Nagasikima, probably still pissed off about being born in a World War II internment camp, even though his family was rich and had been in America for generations, was just waiting for an excuse to exact revenge on any pink-skinned round-eye that happened to cross his path.

After a moment, during which Satan pictured Niro wielding a saber and beheading his delinquent tenants in lieu of the customary THREE DAYS PAY THE RENT OR QUIT notice, Satan realized Mr. McKinney had never been late with a check before.

Sweating as much from his predicament as the heat, Satan stepped up to the entrance of Clancy's Drugs. He stopped outside the door. He wasn't looking forward to seeing Ion. She had taken to staring at him with a disappointed look on her face. He took a second to gaze at the sign over the door—Ol' Clancy smiling away, even though he was still dead. An old woman pushed open the glass door, nearly smacking Satan in the head. Instead of apologizing for almost breaking his nose, she scolded him for not getting out of the way sooner. So much for the heat cheering everyone up.

The instant Satan set foot in Clancy's he knew why. The heater over the door blasted him with hot air. He glanced around the store. The place was a sauna, people sweating, moving slowly, nodding to each other so they didn't have to speak.

It was like hell.

A fat woman wearing grape colored sweats had collapsed on a plastic chair, laying in wait for her prescription of Valium to be filled. She was fanning herself with a heart-shaped candy box, the contents of which she had devoured while sprawled on the seat.

"I'm gonna pay for this," she kept assuring everyone and anyone who passed by, hoping to prevent being slapped with a shoplifting charge.

A smear of chocolate ran across her upper lip and the woman was trying to reel it in with her tongue. She tilted back her head in a vain attempt to get her face and mouth closer together. Satan had been hungry up till now, but quickly lost his appetite.

Ion was helping someone at the counter when she heard the clang of the door chime and saw Vinnie enter the store. He looked almost normal in his cute Cubbies hat. Her heart sank, and she thought about bolting out the back before he could see her, but she was the only cashier on duty.

She had let him down.

While the customer wrote out a check, Ion thought back to that first day when Vinnie came into the store looking for just the right pen to address his letter to the President. It seemed so long ago, years away, even though it had been less than two months. So much had changed since then.

Ion glanced up to see Vinnie staring down one of the aisles in the direction of the pharmacy.

The average man would have noticed something was wrong with her by now and said something, but Vinnie wasn't an average guy. He was part idiot, part genius, and you never knew which one was going to show up at any given moment.

Ion took the woman's check, slipped it into the register, then bagged her hair coloring kit and denture cream.

"Thanks for shopping at Clancy's."

The woman took the bag with a smile. She seemed like a nice woman, an attractive grandmother-type. She cheerily made her way out of the store. As Ion heard the tinkle of the bell above the door, there was a moment where Ion thought she might cry.

Running her hand through her long, blonde mane, her blue-green eyes greener against the pinkness surrounding her irises, she had an irresistible beauty about her. Many men would die for a woman like Ion. Many men would kill for a woman like her. And yet all those men could never have touched her like Vinnie had. In the thought of leaving him, there was an emptiness in her stomach, a void as deep as the blackness of sleep.

Since the death of her mother, Ion had been unable to feel a strong emotional tie to anyone or anything. Leaving became a process and a pattern, just one of the things she did, like breathing or sleeping.

She didn't love Vinnie, not the way a woman loves a man, not completely anyway.

A sharp pain shot through her chest.

What she was experiencing was more like the feelings a mother had for her child. Ion passed backward through time and imagined how her mother must have felt leaving her daughter, her husband, her life behind. Much the same way, Ion thought.

At that moment, she missed her mother more than any other time in her life.

"Hi," Satan said.

Ion seemed to be staring right at him—through him would be a better description.

"Hi," she said, softly.

"I came by to get Vlady's medicine." Satan was picking at an old price tag stuck on the counter. Once he got the thing off, he noticed another, and started picking at that one.

"How's he doing?"

Satan glanced up at Ion from his meticulous work. "Better. His fever's dropping." He paused, then touched the brim of his hat. "Thanks for the cap. It's great for warm weather. I always used to wear the knit one all year round. It wasn't very comfortable." His attempt at small talk was waning. "I used to get laughed at all the time. Surface dwellers are often like that."

"Jesus Christ. Don't start with that crap again, Vinnie. You know how much I hate it when you talk about those fucking little people and their molten lava sun."

A tiny victory. As long as she was scolding him, things were okay. Not that he was a masochist or anything. He just knew she'd never walk out, never to see him again if she was angry.

"You know, they're not small. The people inside are actually—"

"*Hate* it!" She stormed out from behind the counter. "What are you doing here, anyway?" Her tone had an unpleasant, menacing manner to it.

Satan was as happy as could be. Perhaps, he was a masochist after all.

"I told you, picking up Vlady's medicine."

She sighed, "Fine," then turned down one of the aisles heading toward the back of the store.

"Are you coming over tonight? Lilly's making spaghetti. I think Vlady's going to try to eat."

She glanced back at him. "Oh, gee, can I? That ought to be an immense amount of fun, watching some ailing Russian puke up Italian food. Thanks, I'll wait for it to come out on video."

He was chasing after her, a kid after his mommy. "I've missed you."

Turning away so he could no longer see her face, Ion closed her eyes and winced. "I'm working late," she said after a moment.

"How late?"

"Late late."

"What does that mean, late late? Midnight? Two a.m.?"

"Later."

Ion steamrolled toward the obese woman who was still trying to get the chocolate off her lips.

Spotting Ion coming at her, the woman sat up a little.

"I'm gonna pay for these," she said, waving the empty box.

"That's nice," Ion replied, annoyed.

Satan closed the gap. "I'm trying to talk to you," he said once he finally caught up to her. She was standing outside a door that led to the pharmacy counter.

She pulled out a set of keys and slid one of them into the lock. "I'm getting the prescriptions for you," she said.

He stopped her from turning the key. "I thought maybe we could, you know, watch TV tonight or something."

"Or something?" She wrinkled her nose in disdain. "What else might we do, play Jacks? Discuss quantum physics?"

She unlocked the door and pulled it part way open.

"Are you saying, you don't want to, you know, do that anymore?"

"*That?* Fuck, Vinnie. It's called fucking."

The fat woman stopped the onslaught of candy entering her body long enough to take notice of what Ion had said.

"You can say it. You're a big boy now," Ion said.

"I simply choose not to be crude."

"Bullshit. You can't even say it, can you? How can you do it, if you can't say it?" Ion still had the door half-open, but wasn't making any move to go through it. "Haven't you screwed my cousin yet? The girl's in heat, *and* she finds you attractive. Who knows, she might even be good."

Ion and Lilly weren't interchangeable objects for Satan's newfound libido and Ion knew it, but he didn't offer any opposition. He simply lowered his head.

Finally, he spoke: "She's been busy. Taking care of Vlady." He averted his eyes away from hers, glancing at the obese woman instead. "He really is sick, you know."

"I know," said Ion, suddenly tender. Ducking through the door, she disappeared for a moment, then returned with the pills in a white bag. "On the house."

"What am I supposed to do, Ion? The factory's destroyed. I have no money. And I'm running out of Arnolds. I was counting on you."

Ion stared into his eyes for a moment. Lowering her gaze, she slipped into the back once more, reappearing a few seconds later with a box of foil.

"I saved you the last one." She held out the box. "As for the rest…I don't know."

Satan took the foil from Ion's outstretched hand, then turned on his heels and headed toward the front of Clancy's. A tinkle-tinkle and he was out the door. Ion watched the spot where he last had been long after he was gone. Her eyes went completely out of focus and she could almost see the imprint he left on the air.

Men were always wanting her body. And Ion had always been a willing partner. She loved sex, loved the smell of a man, his skin, his musky sweetness. Funny thing was, though, the more they wanted her, the less she wanted them.

Ion refocused and glanced at the chocolate-smeared woman. "The candy's on the house, too."

•

When Kenny Odorman woke up, he opened his eyes to find himself surrounded by a bright light. A whiteness so brilliant he could hardly keep from pulling his lids closed again. It took him a moment, but he adjusted to the radiance. A woman with absolutely no chin leaned over him, then jabbed a finger in his side once she saw him blink.

"You 'wake?" said the woman, dressed all in white, as white as everything else in the room, except the man by the door whose skin was black—sort of brown, actually.

"Where…where am I?" Kenny asked.

"Hospital. You had a mighty bad fall there. Broke three ribs." The woman's chin never moved as her mouth opened and closed. Kenny wondered how that could be, but there it was. "Lucky for you, we was right 'cross the street. The Father brought you in."

It was beginning to brighten inside Kenny's head, shedding a little light on the most recent past. Something about bells, he thought, but he wasn't certain.

"My father brought me here?" There was a bit of surprise in his voice. Kenny and his father hadn't spoken in a year and a half, and even then it was just a "Hello," and "Can I talk to mom."

"It *were* a bad fall. No, no, Father Leery…from St. Augustine's," said the woman, who Kenny was beginning to realize was a nurse of some kind.

"The priest?" asked Kenny, suddenly agitated. It was all coming back to him. Soup, bread, and stairs. Lots and lots of stairs. "Which hospital?"

"Clearwater, babe. But don't you worry. We have lotta patients falling all the time. We know what to do."

Terror washed over Kenny Odorman's face like any number of actors from "B" horror movies. "I'm in a loony bin? A funny farm? An insane asylum? For broken ribs?" There was a pause where the man and the nurse stared at him blankly. "I got to get out of here!"

Kenny was squirming now, and the nurse motioned to the man by the door who rushed over and grabbed Kenny's wrists, pressing his flesh into the cushion of the bedding. A sharp pain ran up Kenny's arm.

"We prefer to call it a sanitarium. And you broke your arm, too," whispered the nurse, far too calmly to be of a normal mind.

Suddenly, there was a loud crash as someone burst through the door. The force of the entrance slammed the oak door against a chair set by the wall, sending it sliding across the tile and into a nightstand. A tall, thin silhouette stood in the doorframe, twitching slightly.

"Leland! Cassie!" screamed the shadow. A cane or stick was now visible. "Get away from him. Get away right this instant or I'll call security. You hear?"

"But Dr. Tim, we was just helping the man. He had a bad fall," said the black man. "Right, Cassie?"

"Leland made me come in here, Dr. Tim. He did. He said he'd cut me into pieces and put me in tomorrow's stew."

"I did not! Dr. Tim, she lying."

There was a loud THWACK!!! as the figure came closer and hit the black man across the back with the cane or stick or whatever it was.

"Oouuww. But she lying!" shouted the black man as he was hit two more times.

"I know she is, Leland. We don't put meat in our food, not since the Kowalski incident. But I can't very well hit a woman, can I?"

"I guess not, Dr. Tim."

"Good," smiled the doctor. "Now get back to your rooms, before I decide to give you both a demerit."

In a hurried jumble of flesh, the black man and the chinless woman raced out the door, arguing in whispers as they left about whose fault it was.

After they both were gone, the doctor stepped into the light. His face was gaunt with hollowed eyes and a day's stubble around his jaw line. He twitched his head every few seconds, jerking it to one side, then slowly bringing it back to the center. Between the head jerks, he would scrunch up his face like a rabbit sniffing for food or a human smelling something awful.

"Well, hello there," he nodded.

Jerk, jerk, bob.

"I see you've met some of our patients."

Twitch, scrunch, scrunch.

"I hope they didn't frighten you."

Jolt, blink, blink, twitch.

"They're rather harmless for the most part."

Scrunch, twitch, jerk.

Dr. Tim prodded Kenny with the stick in the way someone might check a dead body, and with about as much care. Glancing down his side, Kenny realized it was not a stick or a cane but a sonic prod, which seemed fashioned out of electric toothbrushes. A severe pain shot through him and he jolted off the mattress for a brief instant.

The doctor had his own personal earthquake—an 8.3—which lasted about ten seconds.

"That hurt?" he asked when the tremor subsided.

"Yes, that hurt! What kind of doctor are you?"

"Psychiatrist." The man leaned on the edge of the bed. "I think we got the arm back the way it's supposed to be. That's just a guess, of course. Don't quote me on that, malpractice and all."

Finally, Kenny Odorman's brain zeroed in on who he was and what he had done for the thirty-one or so years before this moment, and he knew what he had to do now.

"I want to get out of here. I want to be transferred to another hospital this minute. Do you hear me!?!" Kenny's ribs reminded him to calm down with a stab of pain.

"Now, you just lie yourself back and get some rest, partner. This here's my territory. And we can hold you for seventy-two hours once somebody signs you in. After that, we have to go to the judge and prove you're crazy."

"I'm not *crazy*. Haven't you been listening? I simply fell down some stairs!"

"I'll be the judge of whether or not you're crazy."

Twitch, twitch, scrunch, scrunch, jerk.

•

Kelsey sat on the floor by the dormant fireplace, looking around the room, surveying all the things that belonged to her, all the things she'd pack up and take with her, which was pretty much everything. Only the refrigerator and the two hundred or so yellow writing pads, most of which were blank, would remain behind.

She settled back on several pillows she had tossed on the ground. Night brought comfort to her, and she felt better after the long day, even though Barris was always home. She could curl up in a corner or in bed with a book and let the stress of the office wash away. Sometimes she'd read romances, usually ones set in the Caribbean or Mediterranean. Other times she'd read science fiction that would take her on a journey to far away worlds. That's what she really wanted, to be far away. And if it took indulging in a few hundred pages about little green men, so be it.

Putting her hands to her head, she rubbed small circles around her temples and tried to slow her breathing.

Leo had been acting strangely ever since the explosion, making life at work hell. One minute he'd be happy, the next he'd be paranoid that someone was out to get him. Most of Leo's behavior was linked to Armand Arnold who hadn't caved in yet. In fact, the man's resolve to hold on to his property—even though it meant certain bankruptcy—had become stronger. Something about the way Leo looked when he first heard about the explosion made her suspect he had something to do with it. Leo wasn't a very good actor.

Suddenly, Kelsey realized the refrigerator was hers, as well. She glanced around the room to see if she had missed anything else.

Two dozen bags of tortilla chips, various brands, were scattered about the living room. Under one bag, Barris sat, scribbling his impressions of the various chips onto a notepad.

"Barris," Kelsey said, trying to get his attention. "Barris—"

"Huh?"

"Close your mouth."

Barris glanced down at her from his perch on the sofa. "What?"

"Close your mouth when you chew. That crunching is driving me crazy."

"Sorry."

Barris tried testing a few of the chips while keeping his lips together. The crunching became much louder in his head, and he had to breathe through his nose. It didn't feel right. There was something unnatural about it, eating Doritos politely.

"Kids don't chew with their mouths closed," he said after a minute or two. "I can't get the full effect. They taste different."

Kelsey sat up and stared at him. The time had come to get everything out in the open, to tell him how she felt. He deserved at least that much from her.

"Barris, we have to talk."

"I know," he said with a mouthful.

For an instant, she was startled by his acknowledgment of the problem. Perhaps, she had been wrong about him. Perhaps, deep down inside, Barris understood everything and just had trouble, like many men, in communicating it.

"You're still disappointed I've stopped writing."

Perhaps, not.

"Believe me, Kelsey...it wasn't easy for me to stop, but I'm doing something now that's just as important to me. I only wish you could be supportive of that."

Kelsey shook her head to clear it.

"Barris, you are the worst writer I have ever read. I'm sure there are others out there equally as bad, however, they too will never be published, so I can say in all honesty, that I shall never see a book as horrible as yours. I could care less if you never put another word to paper in your life." Kelsey stood and went to his desk that was actually hers, a gift from her father. She picked up one of the yellow pads and flipped through it. "Listen to this:"

> *The barren landscape of her shoulders were his to explore if he wanted to. She lay sleeping under a thin sheet, bathed in the soft light of the moon that filtered in through a curtained window. All he had to do was reach out and touch her and she would be his. But he was too afraid, too used up to ever be worthy of this woman's love—*

Kelsey looked over at him. "Barris...when did you write this?"

"A couple of weeks ago. I'd been tasting cereal for three hours. I needed a break. I was on a sugar high."

Kelsey read a little more to herself, thumbing a few pages ahead and reading that as well. And for a brief instant, she remembered the first time they met, the feelings that ran through her body when she thought about him.

These words were about her.

Kelsey leaned back on the desk and fingered the corner of the notepad, running her nail along the edge of the pages, which made a zipping sound.

Barris watched Kelsey for a moment. Her hair was a tussle of blonde and browns and he swallowed hard the remnants of food in his mouth. Placing down the bag of chips, he went to her and caressed her cheek softly with the back of his hand.

"I'll do anything to make you stay," he said.

Kelsey stared at him, shaking her head at the shock of his words. A pool of liquid formed at the side of her left eye and fell in a tear down her face. For several weeks now, she had been planning her departure, what she would say, when she would say it. She forgot every bit of it.

"I'll do anything, Kelse. Just don't go."

Kelsey shook her head, this time in answer to him.

"I can't, Barris. I don't have anything left to give you."

He nodded, gazing at the carpet and digging his toes into it. He took in a deep breath and sniffed back a tear of his own.

"I'm sorry," she said.

Kelsey brushed past him too quickly for him to reach out and stop her. Marching into the bedroom, she closed the door without a sound. She rested her brow against the back of the door, locked it, and fell into the soft comforter that lay atop the bed, letting it surround her. Memories and doubts flooded her brain as she retreated under the safety of the bedcovers. And then she cried. Cried herself to sleep.

•

A bulldozer pushed a pile of debris toward an even larger pile.

The noise emanating from under the blade, clinking glass, squeaking metal, and sifting dirt, echoed off the remaining walls of the Arnolds Aluminum factory. Dust filtered upward toward the bright magnesium floods that the demolition crew had erected around the work site.

The night air was thick with the smell of diesel exhaust and crumbled masonry.

Armand Arnold sat on a wood box and poured three fingers of scotch into a glass. He held it up to the lights.

"Here, here," he toasted, then gulped the entire contents of the tumbler.

Armand was folded over, his elbows on his knee, holding the bottle and glass poised in the space between his legs.

"Yeah!" he shouted, "Woooiiiie!!" as they plowed down a wall that no longer had a building to support. "All right!!!"

Humans have a curious interest when it comes to watching things get destroyed, and Armand was very much a human at the moment.

"Tear the whole thing down," he howled. "Go ahead. See if I care. What is it anyway but a bunch of tubes and wires and brick and blood and sweat and..." Armand began to cry. "Who cares? I always hated the color of those walls anyway."

Armand emptied the bottle into his glass, then tossed the spent container into the pile of debris the bulldozer was crushing at the moment. It landed safely only to be smashed by the metal tracks of the machinery.

Armand let out a howl as he poured the remaining scotch down his throat. Everything he'd worked for lay in ruins before him.

"I'm sorry," he said into the bottom of the glass, although it was meant for his father. "Very sorry."

XXII. DE-IONIZED

Two weeks of unseasonably warm weather was wreaking its havoc. Flower buds were beginning to slowly break their way out, the plants and Mother Nature having a tiny communication problem. These fragile seedlings had unfortunately mistaken Indian Summer for Spring. Soon, they'd be paying for their little blunder.

The time and temp sign over Kresgees flashed "-14 F", although everyone knew it was closer to sixty. The sign had literally frozen several weeks back after a particularly cold night. The entire city was just slightly off balance. People kept knocking into each other as if Chicago had tilted. Everyone was going without coats, smiling, looking happy, and then the final blow to the winter mood came—the Sweethearts' Skate scheduled to take place outdoors on the rink set up by Soldier Field, had to be held instead in the United Center after a Blackhawks game the Saturday before Valentine's.

Which turned out to be a good thing. A few of the guys got sent to the box for mishandling a woman.

Walking the streets around Lincoln Heights, Satan wasn't thinking much about the weather. For those very same two weeks, while everyone else was out enjoying the brief and unsettling respite from Winter, he had been pacing back and forth the length of his home, wondering when the check from the government, and the one from McKinney—he'd dropped the "Mr." three days ago—would come.

Last night, at about seven in the evening, the lights went off as the power was cut. The heat had been off a few days now, but luckily, the weather had remained mild. However, with the paper forecasting an approaching cold front, Satan was unable to wait any longer for the money to arrive whenever it pleased. So, he was on his way to see his former principal, mentor, and father figure…to beg.

Even with the threat of freezing to death hanging over him like a dark cloud ready to burst, Satan was having trouble keeping his mind on getting the money. Women were clouding his thoughts. Two women in particular. One was Mrs. McKinney. What would he say? Would he be able to look her in the eye? Could he keep from throwing up? Then there was Ion. She was slipping away from him, taking most of his reasons for living along with her. He felt nauseous, like someone was holding a professional wrestling tournament in his stomach.

Eye gouge. Headbutt. Kidney punch.

One hundred and thirty-seven times on the way to the McKinney's, Satan turned around and started back home, choosing the quick, painless demise of hypothermia over the slow, tortuous death by humiliation. And all one hundred and thirty-seven, he turned right back around.

Not because he wanted to—it would be easier freezing to death—but because of Vlady. Vlady's health depended on a warm environment. He was stronger, but not fully recovered.

As Satan strolled the sidewalk, he glanced down at a piece of white note paper with an address scribbled on it. Just a few more blocks.

He thought of Vlady, and immediately kicked a paper cup lying innocently on the concrete about thirty feet, pretending it was his Soviet friend's head.

Last night, just before the lights went out, Satan came home after spending the day by the freight yard, watching the trains come and go, hook, unhook, and generally rearrange themselves for no apparent reason. A hobby which occupied most of his days since the blast. Climbing the stone steps of his house, he glanced back and caught a glimpse of the sun between two buildings across the street as it sank below the horizon to the West. There was a still feeling to the air, a heaviness that made him sleepy. All he wanted to do was get inside, eat, and jump into bed.

Once in the house, he took off his Cubbies hat and placed it neatly by the pile of bills from Clearwater. A few days ago, he'd gotten tired of the way it looked and reshuffled the stacks to look more like a Frank Lloyd Wright creation, reminiscent of Falling Water, low, rectangular, with lots of squares poking out all over. Lilly and Kelsey had noticed the change in the pile's design, but when pressed for an answer as to what they thought it was, both said "a pile of bills."

Creativity was dead in America.

No wonder a country the size of Taiwan was destroying us on the economic battlefield.

"I've got some food," he shouted toward the stairs. Vlady was eating now, and as the doctor had predicted, there was seemingly no end to his appetite. "Chinese…I think." Satan glanced in the bag and intercepted a burst of smells all jumbled together racing to be first into the open.

No one answered.

It was too early for anyone to be in bed, and Vlady wasn't feeling well enough to be taken on any excursions yet. Satan refolded the top of the bag and put it down next to the baseball cap.

There was only one explanation for there being no answer.

Satan tiptoed his way into the kitchen and slid a huge knife from the wood block that was its sheathing.

Someone had broken into the house and murdered Vlady and Lilly.

The television news was always beaming some horror directly into his living room night after night—this person shot, that person robbed—only a fool would think he could avoid such an onslaught of crime. And Satan wasn't a fool. He knew his time would eventually come. Lucky for him, he'd stopped off for food on the way home and had missed the whole thing.

However, the killer might still be in the house. Caution was advised.

Satan pushed past the kitchen door and crept toward the stairs. He listened for any sound that might indicate a blade or bullet cutting through the air. He heard nothing except the steps creaking under his weight. Reaching the top of the stairs, he wielded the knife around to catch any prowler that might be lurking surreptitiously behind the banister.

Pictures began to flood his brain, pictures of Vlady and Lilly. He had never really told them how he felt, how much he cared. She was beginning to grow on him. Like mildew. And he…he had never left his heart. Vlady would always be his first and dearest friend.

Satan stepped into the guest bedroom. The sheets were mussed, but there was no sign of struggle. Backing out, he headed toward his room. No one there either.

Then he saw it, the light escaping from under the bathroom door. And something else, water, lots of it, spilling into the hall from the space underneath. Just like *Psycho*, he thought, and suddenly, Satan became very sick. A queasiness washed over him like an April rain.

He pushed back the overpainted door.

Lilly was cheerfully giving Vlady a sponge bath. She seemed to be paying particular attention to that area halfway between his head and toes. She turned and smiled as she saw Satan.

"Hi," she said, still rubbing Vlady's penis with a vigor never before witnessed by Satan.

Vlady seemed to be taking the manipulation in stride, his head resting on the back of the tub, a spittle of drool escaping the corner of his mouth.

"What...what are you doing?" Satan said.

"Giving him a bath," she replied, not understanding why he couldn't figure it out for himself. "You want one?"

"No," he said, with a hint of disdain in his voice. "Why would I want that?"

Lilly shook her head knowingly. "I figured you wouldn't. You and my cousin are made for each other. Neither one of you knows how to have fun."

"We know how to have fun."

"Yeah, right."

Vlady, meanwhile, was enjoying every nuance of the discussion. The more animated Lilly got, the more vigorous her cleaning.

"Then have sex with me," she yelled at Satan.

"Why does everything with you eventually boil down to sex."

"Because," she began, "when you get right down to it, the only thing men and women really have in common...is sex."

Vlady let out a little sigh as he came.

•

"Who is it?" asked the sweet, subtle voice that came from behind the door.

Satan felt uneasy about his decision to come here and was wondering if this wasn't the worst mistake he'd made in the last decade and a half. The last BIG, really BIG mistake was coming to this very house thirteen years ago after Graduation ceremonies and getting laid by Mrs. McKinney, while everyone else, including Mr. McKinney, was out getting drunk.

Nevertheless, he was here, and he had already knocked. There was no turning back—unless he tried passing himself off as an encyclopedia or vacuum cleaner salesman and pray she didn't recognize him. Only neither of those two items seemed to be handy at the moment.

"Sa—" Satan caught himself. "Noel...Noel Dorobek."

There was a brief second where Satan heard no sound. The wind had suddenly faded. The side street was deathly silent, no cars or people. And his heart stopped. In that moment, in that absence of sound, Satan achieved a clarity of thought he had never before experienced. He saw his life as one continuous stream of light rushing past him at about that speed, and he knew what he had to do.

But before he could spin around and break into a sprint, Mrs. McKinney opened the door.

"Noel," she said, dragging his name out like people do when they haven't seen a person in a long time. Her voice was warm and welcoming. "Oh my God."

"Hi, Mrs. McKinney."

Satan's eyes were focused on the ground just in front of her feet, but in his peripheral vision he could see that she was still beautiful even after a dozen years of wear.

"I think you can call me Robin. We're adults now."

"Yyyyes, that's true…Robin." Satan was incredibly uncomfortable and it felt like one of the wrestlers in his stomach was about to get tossed out of the ring.

"Why don't you come in," she said, so sweetly, so innocently—like a spider to a fly.

She led him deeper into her web, which was modestly furnished in a taste and style that was definitely hers and not her husband's. He sat on the plush sofa as far to one end as he could. She smiled and joined him, sitting only a few inches away. He realized he had made an error in judgment, leaving himself no room for retreat.

"What brings you by, Noel. It's been what—ten years?"

"Twelve and a half." Satan tried to swallow the tractor-trailer in his throat. "Can I have a glass of water, please?"

Mrs. McKinney stood. "Of course. Do you want something else? A drink, perhaps? Wine?"

So that was her plan. She was going to try and get him drunk, he thought. Not this time.

"Water's fine, tha…thanks." He cleared his throat. No use. The eighteen-wheeler was making a wide right turn in his esophagus.

After a minute, Mrs. McKinney returned with two goblets. One with ice and water, the other with Chardonnay. She handed him the water and sat, taking a sip from the wine once she was settled.

"It's a pleasant surprise, you stopping by. It's nice to have someone to talk to."

There was a sadness in her eyes that could not be hidden by her smile. In fact, she looked as though she might cry. She took another taste of her wine and turned her head away, pretending to gaze at something out the window, but he could see she was wiping a tear from her bottom lash.

"I suppose you've come about Tom. You were always one of his favorites."

"Tom?" Satan said out loud, before he realized whom she was talking about.

She laughed a melancholy laugh.

"Where is he?" Satan said, surveying around the house for any sign of his former principal. There was nothing out of the ordinary, except a stack of bills—not as large as the stack from Clearwater, but sizable just the same—that were piled on the dining room table. Still, the place definitely lacked a masculine touch. No coats over chairs, no shoes lying around. No male debris of any kind.

"You sure you don't want something to drink," she said, finishing her glass and standing about to get another.

"No, I'm fine."

"I'll be right back."

She disappeared into the kitchen for a long, uncomfortable few moments. When she returned, her eyes were red.

"Is Mr. McKinney okay?"

She shook her head and silently mouthed the word "no."

Wiping her eyes, she sniffed back a tear. "He's in County Medical." She paused. "He's dying."

Satan stood by the hospital bed for a long while, staring at his old mentor—father-figure, guardian—before making up his mind whether to sit or not. As he gently lowered himself onto the edge of the bed, the mattress gave under his weight, letting out a crunching and crinkling sound.

The lights in the room had been dimmed, making Satan feel safer for some reason. He tried not to move or breathe or make any noise. He just sat and stared at the man in the bed. Several tubes were sticking out of Mr. McKinney. An IV in his arm. One in his mouth. Another was taped under his nose. The mechanical inhale and exhale of the respirator gave a soothing, melodic feel to the room. The sound was somehow comforting, reassuring.

"Dying?" Satan had asked her at the house.

"Lung cancer," was her reply. "It's been about a year. Nothing seems to be working." She stared at him sitting on the sofa, watching his dismay. "I thought you knew."

"No," he said. "I didn't." He felt very alone sitting next to her as if she were a whirlpool sucking him downward, downward until he couldn't go down anymore. She reached out and placed a warm hand on his shoulder, and although his first impulse was to pull away, he was consoled by it. "How long?"

"A few weeks...maybe less."

A tear formed in the corner of Satan's eye as he slowly slid his fingers across the smooth white sheets and gently touched Mr. McKinney's hand. It was cold and frail and bony. It had the feel of a leather coat after a walk in December. It almost didn't seem human.

The man that lay sleeping before him was not the man Satan knew. Not at all. The McKinney he knew was grouchy, animated and always in motion. He was slender, yet well built. He was strong.

The person resting in bed was feeble and drawn, weighing less than ninety pounds. There were clumps of hair missing from his arms and patches of baldness on his head. His nose and cheeks seemed too large for the rest of his face, and his lips were wrinkled and tight.

Satan patted his mentor's hand, staring down at the thin fingers. All he could do was sit and keep him company. His head was empty. He couldn't think of anything. It was a strange sensation, a dullness that kept him from focusing on any thought for more than a few seconds.

He gazed at the white tiles for some time, thinking that the room was too cold for someone who was sick, thinking of nothing for the most part. Then Satan felt the gaunt hand stir, and he turned to look at Mr. McKinney. The principal was moving his fingers, waking them from their slumber. For a moment, he seemed to choke on the tube running down his throat, but the episode was over in a few seconds. Finally, the man opened his eyes.

Drugs and pain dulled his senses, but the shock of seeing his former student and sometime adversary jolted Mr. McKinney, once again causing him to momentarily gag on the tube in his mouth. After allowing the respirator to breathe for him, Mr. McKinney rested his head on the pillow and shifted his eyes in Satan's direction. Several seconds crawled by where Mr. McKinney thought he was hallucinating. When it became clear the image of Noel Dorobek was real, his eyes changed, almost smiling since his mouth couldn't.

He nodded a greeting.

"How are you feeling?" Satan said, holding the man's hand alternately tightly, then loosely.

The principal mumbled something.

"Good, I'm glad." Satan had no idea what the man had said, but he figured it best to be positive under the circumstances.

Suddenly, Mr. McKinney began having what Satan at first thought was an epileptic fit. He was pointing up toward something, then at Satan's chest, then back up at whatever it was.

Turning his head, Satan realized Mr. McKinney was motioning toward the television.

The man's eyes were beaming.

Satan understood and gave him a nod.

"You saw me."

The principal squeezed Satan's hand.

"It was nice, huh?"

Mr. McKinney nodded.

Satan knew he should say something about the check, after all that was why he had come in the first place.

"Mr. McKinney..." He paused. "I...I just wanted to tell you how much I appreciate everything you've done for me over the years. I couldn't have done it without you." Satan was on the verge of tears. "You've been like a father..."

Satan fell on top of his former principal and held him tightly. As best as he could, Mr. McKinney hugged his pupil back.

"That's why it was so hard realizing I'd slept with your wife."

There. He'd said it. It was out in the open. A huge weight was lifted from his shoulders. He loved—really *loved* this man, not just for the money he'd given, but everything he'd done, and it killed Satan to know that he'd betrayed that love.

Satan waited silently, his arms still wrapped tightly around the frail man's body. He waited for the inevitable.

Mr. McKinney patted him on the back, gently.

Satan pulled back from his hug and gazed at the principal's face. It was a remarkable face, strong, beaming, even in the shadow of death. Even with tubes and wires dangling from nearly every opening, nothing could dull the brightness in those eyes.

Mr. McKinney nodded a sad, sweet acknowledgment to Satan. A look that seemed to be saying, "It's okay. I understand."

Satan emerged from the room a few moments later to find Mrs. McKinney waiting outside the door. They gave each other a quick glance, then started down the hall in silence. Halfway to the elevator, she put her arm through his and leaned her head on his shoulder.

With all the hissing and beeping going on from the life support and monitoring equipment, Mr. McKinney sometimes had trouble understanding people. But he was glad he was able to hear his former student's words. They were welcomed and made all the years of scrimping and saving to help this boy worthwhile. They were sweet words, an apology, a thank you. As Mr. McKinney drifted back into his sickly slumber, he replayed them in his head, "That's why it was so hard realizing I hadn't kept up with your life."

•

Ion sat in the dark.

She surveyed the two rooms that had been her home for the past eight years. In the moonlight, the place seemed much larger to her. She had spent most of those years putting together the pieces of other people's lives. All she had to show for it were a few thank you gifts and some memories. Maybe that's all life is, a collection of moments, a scrapbook of feelings and events and remembrances. Let everyone else enjoy the fruits of her labor, she didn't care. She wasn't bitter. Because she knew it wasn't that the world was unfair, or that people took and took and never gave. She had been offered jobs and money and houses, so many houses, and cars and jewelry and positions of power. She turned them down. She turned them down because they came at a price. Even when they were a reward for something she had already done, there was always the expectation of more. Either more of her time, her efforts or more of herself.

So what if no one understood. She didn't owe anyone, wasn't in anyone's debt. She was free. Free to do what she wanted. Free from everyone and everything.

Except maybe herself.

She stared at a stack of boxes resting against the far wall. They reminded her of Vinnie's stupid pile of bills.

She took in another deep breath. It was nearly time. She went back to packing the box set on the floor in front of her.

Ion tried not to feel old. She tried not to feel tired. She tried not to feel like a little girl.

But mostly, Ion tried not to feel alone.

•

The ride home was excruciating. Not only was he alone with Mrs. McKinney for the third time in as many hours, he was in an automobile—a foreign one, which made it even worse.

Satan hated cars, thought they were the bane of our society, thought the horse and buggy should be brought back if only somebody could do something about all the horse shit in the middle of the road. He hated horse shit more than he hated cars.

For most of the drive to the hospital and again as they headed toward his house, Satan had been silent, choosing to occupy his brain in the pursuit of mundane thoughts, such as how easy it would be for a car to veer off course and smash into a telephone pole or parking meter and take him and a few pedestrians to the scrap yard with it.

Whenever he wasn't musing about auto accidents and horrible deaths, Satan was thinking about Mrs. McKinney. This woman had scarred him and he wasn't sure how or why.

"Turn down here," he said, pointing right.

Mrs. McKinney steered the car in that direction. Making the turn, she snuck a look at him. His face had changed relatively little, although he was older, more mature, more worldly than when she'd seen him last. But that's what made men men. Robin hoped in some small way, she had helped bring about this metamorphosis. By giving her body to him, she had offered something very special—the knowledge that he was attractive, that he was worthwhile. Most teenage girls couldn't spot a diamond in the rough. And he *was* a very special gem. She had plucked him from the depths of despair that Graduation Day, alone, off in a corner, and provided him with a small token of love and friendship and sex.

Satan caught her staring at him, which made him feel even more uncomfortable. Which wasn't easy. Besides everything else, Mrs. McKinney was one of those people who always "needed air." It was an odd affliction that his mother had suffered from, leaving windows and doors open and turning fans on in the dead of Winter. As if to say, if the air wasn't moving, it was somehow no good. His mother loved tornadoes. "Those folk's had themselves a good airing out," she'd say whenever she saw a news report about a twister running through some small town and wreaking a few million in damages.

Mrs. McKinney had her window rolled down and the vents wide open, blasting several cubic feet of cool air per second in his face. Traveling to the hospital, this peculiar set up was a minor inconvenience, but now, several hours into night, the warm spell suddenly mutating into a cold front, it was a bit more bothersome.

Eventually, he got to thinking about her again and what she had done to him. Stupid things seem so smart when you're doing them. And sleeping with Mrs. McKinney seemed like the most brilliant idea at the time.

As soon as it was over, however, it started. Guilt. Tremendous guilt. And betrayal.

It was difficult to explain, but now that it was okay with Mr. McKinney, now that he knew everything and understood, Satan felt lighter, his mind clearer. He was no longer angry with Mrs. McKinney. Strangest thing was, he hadn't realized he was angry in the first place. But the relief he experienced in the telling, the appreciation of that release of tension, proved how strong his resentment had been.

"I don't get it, Vinnie," said Ion, the last time she'd been at the house only a few days earlier. "What's the big deal?"

He didn't have an answer.

"An older woman coming on to you, that's like a teenage boy's fantasy, isn't it?"

He nodded. "I guess."

"C'mon, Vinnie. So, you slept with her." Her voice was very tender. The most tender it had been in weeks. "It wasn't like she forced you to do it." Ion paused, her eyes watching him for a moment. "Did she force you, Vinnie?"

He shook his head, no.

"Then what?"

Satan turned toward Mrs. McKinney.

"You took him away from me."

"What?" Robin said as she pulled the car to a stop in front of Satan's home.

"You took him away," he repeated, enunciating each word this time. "In here." He pounded on his chest right over his heart. "He was the only thing I had. He took care of me, made sure I had enough money, enough food." Satan tried not to, but he began to cry. "He was the only person who ever asked me how I was doing. The only one who ever cared what happened to me. He was the closest thing I had to a father back then." Satan sat shivering for a moment, silent, his eyes staring down at his hands that were clenched into fists. "And you took him away."

•

In the flickering light of three candles, Satan lay staring at the ceiling, wondering who came up with the word ceiling and what the person was thinking when they thought it up. Did someone one day point toward the rafters or apex of the cave and say, "That's a ceiling," where in which everyone else present went, "Ah-*huh*, 'ceiling'"? He didn't know. And it bothered him that nobody could ever satisfactorily explain how things got their names.

Oh, his teachers would pull out the dictionary and show him the derivatives of words, tracing them back to Latin or Greek or Phoenician or Sanskrit or whatever, but who came up with *those* languages? Who was it that first picked up a rock and said, "Mmmmm ROCK!"? Whoever it was deserved a little credit.

"What are you thinking about?" asked Lilly, stringing together a whole bunch of sounds he'd never know the origins of as she sat on the edge of his bed.

"I think it's amazing that we can speak," he said, still staring at the ceiling. The heaviness that had been weighing him down since the explosion had been lifted in revealing the truth to Mr. McKinney and in confronting his wife.

"I'm very easy to talk with. People tell me that all the time."

Satan lowered his gaze to look at Lilly. She was smiling, which annoyed him somewhat. "What are you doing in here?" he said.

"Checking up on you. Without any power or heat, you can get really sick." She put down the candle she was carrying and touched his forehead, gently caressing it with slender fingers.

Her hands felt wonderful across his face, but he attempted to maintain his look of disdain otherwise she might get the wrong idea and think he liked her.

"I don't need checking up on," he said as she handed him a notice from Niro to pay the rent or quit. He glanced at it and put it with the rest of the bills, disconnect notices, and service interruptions. He was waiting for a stone tablet from God to complete the picture.

"I just like taking care of people. It's this maternal thing I have. I figure I better have some kids soon or I'm gonna blow." She pushed back several strands of hair that were draped over his eyes. "You wanna have sex? Might solve both of our problems."

"No, I do not want to have sex with you." Which was a complete lie. Ever since he and Ion had done it, a major goal of his was getting more. And seeing Lilly's manipulation of Vlady in the bathtub hadn't helped things. "And I don't have a problem. Except for you."

"Why don't you like me?" she said, the soft, warm light of the candles dancing off her eyes.

He really didn't know what annoyed him about Lilly or why he couldn't bring himself to like her. It would be very simple to lift the sheet and have her climb into bed with him. She had made that abundantly clear. Over and over he asked the question—what was it about her he found so horribly repulsive. Lilly was sweet, innocent, sexually aggressive, responsive, endearing, and, in her own way, attractive. Perhaps, it was simply this: she wasn't Ion. It was the only reason he could come up with.

He stared back at the ceiling. "I don't know."

"I don't know? That's it? What kind of answer is that?"

"I don't know."

"I've tried everything on you. Wearing no underwear, wearing a lot of underwear, too much makeup, no makeup, being aggressive, not aggressive at all. Come to find out, you don't know."

"I don't."

"That's pathetic."

Satan sat up and leaned against the wall. He felt he should clarify his answer. Lilly deserved a bit more explanation than "I don't know." She was cooking and cleaning and taking care of Vlady. That had to count for something. He pulled the covers up over his knees and rocked back and forth slightly on the bed. "I'm in love with your cousin."

"Ion?" she said, as if the thought of someone loving Ion was akin to eating a bowl of live worms.

"You have another cousin I've slept with?"

Lilly gazed into Satan's eyes for a moment. So innocent. So naive. So *stupid*. "You don't understand, do you? She's leaving." Her tone was cold, matter-of-fact.

"What do you mean leaving?" he said, rocking a bit more now.

In the weeks since Lilly first began staying at Satan's, she had grown up a great deal. Being around men up close for an extended period was a lot different than viewing them from a distance. They weren't as appealing in practice as they were in theory. Their habits, as far as hygiene, grooming, housework and cooking were concerned, were substandard. They were loud, self-centered, but most of all, they always wanted what they couldn't have.

"She's making plans to leave, probably packing right this minute. I'm here." Lilly tapped herself between her breasts. "She's leaving. Don't you comprehend the value of proximity?"

"But I bought her a Valentine's gift." He glanced across the room at the box wrapped in yellow and white resting on the chair in the corner. It looked elegant in the moonlight, if not a little lonesome. Maybe Lilly was right. Ever since Ion met him, she had been pulling away. From the first moment, even as she appeared to get closer, she kept moving further and further from him.

When Satan turned back to Lilly, he found she was gone. He sank into his pillow and decided that even though chances were high that he would be humiliated, he was going to fight to keep Ion.

•

The air had grown much colder and the Westerly winds were whipping in from the Lake, burning through layers of clothes like an icy blowtorch. Clouds were forming overhead, the nimbus variety, and it appeared as though it might snow soon.

There was an odd quietness, a muffled quality to the sounds of the city. The kind of effect that fog brings, or a hot, humid, still day. But it wasn't hot or humid or even foggy, just still.

The day was winding down, with the sky a pinkish-gray as the edges of dark clouds refracted light from the dying sun.

All in all, not the perfect Valentine's Day.

But it was the only one Satan was going to get to try and woo Ion back from the brink of leaving. And that was his first mistake. Ion wasn't the wooing type. Strength was what excited her. Self-assuredness, confidence— not silly flowers, candies and tired clichés from a greeting card. Yet, that was exactly what Satan was packing as ammunition in the battle to win her back. They were Lilly's idea. Which was the second mistake he made, taking advice from someone who had a direct interest in the outcome. Whether in business or personal relationships, it was always a good idea finding out what somebody had to gain from a situation before running headlong in the direction they've pointed you.

Although, the heart-shaped sapphire ring he was originally going to give Ion wouldn't have been any better received.

The wind started to pick up and he held the top of his coat closed with his hand. A homeless man was begging for money on the sidewalk up ahead and Satan immediately tried to find something to do to make him seem too busy to bother. He began studying the roses he bought for Ion and nearly got a thorn in the eye when a gust of wind blew the flowers into his face.

The third mistake Satan made was in getting up this morning.

"Spare one of your roses," the homeless man said.

"Excuse me?"

"Spare one of your roses."

"You're begging for roses? How hideously sad."

"You look down on your luck, friend. I thought it best not to ask you for money," the man explained.

Vagrants had an unnerving way of giving Satan the impression that they were feeling sorry for *him*.

"'Sides, my girlfriend likes flowers. Course, she don't have no teeth, but she do like them roses."

Satan handed the man a rose. He took it and sniffed at the petals, gently running his fingertips over the soft interiors.

"Can I have me another? I got another woman I kinna like."

Satan stared at the man, his brows furrowed low over his eyes. Letting out a defeated sigh, he gave the man another rose. The man nodded a thank you as he grabbed the second flower and continued down the sidewalk.

"Roses for sale," Satan heard the man say as he turned the corner.

Approaching Clancy's Drug, the street crowded with people all bundled in coats, grumbling, swearing, snarling, more typical of Chicagoan behavior than the last few weeks, a sudden wave of terror washed over Satan, freezing his feet to the sidewalk outside the store. He almost turned and went back home, and he might have, only he couldn't move. Instead, he stayed put, not budging a muscle until Ion emerged from the front door half an hour later.

"Vinnie…hey," she said, smiling at him until she saw the armload of gifts he was toting.

"Happy Valentine's Day," he blurted out as he snapped out of his daze. He thrust all the presents in her direction at once, hoping she might find something to her liking and accept it as an example of his everlasting love.

Ion dodged a thorny stem lunging straight at her face. "You're gonna poke somebody's eye out with that stuff." She knocked the roses away, then pushed her hair back and regained her composure. "I'd just as soon not have it be mine. What is all this shit, anyway?"

He tried to remember what it was he was shoving at her. "A Valentine's Day card. Ah, a box of candy. And a dozen roses. Well, actually, there's only ten, but that's sort of a long story."

"Ten roses. I see."

"I'd rather not get into that at the moment. Happy Valentine's," he said, offering the gifts once more.

Ion glanced at the people strolling past, at the threatening sky, and sighed. She wondered if she'd miss them. Chicago had been home her entire life. It had been a good place.

Returning her gaze to Vinnie, she reached out and took the flowers, holding them toward the ground like a baseball player holds his bat coming to the plate. She had never known anyone as odd as him, not in all the people she'd met. Not even amongst Slag's circle of friends.

This was not going to end as neatly or as cleanly as she had hoped. Her plan had been to slip away and let him discover her escape in a few days when he came to the store or went looking for her at her apartment. She meant to be gone already, but someone had gotten sick at Clancy's and she agreed to work one more shift. They paid her double time, and she needed the money. Because she didn't know where she was going, but she knew it was far from Chicago, if not in miles, at least in spirit.

"You keep the candy," said Ion.

"What about the card?"

"I'm not very big on anything that encapsulates the human condition in ten words or less."

He nodded, sadly.

He stared at her. She seemed tired, but she still possessed a radiance that made men passing them turn for a second look. Her eyes, which like the surface of the ocean changed color with the weather, were steel blue under a sky that was turning gray.

Ion began walking, motioning for him to follow. As they made their way down the sidewalk, Satan dumped the card into a trash can.

She thought maybe she'd go to Los Angeles where she had spent some time with that actor, the guy that turned out to be a jerk, but L.A. seemed so...obvious. And New York seemed too cold, not the temperature of the place, but the attitude. Cliquey. Elitist. A caste system, a social stratum that dulled and diminished genius, compartmentalized humanity into small, manageable and easily labeled portions and paralyzed creativity. At least in L.A., anything was possible.

Ion *would* miss this place.

Beneath the darkening skies, the air, the street, the buildings, everything, seemed to become the color of tarnished silver. It made the city feel that much colder, as if the buildings could suddenly paint themselves red or green, the cold might simply disappear.

A shiver ran through Satan's body and he wanted more than anything just to hold Ion, to feel the warmth of her body pressing against his. But he couldn't get himself to take her hand.

A couple in love was coming toward them. The woman wrapped in a long blue coat had her head resting against the man's shoulder, her arm through his. They both were smiling and marching in step as they passed. Satan wanted that to be him with Ion's arm coiled around his.

"Vinnie," Ion began. "There are things in life that require subtlety, and things in life that just need to be said."

Satan glanced down at his feet, hoping he could find something there to give him a little strength.

The words languished on Ion's tongue. "I'm dying, Vinnie."

"What?" His heart smashed onto the pavement.

"I've got a tumor the size of a honeydew in my skull and I have to go away to get treatment. Chances are, I won't make it. My head's going to probably explode, so I figure I should be someplace far enough away from Chicago so that no one has to see me blow up."

"What?"

"Vinnie don't make me have to repeat myself." She wasn't sure she could remember what the hell she had said anyway. She hadn't meant to lie, but it just seemed to spring from her mouth before she could stop it.

"You're dying?"

"Think of it as me just...going away."

"Are you out of your head!?" he said, wincing as he regretted his choice of words. "I mean...you know what I mean. I want to help. Everyone would want to help. Lilly, Slag..." He struggled for some more names. "...that pharmacist guy at Clancy's…" His face lit up. "…your dad! He'd want to be there…to support you."

"Nobody's to know about this, Vinnie. Nobody. That's the way I want it. Do you understand? Just respect my wishes on this one—" she milked it, "—possibly *last* request."

Satan stood in the middle of the sidewalk, stunned and bewildered. His body was numb and a tingling ran through his limbs.

"I…" He couldn't speak.

"There's nothing you or I can do about this. Just like there was nothing we could do about Arnolds. That's life. It doesn't always work out the way you want." She thought of Armand and Peter, Slag and Lilly…her father. All the people she was giving up.

She touched Satan's face and tried to hold back a tear, but it slipped out and slid down her cheek.

"You were the best of them all, Vinnie." She took his hand and held it. "You just might be a genius. You don't need me. You never did. Just…go do something great with your life."

Closing her eyes to dam any more tears, she squeezed his palm, letting all the tenderness and affection she had for him flow through her fingers and into his. After there was nothing left, she released her grip and pulled away.

"Ion," he said. "I…I…" He was having trouble. "…hope your head doesn't blow up."

Ion glanced back, but said nothing.

"I'll miss you," he added.

The wind blew and the crowds strolled past. But nobody seemed to notice or give a damn that his life was being destroyed. Finally, she turned, and holding her head high and her tears back, began down the sidewalk without another look.

XXIII. SOME HELPFUL HINTS ON WHAT TO DO WHEN SOMEONE HAS STOMPED ALL OVER YOUR HEART

XXIV. PLEASE PUT TRASH IN ITS PLACE

It was cold. And he shivered as he watched her walk away, her heels clicking on the icy sidewalk. He was sad, knowing this woman had entirely changed his life, and embarrassed that all he could do was stare after her.

•

The coolness of the air seemed to make everything a little clearer. And the sterling hue the buildings, the people and the city had taken on allowed Satan to see Ion for several minutes. She stood out against the gray backdrop, a splash of color in the dullness.

He watched her for as long as he could, watched her leave him. He wasn't sure if she was telling the truth. Wasn't sure if she really was dying. It'd be just like Ion to pull something like that—get a tumor in her head the size of a small dog just so she could make a clean getaway.

Deep in his chest where his heart could have been, should have been, he didn't believe it, but then it didn't really matter. By giving him that tiny seed of doubt, she had set him free. She had given Satan that one chance, that one in a million, that it wasn't *him* she was leaving. That *he* wasn't the reason.

Finally, after almost an eternity, it happened. A CTA bus belched eight pounds of soot in Satan's face as he stood on the edge of the curb for a better view and by the time he got the exhaust particles out of his eyes, he had lost her in the crowd a few blocks down the street. Frantically, he bobbed and stretched and squinted, moved and jumped and shifted, trying to catch a glimpse of her golden hair or her prismatic jacket, one last look, but…she was gone.

Satan held still on the busy sidewalk, not moving a muscle. The concrete under his feet was freezing and he could feel his knee joints creaking. There was a hole where his stomach had been only a few moments ago, and a simple blood pump where his heart had once resided.

Ion was surely gone.

He stood beside a parking meter set adjacent to a street he couldn't remember the name of, even though he'd been on it a thousand times before. Chicago seemed alien to his eyes, the buildings of the Loop malformed and out of place as if God were playing a grand joke on him, rearranging the cityscape so he couldn't find his way.

Satan was down and God was kicking him in the gut.

Squeezing the blood from his fingers as he crushed the outside of the candy box, Satan sucked in a quick, deep breath. He shuddered, letting the air out almost in a sob. Glancing down at the mutilated heart that nearly duplicated his own, he ripped off the top and began popping the chocolates in his mouth in an attempt to fill the empty feeling he had inside.

One after another they slid down his throat—cream-filled, peanut clusters, chocolate covered cherries—until he thought he might be sick.

When he finished the entire box, he started to walk back the way he and Ion had come. He grabbed the paper wrapping that held the last candy in the box, popped the caramel-toffee chew onto his tongue and tossed the paper liner into the air. The chocolate brown wrapper floated toward the concrete, tumbling over and over as it journeyed toward the sidewalk. Finally, hitting the pavement, it crumpled and bounced. Before the liner could hit the ground again, Satan was surrounded by two dozen men and women, their guns outstretched and aimed at his head.

Some had uniforms, most did not. But all of them seemed very, very unhappy.

"Freeze! Keep your hands at your side!" screamed one of them.

Satan cautiously glanced around, trying not to move too quickly in any one direction.

"Is there a problem?" Satan said to the crowd of police and federal agents.

"I said freeze!"

"I'm freezing," said Satan, suddenly feeling colder and throwing his hands into the air, making just the kind of abrupt gesture he'd been hoping to avoid. The kind of gesture that got people shot or killed or worse.

"I told you to freeze and keep your hands at your side!"

Satan put his hands back down.

"Stop moving, Goddammit!"

"Okay, okay, okay. What's going on?"

"Noel Dorobek, a.k.a. Satan, you are under arrest," shouted someone, flashing a badge and waving a very large gun as he moved in closer.

"Arrested? For what?"

Another man with rubber gloves and a set of tongs bent down and picked up the candy wrapper and dropped it in a plastic baggy, then sealed the top with a zip across the edge.

"Littering," said the guy with the badge.

"Littering? Jeez, you cops are getting tough."

•

Kenny Odorman was creeping along the cold linoleum floor, his bare feet slapping on the tile like two steaks dropped in a frying pan. He had survived the giant sonic toothbrush-like prod and so far had avoided any of Dr. Tim's other inventions. Everyone in the Clearwater Sanitarium was down at supper at the moment. He had slipped out of his room after pretending to be asleep. None of the nut cases ever missed a meal. It was the only time he got any peace. He gladly ate cold leftovers for the fifty or sixty minutes of quiet he got three times a day.

Kenny snuck past the hall guard who was flirting with Hilda, a strapping six-footer, at the nurses' station. Hilda outweighed the guard by a good sixty pounds and stood nearly a foot taller. In fact, Kenny couldn't imagine what the guard thought he would do with a woman of that size or, for that matter, what help he could be in the event that one of the nut cases tried anything funny. Guns weren't allowed on the hospital premises for fear that one of the patients might accidentally get a hold of one and do something extremely unsavory. This guy looked like he'd be outmatched by a ten-year-old with a straw and a halfway decent supply of paper napkins.

Making a totally unnecessary set of expressions running the gambit from pained to astonished, Kenny tiptoed around the corner. If the information he'd gotten from one of the loonies was correct the records room should be just up ahead. But then, these whackos had a retarded sense of humor.

This was his nineteenth attempt at locating where Clearwater kept their files.

Sneering slightly, he saw it—the records room—just a few yards away.

Reaching for the door, he twisted the knob, feeling a power he hadn't felt since he trashed Gary J. Somebody's credit the last time he had been at work.

Work. He missed it so intensely. Like an addict craving a fix of heroin.

Kenny pushed open the door, revealing a cluttered, claustrophobic cube of 6 by 9 by 8 feet high. At least thirty trees had courageously given their lives for the piles of forms and files.

Effortlessly, he slipped inside.

Finding the paperwork on Dorobek's mother among this mess wasn't going to be an easy task, but then, Kenny Odorman had been training his entire life for this. And he wasn't going to let little Noel off if there was any way of sticking him with his mother's bill.

Not wasting any time, Kenny started searching the room.

He smirked as he sifted through the stacks of uncollated, half-processed records, getting far too much pleasure out of it than a sane person should.

•

Ion's father stood pacing the room like a husband waiting for his wife to give birth. He'd been released from the hospital twelve days ago and was starting to get back into the swing of things. The limp was hardly noticeable unless you were looking for it. Still, each step was painful.

He was finally going to get to meet the man who had caused him all this suffering. Oh, he wouldn't do anything illegal, but he might inadvertently rough him up a little. His daughter was right, this guy Satan was relatively harmless, but he had beefed up the surveillance reports to make him look a bit more dangerous so he could keep tailing him. The President's order to arrest him was put on hold when he saved the cop, but it was back in force after the explosion made him appear even more of a threat.

Still, Ion's dad was a bit surprised at how much manpower they used, but then, the Old Boys liked to be thorough.

Ion's dad would let the guy go soon enough—after he'd given him a good scare. That's all he really wanted—just a little payback for the torment he had endured, both physically in terms of pain, and mentally, in being the butt of everyone's jokes.

One didn't get hit by a bus and not take a little ribbing, but he had grown tired of it.

Ion's father paced back and forth, back and forth for the better part of six hours. And still, there was no sign of this Satan character.

When he finally received a communiqué from Special Operations stating that the arrest had never taken place and that all records of said non-arrest were being destroyed, he realized some wingnut agent of some off-budget agency had taken his beefed-up reports far too seriously.

•

Satan sat in the dark.

Somewhere water was dripping. For the past ten hours, he'd been triangulating the source of the sound by slowly turning his head, thus his ears, to find the direction and distance of the dripping water. And as best he could tell, it was coming from inside his skull. Although in the beginning that seemed extremely unlikely, as time passed, he had grown to accept, and then, embraced this belief.

The plip-plip-plip of the droplets hitting the ground continued.

There was a faint ribbon of light etched along the floor just outside the bars of Satan's cell. An anonymous yawn flittered past his ear from somewhere. He realized as he closed his mouth, it was from him.

The charge was *littering*...the city was obviously cracking down.

He had spent twenty-three hours under a hot lamp that burned through the back of his retina, so that after awhile all he could see was the light itself, simple shadows beyond it, and a bunch of really neat spinning fireballs. Questions, questions, questions, so many questions he forgot what they were, and what he answered.

Finally, the questions stopped. And a woman wearing next to nothing came in and tried to seduce the information out of him, only the lamp had burned its patterns in his eyes and he couldn't really look at her exposed body directly, only through the edges of his vision, which is probably why the woman went away unsuccessful.

A cockroach scurried past his feet, causing Satan's body to involuntarily jolt upright and twitch for several seconds, a reflex action left over from the early pre-humanity days when we were little more than amoebas with feet and insects were giants that liked to eat us. Satan winced at the thought of having to blindly slide himself under the covers of the bunk on which he sat, perhaps that's why he hadn't gone to sleep for thirty-six hours. God only knows what lurked under there. He had read one day while waiting in line at the grocery store that a woman in Idaho had three-quarters of her foot eaten off by a band of locusts. Cockroaches weren't written about in the Bible—a fact that made him doubt the validity of the entire tome. Of course, the Bible didn't say anything about super-rats, either—one of which was on the other side of the cell, eyeing the cockroach.

Satan looked around the room, wishing he had a tin cup to drag across the bars, only he feared some of the rat's pals might think it was a dinner bell and come calling—and then where would he be? He was also searching the area in hopes that he might find some indication that a cat was nearby. Unfortunately, there was none. Most likely, because the rats had eaten them all.

Still, something wasn't quite right about this place. Everyone was always complaining that the penal system was overcrowded, that prisons were brimming with inmates, so much so that they even had to set some of them free to compensate. But this place was oddly silent, and he couldn't see anyone or anything remotely human in the adjoining cells.

Suddenly, there was a creaking sound that echoed at the far end of the cellblock, making its way through the empty spaces, finally reaching Satan. It was the rusty hinges of the cellblock door.

He sat there, in the blackness, waiting for whomever it was to come, thinking how much better he'd feel if he were in the center of the planet.

At first, some of what Ion said seemed to make an odd sort of sense, but lately, he couldn't help but notice that, pitiful as it may have been, his life had been much less complicated before he met her. Actually, Ion herself wasn't to blame. It was just people in general that tended to agitate the fabric of society. Without people, civilization would be much better off.

Satan glanced down at his hands, hands he could barely see in the dimness. They were swollen from having ingested too much MSG. It must have been in the Chinese food that the jail had sent out for.

This had thrown him for awhile. He was expecting bread and water, or, at best, overcooked, re-cooked, pre-cooked cafeteria food. The thought never crossed his wonderfully immense brain that he'd be feasting on Kung Pao Chicken and Moo Shu Pork. The food came in four paper boxes with meaningless red swatches on the outsides, supposedly some sort of identifiable language that resembled more than anything what pick-up sticks looked like when they were tossed on the ground.

Of course, no eating utensils were given, just two wooden sticks. It took him nearly an hour to eat, and by the time he finished he was hungry again.

Maybe it was someone bringing more food. Chop Suey, he hoped.

A rotund man stepped up to the door of Satan's cell. He was let inside by a shadow that closed the door behind the round man and clicked off into the darkness. The man stepped into the tiny beam of soft light that had found its way in somehow. He wore a tight smile on his face, more a look of deep, considerable thought than a grin. The man drew in a breath that sounded off every wall and seemed to come from everywhere.

"How's everything, Noel?"

It took Satan a second before he realized the man was talking to him.

"Ah," he stuttered. "My fingers are a bit swollen from the Chinese food… but other than that I'm…fine. I guess."

The super-rat was getting ready to spring on the cockroach.

"Good, good," said the man like someone who really wasn't listening.

Satan kept turning his head to get the man in focus.

"Am I going to get to speak to a lawyer? For some reason, out of the dark recesses of my educational career, I remember something about that in the Constitution."

There wasn't any answer.

"I could be wrong." He paused. "Are we still *in* the United States?"

The round man touched his chin. "Do you know why you're here, Noel?"

"Listen…I didn't *mean* to litter," Satan began, defiantly. "I mean, I was emotionally distraught at the time. I wasn't thinking, okay?"

"Forget the candy wrapper!" The man was trying to keep his composure. In the stingy light, he looked like Oliver Hardy minus the mustache. "You're here because every fucking bureaucratic idiot from the Pentagon on down to the Energy Department thinks you're dangerous. They think you're some threat to national security."

Satan squinted. "What?" This was a monkey wrench into the situation. Government interference.

"They've been watching you for weeks. Bugging your house, tapping your phone. Got some good video of you and Blondie…tough to keep that one in stock."

"Video tape? People really are watching me?"

"Big time."

"What did I ever do to deserve this kind of scrutiny? I've never even gotten a traffic ticket!" he said, loudly, indignantly. Of course, he had never actually driven, so this was a moot point, but he went with it anyway.

"I know. I've been over your file."

"Excuse me, but could you move a little to the right? Your interrogation lamp seems to have burned away any chance for direct eye contact."

"Sorry about that," said the man as he shifted himself into Satan's peripheral view. "It was the letter you sent them. They have you pegged as some nuclear terrorist."

"My letter? I didn't say anything about bombs."

"You stated that you knew the government has been hiding the truth about people underground and that you're going to reveal them." He paused. "They think you mean the people we have in the missile silos under the city."

"There are missile silos in Chicago?"

"Chicago, New York, Cleveland, you name it. You remember all those casinos Donald Trump built in Atlantic City? Trump Silos, we call them." Oliver Hardy chuckled to himself. "Everybody kept sending observers to the silos in the Dakotas, Montana, New Mexico, making sure we destroyed them. So, we moved them to the cities."

"Why are you telling me this?"

"Well, we know all about *you*, so I think it's only fair. These Federal guys think you're some kinda fucking crackpot. But then they're all *crazy*!" Hardy snickered. He cleared his throat just as the super-rat pounced on the cockroach. "That's why I stole you away from them…because you don't know shit about silos, do you?"

"I do now."

"That won't matter soon." Hardy put his hands together and rubbed them. "I know you don't know shit, because I know who you really are."

Satan waited.

"You're Noel Kevin Dorobek."

"I could have told you that."

"Ah, but could you have told me that you're the twice abandoned supremely fucked-up offspring of a no-good, tattle-telling lowlife felonious thug?"

"No, I don't even think I could say that." Satan was having enough trouble trying to make sense of it.

Oliver Hardy put his hands to his face, rubbed the start of some stubble and blew out a lung full of air. "You ever wonder what happened to your father, kid?"

Satan took a moment. It was strange. His father was always on his mind, but he never really crossed it. What happened to his dad, why he never showed up at Union Station were questions he asked himself all the time and yet, the lack of any answers had little effect on his life, or so he believed. The years had dulled the queries and thinned them out. Sometimes he'd go a whole week without wondering. But never more than that.

"Not really," said Satan.

"Not really?" echoed the man. "Huh. I would have thought a curious, intelligent person such as yourself would have wondered why his father would just up and take off."

For a moment, the tap-tap-tap of the dripping water was the only sound.

Finally, Satan cracked. "Alright, alright, alright, what happened to him? Christ!"

The man gave out a little laugh. This was so much fun.

"He made it inside, didn't he?"

"He wouldn't have made it inside a week." Hardy paused. "Kid, your scumbag father was a little fish in a very big pond who got his hand caught in the cookie jar—"

"Fish don't have hands."

"A little *thug* who got *caught* skimming profits off the top…and then came running to the FBI for help, willing to testify to anything just as long as the Feds put him in a witness protection program."

Satan sat in silence.

•

On those nights when Henry Dorobek would creep into his son's bedroom, hours after the young boy had been read a story and put to sleep by his mother, he began to find more and more that his child was already awake, only pretending to be asleep.

He longed for those nights in the past when he would come home, sneak in the room and stare at his son for hours. It gave him great comfort because Henry needed to know that he was doing what he did for something important, something special. He never realized it was the poem from Blake he would recite and the line "Why wilt thou sleep the sleep of death?" that kept his son from his slumber.

Henry was an imposing figure, a dweller of the netherworld, a citizen of a completely other realm than our own. He preferred these twilight sojourns with his son because many times his hands were bloody and covered in dirt from digging and all the other things one must do to find their way into the Underworld.

These were often the only images of his father that Satan could conjure up. He couldn't remember ever seeing his dad in the day or under the warm glow of a light bulb, only there, in the blackness of the night.

It was in an attempt to lull his child to sleep that Henry began telling Noel stories—tales of such incredible intricacy. Adventures, chases, rescues and, most of all, tales of hope. As his father told it, the Underworld was full of all these things and much, much, much, much more, and that it was the Underworld that offered a better kind of life for people like them. It wasn't easy, you had to dig down deep, but you could make it if you really believed.

As a boy, Satan didn't believe in Santa Claus, or the Easter Bunny, or the Tooth Fairy. But he was convinced that the Underworld was a pretty cool place, and that when he grew up, he wanted to go there.

•

Underworld.

The word echoed in his head, transporting him from the short salad days of his childhood to the harsh reality that was quickly engulfing him. And suddenly, that one word undid three decades. The years lay in a pile on the floor, unwoven like a long string of yarn that once had been a sweater.

"You mean," his anger simmering into a boil, "I've spent my entire life believing there were people *inside* the Earth, when all it really was, was a bunch of gangsters?!"

Satan got to his feet and kicked the super-rat across the cellblock.

"Is my father still alive? Because if he is, I'd like to take his head and twist it off."

"I can't give out that information."

"Fine. Just let me out of here so I can search to the ends of the Earth, to the end of Time to find him. C'mon, c'mon, don't I get some sort of phone call or something? What is this, Haiti?"

"I don't think you understand, kid."

"Oh, I understand perfectly. My father—who, all this time, I've been mourning his loss, believing that, at least, he had found his way to a better place—is single-handedly responsible for most of the day-to-day hell that is my life."

"No, I mean, you don't understand your situation." Hardy motioned to the surrounding room in all its frightening perfection. "This isn't a prison. At least, not anymore. Nobody's been in this place in twenty or thirty years."

"I'm here."

"Yeah, but see, nobody *knows* you're here. There's no record of you ever having been arrested. Oh, maybe in a few days or so, someone might notice you're missing, but by then it'll be too late."

There was a tone about the man's statement that unsettled Satan.

"How can you say nobody knows? There had to be a hundred people trying to handcuff me."

"I've taken care of that."

"And who are you?"

"I'm a go-getter. A responsibility taker. A man who gets things done." Hardy paused for a moment, proud of himself. "Besides, you know too much now. The silo thing," he said just seconds before he lifted a gun out of the darkness and aimed it at Satan's head—right about as dead center between the eyes as one could get without measuring.

Satan stared down the barrel, wondering what nothingness felt like, wondering how much the bullet was going to hurt. Wondering if there were such things as ghosts, and if there were, if he could petition to come back and haunt the man he once thought of as father.

"Aren't there laws against this?"

"I'm sure there are. But what nobody knows about...nobody knows about."

Unfortunately, there seemed to be a strange logic to that statement which Satan couldn't argue with.

The man clicked the hammer back.

"Don't I at least get one last request?"

"What is it?" said the man, loosening up his trigger finger and clenching his jaw, which made the ever-growing tufts of hair coming out of the man's ears waggle a bit, something that should have enlightened Satan as to who this man was or at least who he was related to.

But Satan was too busy trying to come up with something for his last request, only there was nothing he wanted at the moment, except maybe to be anywhere but where he was.

"Well?"

"It's a little hard to think with a gun pointed at your forehead."

"Get used to it."

Satan's life rushed before him, a river flowing past his mind's eye, a sea of images and emotions, of bits and pieces of an existence that added up to very little. He was saddened by this.

Ion had tried to help him see what life was all about, but she was gone. And soon he would be too, only much farther away.

"I can't think of anything."

"That's pathetic." The man sighed, "All right, listen, I'll give you one. Your father...he is alive. He's got three kids and a big house in Washington state." Hardy smiled, feeling better for having done a good deed.

"Alive?"

"Yeah, now let's get on with this."

"Washington state."

"Ah-huh."

"Three other children?"

"Yes, yes, yes!"

Satan sat there fuming, wondering what the turnaround time to become a ghost was. He was so mad, in fact, that he even thought about grabbing the gun himself.

But Oliver Hardy was too fast for Satan. He began to squeeze on the trigger just as the super-rat, searching for whomever it was that had punted it across the room, found the wrong foot and bit it.

Hardy's arm shot straight up with the shock of rodent teeth gnashing at his heel. Tightening his muscles in response to the pain, he involuntarily fired the gun toward the cement ceiling, causing the bullet to ricochet back down on his head.

•

There are many observations regarding the effects of gravity, one of the best being that what goes up, must come down. A corollary to this is that what goes up really fast, must also come down really fast and will probably hurt if it hits you.

XXV. FREE RADICALS

He had put on ten pounds or so, weight he needed badly. His strength had returned and so had his spirit. There was plenty of food and Lilly's constant attention had pushed the ghosts of the last few years deeper into his past.

With his face not as drawn out, his strong features enhanced his looks instead of seeming too pronounced, and caused several of the young women in the neighborhood to follow him whenever he went out for a walk.

All of which should have made Vlady feel better. But it didn't, not really.

Lilly kept his appearances on the street short and infrequent, which instead of frustrating the hopes of the local females had the opposite effect. Their interest had been piqued, and now, every time he appeared, it was an event.

Vlady was walking with Lilly, having just picked up some things at a small grocery store a few blocks away. The air was crisp and the wind was steadily blowing in off the Lake. He was beginning to think again. Think real thoughts, not the boxed-in unrealities he had been replaying in his mind since his life turned sour. He had nearly gone mad, but somehow he had been saved from the pit of insanity.

One of those new thoughts crossed his mind.

"Where's Noel?"

"Who," asked Lilly who was too busy shooting discouraging glares in the direction of any female—or even male, for that matter—that gave Vlady more than a passing glance.

"Noel...ah, 'Satan' as you call him."

"Oh, him..." Lilly said, flatly. A passel of thirteen-year-old girls walked by, giggling and pointing self-consciously at Vlady and she wished she had a cluster bomb to lob at them and take care of the whole group at once. Instead, she growled in their direction, eliciting a shrill from one of the girls and laughter from the rest. "I don't know. Why do you ask?"

"Well, he hasn't been around for...what," he counted on his fingers, "three days."

"He's probably off chasing after my cousin." Lilly sneered at an old woman pushing a handcart full of groceries. The startled woman slipped on a patch of ice, falling flat in the middle of the intersection and spilling the contents of her bags.

Vlady turned to help the woman to her feet, but was stopped by a force he had never encountered before—the strong arm of a jealous woman.

"Keep moving," Lilly ordered.

"But..."

"Forget her. The woman's depraved."

Vlady wasn't quite sure what that meant exactly—he was probably on a plane bound for Russia when the word came up in class—but it didn't sound pleasant. He mouthed a polite "I'm sorry" to the old woman and let himself be led back toward the house.

It was several minutes before the conversation returned to Satan's whereabouts.

"I thought you said she was planning to dump him."

"She is." Lilly's responses were as curt as she could manage and still get her point across. She wanted to avoid wasting time, and keep her attention peeled on anyone that appeared threatening. She no longer enjoyed being with Vlady—she never dropped her guard long enough to experience the pleasure his company used to afford—but she wasn't going to let anyone else have him.

"Well, maybe he's gone and done something stupid," Vlady said, worried about his friend's safety.

"I don't think there's any *maybe* about it. Everything he does is stupid."

"No, I mean, like..." he motioned with his hand across his neck. "...hurt himself. He might need us."

"I'm sure he's fine. Now—"

"We're living in his house, aren't you a little curious why he isn't there?"

Lilly stopped and put her hands on her hips. They were nice hands and even nicer hips, and Vlady had become fond of climbing between them.

"First of all, who paid that Japanese guy?"

"You did," answered Vlady. "After you deposited Noel's check into your account." He had told her not to forge Noel's signature on the Government check that arrived after Congress and the President finally agreed on a budget, but when she signed it anyway, Vlady didn't complain. He was happy to have a place to stay. Soon he would go out and get a job and pay back all that Satan had done for him.

"Exactly," Lilly said, as if *she* had paid Niro out of her own pocket. "Second of all, I want to have sex the second we get inside the door."

"Okay," said Vlady, with a hint of indifference, wondering why they couldn't just do it like normal people and wait at least until after dinner.

"Don't you find me attractive anymore?"

"Of course, but—"

"Fine, then it's settled."

Lilly grabbed Vlady's arm and dragged him toward home like a kid being forced to tag along on a ten store, six-hour shopping spree.

•

Armand Arnold stared out over the cleared landscape that had once been his company. The damage didn't look as daunting with all the rubble removed and the area swept clean. It reminded Armand of a field or parking lot after the circus left town; some litter and a lot of broken dreams the only things left behind.

As his eyes lost their focus, his mind became calm for the first time in several weeks, and some of the events surrounding the explosion began passing in review through his consciousness. He remembered how much hope he had held in his heart as Peter Marks' ad campaign began showing definitive results, as the orders for Arnolds Aluminum skyrocketed in the Chicago area. But then the World had very little interest in the plans of human beings—or any creature for that matter—and didn't care that you had it all figured out on paper with tabbed columns and numbered paragraphs. In fact, given something concrete to thwart (such as a carefully drawn business plan with tabbed columns and numbered paragraphs), the World was just as likely to grant all the wishes as it was to go point-by-point down the list and throw a wrench or a car—or anything else it could pick up and heave—into the machinery of your meticulously organized life.

Redirecting his stare, Armand watched a truck full of debris pass in front of him on its way out the main gate toward a dump where much of his factory lay in pieces. He thought, he'd have to visit it someday to see what had been made of the landfill that contained so much of his heart and soul, and that of his father's and his father's father. He hoped it would become a nice park with a tree-lined jogging path.

Once the truck was out of sight, Armand pulled back his gaze to where his office had, in the past, stood. There was just a big empty space there now. However, the explosion had imprinted the shadows of several pieces of office equipment on one of the remaining walls, the one between the factory and the corporate suites. The patterned brick strangely outlined a Xerox copier, a FAX machine, several computer monitors, and an air purifier.

Armand always hated that air purifier and its annoying whir, and was glad to be rid of it. It was the one bright spot of this whole ordeal.

One of the workmen strolled up to Armand and handed him a small rectangular box, its cover scorched so that you couldn't make out what it was. Armand took it gingerly and, after a long beat, cautiously lifted the lid. He peered inside. To his surprise, it didn't contain anything dangerous, just fourteen nearly intact Cuban cigars out of the twenty Peter had given him. The workman had unearthed the box under a pile of debris that was found over a quarter-mile away in the middle of the old Clark Plumbing parking lot. It was buried under what was left of Armand's desk—the one his grandfather had used—and the seatback of his new chair. The whereabouts of the rest of the chair had not been located. And the search had been abandoned.

After passing along the find, the workman nodded, but didn't turn away. It seemed he wanted to say something, to offer some comfort, but he couldn't think of an appropriate remark, so he simply nodded again and headed back to work.

Armand sat on his wooden box in the middle of all the commotion, watching the progress as he had since the first day after the explosion. Coming here had become a ritual for him, and he took great comfort in it. He no longer used a bottle of scotch or gin to take the edge off the pain. He didn't need it anymore. He had found the strength within himself to deal with this tragedy.

Take it like a man, he thought.

And he did.

Luckily for Armand, the World was off wreaking havoc on someone's life in Bolivia and wasn't paying attention.

"What do you hope to find staring into this debris," asked a voice that came from the side and slightly behind Armand.

Surprised by both the question and the questioner, Armand swung himself around to face the inquisitor.

"What?" Armand said to the man who was thin, unshaven, and looked as though he'd been sleeping in his clothes for some time.

"What do you hope to find staring into this debris?" Jesus asked again. "I've been watching you for almost three weeks now. And all you do is sit and watch this place be torn apart. I don't understand."

"Neither do I," said Armand, more in response to the man than the question.

"Was this place of importance to you?"

"It was my life." Armand hung his head. He opened the box of cigars and pulled one out. Slowly, he lit it. "Who the hell are you?"

"I'm Jesus."

Armand took in a deep pull from his cigar, raising his eyebrows. He thought about this for a moment. He'd never been a religious man, but the name gave him some pause. There wasn't any thunder or lightning, but he felt it best to give the man a measure of courtesy. The name alone deserved that much. He offered the box to the man, who took out a cigar. Armand lit the man's Cuban.

"I see."

"You are tired. I will leave you to your grief. Thank you for the smoke."

Jesus turned and began to walk away.

"Hey, wait a minute," Armand yelled after him. "That's it? 'I'll leave you to your grief?'"

"I can give you no pity that you haven't already given yourself." Jesus had stopped, but not come back. He stood his ground, choosing instead to draw Armand out.

Armand got to his feet and went to the man. He held out his palm and introduced himself. "I'm Armand Arnold. And this used to be my business." After shaking hands, he spread his arms out in the general direction of the factory.

"You do not own it any longer?"

"What I own is rubble, and most of that's been sent to a dump in Indiana. One more reason to hate Hoosiers."

Jesus looked at the remaining sections of the plant and got an idea. He was convinced that the explosion was the sign he'd been waiting for. But whether or not that was the case, Jesus was also a realist. He had no money, he had no job, and he was quite hungry.

"In the winter, the fields are cleared by the bitter cold. Everything dies. And in the Spring the land is tilled until fresh. That is how the new season of growth is planted."

"Excuse me?"

"Your field has been cleared, and now it has been tilled. It is time to sow your seeds."

"Listen, Jesus," Armand said, blowing smoke to the side so as not to be rude, "I don't have any seeds to sow, pal." All he did have was one furnace still operational and a few dozen uncut rolls of foil. They were about forty feet wide and a few thousand feet long. Not very practical for kitchen use. That is if you could even get them in somebody's house. In the months prior to December, prior to the upswing in sales, Armand had been stockpiling the foil to keep his minimum staff working nearly full-time. In fact, he had forgotten all about the surplus foil until just a week ago when the cleanup crews were clearing out the warehouses. There were also a few hundred boxes of foil in various sizes, hardly enough worth the effort to ship out.

Armand paused and gave Jesus a tiny smile.

"Listen, Jesus, I'm sorry. But I just don't have the will to rebuild this thing from the ground up."

Jesus nodded his head solemnly for a moment. "Your grandfather must have been an extraordinary man." With that, he turned and started away again.

Armand stood and let the words plow right through him. He tapped at the cigar with his fingertip, causing the ashes to drift to the cold asphalt. Armand Arnold hadn't come this far in life without the ability to recognize a challenge—a dare—when he heard one. Even one that was couched in politeness.

He bit into the cigar.

"All right, Jesus…you got yourself a job."

•

Clearwater Sanitarium stood out from the rest of the buildings on the quiet street. Across from it, St. Augustine's lay silent, its bells waiting for the top of the hour to sound. The Sanitarium was situated at the corner of two streets that for the better part of six miles ran mostly parallel to each other. The roads didn't meet at right angles. Instead, the street running behind the hospital seemed to have lost its way and veered into the other purely by chance.

It was in much the same way that most of the patients came to be at Clearwater.

Kenny Odorman was no exception.

Now, he was trying to make the best of his situation.

He entered the white, white room to find the woman asleep. The television was on, playing and replaying a succession of commercials for Arnolds Aluminum, some featuring Satan, others showing families and business people wrapping their heads in foil. Even one which was a truncated version of "Wrap Music," the current #2 song in the country by hip-hop artist Kid Rah.

The flickering 30-second spots repeating over and over gave a surreal feel to the room.

Kenny crept up to the bed and leaned against the rail, which held the woman inside and kept her from falling to the cold linoleum floor.

The records room had been no help at all to him. It was like sifting through a landfill to find the ring you accidentally tossed out with the garbage a month before.

And Kenny needed help.

Dorobek's mother slept before him. She had a pretty face, wrinkled from time, but still pink with life.

He glanced at the television, felt unnaturally drawn to it, then snapped out of the trance and reached for the remote to turn it off.

"No," she whispered groggily, waking from her slumber.

Kenny removed his hand from the controller and gave her a tiny smile.

She gazed at him sweetly. "I knew you'd come," she said. "I knew you couldn't stay away forever."

Kenny had met Mrs. Dorobek only once, when he had punched Noel in the head during chorus practice and she had to come in and pick up her woozy son. Kenny was sitting in the principal's office, an animal at the zoo, an example of delinquency, of what could happen to you if you misbehaved. The poster child for a generation. He had to admit the principal's logic was impeccable. Kenny's fate had deterred many a student away from a life of undying shame. It was something he was proud of in an odd sort of way.

Still, he never expected the woman to remember him, especially not as fondly as this.

"Let me look at you," she said, touching his face. "You look as young as the day you left."

This fact was definitely in dispute. He had moved out of the city in the middle of the fourth grade. The woman hadn't seen him in twenty years.

"Henry," she said with love and tenderness. "Henry, take me away from this place. I'll be all right now that you're home."

Kenny's heart skipped a beat and pitter-pattered merrily for several more. A wave of universal happiness jitterbugged through his veins and he felt a tingle in his fingers and toes. Karma and joy surrounded him.

This turn of events fit perfectly into his vengeful plans.

"Soon," he said patting her hand gently. "We'll get you out of here very soon." He turned his lips up in what she perceived as a lovely smile, but to anyone else would have been a smirk. "Now, if you would be so kind as to tell me…where have we moved to?"

•

The place smelled of fresh paint and the gluey aftermath of newly laid carpet. It was bright in the room, the sun coming in off a large veranda. The curtains on the French doors were pulled back, letting in as much of the morning light as possible. Feathers of sunlight tickled Kelsey's bare back and the warmth finally woke her gently from her cozy sleep.

With squinted eyes, she rose up on one arm, pulling two pillows under her breasts for support. It was a great way to start the day. The new sheets and comforter smelled fresh. Her hair was a tussle of blonde and a few wisps of brown lurking here and there.

"Good morning," she said to the cat she had acquired during the move. The stray had been coming to her window at the other apartment for months, so she didn't feel bad in leaving with it.

"Yeowmeow," answered the cat from some hiding place under the covers. "It's time to get up, honey."

Kelsey practiced a lazy stretch, the cat mimicking her. The warm sheets fell from her shoulder, exposing a beautifully sleek figure. Leaving Barris had done something wonderful to Kelsey. Her skin glowed, her eyes burned brighter than ever, and her nights of slumber were filled with the sweetest dreams.

Climbing out of bed, she walked naked to the kitchen and made herself a cup of coffee, and for the cat, poured some cream.

A moment later, both she and the cat were sitting at the table purring. Half her life was now in order.

•

Plish, plish. Plish, plish. Plish, plish.

The sound echoed off the walls of the tunnel as Satan sloshed through the thick, stale water.

Plish, plish. Plish, plish. Plish, plish.

He couldn't see anything ahead or behind. There was total darkness.

Plish, plish. Plish, plish. Plish, plish.

But this was more than simply darkness; this was the absence of light. And very few people in the history of man have ever found themselves truly in the absence of light. But that's exactly where Satan found himself. And in the dark, the mind plays incredible tricks on a person. Every step sank him deeper into a muddy slime that made the imagination wonder what it contained. He grew sick at the thought and shuddered, stumbling into the wall. Righting himself, he could hear the screech of rats and other creatures nearby, just waiting for him to fail so that they could feed off his smooth, white flesh.

Satan had made his escape shortly after the bullet boomeranged off the ceiling and struck Oliver Hardy in the head. The bullet meandered through his body and finally exited his left foot, killing both him and the rat.

That was the easy part.

Satan knew he couldn't just saunter out the front door. These government guys never worked alone and who'd believe him if he told them the truth. It'd be another couple of days under the bright light, and he didn't think his retinas could stand it. So, after a good deal of thinking, a lot of searching, and a bit of luck, Satan found a hole that had been carved out of one of the cells at the end of the block. That hole led to a series of tunnels, which in turn led him to here.

Wherever that was.

There were several things that drove him to escape: 1) he wanted to find his father so that he could tell him what a jerk he'd been, and maybe pop him in the mouth, 2) he felt that the man accidentally killing himself was a good sign, and since there were always an ample supply of government agents willing to shoot citizens with little or no provocation, this was a good time to leave, 3) the rat's husband had shown up and was pretty pissed that his wife had been shot.

Thus, the decision to leave was a relatively simple one.

However, there is a vast difference between coming up with a theory and actually putting it into practice.

Continuing blindly in the dark passage, Satan sent his right toe out as a scout. If the ground seemed firm enough, he'd take a step. So far things had proceeded uneventfully. In fact, he began to notice that the depth of the water was becoming more shallow. After an hour or so, it came up only to his knees. Two hours later, the water was at his ankles. Satan's spirits were rising. The air grew warmer, and finally, he spotted a dim, flickering light up ahead in the distance.

It was likely the core of a nuclear power plant, but he didn't care. He had gone nearly ten miles completely underground, and he wanted out.

As he neared the light, his leg muscles began to burn and cramp up. The closer he got, the more painful it became. There was a tightness in his chest and his breathing became quick and short. Like a marathon runner finding the last hundred yards the worst, he stared ahead at the light and wished with all his might he was already there.

The source of the light was growing nearer and seemed just around the corner. At last, he knew he'd make it. He'd survive another grueling day.

Satan turned the corner and stopped. He leaned against the wall of the tunnel and tried to catch his breath. It was difficult—so much light after so much darkness—but he concentrated on focusing his eyes past the fire.

When his eyes finally did their job, Satan clearly saw the old man and the metallic briefcase.

"It's you!" screamed Satan about a fifth-of-a-second before Jimmy Hoffa smacked him across the jaw with a shimmering purple and gold and cobalt blue rock.

XXVI. NEXT STEP, THE END OF THE WORLD

Slag was meandering through the streets of the Westside. He'd traveled these sidewalks many times in the past, which made him feel a bit more confident here than in most places that he wouldn't fall off the edge of the earth.

Still, he kept his head down and his eyes peeled, watching carefully the road ahead, ever ready for that one-in-a-million chance.

As he mapped his steps, Slag thought about the guy with the foil on his head. He hadn't seen him in awhile. The guy was pretty cool and he always made it more fun at the blues club when he was around. The club wasn't the same since he'd been gone, which Slag mistakenly thought had been months, when, in fact, it had only been days.

He hoped the guy would come back from wherever he was.

Slag was wondering where he could find the guy with the foil and wasn't paying attention to where he was walking. He stepped off the curb and plunged into a dark abyss, which for a second he thought was the end of the earth, but turned out to be an uncovered sewer.

•

It sounded like a raging river and smelled like his bathroom toilet. Darkness surrounded him. There's a strange feeling about waking up in complete and total darkness almost entirely submerged. Something unsettling. The body wants light when it comes out of its slumber. And it wants to be dry.

After a few moments, Satan's body got its wish as he was thrown, suddenly, into the light. It was a blinding, harsh glare and it was painful for him to be under it. He had never seen light hurt anyone except in Star Trek episodes. And right now Satan felt like Kirk with pins in his eyes.

Tossed onto the sandy ground like a humpback beached by a surging brown-water wave, Satan came to rest with a hard THUD, his face marinating in several inches of sewer water.

When the blazing whiteness cooled down and his eyes could make out actual items, shapes and colors, he saw an unidentifiable sewer creature taking a snap out of some equally unidentifiable decaying food drifting on the surface of the water a few inches from his face. Normally, a sight such as this might cause involuntary spasms as the person tried, vainly, to get as far away as possible. Satan didn't bother to flinch. He had been through too much to care. He glanced up as a shadow passed over him.

Jesus stood over the odd looking man with a McDonald's wrapper stuck to his forehead. "Welcome," he said.

Satan stared at the tall, thin greeter who wore gray overalls with the name "Jesus" embroidered on the chest.

Well, there it was, Satan thought, confirmation.

He was dead.

It was testimony to the ironic nature of his life that he, the son of a Mafia turncoat, had been killed by a guy everyone was convinced the mob had offed more than a quarter century ago.

Satan looked around at Heaven, which looked a lot like a run down neighborhood in Chicago.

"I'm a little disappointed," he said as a Big Gulp, then a half-eaten Whopper floated past him out of a pipe and into the Pearly Gates.

The trash was followed out of the pipe by another new arrival, who slammed into Satan, causing pain, something he didn't expect from death. This person had long hair and pale white skin.

"And what is your disappointment?"

Satan thought about it for a moment. "I'm not in Heaven am I?"

"No."

"Oh, my God, I'm in *Hell*?"

Jesus looked solemnly at the man. "Chicago."

Suddenly, the person in the water sat up.

"Slag?"

Slag pulled several soggy hot dog bun remnants from under his shirt and nodded to Satan as if he almost recognized him. The poet's clothes were soaked and he smelled terrible, but surprisingly, his hair looked great.

"Jesus! I'm alive?" said Satan, less glad than one might expect.

"Not for long, man. Time is smashing past." Slag flipped several pounds of that hair over the back of his head and Satan could see he had a large bump on his forehead. "We'll be dirt soon."

"Thank you, Slag. It's always inspirational to hear you string words together into near-sentences," barked Satan.

"It's cool, man." Slag looked at the man and had the impression the man knew him.

Satan shook his head sadly as he climbed out of the sewer channel with the help of Jesus. As he reached the top of the cement drainway, Satan's jaw slackened slightly as he glanced out over a mostly barren piece of land that had once been Arnolds Aluminum.

Armand Arnold sat behind a dented metal secretary's desk that had been salvaged from the rubble. He had his feet up on the desk and was smoking the last of his cigars as he held a cellular phone to his ear.

"No? What do you mean no? We need the loans to rebuild so we can pay off all the other loans. Sixty years of business has gotta mean something." Armand was quiet for a moment as he listened. Then he cut in, "We're not completely destroyed, I've got a dozen rolls—" Armand grabbed Jesus as he walked up with Satan and Slag. "Talk to my Director of New Business Development." Armand handed the cell phone to Jesus. "Here."

Jesus put his lips tentatively to the phone. "In the winter, the fields are cleared by the bitter cold. Everything dies. And in the Spring the land is tilled—Hello?" He tapped at the phone. "Hello?" Jesus listened for a moment, then offered the phone back to Armand, who was shaking his head. "I think they hung up," said Jesus just as the bulldozer smashed through some debris in the distance.

"You're fired!" Armand shouted at Jesus.

Satan looked at the bulldozer, then at Jesus, then at Armand. "Have you gone mad?! What are you doing? They're obliterating your factory!"

"Son, let me put it to you like this. Explosives, in general, have a negative effect on business."

"You're just giving up? You can't do that."

"Yes, I can. The Chinese have a proverb. 'At birth we come, at death we go…baring nothing.' My crack team and I here," he motioned to himself and Jesus, "are just getting ready a little early."

"But what about me?" asked Satan as he rubbed his head which began to pound like a rock concert was being held in his sinuses, becoming alarmed when he realized he had lost another hat to Jimmy Hoffa. "I *need* your foil. Only Arnolds will do."

"What are you, an idiot? Foil's foil. It's all the same."

Armand's words were heretical and Satan glared at the man.

"Hey, whatever." Armand pointed to the gigantic rolls of foil. "They're all yours. Oughta last you to the next millennium."

Satan continued scowling at Armand even as he swiftly dashed over to one of the giant rolls, tore off a piece and instinctively wrapped it around his head.

"It's not your fault, Son. Just evolution. Survival of the fittest." Armand nodded toward the rendering of Renaissance Village on the large placard across the street. "You and me, we're Dodos."

With a massive dose of religion, Satan turned and rushed Armand who was still seated.

"Get up." Satan waited for any sign of movement. There was none. "Get UP!"

"Leave me alone. You're fired, too."

"You can't fire me. I have a contract. And you can't simply sit there sulking in your misery. I won't tolerate it." Satan was quiet for a moment. "This is the only thing I have left," he said softly, tapping his head.

"I think you might have lost that a while ago, Son."

"The foil! Your foil!" Satan pointed to the remains of the Arnolds Aluminum sign. "What about your commitment to it? Huh? What about that?"

"I don't have the energy."

Twisting Armand's head back, forcing the man to look at him, Satan leaned in close. "Listen to me, you. I've been abandoned by my father, the gangster, seen my mother carted off to a nut house. I've been left for dead by some lunatic fringe of the U.S. Government apparently able to assassinate people without any red tape. I've been whacked in the skull by a dead teamster and I've had my heart torn out of my chest by a female who does this for a living...I'm not a dodo. I'm a cockroach. I just keep on surviving. And you, you have the nerve to tell me you don't have the *energy*! Well, fffff—" He was having trouble getting the words out, then finally they came. "—ffffuck *you*!"

Standing there, panting heavily, Satan looked as if a large weight had been lifted from him. Finally, he spoke.

"Your grandfather built this place, your father built it up, and you and me, we *razed* it! I'm not going to have that on *my* conscious. No, sir. Not me."

Armand was stunned. He had been president of his company for so long he couldn't remember the last time anyone had talked to him like that. Actually, he could remember. But not since his father had died.

"Okay," he said quietly, just like he had all those times to his dad.

Clearly not expecting that response, Satan was startled for a moment. It took him time to recover, and all he could manage was: "Well…" A pause. "Okay."

Armand looked at Satan. "All right, Mr. Passion. You got any ideas?"

Satan looked off in the distance toward the Loop and saw the towering skyscrapers, which were shimmering and vibrating and becoming increasingly out of focus.

"Actually, I—"

Everything went dark as Satan fainted.

•

The Big Red Thing loomed over the busy city street. Kelsey stared up at the building. This was a ritual for her, as routine as waking each morning. After parking her car in the garage just west of her office, she'd cross the street, pause at the base of her building and look up. The clouds moving past the structure made it appear to be falling to the left. In that moment, she felt an instant of sickness in her stomach that was as much from the illusion of the huge red box tilting as it was from the thought that she'd have to spend another eight hours in the presence of Leo Lincoln.

Once inside, the vitality she awoke with each morning soon left her. It usually took a half-hour or so, just about the moment Leo would stroll into the office.

Einstein had a theory about the relative nature of time. He must have worked for someone very much like Leo Lincoln. Time seemed to move excruciatingly slow as the days of February passed. Kelsey had never fully recovered from seeing Armand Arnold's dream go up in a ball of flame and debris. That her boss took so much pleasure from that very same event made her despair all the more difficult to shake.

She was expecting developers proposing a new skyscraper in The Loop that would dwarf the Sears by 600 feet. Every few years someone got enough people fired up to try and fund a bid to retake the title of World's Tallest Building for Chicago.

Kelsey rolled up the blueprints for Renaissance Village and slid them into a tube. At least she wouldn't have to look at them anymore. The zoning board had given the project the green light, confident Armand Arnold would sell the property now that his company had shut down and blown up. Ground breaking would take place at the old Clark Plumbing factory in a week. It was just the news Leo had hoped for. Now it didn't make a difference whether Armand held out or not. Construction would start immediately and the city rarely pulled the permit on a job in progress.

Leaning back in her chair, Kelsey put her hands behind her head. The clock on the wall ticked mockingly at her. Leo was more annoying than ever and carried himself with a smugness he had, until then, only aspired to. And his fits of paranoia had died away.

Kelsey was so sure Leo was in some way responsible for the destruction of Arnolds that she had quietly hired a private detective in the hope that she could find something to link Leo to the deed. The private dick—as she referred to him—had dazzled her with a bag of tricks and a suitcase full of toys, but so far, was doing nothing but papering her to death.

Several nondescript boxes sat in the middle of her office. Papers and files that the P.I. had unearthed in the basement of the old county administration office. He dropped them off three days ago.

Kelsey had been spending her now Barris-free evenings alone with these very same boxes. Some held details about projects Leo had worked on. Others contained papers pertaining to the Lincoln family; birth certificates, family history, school records—some dating back to the turn of the century. Leo's mother had given the records to the county in case they might be of historical importance. Kelsey was hoping Leo had had some education in explosives, but the closest she came was that he got an F and two Ds in chemistry. There were still several boxes she hadn't gone through. And the dick had promised her more.

There was a knock at the door, which gave her a start.

"Yes, come in," said Kelsey. She glanced up to find her assistant standing in the door frame. "What is it, Sandy?"

"There's someone here to see you." The woman seemed a bit nervous.

Kelsey closed her eyes, put three fingers to her temple and rubbed it, making tight circles. "Send them in."

Only it wasn't the developers. Instead, Barris strolled into the room, carrying a leather valise under his arm, an expensive suit covering his frame. He cleared his throat. Kelsey opened her eyes without removing her hand from her head. She nearly fell off the side of her chair when she saw her ex-lover standing in the middle of her office. As it was, her elbow slipped and she smacked her forehead into a PERSONAL & CONFIDENTIAL stamp that was lying on her desk. A red "NAL & CON" was inked into the area above her brow.

"Barris!" she said, as if he'd been a client storming in on her while she was undressing. She pulled the edge of a blueprint toward her chest to emphasize this. "What are you doing here?"

"Hi, Kelse. You look great," he said, in answer to some other question than the one she'd asked.

She rubbed at the inkblot on her forehead with her fingers, making it worse.

"What do you want?" she asked, annoyed. And her day had started out so incredibly well.

"It's business." Barris closed the door to give them a bit of privacy. Kelsey jumped out of her chair and went to open it, when he stopped her. "Wait."

"Barris, we have nothing to talk about. We ended it much cleaner than I thought possible, but now, I want to get on with my life."

"I know." He nodded, then began fishing in his valise for something.

She had to admit the break up had done wonders for him. In fact, she felt a tinge of jealousy over how well he looked. Somewhere lurking deep inside her was a tiny place that secretly wished he had completely fallen apart and had come crawling into her office to beg her to come back to him. Beg her to end his nightmare and make things the way they were. She'd turn him away, of course, it was much too late for reconciliation now, she'd tell him, but she wanted to know, wanted him to know, how much she had meant in his life.

But here he was looking great.

It was beginning to annoy her.

A lot.

She had the urge to spout off all the wonderful things that had happened to her. About the apartment she found, about the half dozen men who had asked her out for a date, but she knew he'd see through the effort.

So, instead, she convinced herself that she wasn't interested in what, why, or how he had changed.

But then Barris, being Barris, made a face or small gesture that reminded her of all the reasons she'd left him, giving her a sharp, heavy feeling behind the bridge of her nose like eating ice cream too quickly.

She wrapped her fingers around her nose and squeezed. Living without a man took some getting used to. Even when she no longer loved Barris, Kelsey drew comfort from his presence. Now, she was alone, and at times, that feeling was more painful than anything she had felt living with him. But her decision was the right one, and she knew it deep in her heart.

Barris pulled out a short stack of papers.

"You still want to pinch Leo Lincoln?"

Kelsey stopped trying to go for the door.

"No," she said. "I want to smack him."

He gazed at her and gave her a wonderful, somewhat evil grin.

•

Vlady patted the back of Satan's hand. "Noel, hey, wake up. You can't go to sleep."

"Quiet, I'm trying to go to sleep."

"You can't. Wake up!"

Satan looked around and found himself in his living room on the couch. "What happened to the factory?"

"It blew up."

"I know that. I was there. But what happened?"

"You got a concussion. Apparently from some blow to the head."

Satan relived the pain all over again.

"Yeah, it's a long story. You don't happen to know anything about the history of the Teamsters Union, do you?"

"Not really."

"Good."

Vlady's eyes seemed so sad, as if a part of him had left his body. Satan started to say something else, but the look on Vlady's face—the depth of the pain he saw—made him draw back the urge to speak.

The two of them sat in silence.

"I owe you my life," Vlady finally said. "I'm glad you're okay." He was quiet again, then said, "C'mon," with a faint smile, "Let's get you upstairs so you can be more comfortable."

"Okay." Satan coughed, sending several ounces of fetid, malodorous liquid into the air, a manifestation that began after being spit out of the sewer.

As Vlady lifted Satan off the couch, Lilly eyed Satan with a deep and simmering contempt. The guy had never actually done anything wrong to her, which was mostly why she couldn't stand him. If just once he'd violated her—or even tried to—maybe she wouldn't despise him so much.

•

"How are you feeling?" asked Kelsey. Softly, she caressed Satan's face with her hand, thinking of her kitten.

Her fingers felt wonderful, and he closed his eyes to bask in her touch. He lazily glanced around his bedroom. It seemed as though he had left this place a million years ago—as if he had traveled distant oceans on a monumental trek as Ulysses had once done. Yet, sitting on his bed, the blankets and mattress were so comfortable and familiar that the feeling nearly made him cry—something Ulysses rarely did.

Kelsey watched him carefully. "We were worried about you."

"So was I," he mumbled into the pillow. "At least, I know who I am now."

Kelsey wasn't sure if that was a good thing or a bad thing. "I know Ion meant a lot to you. It's normal to want to run away. I can understand that. It tears at your heart when you lose someone."

He smiled bittersweetly. "I didn't quite run away. It was more like…I was dragged." Satan eyes fell on the phone beside his bed. After watching it for several seconds, he picked up the black handle, but did not dial. "I know you're listening," he said into the mouthpiece. "I want you to stop following me, stop filming me, stop bugging me…and my house. If you insist on harassing me, I will have no choice but to go straight to the newspapers with what I know. Scandal, humiliation, and a geopolitical crisis will ensue.

"I am not a threat to anyone, except perhaps myself. All I wanted was to fulfill a childhood dream. That was, find a way to get inside the center of the Earth, and maybe locate my father. Not get inside nuclear missile silos or anything like that. Just the center of the Earth. I'm sure you've heard of Jules Verne. Strike that, you probably have no idea who Jules Verne is, but I can assure you that if our educational system hadn't failed you, you'd understand what I'm saying and empathize with me.

"Only now, even that dream is gone. Like Santa Claus and the Tooth Fairy, ignorance washed away in the starkness of truth. So, I'd appreciate it if you just left me alone." He started to hang up, thought about it, then returned the receiver to his mouth. "Thank you."

Satan replaced the receiver on the phone.

Kelsey stared at him, not knowing what to make of his outburst. "I'm glad you're…are you sure you're all right," she said.

Satan folded down the comforter that covered his body. He meticulously creased the fold and patted the fabric when he was done.

"My father was a criminal who testified for the government and then went into a witness protection program."

"A criminal? I don't understand."

"He was a gangster. A 'no-good, tattle-telling lowlife felonious thug' to quote a dearly departed friend of mine. Only now, my dad's the perfect citizen somewhere in Washington state with a new life, a new wife, and three new kids. That's why he didn't show up at the train station. That's why my mother went crazy. That's why I want to find him and twist his head off."

Kelsey tried to process the information. You always had to take what Satan said with a grain of salt.

"How was *your* day?" he said before she could finish.

"Well, the planning commission gave the okay to start work on Renaissance Village. Once that happens, it'll be nearly impossible for Armand to rebuild the factory."

"So, only slightly better than mine."

Satan sat up. He empathized with Armand and his company. He felt that Arnolds Aluminum's failure had been his fault, that he had draped his bad luck over the corporation like a burial cloth.

"Whatever you said or did today got Armand fired up. He's not giving up. But you've only got a week to do something before they begin construction on Renaissance. Barris and Peter thought you might be interested in helping."

"I think I've 'helped' Arnolds enough, don't you?"

Kelsey nodded, sadly. They both sat quietly for a moment. Finally, Kelsey grabbed the silence. "I left Barris."

Stunned, Satan paused before answering. "But I thought you two were so happy."

"Of course you did, Satan. You think everyone else's life is great. And that you're the only unhappy person in the world."

"That's not precisely correct. I simply claim that no one can document a more horrible life than mine." He thought about Barris and his quest to bring forth his inner world. The parallels were striking. "But he's so talented."

"You really think so?"

Satan had never really contemplated the thought. Come to think of it, he'd never actually read anything written by Barris. "Well, yeah, don't you?"

"I think it's for the best. I'm happier this way."

Satan lowered his head, thinking about Barris, wondering how he was taking this loss. "Why do women do this?"

"Because we know better than men when it's right and when it's not."

A picture of Ion flashed in Satan's mind. The wind flowing through her hair as she smiled. Blue, effervescent eyes clicking back and forth as they stared into his eyes.

"I miss her. Sort of like an old soldier misses war." He looked at the broken window. He was going to have to fix that soon or risk pneumonia. "But whenever I try to put how I feel into words, it comes out sounding so...trivial."

"That's cause what you're feeling isn't words. It's in here." She tapped at his chest.

Deep in the recesses of that chest, Satan's human heart beat out a stinging rhythm of love and hate, love and hate, love and hate. These alternating beats, these two words seemed to him to have no meaning outside himself. He had heard them said, heard them shouted from the tops of buildings, splayed across the billboards in pink and red, and whispered in the darkness on the movie screens. Words repeated so often for so long with so little provocation that their meaning had been muddied and obscured. And yet, somewhere in his soul, Satan knew that the original intent that led to the creation of these words still existed.

Language could only lie about the truth, never fully reflecting what the mind saw. Mere words were inadequate to describe the beauty of the earth, its land, its seas, its teeming life, that billions of years had created and refined—and these were tangible things. How could anything so imprecise as language ever hope to describe that which you couldn't even touch?

"She wasn't right for you."

"Yes, she was. But only up to a certain point."

Satan vowed to never speak of love again.

•

A doctor from the hospital called to make sure Satan was not having any complications from his second concussion in less than two months. He asked Satan a series of questions, which Satan couldn't answer. Not because of any blow to the head, not because he hadn't been to sleep in several days and couldn't so much as nap until the doctor gave the okay, but because Satan was unable to understand a single word said in the doctor's thick Eastern European accent. Initially, the doctor wanted to send an ambulance to rush Satan to the emergency since his patient was obviously suffering from persistent confusion, and possible brain injury.

It took some time for Satan to convince the man he was fine. Mostly because the man couldn't understand a word his patient was saying. Frustrated, the doctor finally put someone else on the phone.

A minute later, Satan was told he could finally go to sleep.

Which he did a minute after that.

•

In the corner of the living room, Vlady sat at the computer hosting Satan's website, which was still streaming video that Slag updated every day. Despite the explosion, despite the hours and hours of footage showing Satan sleeping, visitors continued to flock to the site. Perhaps they came out of morbid curiosity. But as Peter Marks said, trying to find a silver lining in all this, "A hit is a hit is a hit, morbid or not."

Vlady was staring at the screen. He hadn't touched the keys or moved the mouse, but Lilly watched him as she vacuumed, ever ready to sprint over and pull the plug if he started surfing the net for naked pictures of women. He had her around for God's Sake. She'd take off her clothes for him in an instant.

Vlady's mind was elsewhere, on the rock atop his friend's dresser. He noticed Ion's gift when checking on Satan early this morning. It wasn't at all like his shimmering purple and gold and blue stone, but it had enough of a draw on him to cause him to steal it.

The rock, which now bulged in his front pocket, brought it all back. The loss. The staggering loss. Of *his* rock. Of the pigeon. Of Sasha.

Pushing back the chair, Vlady stood and walked toward the stairs.

Lilly shouted over the din. "Where you going?"

"I'm gonna try and take a nap."

"Wait," she said, dropping the vacuum after seeing the bulge in his pants. "I'll come with you."

"No," he said, harshly. He took in a deep breath, then softened his tone. "I just need to get some rest."

"Okay." Lilly tried not to sound too hurt. "But if you need me…"

"I won't," he said, then added, "Maybe later."

Vlady turned and climbed the steps, letting out a sigh of relief, realizing that where he was going, he would no longer be haunted by the past, no longer feel any more pain.

•

When Satan woke up the next afternoon, something happened which suddenly motivated him more than even Ion had. He was sitting there under the covers with another bird on his head, thinking how pitiful his life was and that there was no end in sight to the humiliation.

So far, an ordinary morning.

And then it struck him.

Well, actually two things struck him. The first was the bird, who began to peck at the lump on his forehead given to him by Jimmy Hoffa, thinking it was a small pile of seeds. The second was a thought. A wholly unique thought for Satan.

He sat up, sending the bird flying across the room. After grabbing his robe and walking to the mirror hanging over his dresser, Satan looked into the reflection, staring into his own eyes and gazing at himself much longer than he normally felt comfortable with.

"She didn't think you could do it," he whispered to the reflection. "And neither did you."

Satan went to the pile of hats lying in the corner. Bowlers, caps, berets, all kinds of head gear. He took one of the bowlers and back in front of the mirror, placed it on his head. That's when he noticed his rock was gone. Ion probably took it before she left. Maybe it was for the best, there was already enough in his home that reminded him of her. He straightened the bowler, then tipped it to the left.

He still wasn't sure if he believed in himself, but he knew if he didn't do something, the rest of his life would be lived with regret, or worse, the way it had been before.

"Kelsey!" he yelled out as he opened the door to his bedroom. Seven days. What could he do in a week to save Arnolds? Stepping heavily on the creaking wood, he went from room to room. "Kelsey!"

Finally, Lilly appeared at the top of the stairs.

"What are you screaming about? Don't you realize Vlady's trying to sleep," she cried. "He needs his rest!"

Satan cringed at the sight of her. Lilly's face had begun to change, almost to fit her new role as guardian over Vlady. The lines around her eyes had thickened and her gaze was cold as a glacier.

"Where's Kelsey?"

"She went home after you went to sleep."

He grunted, a low, even growl, then brushed past her, deciding to talk to

Vlady instead. His friend would understand tenacity, resolve and maybe have some advice for Satan on how to get some.

He had gotten an idea at the factory before he blacked out. But what was it?

Satan pushed open the door to his mother's old room, which, since they found him on the steps, had become Vlady's.

A breath of frigid air rushed past him. He immediately drew his arms in to keep his body's warmth from dissipating. An arctic blast blew through an open window and sent the curtains scattering for cover.

A few years in Siberia had surely changed Vlady. Polar bears didn't like it this cold.

Satan stepped through the doorway, bundling his robe over his torso as he hurried to the window and closed it. He made a sound, "Brrrrrrrrr," before turning to say something to Vlady. The sentence never left his mouth because he saw the frozen lump on the bed first. He stepped cautiously over to it and touched his hand to the part of the lump that lay on the pillow.

Lilly entered the room in a huff and, immediately, screamed a scream from the fiery pits of hell when she saw the frozen mass resting peacefully atop the covers.

Vlady was gone.

Satan picked up the blue sheet of paper that sat folded on the pillow. Opening it, he glanced at the words, then at the six-foot snowman Vlady had built in the middle of his mattress. With the window closed, it was already beginning to melt.

"Dear Noel..." the letter began:

> *Thank you for your hospitality and your food. By now, you know that I have left with your rock. I am sorry for that. As you read this, I am on my way to South America where I hope to find a bride and raise mangos. It is nothing against you, you have been wonderful to me. I would not have survived without your help. You have allowed me to build my strength and regain my will to live.*
>
> *Having done this, I feel it would be a shame to commit suicide. However, if I had to spend one more minute in Lilly's presence, that is what would come of it.*
>
> *I wish you well.*

Your friend,
Vlady

Satan found five hundred dollars and change under the note.

P.S. This isn't much, but it's all they had in the till at
the liquor store around the corner (less my plane ticket,
of course).
I'm sure it's not marked.

Satan neatly folded the note and the bills and placed them in the pocket of his robe, then walked slowly over to Lilly who was caressing the snowman tenderly.

"What does it say," she asked sadly.

"Get out," he said.

"Excuse me?" She was too caught up in her grief to properly translate his words. She wept at the thought of Vlady's smell and the sparkle in his eyes when he spoke of his life, even the sad times.

"I said, get out of my house."

She sat frozen like a deer staring into oncoming headlights. "I don't understand."

"Have you been living under power lines your whole life? What part of 'get out' don't you understand?" He waited, but she didn't answer. "I'll make it easier. OUT! You're a curse upon my home. Pack your bags and take the pestilence you've brought to this house with you. Round up the wagons and git, lil' darlin'. Any of this getting through to you? Perhaps, if I draw it—"

Lilly stood and pushed past him without another word. He heard her muffled crying as she gathered her things, then heard a series of ear-piercing sounds as Lilly stormed out of the house, breaking a few hundred items as she went.

Satan felt pretty good. He glanced around the room to see if there was anyone or anything else he could exorcise from his life. He picked up the phone, started to throw it out the window, but instead, dialed Armand Arnold.

XXVII. GINGERBREAD CITY

It snowed for four days and nights, and the city was covered in a blanket of white that seemed to make Chicago look less threatening, more like a town than a big city.

After thirty-six inches of the white powder stacked up on the cement and asphalt, the place looked less like a town and more like a giant series of gingerbread houses.

It was the greatest blizzard in the history of Chicago.

Thousands of cars and buses were stranded in the streets, hampering the cleanup. Trains and pedestrians were unable to pass through the drifts. Business came to a standstill. The few people that did venture out found nothing to do and no place to go and sooner or later went back inside to watch the variety of broadcast, cable and satellite channels available on television.

All those commercials had put people in the buying mood. However, most stores were closed and the Mayor told everyone to stay indoors until the roads could be cleared.

All of which benefited internet retailers and the Shop-At-Home network immensely. For people without web access, Shop-At-Home was the only game in town, and sales shot through the roof. Of course, trinkets and gold-plated serpentine chains were no substitute for food, but everyone starved happily, knowing that in 2-3 weeks they were going to get a whole bunch of really neat stuff…if they survived until then.

Happily, on the fifth day, the clouds broke and the sun peeked through, shining its brightness on the ground below, and warming it slightly.

•

During the storm, Kenny Odorman escaped from Clearwater.

Climbing out the fourth story window, he shimmied down a drainage pipe to the sidewalk below. Of course, the subzero temperature made the metal pipe extremely cold. He had several patches of frostbite on his hands and legs, but he couldn't concern himself with that now. He focused himself on the job at hand, and that was: get to his office, input Dorobek's address, and let the system do the rest. Once the computers knew where to look for Noel, they'd spit out threatening letters, legal correspondence, bills and more bills.

Kenny actually got a warm feeling inside as he trudged half-naked down the street. Finally, hours later, he made it to his office. But that was as far as he got. The storm forced him to remain there after a ten-foot drift set up shop directly outside the main doors.

At least he could enter Dorobek's information into the computer and fantasize about the look on his old nemesis' face when the bill collectors and prosecutors came calling with charges of fraud and debts totaling nearly half a million dollars.

Kenny Odorman loved his work.

•

Kelsey sat on the floor of her new apartment. The contents of the seven boxes lay on the ground surrounding her. With Satan back safe at home, she returned to poring over the boxes of documents. When she first learned he was missing, she worried he followed Ion in a vain attempt to win her back. Ion had transformed Satan, mostly for the good. But it seemed to Kelsey that as soon as Ion had taken him as far as she could, she abandoned him.

Ion told her how she'd find these men, see their potential, knead them, mold them into something more than they had been, then exit just as they were beginning to reach their potential. Ion said that if she stayed, they'd always believe the success was because of her. They'd think that in order to remain successful they'd need her. This way, if they made it, it was their success.

Satan hadn't made it, per se, but he was certainly no longer the same person. He looked leaner, older, more like a man than a boy.

Kelsey glanced around the room. There was little in the papers of any historical importance, not that she was rolling on the floor for that reason.

She tried, unsuccessfully, to convince the police that Leo had a hand in the demise of Arnolds Aluminum. The FBI analyzed the detonator, found that it matched those used in several unsolved bombings over the last ten years. A couple benefited Leo's friends, but many did not. Frustrated by her failure to implicate Leo, she held out these pages as her final hope of finding some shred of something, a dark secret, a hidden clue that could unravel her boss' overspun ego. Something to give her a modicum of satisfaction.

So far, no luck. The papers were all very innocuous. Birth certificates, school records, etc. Nothing even the least bit interesting.

Then quite by impulse, Kelsey decided to line everyone's birth certificates up, forming one giant family tree on her living room floor.

Still nothing. Everybody fit where they were supposed to—even Leo. Of course, his certificate was a little shorter and a little wider and a little redder than everyone else's.

Frustrated, Kelsey picked up an old, brittle envelope and carefully tore at the flap. She reached in and gently pulled out a yellowed piece of paper, browning at the edges. A piece of paper that, in it's own way, would ruin Leo's life.

•

Over on the roof of Brisker, Pendry & Marks, only the comb of the metal rooster was visible. After half a day of sun, the beak could be made out just barely, and if you didn't know what it was, you might have mistaken it for a giant hairbrush.

All of this hadn't deterred Peter Marks who was sitting at his desk looking at the plan he and Jesus and Barris and Armand had worked out over the last hundred and twenty hours.

"This isn't going to work. It's crazy," Armand said.

Jesus mumbled ideas to himself as he looked at the elevation plans of the John Hancock Center. A hundred floors straight up. A marvelous feat of engineering and design. Peter had gotten the drawings from someone inside Skidmore, Owings & Merrill.

Barris glanced at the plans. He wasn't nearly as impressed with them as Jesus was. The building had two antenna towers protruding from its roof that gave it the appearance of an enormous stun gun.

"Why are we using the Hancock? Why not the Sears Tower? I mean, isn't *that* the tallest building in America? Instead, we're using the *fourth* tallest building in America?"

"First of all, Big John is more elegant. Everyone loves Big John," Peter Marks said. "Second, the parade doesn't pass the Sears!"

"I think what we're planning is illegal. Has anyone thought about that?" Armand worried aloud. He was against mostly everything they had decided, but even though it was *his* company, he felt he should defer to the majority.

"It was your idea," Peter Marks said to Armand.

Armand nodded his head and shrugged his shoulders at the same time. He didn't recall this being so, but went with it anyway. Then he remembered. "Actually, it was Satan's idea."

Of course, it wasn't this momentous when Satan explained it to him over the phone, but the basic mechanics were the same.

"I think he had something...subtler in mind," Armand added. "Something to put the planning commission's green-light of Renaissance Village on hold and give us more time."

"Subtlety has never been my strong point," Peter explained.

Through the raging blizzard, Peter Marks had somehow gotten one of his employees to trudge over to the eight or so television stations in town and deliver a series of newly and hastily edited commercials featuring Satan. He had them played nonstop. Peter figured that as soon as the weather broke the first thing people would do was go out and buy food. The second thing they'd do is purchase Arnolds Aluminum to wrap up the leftovers.

Of course, with there being no Arnolds on the shelves, Peter was predicting chaos and, hopefully, sporadic rioting. All of which would bring much-needed publicity.

Then he remembered Armand had no money. So, he had his guy trudge back to each of the stations and pull the spots before the bills got out of hand.

Which led to Plan "B."

"The Lincoln Parade will give us good television coverage. This is war. Guerrilla war. We're battling 500 channels, instant web access, the microwave generation with the attention span to match," he said, taking the last Girl Scout cookie in the building and popping it in his mouth. The others eyed him jealously. They had munched through their allotment of snacks nearly a day and a half ago.

A gaunt Jesus nodded his head slowly as he watched Peter gnash at his food.

"We'll webcast the ads, using the site Ion set up." Peter Marks licked his lips as he swallowed the last little bit of cookie.

"She was a wonderful woman," Barris said, thinking not of Ion, but of Kelsey. "An unbelievable and delicate flower," he sighed, under his breath.

Peter Marks gave Barris a shove, sending him crashing to the floor. "Would you shut up about your damn ex! Christ, it's driving me up the wall. With all I hear about this chick, I can't tell if I want to fuck her or puke all over you. Give it up, will ya?"

"It is getting a bit tiresome," added Armand.

Jesus who rarely said anything that wasn't positive nodded in agreement. "You're acting like a loser."

Barris picked himself off the ground, brushed the dirt from his clothes and sat back down. He sulked for a few moments. In fact, all of them sulked. None of them had women. Oh, Armand had a wife, but that wasn't the same thing as having a *woman*. The four men tried to make themselves look busy by shuffling papers and sorting through diagrams and elevation plans, but it did little to hide the void in their hearts left by the lack of true female companionship.

"All right," sighed Peter. "Enough of this angst crap. We're men. We don't care if we have women."

"I had this woman once," began Jesus. "She was a mailman, a mail *person*. Beautiful, sexy. She used to deliver my mail, personally, each day, right to me. Once in awhile, she'd let her fingers linger on mine a bit longer than they should have. Then one day she outright nibbled on my thumb, sucking it like a baby would."

He paused. The others waited silently for him to begin again, but he didn't.

Finally, Peter had had enough. "So, then what?"

Jesus lowered his eyes toward the floor.

"Turned out to be a transvestite."

There was a collective groan/cringe as each of them was hit with the visual. Barris actually stopped thinking about Kelsey for a moment.

"Thank you, Jesus. I think we all appreciated that little diversion." Peter picked up a pad that had a series of notes scribbled on it. President's Day was the day after tomorrow. And there was much to do before then. "Okay, so who had the idea involving the midgets?"

"That was Satan's as well."

XXVIII. VERDAD

A thick, white layer hung over the room, smoke from the morning's half-pack of Camels. Yellowed fingers tapped ashes into last night's whiskey glass. The gray flakes floated on the remnants of a whiskey sour.

Brian Verdad inhaled the last of his cigarette, then flicked it into the glass where it died with a faint hiss.

He had spent the last twenty days in his room, in bed, the covers drawn up over himself. The air was stale and his musky smell was drowned out only by the stench of cigarettes. He couldn't seem to motivate himself to get up, however, now that his one dozen carton supply of Camels were spent, he'd have to do something—he wasn't very friendly without nicotine in his blood, and the marijuana growing in his basement hadn't budded yet.

Last night—like the others before—hadn't been very restful and all he could think of as he lay under his comforter sucking on a cig was how very small a prison cell would be.

He stared at his High School diploma from Parkinson High and realized he had ended up exactly where his principle, Mr. McKinney, had said he would. On his way to jail.

He brushed his stained fingers across his eyebrows and picked at a mutant hair that was nearly twice as long as any other. He winced as it finally came loose, then placed the strand in his palm to look at it.

The hair became a source of entertainment for him. He stared at it for nearly fifteen minutes, thinking it was surely the most exciting thing that had come along in the twenty days. How odd, he thought. That his body could have screwed up so badly on something as simple as an eyebrow hair.

Suddenly, an errant breeze blew the strand from his hand, and that was the end of the show. With the hair gone and the level of nicotine dropping, Brian Verdad went back to worrying. Ever since the Arnolds Aluminum explosion, he'd been living in never-ending fear. He was mortified, terrified. Clumps of hair were coming out of his scalp the mornings he could get himself motivated enough to shower. A rash had developed under his left shoulder blade—in a place he couldn't quite reach to scratch.

He had never built a device for something so public. Torching restaurants for insurance, or scaring off 'certain people' from buying homes in discriminating wealthy neighborhoods was the extent of his work. Occasionally, he'd do a job for Leo Lincoln, who more than a few times had hired him to build explosives to force one or two last holdouts into selling to developers. But that was a house here and there, a store every once in a while.

But Arnold's...

He had no idea Leo meant to completely obliterate an entire factory. It was so obviously a torch job that the cops and the arson squad would figure out where the parts were purchased, when, and by whom, which would eventually lead to him. He tried to cover his tracks by having friends innocently buy the items not knowing what the whole would make, but still, he wasn't convinced he'd come away from this without doing some time.

So, for the last three weeks, he'd been holed up in his bedroom, sure that any moment the cops would be knocking on the door.

He had to do something. He just couldn't sit around any longer. His food was dwindling, his cigs were *fini*, and he'd run out of toilet paper two or three days ago.

With a tremendous amount of resolve that had been storing up over the past four hundred and eighty hours, Brian got to his feet. His legs ached from disuse, and his head felt light as he stood too quickly. After a moment, he regained his balance, then walked out of his house and into his garage. He piled up all of the supplies and equipment he'd gathered over the years, all the tools and papers and hardware, and loaded them into the trunk of his Pontiac GTO.

The back end sat low under all the weight, so he pumped up the air shocks so it wouldn't be as noticeable.

His plan was to find an isolated spot and dump everything.

Give it up. Start fresh.

Once the last fifteen years of his life had been erased from his garage, Brian Verdad climbed behind the wheel of his car, turned the key and pulled slowly out of the drive, checking each way before backing into the street.

His speed never went above 25, the limit for city streets unless otherwise posted. At stop signs, he stopped completely, looked both ways, then, and only then, proceeded cautiously through the intersection. He made sure he did nothing illegal. His biggest fear now was that he'd be pulled over by some cop for a traffic violation and then he'd be in deep shit.

About halfway out of the city, a cop taking a reading break on one of the side streets noticed the overly cautious driver heading past him. Immediately, he became suspicious. After following the Limelight Green GTO for a few miles, the cop was sure something big was up. He called for backup, set up four major roadblocks, then moved in for the kill.

The lights and siren went off, startling Brian, who was thinking how smoothly the whole thing was going. He stayed calm and pulled the car gently over to the side of the road, making sure it was safe to do so first.

As Brian saw the cop step out of his cruiser and approach him on foot in his rear view mirror, he listed off his options in his head and chose to set off a detonator cap and blow himself and the car—and maybe even the cop—to smithereens.

The cop stepped up to the driver-side window just as a dozen police cars pulled up, the officers with their guns at the ready.

Brian Verdad's finger played with the switch to blow the trunk. A bead of sweat rolled off his nose.

But he didn't have the guts to go through with it.

It was the bead of sweat that tipped the cop off, making him decide to look in the trunk.

XXIX. WRAPPING IT UP

Leo Lincoln woke up early that morning. He couldn't sleep. He had set the alarm for five-thirty, but he'd gotten up well before then. Today was a special day, and he looked forward to it more than any other day during the whole year.

President's Day.

And that meant the Lincoln Parade. He rubbed his hands together in anticipation. He'd get to sit up in the VIP grandstand with the Mayor and the Governor and his grandmother and the rest of the Lincoln clan.

He paced the length of his apartment, getting more and more excited with each passing second. Power suited him well, he thought. He just had to keep busy until the festivities began. Otherwise, he'd go out of his mind. Searching for something to do, he walked from room to room. His clothes were already laid out on the bed—he'd chosen them a week ago. His stomach was empty, but he wasn't very hungry. And his maid had done the dishes and scrubbed his bathroom.

At five-thirty, the alarm started beeping, which gave Leo something to do for nearly thirty seconds.

•

A passel of clouds drifted over the city. They were pretty white ones that exploded out from their centers, like those after a heavy rain. There was a horse and buggy, an elephant with a stubby trunk, and a man urinating with an uncomfortably large penis. But soon the horse, the elephant, and the man's penis disappeared to the east, and the sky became as clear and as blue as a sapphire, eliciting a sigh from all those gazing toward it.

A temperate breeze blew in from the west, keeping the cooler air over the Lake from spoiling the day's festivities. The roar of snow blowers and the scraping of snow shovels filled the air as evidence of the blizzard was cleared away from the streets and sidewalks.

Shut in their homes for days, Chicagoans poured into the streets. Although only a few hundred spectators lined up to witness the Presidents' Day festivities. Most people were more interested in getting to the grocery store to replenish their cupboards and refrigerators after the long storm.

In fact, for a while, the onlookers were outnumbered by protesters standing along Michigan Avenue waving a repertoire of signs and banners.

None of this diminished Leo's mood. He sat proudly at the far end of the grandstand in the last seat reserved for the Lincolns. He was wearing his finest suit, an Armani, which looked more like it had come from Sears when he was stuffed in it. He hated bands, except for the little majorettes that marched in front holding the banners—he liked them. A few years ago, he even took one of them out on a date, promising her a key to the city. Of course, it was just the key to his laundry room, but the girl was so impressed she wrote about it in the school newspaper. He had to do a lot of explaining to get out of that one. He was surprised by how many people actually read the high school's paper. But in the end, as always, he triumphed over adversity.

And all the while, the Hancock towered over the plaza, casting its shadow on the grandstand and making the air more brisk. The temperature caused Leo's cheeks to be a bit redder than usual. But it didn't matter. This was *his* day.

It didn't even bother him that the old woman at the end of the row kept shifting in her seat, staring upward, and just generally making a nuisance of herself.

"What the hell is that?" said the woman, who happened to be his grandmother. "Leo, did you have something to do with this?" she yelled over the dozen or so people between them. She always liked to put a little distance between Leo and herself.

A woman sitting next to his grandmother waved to Leo.

"Hi, Leo."

"Hello, Mother."

"You're making a spectacle of yourself," said the grandmother as she slapped her daughter's hand down.

"He's my son."

"Yeah, well...I wouldn't go bragging about it," the old woman said as she shot Leo a rather stern glare, which he didn't appreciate.

"What is *what*, Grandmother?" replied Leo, trying not to lose sight of one particularly cute majorette.

"That," she said, pointing west.

Frustrated that a balloon seller was blocking his view of the young majorette, Leo turned toward his grandmother.

"What?" he said as he looked in the direction of her finger. His eyes shot open in horror as he saw what she was pointing at. The blood drained from his face, and he let out an involuntary, "Oh, shit."

"Watch your God Damned language," the elder Lincoln said to him.

•

"I don't think you're supposed to be doing that," said a small, frail man as he rubbed his scalp between the few hairs he had left on his head. He wore a white shirt, and his pants and tie were dark blue. His name, Andy, was embroidered on the pocket in red. "I mean, I don't really think this is kosher, if you know what I mean?"

"What seems to be the problem?" Peter Marks said to the building superintendent. Peter was standing precariously atop a forty-foot roll of aluminum that hung half over the edge of the Hancock's roof. A strong breeze quickly caused Peter to lose his bravado and he frantically grabbed for the guide wires attached to the pulley over his head.

"I don't think those things..." Andy pointed to the window-washing platform that was being used to hold the roll of foil Peter was standing on along the side of the building. "...are made to handle something of this nature."

"It's a simple household product, Andy, but in the hands of a genius..." He paused considering himself fondly for just an instant. "Stand back and watch history in the making, my friend. God, I love this job! We are going to bring Arnolds Aluminum back from the DEAD!" Peter gave a howl as he shook his fist.

Standing at the base of one of the two huge radio and television antennas that sprouted from the roof of the Hancock, Andy wasn't convinced history had anything to do with what was going on. He also felt a bit insecure about having let all these people up to the roof in the first place. He nervously watched as several dozen workers fixed another roll to a second platform, this one on the west face of the building. There were three platforms to a side, twelve in all. Large foil rolls were being loaded onto each one.

"I don't understand what this has to do with President's Day or the Lincoln Parade," he said, thinking how easily a pink slip could find its way into his inbox.

Armand pressed himself against an air duct a few feet to the left of Andy, looking a bit pale. Armand wasn't fond of heights. In fact, he'd never visited the Hancock Observatory on the 94th floor because it was just too damn far off the ground. Unfortunately, he now found himself six floors higher, *outside* and on *top* of the Hancock. "It's very complicated," he explained in an overly calm tone after Andy looked to him for an answer.

Peter was whistling and motioning to the workmen. "Let's see him!"

An annoying groan emanated from somewhere behind the air ducts. In a moment, Satan was dangling over the center of the roof between the two gigantic spires, his feet unable to touch the ground.

"I look ridiculous," Satan sighed.

"You look wonderful!" screamed Peter, nearly falling to his death as he jumped up and down with glee.

Satan glanced over to Barris, who was controlling the hydraulic winch which held him above the rooftop. "Barris, tell him I look ridiculous."

"It's not that bad, Satan. Really."

"I look like a baked potato."

"No, you don't."

"Yes, I do."

The suit had been Jesus' idea, or so Peter claimed. Jesus said Barris was the first one to mention it. Barris recalled Armand bringing it up. Armand refused to take responsibility for anything. Well, no matter. Whoever's idea it *had* been, Satan was the one stuck with it now. He was clad from head to toe in a suit made of triple-ply, industrial grade aluminum foil.

"Barris, put me down. I must've lost twelve pounds already." Satan poked at his side. "I think I'm done."

Barris looked to Peter who shook his head.

"I can't."

"Barris, put me down or I will kill you and take your book and have it published as my own."

Barris thought about this for a moment. He didn't like the idea of someone else getting credit for his sweat and blood. He might have been forced to comply with Satan's demand had the book been anywhere near finished. "Satan...think of what you're doing for Mankind."

"And just what is that, Barris?"

Jesus stepped in after Barris couldn't come up with anything that even remotely tickled Mankind, let alone helped it.

"You are informing the public..." Jesus began. "...that foil can protect you from gamma ray bombardment. You might not age as quickly, or you might keep your mental faculties longer. You're also putting folks back to work. These men and women have families. Families who will be eternally grateful."

All of the workmen nodded in agreement as though at any moment, they might break out and start singing, "Just look for the union label..."

"And if the foil these men and women make can protect just one child. Allow just one person to live a fuller, happier life...well, isn't that worth it?"

Jesus' speech seemed to resonate with everyone on the roof.

Except Satan.

And Peter Marks. "Besides, you're gonna be stinking rich," he said.

"I'm going to be dead."

"You're not going to die," Armand said, hopefully.

The meek tone of his voice echoed in the air duct by his head. When the sound returned, he heard himself and found it unappealing. He suddenly realized that he'd become a complete wimp since the explosion. With the exception of that one moment when Satan forced him to stand and fight for his company—a resolve that lasted less than a day—Armand had let events happen to him and not for him. Slowly, he took a step away from the protection of the duct. After a moment, he found himself standing directly under Satan.

"You are not going to die," Armand said, forcefully. "You're gonna be famous."

"I'm not interested in being famous," Satan answered as a bead of sweat rolled into his mouth. He heard Ion's voice in his head as if she was standing right behind his ear. He remembered saying those very words to her. It was a Friday, and she had just begun her makeover of him. He knew it was a Friday because he recalled thinking about his mother eating fish somewhere uptown. "I don't want fame" was his exact quote that day. Ion turned from what she was doing—measuring Slag's head for a Gamma Cap—and slowly, methodically strolled toward Satan, until they were finally face to face. "That may be true," she said, just as slowly as she had walked over. "But you dream about the whole world knowing your name…acknowledging what you've done…realizing what a genius you are." He didn't acknowledge it, but she was right. "Fame is the price for that," she added. "And when the time comes, you'll pay it gladly."

As he twisted above the ground, Satan lowered his head, resting his chin on his foil-clad chest. He was paying. Dearly.

Losing his conviction for a moment, Armand looked over to Peter Marks. "Why are we doing this again?"

"We're making a statement, Foil Man. Your factory might have been reduced to a pile of rubble, all our hopes may have been crushed, but you can't kill the human spirit. Who knows what'll happen. Who knows if we'll force the city to put a hold on Renaissance Village. Who knows if we'll sell one box of foil or bring in even one investor. Who cares? This just might be the most important thing we ever do in our lives. Ever. We're going to show the world something about dignity and principal. We might expend every last resource Arnolds Aluminum has, every last dollar, every last scrap of foil. I might not receive a cent for all the time and effort and man-hours we've spent. But wouldn't you rather go out with a bang, than go out with a whimper?"

Armand felt a surge of religion course through his veins. Even Satan had to admit that Peter's speech had moved him. This probably *would* be the most important moment of his life. Something that would be remembered forever. He felt better knowing that it didn't make a difference what the outcome was.

"Nobody's ever seen anything like this before." Peter spread his arms out toward the rolls of foil.

Meanwhile, Andy had gone over to a phone to ask his deputy for advice, but had gotten little more than "you're the boss" as an answer, which wasn't any help because he already knew that. Now, walking back, Andy took one look at Satan and said, "He looks like a baked potato."

"That's it! Get me down from here. Right now!" Satan put his hands on his hips, indignant.

Andy nodded in agreement. "I don't think this is…*copacetic*." He had just learned the word yesterday on his way to work, listening to the Verbal Advantage tape program he'd gotten for Christmas and was glad, even in the midst of this turmoil, to find an opportunity to use it. "Nothing in the manual seems to cover it. I don't know if I can allow you to continue."

Peter was busy directing the workmen as they placed the last of the twelve rolls on the northern face of the building. He stopped when he heard the sniveling little superintendent attempting to put up some resistance.

"Listen, Andy, our papers are all in order. It doesn't appear to me that you have any choice in this matter. So, if you could just move out of the way before you are accidentally crushed under a half-ton of foil, we'll be able to get on with our business."

"What papers?" asked Armand, who got a kick from Jesus before he could say anything else.

After moving a safe distance from the rolls, Andy pulled the papers out of his shirt pocket, unfolded them and held the pages toward Peter in what, for him, was a fairly dramatic fashion. "That's just it. These are signed by the Mayor."

"The Mayor?" mouthed Armand. He didn't need to be kicked twice.

"Exactly. So, what's the problem?" replied Peter.

Andy scrunched up his face in a frown. "The city doesn't own this building. I think I oughta check with my superiors. Make sure these documents aren't…" he searched for the right word. "…*spurious.*"

Sensing that the moment was fast slipping away, and not really prepared at this moment to explain to Armand that he'd secured the Mayor's support—and signature—by promising him a large campaign donation from Arnolds Aluminum, Peter decided this was as good a time as any to get started. He pulled a transceiver from his back pocket and put it to his lips. "All right, let's put him over the side."

Leo stared up at the shining, silvery object as it appeared over the edge of the Hancock. Immediately, he grabbed the opera glasses of the woman sitting next to him. "Excuse me, Aunt Mimi."

"Leo, what's gotten into you, boy?" said the woman as she wrestled with her nephew for the spectacles.

Eventually, Leo tore them from her wrinkled, bony fingers and put them up to his face. Avoiding his aunt's swinging purse, he peered through the glasses, squinting to get a better view of what it was that was hanging over the edge of the tower. It looked like a baked potato.

The view was spectacular. The sun was warm and the sky was clear. If he hadn't been dangling a thousand or so feet off the ground, Satan might have thought it was a nice day.

But he didn't, because he was.

A mechanical jolt was sent through the steel cable as the winch lowered Satan toward the observation deck six floors below. He gripped the chains hooking him to the cable as tightly as he could and not cut off all circulation to his fingers. He jerked the chains in a vain and belated attempt to check the safety of his situation until he realized if there *was* something wrong he'd only speed up the process by yanking on the cabling. He let out a tiny squeal as the winch lurched to a stop right in front of several hundred tourists staring at him through the windows.

After a moment, where he cursed Ion and God, in that order, Satan summoned the courage to take a peek toward the ground. The pavement, a hundred floors or so below, spiraled toward him. In an instant, every meal he'd ever eaten violently evacuated his stomach.

"How's it look?" asked Jesus excitedly as he stood atop of one of the winches.

"Like a Nazi propaganda film," answered Satan as he wiped his mouth.

Peter Marks was on his perch ordering the workman to fix the end of the foil rolls to the roof. "I take it you mean there's a whole bunch of people waiting to be brainwashed," he said.

"Actually, it's not very crowded," said Armand, his newfound confidence a little shaken—more by the lack of people, than the height.

"Not to worry, Foil Man. We've got an ace-in-the-hole." Peter mimicked clicking a camera. He pointed to one of his people with a wireless webcam fixed to the top of a PowerBook, and toward several helicopters hovering over the parade. "The Big Eye's watching." One of the craft seemed to have taken notice of them and moved closer. Peter turned and looked over the side. "How you doing out there, Satan?"

"Has anyone checked this equipment lately? I'm certain that within minutes, I will be plunging to my death. I can almost guarantee this machine was assembled by the lowest bidder in some Third World country with inferior parts and workmanship."

A thought crossed his mind.

"If I *am* killed...please don't let them bury me in this suit."

"You're doing fine."

"Then you get down here," Satan said, suddenly less interested in being part of the 'team.' "At a hundred stories, nobody's going to know me from a dog in a prom dress."

"We need you for the close-ups, babe," Peter said, pointing toward the helicopter that was closing on the building. "Hang in there." Peter Mark's put the transceiver to his lips again. "Fire it up and let it down."

Suddenly, a loud THWACK echoed from the top of the building, which startled everyone on the street and caused Leo to drop the spyglasses on two teenagers necking under the grandstand.

"Hey, asshole," screamed the boy, who was drowned out by the ensuing noise.

Streams of red, white and blue, then yellow, green, and orange shot from the tower, spreading across the sky and raining down toward the crowd. There was a collective "oooooww" as the fireworks dissipated halfway down the building.

The crowd applauded as several more bursts went off in the bright blue sky. A distant sound, a creaking of stressed metal was heard as twelve hoists kicked into gear and the giant foil rolls began to unfurl on all sides of the building.

Leo Lincoln's face turned purple.

The display was short, although it didn't seem that way to Satan. Embers floated past him, some landing on his arm. He patted them out, sending tiny trails of smoke into the air, but the gesture was meaningless. His foil suit was all the protection he needed.

One of the giant sheets of foil slid behind him as it was unrolled, passing close enough to brush against his back and send him swinging. Satan hung twisting in a wind that was much stronger and cooler at this height than on the ground.

This was it.

His pulse hammered in his head. The popping of the fireworks added to the beat, but did not overpower it. His heart was racing, running far above recommended levels, he was sure. In no time, he'd be dead—whether from a thousand-foot swan dive or a blown artery.

And yet...

...he felt more alive than he'd ever felt in his life. Maybe Peter Marks was right. As painful, annoying and dangerous as this moment had become, Satan began to relish it. Like falling in love and having it taken away. There was discomfort, but he accepted it and after awhile, he couldn't imagine it not being there. He had lived more in the past two and a half months than he'd lived in thirty plus years. He'd experienced more fear, more pain, more love than a thousand lifetimes at the pace he'd set before meeting Ion. She had ruined his life. Absolutely. But in doing so, she had allowed him to understand what that life was worth. Maybe he'd never fall in love again. Who could say? He never thought he would fall in love a first time, but he had. Who really knew what the future held? The only thing he was sure about was that he felt alive. Life was coursing through his veins. And as he dangled on the edge of that life, flirting shamelessly with the Grim Reaper, he let out a laugh that echoed in the silence that followed the fireworks. A boisterous roar that could even be heard on the street.

A half-concerned Peter Marks stuck his head over the side again.

"You okay?"

"I'm great."

Peter was ready for any response but that one. He opened his mouth, but nothing came out.

Satan was excitedly tugging on the chains, trying to get a better look at Peter. "I might be about to die, but I feel *alive* for the first time."

Peter gave a faux smile and an obligatory nod. "That *is* great. Let's talk about it when this's all over. I'll buy the beer and cheese snacks, you provide the Temple of the Feel-Good commentary."

"No, you don't understand."

"No, I do understand. I understand that we're gonna miss the News at Noon if we don't hurry."

Satan laughed again. "It doesn't matter. Like you were trying to tell me, it's the journey. Not the destination."

Peter motioned toward the cameras. "Unless the destination is two million homes."

"So, we fail. So what? I've been doing that all my life without even trying. I'm an expert at it. I've spent all this time trying to avoid pain, avoid risk. I've survived, but I haven't lived. I mean, we're just supposed to try, right?"

"Listen, Satan…" Peter took a breath and restarted more calmly, his tone more open and caring. "Life isn't supposed to be easy or safe. Yes, victory comes in the attempt. That's what we're doing here. We're putting it on the line. But you can't *talk* about doing things, you have to just do them. And right now, we have to stop talking and do this. Okay?"

Satan smiled. "Okay." He patted the foil hood covering his skull, then glanced out at the Lake and the city and saw all the magnificent things that mankind had built. "Peter," he yelled up.

"Yeah?"

"I've been thinking about dropping the whole Inner Earth, Satan name thing...since it became pretty clear that was all just a—"

Peter interrupted, "What are you trying to say, my foil-clad friend?"

"I'll tell you later."

"Okay...you're on, babe."

As the window washing platforms made their way down the side of the Hancock Tower, the foil covered more and more of the building till nearly all of it was sheathed in aluminum.

And that's when the trouble began.

•

Like Leo, Kelsey had awakened early. She made herself and the kitten breakfast, then slipped on some comfortable clothes. She'd gotten Satan's message the night before. It gave vague references to "something big" that had to do with Arnolds Aluminum and the Lincoln Parade. Leo would be there, so would Barris, she figured.

She got an early start to miss the traffic, choosing to wait for *whatever-it-was* in her office—the first few days after a heavy storm were always a treacherous commute, even if the roads were clear.

She'd been staring out the window when she saw the fireworks and the tiny silver dot. Then the metallic sheets began to unfurl. It was about this time that the reception on her television started to get a bit fuzzy, so she shut it off and went down to the street where she made her way through the crowd, a manila envelope held close to her breast.

Time to ruin Leo's life.

•

Fortunately for Kenny Odorman, the door to the cafeteria was easily jimmied. He snuck in and ravaged the cupboards and freezers and fridges, gathering food like a squirrel with a glandular problem.

Strolling back to his workstation with his booty in tow, Kenny sat in front of the computer and typed in Dorobek's name. He wanted to see the file one last time before he printed out a hard copy and hand delivered it to Noel himself. He wanted the pleasure of seeing the look on his face, something he had—with the others whose credit he'd trashed—only dreamed about.

He shoved a half-frozen Armour hot dog in his mouth and snapped off a bite.

God, he loved his work.

•

The crowd applauded enthusiastically as the entire building was draped in foil, shiny-side out. In perfect synchronization, a Goodyear blimp wrapped in Arnolds appeared over the plaza, the message "ARNOLDS…KEEPS THE GAMMA RAYS OUT, AND THE FRESHNESS IN" ran repeatedly across the bottom of the airship's belly in green letters.

There was a general sense of awe in the area, which should not be confused with the specific sense of awe one feels when all their checks clear at the end of the month without a hitch. No, this was far grander in scope and, therefore, less definitive.

There are singular moments that occur rarely in the course of history, and this was one. History is said to be that portion of time which has been recorded by man. Thus, dinosaurs are *prehistoric*. However, beginning in the latter stages of the twentieth century, a new and more restrictive definition of the word had come into play: That which is not recorded by video camera is subject to interpretation, hence, cannot be considered incontrovertible, and, by extrapolation, never occurred in the first place.

Fortunately, television was broadcasting the event into every home in Chicago. However, many of the people that had been watching turned off their sets to go downtown and see the action for themselves—especially after the reception grew fuzzy when all the foil began interfering with the transmitters.

The crowd on the street began to swell. It doubled, then tripled, then doubled again. The streets were teeming with onlookers, all gazing upward at the shiny, shimmering, silvery sheath on the Hancock.

On cue, Slag and the rest of the "protesters" threw down their signs and proceeded to spread out, handing hundreds of aluminum hats to the people in the crowd.

"They're cool, man," Slag would say to each recipient.

A homeless man climbing out of a cardboard box asked for six. "Six iterations at most. Lou is waiting under the arch."

"Cool," Slag said as he handed the man in the platinum wig more hats, suddenly wondering where the chick with the blonde hair was.

Some thought the hats were bag lunches after seeing the vagrant take a half dozen and got indignant that someone had mistaken them for homeless. Others were more receptive. And after awhile, over two thousand people had foil on their heads. Everyone was milling about having a good time and laughing at one another.

And this was when Harmonic Distortion came into play.

With all that foil on the ground, on the building, in the air, and on people's heads, reflecting the radio and television waves radiating from the antennas, a peculiar phenomenon occurred. The frequencies began to merge which caused the two huge antenna towers on the Hancock to hum, turning the entire structure into a giant tuning fork.

At first, it was faint, but soon the sound grew audible to those on the street.

Kelsey popped at her ear with the palm of her hand and stretched her jaw a number of times to clear the buzz out of her head. Once she noticed several others in the crowd doing the same, she realized it was clearly not a problem unique to her. Something, somewhere was humming and the sound was becoming louder and more unnerving with each tick of the clock. Within a few moments, it was uncomfortable. When the pitch reached a constant tone, it was like having a wooden stake driven through the side of your head while seeing your mother stark naked at six a.m.

•

Satan could see the crowd below growing increasingly restless. They were ants scattering in every direction in search of food. He couldn't quite determine what all the commotion was about. Because of a mathematical equation understood by only three physicists, all of whom were dead, Satan's suit was refracting the sound waves, making them hardly noticeable to him. He glanced at the pandemonium below. Someone must have announced a half-price sale at Filene's Basement around the corner, he thought.

He felt a little left out, even though he really didn't like Filene's.

Suddenly, several windows behind Satan burst under the stress of the noise, ripping through part of the foil. Windows on several other nearby buildings began to rupture as well. It was the first indication that all was not well in the Windy City, and that it wasn't simply a red tag special causing the ruckus. He watched numbly as glass rained down on the crowd, further sending the place into chaos.

The high from his "Life Is To Be Lived" nonsense had diminished significantly, if only because it was becoming clear he had very little time left to enjoy his newfound—obviously stupid—philosophy.

•

Eight minutes after the humming started, Kelsey reached the grandstand. It was close to empty as everyone tried to find cover from the noise and shattering windows. A minute later, she found Leo under the seats, cowering beside his grandmother in the far corner, doing his best to avoid the falling shards of tempered glass.

"Kelsey!" he screamed up in her direction. "Thank God, you've come to save me. Please, we have to get out of here."

"Here," she said, handing him the envelope through the space between the bench seats.

"Kelsey, I don't have time to look at my mail. Armand Arnold has snapped and he's decided to take me and the entire city down with him. What does he think, destroying the Hancock will sell more foil?"

Leo's grandmother shoved him. "Let the girl under here for Christ's Sake. It's dangerous out there."

"Yes, Grandmother."

Kelsey climbed through to get under the grandstand. She tried to hold back a giggle, but it slipped out. "Open it."

"Why?"

"I'll tell your wife the name of everyone you've ever had an affair with," she yelled in his ear.

"She already knows," said the elder Mrs. Lincoln. "Open it, Leo."

Somehow, his secrets weren't all that secret anymore. He unsealed the package, begrudgingly. "What is it?"

"Your birth certificates."

It was becoming difficult to hear. The pitch was more painful than pleasant, but his grandmother raised her eyebrow as she realized what the young woman had said. She nodded, knowingly.

"Certificates?" he said as he pulled the two pages from the envelope, not sure he'd heard her correctly. He glanced at the one with his name on it, then the other that seemed to belong to someone else, 'Boy Wolinski.' "Only one of these is mine."

"No, they're both yours," said his grandmother.

Leo shook his round, red face. "I don't understand."

"You're adopted," smiled Kelsey.

A look of sheer terror came over Leo.

His grandmother nodded, wearing a thinly veiled smile of her own.

Leo turned blue and passed out.

•

It took sixteen minutes for the din to reach a level resounding enough to render a human unconscious. Each person was affected in their own way and at different degrees of severity, but it was only a matter of time before everyone was knocked out.

Of course, it took considerably less time to kill off the entire rodent population within a thirty-block radius.

Peter Marks held his hands to his head. Glancing toward the base of the antennas, he saw that Armand and the workmen were already out cold. He couldn't help but wonder if all this was going to hurt sales. And everything had been going so well up to then. Finally, he fell limp and slipped off his perch.

Barris slumped over next and landed on the controls of the winch holding Satan.

As the tiny crane lurched, Satan looked up to see Peter's body hanging partially over the edge of the building. Peter was being buffeted by the wind, and it wouldn't take much to send him plunging to the pavement. But for the moment, he seemed stable.

Which wasn't as true for Satan.

Once the panic was well under way inside his head, Satan realized there was no one controlling the winch that held him precariously over the street. A street that from this height looked very much like it was out of a satellite photo.

A faint fluttering was heard as the TV helicopter kept its distance. Satan could see the helmeted cameraman leaning out the side door capturing the action. Unfortunately, none of the local stations were able to transmit any longer because of the interference, but the feed was going out live on CNN and MSNBC.

The craft hung there, just out of range—as if the Hancock might reach out, grab it and toss it to the pavement.

The other helicopters were circling the area, showing on the broadcast networks what must have appeared from the air as a mass suicide.

Directing his attention past the helicopters and the blimp that was drifting aimlessly, its helmetless pilot unconscious after getting too close to the Hancock, Satan stared at the white caps on the Lake. A few ships were visible farther out. He felt peaceful, tranquil.

"Thank you," he said toward the Heavens. "Thank you for all the wonderful things, for all the horrible things, for every last moment I've been able to remember...Thank you."

He wiped at his face to brush away a tear that had escaped his eye.

"I've been asleep...all this time, asleep." He glanced up and watched as the two antennas shook wildly above the top of the building. Part of the air conditioning system went rushing past him and, twenty seconds later, flattened a grinder shop. "But I'm awake now."

Satan could feel the winch giving way. It was time to figure out how to get down from his position. He took a quick inventory of his options. He noted two: Jump and hope that a tremendous updraft occurred to cushion his plunge; or, unhook himself and climb up the chains and the cable to the roof.

Neither elicited a very positive response from Satan.

Unfortunately, he didn't have time to sit down and come up with other alternatives. He had to act soon. The hum was beginning to affect him, making him feel sluggish and dizzy. He rubbed his temples to rid himself of the pain, but as soon as he took his hands away, his headache returned. Gripping the chains as hard as he could, he leaned his head back and sighed, thinking how much he hated the thought of climbing up a metal chain a thousand feet off the ground. A hate remedied only slightly by the thought of his other choice.

He had to do something. The humming was inside his head now.

As he pulled himself upright, an odd thought occurred to him. A fleeting impression of the little swing set his father built for him in the back yard of their first home. It was red and yellow and two of the feet would lift off the ground if you got the swing high enough.

He studied the cable above, then stared at the broken windows behind him. It wasn't impossible, he thought—better than climbing. He clicked his teeth together, then unhooked himself from his harness and began to swing his feet. After a few failed attempts, he started to sway—slowly at first, then with each try, a little faster, a little farther.

The crane pulled free from the roof, dumping Barris onto the gravel, and was beginning to slide toward Peter Marks and the edge of the building, picking up momentum as it went.

Within a minute, Satan was swinging far enough so his feet advanced through the large tear in the foil wall. A moment later, his shin passed the plane of the window frames. He pumped harder and harder, swaying higher and higher. A few more giant swings and he'd be far enough inside to jump.

Brushing past Peter Marks, the winch slid out halfway over the edge, making a loud metal groan that caused Satan to look up.

Knowing he had only a few seconds left, Satan swung himself toward the building as hard as he could. When he reached the apex and nearly had his whole body inside, he let go.

•

Jesus stood at the highest point on the Hancock's roof, the antenna towers rising on either side of him.

Somehow, he remained conscious, but the sound was definitely affecting him. His brain became more clouded with every second.

He was well over ninety-three percent mad by the time Satan arrived on the roof.

•

Swinging into the building had been one of Satan's better ideas in the last thirty years, and also one of his most fortunate. Seconds after jumping inside, the winch tumbled off the roof and raced by the open window.

With a tremendous sigh of relief, Satan watched as the huge crane careened toward the ground, that was, until he realized his safety rope was still attached to the plummeting wreckage.

Fumbling with the hooks, his fingers working as fast as they were able, Satan finally unfastened the lanyard the same instant the slack ran out, ripping the cord out of his hands and down the side of the building.

Satan was knocked to the floor as the crane landed with a tumultuous impact, smashing into, and completely destroying, a fully loaded Good Humor van. Dozens of Fudgie-Wudgies were sent hurtling through the air, covering the unconscious bystanders with a thin chocolate coating.

Satan picked himself up off the ground of the lovely ninety-second-floor apartment, went into the hall, found the stairwell, made it to the top, only to find himself face to face with a roof access door that was armed to the teeth with gadgets.

The door had a huge sign on it warning that an alarm would sound, the police would be notified, and his picture would be taken if the passage were breached. Satan never came out well in photos, at least it never looked like him, so he didn't worry about that. He assumed that with everything that had transpired, the police already knew, and with the sonic disturbance in full force, what harm could a measly little alarm do.

Unfortunately, it was the sound of that very alarm that sent Jesus over the top.

"Do you see it?" Jesus said wildly as he viewed the city, making quick movements from side to side with his head. "Do you see it crumbling to dust all around us?" He extended a finger toward the ground. "This is it! The end is near. I can feel it!" he screamed.

"Jesus..." Satan groaned, more a curse than an acknowledgment of the man's name. "What the hell's wrong with you?"

"Nothing is wrong. This is the way. This is how it is to be."

Frustrated as he tried to maneuver in his foil suit, Satan began to shed himself of it. Getting it halfway off, he was smashed by the sound waves that, until now, had hardly affected him.

"Whooooaaaa!" he said as he zipped the suit back on.

Once he recovered, Satan looked around the roof, noticing that the structure was coming apart from the intense vibration. The foil was causing the disturbance, he reasoned, and he had to cut it down before the whole building hummed itself out of existence.

"Listen, this place is gonna crumble to dust if you don't get down from there and help me get rid of this damn foil!"

Satan went over to the west edge and searched about for something sharp to tear into the forty-foot sheets.

"Do not touch that!" Jesus ordered, motioning to the foil beneath Satan's feet. "This is the end. I will not allow you to stop it."

"Well, I really didn't ask your permission, did I?"

Jesus spread out his arms. "I am here to claim my seat as Judge over the sinners of the world. To decide who will join me in everlasting life, and who will remain behind to die a thousand deaths."

Satan stopped his search for a moment to stare at Jesus. This guy was seriously off his rocker.

"Listen, Jesus..." He spoke slowly at first, choosing his words carefully, so as not to agitate the man further. "You've got the name thing down—and that's kind of freaky in its own way—but I've read the Bible, and I don't recall anything about freezer wrap having a major role in causing Armageddon."

"My mother said I was destined for great things."

"Well, mothers have a way of being wrong."

Satan returned his attention to the foil.

"Do not interfere in the natural order of things," Jesus shouted as he hopped on top of an overturned pail, enabling him to stand a little bit taller.

"Jesus…this is *not* the natural order of things. This is freezer wrap! Now, I'm going to cut this foil down with or without your help. It would be easier with your assistance, however, whether you help or not, I'd appreciate it if you would *shut up*, so I can concentrate."

"The hand of God forbids you." Jesus tried unsuccessfully to summon the power of Heaven in his fingers, aiming them toward Satan in a threatening fashion.

Satan sighed. "Would you get down here and help me!"

"No," pouted Jesus, his shoulders dropping. Regaining what little was left of his mind, he returned his arms toward the sky and continued to spout off incantations and predictions of doom.

All of this was starting to annoy Satan, who had lifted one of the worker's cutting tools and was halfway through the center roll on the east side of the roof. Jesus' howling was more than inconvenient, it was unnerving. No matter how much he tried to convince himself that this guy was a wacko, Satan felt uncomfortable. Once he realized the Roman's had pegged the other Jesus as a nut, he really got nervous.

Finally, Satan stood up, let out a heavy sigh, picked up a pipe that had come loose from somewhere, strolled up to Jesus and, while he was in mid-sentence, whacked him in the head.

Even though the hum was nearly unbearable—and the end *was* imminent—everything seemed more pleasant without Jesus ranting on his pulpit. Satan skipped to the roof's edge and sliced through the end of the sheet. It floated gently toward the ground, slithering like a flat snake as it fell.

One by one, Satan freed the twelve rolls. He ran from one corner of the roof to the other, staying focused on what he had to do. As the last roll was cut loose, a tremendous sonic backlash occurred which sent a powerful wave of energy surging through the towers. A thunderous crack punctuated the event, shaking the Hancock as if a hundred bolts of lightning had struck it.

•

Kenny Odorman was staring at his computer terminal when the power surge hit. The lights dimmed and the screen fluttered for a moment, then both quickly came back to life. Kenny yawned as he typed in the sequence to bring up Dorobek's file. Brownouts and electrical spikes occurred all the time at the office, but the mainframes were safeguarded by a sophisticated surge protection system. He pressed the enter key to retrieve the data.

NO SUCH FILE, the screen said.

Kenny tried once more.

NO SUCK FILL was the second response.

NU SICK FELL came up on the third try.

A bead of sweat rolled off Kenny's forehead, stinging his eye. He entered the names of several others who were considered poor credit risks.

NA SACK FUEL.

For more than an hour, Kenny entered name after name in an attempt to get credit information. He even tried to call up his own file, which he knew was good because he had cleared it himself.

NI SEXX FULL.

Nothing.

Sweat streamed down his face. His heart rate skyrocketed. His lungs felt as if they were filled with water. He rolled his chair over to the next cubicle and tried to get something on that terminal.

Still nothing.

In a single instant, with more than a terajoule surging through the lines, every CreditDat file had been wiped out.

Kenny Odorman collapsed on the floor and began to weep.

•

The shock of the blast caused Peter Marks to slip further over the edge of the Hancock. Like the rock that starts a landslide, the tiny shift in Peter's position caused him to begin sliding off the roof. The movement was slow at first, but it quickly picked up speed. A few more seconds and he would plunge to his death.

It was only by accident that Satan noticed the man slipping over the brink—he'd been thrown to the ground by the surge, landing just a few inches from Peter. That Satan was close enough to grab Peter's collar as he disappeared over the edge was unbelievable. That his reflexes were still intact enough to do so was simply amazing.

Unlike his saving the policeman from plummeting off the billboard, this was less instinctive, more a conscious effort to save Peter even at the risk of his own safety.

Satan hooked his feet around a valve sticking out of the roof, then dragged Peter's limp body back over the lip on the building.

Exhausted, he collapsed onto Peter's back.

Peter Marks never knew how close he'd come to being splashed all over

Michigan Avenue, and perhaps it was best. No man needed to know such things.

Satan lay there not moving for several minutes. The ear-piercing hum steadily declined so that, after awhile, it was bearable. He noticed that the camera crew in the closest helicopter was getting more daring as the sound subsided. He covered his face and crawled inconspicuously to where he'd left Jesus. He grabbed hold of Jesus's leg and towed him over to the edge of the building, then positioned him so it appeared he saved Peter.

Satan crawled back to the roof access door and slipped inside before the TV crew got close enough to get a good shot of anyone's face.

•

It took nearly ten minutes for most people to come to. Some stayed out for as much as twenty minutes. Leo Lincoln woke up after about fifteen. His head pounded as if a scratched disco record was skipping inside his skull. There was even a moment when he thought he saw the lighted dance floor from *Saturday Night Fever*. As it turned out, the lights were from a police car that had pulled up next to the grandstand.

Leo opened his eyes to find two officers glaring down at him.

"I'm glad you two are here," Leo bellowed. "I want those people on the roof arrested this instant! Do you hear me?"

The two cops stood with their hands on their hips, which put them in a good position to grab their guns if this guy gave them any trouble.

"Is your name Leo Lincoln?" asked one of the cops.

"Yes!" he said, indignantly. "You're wasting time. They're probably getting away as we speak."

"Do you know a Brian Verdad?" asked the cop.

Leo's face did a little jig as he tried to hide his surprise. He feigned a puzzled look, unsuccessfully.

"Ah, no...never heard of him."

The two cops glanced at each other.

"Would you come with us, please," said the second cop as he handcuffed Leo's arms behind his back and tugged him toward the car.

"Actually...to tell you the truth, my name isn't Leo Lincoln."

The cops stuffed him into the back seat.

"And I have the papers to prove it!" Leo said as they bumped his head on the roof of the car. "Kelsey!"

•

Satan emerged from the revolving doors at the foot of the John Hancock Center. He wore a suit he'd stripped off a tax attorney on the sixteenth floor. It was several sizes too small, but no one paid any attention to his clothes. He could, he realized, be wearing a thong bikini and only get a passing glance after what just occurred.

He maneuvered quietly past the fountain, up the stairs to the street and through the dazed crowd, slipping away unnoticed. For a few blocks, he didn't have to think, a herd of bewildered people all following the person in front of them took Satan where it wanted to go. After a while the crowd thinned out, and he found himself on the corner of Dearborn and Adams at the exact spot where the guy with the scar and three moles on his face driving the huge car sporting the metal dog atop the hood had nearly run him over.

He stared down at the ground, noticing broken glass on the sidewalk. Gazing up at the buildings, he saw that windows all up and down the street had been shattered.

"Vinnie," shouted a female voice from behind.

Satan's heart was in his throat. He had done everything he was supposed to. Had become the man she had wanted him to be. He had earned this.

Satan turned toward the voice, his heart pounding up near his throat, his eyes closed like a young child awaiting his present. When he opened them, he watched the young brunette run past him into the arms of a dark-haired man. "Oh, Vinnie," she said again. "I was so scared."

"It's aw right now, baby. It's allll right," the man said, holding her close to his body, comforting her.

Kelsey stood at the corner. She was framed by a light post on her right, a parking meter on her left, and a walk sign above her head. She still looked wonderful, although several hundred pounds of shredded lettuce and tomatoes from the grinder shop had landed on her, a few ounces of which clung to her body here and there.

Gazing past the couple, Satan saw her.

"You're okay," she said as she hurried up to him and kissed his cheek. Wrapping her arms around him, she whispered into his ear, "I'm glad."

He wanted to ask her about the salad she was wearing, but she jogged across the street to make the light before he could.

"Where are you going?" he shouted across the traffic.

"Police station."

"Oh." He nodded, knowingly, then decided that wasn't getting him anywhere. "What for?"

She blew him a kiss. "I'll tell you later. Call me."

He wanted to tell her that he didn't know the number to her new apartment, but she was gone before he could get out the words.

Satan stood for a long time on the gray-white sidewalk, surrounded by the city and its buildings new and old, which suddenly made him feel very small. He remained motionless but not without emotion, watching the brunette and *her* Vinnie, wondering where Ion was and who she was holding now.

XXX. P.S.

The snow was nearly gone. There were patches of it here and there, mostly in the shadows.

Satan made his way along Michigan Avenue. It was windy and a few errant scraps of aluminum foil skipped past. He wondered if they were remnants of the rolls he'd cut loose from the Hancock, or if they were simply blown into the street from an overturned garbage can somewhere. He didn't know, but then it didn't really matter.

Within hours, the events atop the Hancock took on the status of legend, along with its strange side effects; the mysterious and complete disappearance of all rats, mice, and cockroaches, the destruction of records at the three major credit reporting agencies, the roughly one million dollars that poured out of overflowing storm drains the next morning when all the snow melted, and a thousand other things people claimed were caused by the Harmonic Distortion.

As Satan turned the corner, a man strode past wearing an "I survived the Great Chicago Foil" T-shirt.

An odd feeling raced through Satan's body as he realized he had a part in causing all this. The feeling was pride. And nausea.

Ion's face popped into his head, and he wondered if she had heard about the Great Chicago Foil wherever she was, wondered how she felt knowing that he had succeeded where she thought he would fail. Something deep down told him he had touched her as much as she had touched him. But he also knew that she was weak where he was strong. A fact that all her attitude and flash obscured. A truth that had taken him until now to accept or even recognize.

He felt sad. Very sad. Mostly for her.

Satan took in a deep breath. The air smelled sweet, like Spring might not be too far away. With it would come flowers and allergies and sneezing and the ten thousand hornets that nested under his back steps and attacked him whenever he took out the garbage.

And yet, he felt he would be blossoming as well.

He stopped and glanced around. He had nothing to do—nothing he had to do. For years that never bothered him. For some reason, it did now. He didn't have to work. Armand Arnold made it clear he'd never have to worry about money again.

[Once Leo Lincoln, née Wolinski, started talking to the police, the developers of Renaissance Village mysteriously disappeared, leaving Armand free to rebuild his factory. And since Leo was an employee of the municipality of Chicago when he set the explosives, the city agreed to pay Arnolds Aluminum an undisclosed sum (rumored to be in the tens of millions) in an out-of-court settlement. The plant would be fully operational by the end of Summer. Armand was even thinking of buying the old Clark Pipe factory and expanding...into plastic wrap.]

Still, Satan felt he should do something with his life. For a brief instant, he entertained the idea of searching for Ion, only he knew that even if he *could* locate her, he would never really find her.

He had once been on a quest to discover Utopia. Perhaps he didn't have to go so deep within the planet to find it. Just deep within himself.

There were so many things he hadn't seen, so many places he hadn't been. One place he wouldn't go, though, was Washington State. Satan decided pursuing his father any longer wouldn't do anyone any good. What could the man say that would make any difference after all these years, after all the illusions, deceptions and misinterpretation? He thought about visiting his mother—perhaps the millionth time he'd done that in fifteen years.

Only this time, he felt he really would.

Anything was possible.

Anything at all.

He pulled out a piece of paper with several phone numbers scratched on it, a name beside each. Kelsey, Barris, Peter Marks, and Armand. Slag didn't have a phone, but you could reach him by dialing the payphone on the street below his apartment, letting it ring till someone finally picked up, then ask the person to scream out Slag's name. The surprising thing was, it usually worked. You could even leave messages for him.

Satan stared at the names. These were his friends. More than that, this was his *family*. The only one he had.

He removed his bowler and placed it on a parking meter that had just expired. The air felt strange as it brushed against his bare head. But it was somehow comforting. As if it was supposed to be this way.

Satan strolled over to the payphone set next to Modi's Newsstand. He glanced at the stacks of papers piled on the ground. There were a bunch of articles on how the economy was growing once again—housing starts up, car and other big ticket purchases up, retail sales up—now that most people had good credit again after their records were destroyed.

As Satan fished in his pocket for some change, he spotted a familiar face on one of the magazines in the rack. It was Peter Marks smiling on the cover of Adweek.

Satan gave a little laugh, then inserted the change in the slot in the phone, and dialed the first number.

It rang only once.

"Hello," Kelsey said.

"Hi, it's Sa—" He paused. "It's Noel…and I was thinking about having everyone over for dinner."

•

Noel stood at the entrance of the Food King. He hoped the manager/maniac had been arrested or killed or had forgotten him somehow.

Unfortunately, he realized it was unlikely any of these wishes would come true.

After everyone agreed to come to his house for dinner, he decided he would cook the meal himself. And hope to God that no one got food poisoning. It was a risk. But he wanted them to know how grateful he was that they were in his life…without having to actually say so out loud.

Besides, risk taking was good. It added to life.

At least, that's what Noel kept repeating to himself as he stepped up to the automatic door leading into the market, wondering if the thing was watching him. It was, apparently. It opened, and he walked inside. Immediately, he was confronted by a problem: getting a shopping cart. He attempted to extract one from the line of them laying in wait at the front of the store. They were reluctant servants, slaves to the whims of men and women in search of grocery bargains. He finally pried one free. It had two bad wheels—one didn't work at all—and there was a used diaper sitting in the bottom. Not in the mood to wrestle with another cart and wrench his back further, Noel decided this one would be good enough. He calculated that he could probably fit the ingredients for his meal in the top rack and never have to deal with the soiled Huggie stuck to the metal caging.

Noel made his way up and down the aisles.

The bad wheel that wouldn't turn was giving him trouble. He adjusted his stance and leaned into the handle. That seemed to do it.

Staring at the rows of neatly stocked food, Noel wondered what kind of food he should make. He never paid much attention to what other people ate. It didn't interest him. He tried to remember what Kelsey made whenever she had people over.

Something fowl, he thought.

A young woman at the end of the aisle caught his attention. She had a bright smile and stunning eyes that reminded him of Ion's.

He immediately wanted to strangle her.

Noel was lost in his somewhat misplaced homicidal revenge fantasy when the young woman's annoyingly adorable three-year-old son whacked him in the groin with a toilet brush, causing Noel to lose control of the cart, which veered off to the left and plowed into a shelf full of organic prune juice.

Several pops echoed through the store. The distant sound reached the manager and somehow passed through the thick tufts of hair that blocked the openings to his ears. The man, having just returned from the funeral of his brother who'd been fatally wounded in a freak accident involving a rat and a pistol, was in no mood for troublemakers. He grunted loudly as he realized what was afoot.

And the chase was on.

ABOUT THE AUTHOR

Edward Savio grew up in Connecticut. He is a screenwriter, novelist, and creator of the political cartoon, "Ourmageddon." He has written numerous film projects for Walt Disney Studios, Sony Pictures Entertainment and others. He makes his home in San Francisco with his family where he is known as the "idiot upstairs."

You can send comments to the author at: writeme@edwardsavio.com

See edwardsavio.com for more information on his books and comic.

"Crude...vulgar...authentically illuminating at times...weaves a tapestry that's part *Portnoy's Complaint*, part crash-course in world economics."
—*Kirkus Reviews*

THE VELVET SLEDGEHAMMER
Sort of a Novel

Billy Gerrick has been raised since childhood to be the best in the world at what he does.

Argue.

The Wall Street Journal calls him "The best thing to happen to world trade since the boat." The President praises him as a "Great American." His wonderfully perfect girlfriend thinks he's the kindest, most generous man alive.

Only Billy Gerrick knows the truth…he's a deeply flawed hero who has held it together all these years by sheer will. A man haunted by a zany childhood, an overactive libido, and the girl-that-got-away. As the youngest Cabinet member in United States' history, his personal demons are about to collide head-on with his professional obligations.

On the eve of finalizing the most complex international agreement in the history of mankind, his girlfriend chooses this historic moment to pressure him about settling down and having kids. If Billy Gerrick knows anything, he knows he's the last person on earth that should be in charge of raising a child.

A hilarious, unbridled, unapologetic journey through the loves, the loses, and the triumphs of a man who is part Holden Caulfield, part Alexander Portnoy, and part Sun Tzu all rolled into one.

A man who may have finally met his match.

Available wherever books, ebooks, and audiobooks are sold.